Inv

Volume I
The Orion War

by

Kali Altsoba

Second Edition

About the Author

Kali Altsoba is the pen name used to publish future military fiction by the award winning teacher and military historian Cathal J. Nolan (Boston University). The author of many books and scholarly articles, he received the top award for military history, the *Gilder Lehrman Prize,* for *The Allure of Battle: A History of How Wars are Won and Lost* (Oxford University Press: 2017). *Allure* also received the first ever *Distinguished Book Award* from *War on the Rocks* (2018). His books are feature reviewed in academic and military journals, and the *New York Times, Wall Street Journal*, and *The National*. He has spoken to think tanks and historical associations in Afghanistan, Argentina, Britain, Canada, Israel, and across the United States. He has appeared on CBS Radio, Fox Radio, Radio Free Europe, BBC *Mundo*, Newstalk (Ireland), PBS and C-Span. He advices on military history issues for the PBS series *NOVA*, and was featured in the *NOVA* documentary on the evacuation of Allied troops from Dunkirk. He participated in podcasts by *The Dead Prussian, New Books Network*, *Historically Thinking*, *Dangerous History*, and others. He now hosts a military history podcast series for *New Books Network.*

Author's Note (First Edition)

Some events in this series derive from real world acts of war, including war crimes and atrocities adapted from After Action reports, combat memoirs and eyewitness accounts. They come from widely varied armies, times and cultures, in dozens of wars across many centuries. The result is often grim and not for the fainthearted, cruel and pitiless, but true to the wide human experience of war waged over time. As dark as the tale becomes, as savage as some characters and combat depictions are, I hope my effort to root this series in a deeply human experience of the high politics of empire and the brutality of war will be rewarding to some readers.

Author's Note (Second Edition)

This book is reorganized, rewritten, and greatly expanded. Four new chapters are included, along with character and situational development in all other chapters. The story anticipates major themes in the Orion War series, adds plot twists and enhanced character arcs that continue in follow on books. Combat depictions may echo real events and veteran experience, but are reset within a complex weave of character development and future war that marks the history of the Thousand Worlds of Orion yet to come. There are numerous literary references woven into names, plot motifs, characters, and developments. Some are explicit. Others have been left implicit, as "easter eggs" for curious readers to discover and explore.

Contents

"Then it's good that you, sire, are the greatest of all the fishes in Orion, and have the strength to bend Nature to your purpose." In their early intimacy, it was still common for Takeshi to serve up a too thick sauce of gaudy flattery to Pyotr. Before he learned Pyotr's hot bile words, and thus to do it more subtly.

Pyotr let the praise slip past without retort, as unworthy as the chalky paste he pushed to one side of his plate. Then he instructed Takeshi on Imperium politics, a habit he fell into rather too easily, as his mother the Dowager had with him. He found himself eager to teach this special young officer the inner ways of the Jade Court, and his pride of place atop it. It was the first time he did it, but not the last. "You steel gray men in SAC cannot survive without Oetkerts and the old elites. Without me, specifically. You are strong but you need a stronger ruler. Otherwise a hierarchy of devouring in the oceans becomes a monstrous chaos."

"An interesting view. I agree, sire. SAC must be mastered."

Pyotr ignored him, continuing as if he never spoke. "You need the stability of the Oetkert line and support from the three noble castes. Who else will save the schools of little fish from predator fish like you, and save you from yourselves? Left unchecked, SAC will devour everything in the ocean of my people in which it swims. Then you would turn on, and you would consume, each other."

"While that is likely, sire, if it proves so, the trick is to be the last to eat."

Pyotr Shaka's narrow smile was like an *iklwa* wielded by his most famous ancestor, sharp and short and leaf-bladed, thrust not thrown into vital organs at eye-to-eye distance. It's the best way to kill a man, looking him in the eye to be sure he's dead before you let his standing corpse drop to the jade tiled floor. "How will *you* play that trick? You have no power without me, no great lands or wealth. At least not to compete with my barons and generals. You, colonel, are nothing but my shadow. No, even less than that: my shadow puppet."

"That is true, sire. That's why for a powerless, lowborn man like me *balance* is everything. Only through balance can one rule an empire or a chaotic Universe that's always seeking imbalance by its nature." Takeshi thought he made a real impression. He had, but not the one intended.

Pyotr visibly winced, clearly cut deep by the sharpest of memories. Takeshi watched his left hand move down to where he knew Pyotr wore a black *degen* inside his robe. The so called 'holy blade' was taken by a Palast Wache bird guard from the hand of a dead assassin and handed to his mother, the Dowager Empress, on the night the Broderbund murdered his father and holy assassin monks crept the halls of the Waldstätte Palast looking to kill him and his siblings. All but one. It was the way the old Brethren controlled the Oetkert dynasty and succession for over 1,500 years, choosing who would rule and who must die with an assassin's sleek and holy knife, forged from the Black Stone itself.

Pyotr preferred the black dagger to the heavy 1.5 meter *iklwa* carried by Shaka predecessors whenever they walked into the Jade Court or sat the Throne. It was the rule and tradition for centuries, until his mother the Dowager Empress said: "How ridiculous! I'm not carrying that *thing* around all day. I have real work to do!" And cast it aside. Pyotr was happy she broke precedent. The short staffed, ancient spear was too awkward for him, and he was afraid of it as a boy. Now, he only carries it on the most formal state occasions. But he's not unarmed. Ever since his mother's death brought him to the Jade Throne the captured *degen* that he found hidden on her cooling corpse has been strapped tightly to his nakedness. He never takes it off, not to wash or dress or even to rut. It reminds him never to forget his hate and power. Or his most terrible crime.

That night, he couldn't hide the thought fast enough, not before he showed Takeshi sudden anger in his royal, green eyes. '*And guilt? Why guilt?*' Takeshi knew the old stories, the whispered tales that Pyotr was a matricide. He wondered then and later if what he saw that night in Pyotr's jade eyes was a silent confession. He missed Pyotr's thinking entirely. It wasn't about his mother's death, it was about her secret words, delivered sternly to him a year earlier in the last long talk they ever had. A warning she made to always seek balance in his pursuit of power.

A warning he ignored all his life.

A warning he ignores now, on the path to war.

A warning he's too proud and vain to ever heed.

Pyotr threw a second *iklwa* smile over the table, thrusting a real threat while looking to see if Takeshi knew, if he'd pushed a rhetorical point about 'balance' to goad or mock his Tennō into letting his secret vanity and secret doubt slip out. Takeshi kept his own face utterly blank as he watched a second flash of angry guilt cross Pyotr's visage. He didn't know what the painful thought or trigger word was. Neither man was what he seemed. Both men knew that. Yet there was no mistaking the curt and silent dismissal, a quick wave of the back of Pyotr's hand in the direction of the chamber's heavy, inlaid jade door. '*He's angry, even hurt. Time for me to go.*'

Pyotr pushed away his partly eaten fish and stood tall in his blue ermine robe. It dropped tumbles of black spiced snuff on the floor as it opened partly, to reveal a surprising fat belly and sagging genitals. He called angrily for a cleaning servant, then for guards to seize the cook who prepared the disgusting white sauce that ruined his carp. Later, he ordered the cook whipped, then exiled from Kestino. '*He is grown as corpulent as he is corrupt,*' Takeshi thought. But he said nothing as he bowed before the brooding monarch, who scratched at himself vigorously beneath his robe after drawing it closed with a sweep when he saw that Takeshi could see his oily nakedness.

The next day Takeshi accessed the official Jade Court library. He scanned the *History of the Oetkerts* and of the *Third Zulu Empire.* He reread *The Shakas in Orion History*, and browsed thirty other tomes. He was sure that somewhere in all the gallant, official lies about the twin dynastic families he could find some clue to the Tennō's odd flash of anger. He failed. It was all lies and fabrications. A host of pretty and heroic lies written by generations of whorish court historians.

He wasn't allowed back to see Pyotr for six months after that. He thought his career on Novaya Uda had ended before it really began. Then another call to chambers came, and Pyotr said nothing at all about what happened before. Talk soon turned back to power and politics, and by slow turns Pyotr revealed that he needed Takeshi's help to take the Imperium into war.

Takeshi still hasn't found the trigger word, doesn't know the origin of the oozing private wound that hurt Pyotr so much he cut him off with a wave and implied threat. He's determined to find out. He knows it's important. '*It's a weakness I must discover. I may be able to provoke him with it, use it to turn him over and perhaps one day to turn him out. The Oetkerts and Shakas have sat too long upon the Jade Throne.*' It was the one, certain conclusion he came to after reading all those histories. That he was the better, more worthy man in the room that night; that he therefore had as much right to ambition and power as any royal.

***

The fifth time they were alone Takeshi watched Pyotr gorge on a huge meal of fire roasted mockfish, yams and sweet onions, washed down with a carafe of finest Zug wine. He studied the Tennō's ebony face. Traced the infamous, thin white scar running down the line of his left cheek and neck, stopping short of his artery. Rumor said a whore's knife reached bone before young and slender, and arrogant and enraged, Pyotr cut her down with his white diamond blade. Others said a rent boy did it. It was the same sordid tale, told either way. '*Oetkert men can have any beauty at the Jade Court they want. Or a slave girl or boy spotted out a window of a passing black hover. Yet the Tennō in his youth consorted with whores in the Old City. Pyotr and his father gave in to their lowest lusts. It's a real weakness of the line.'*

He explored Pyotr's jade eyes, set deep in a high cheeked Oetkert face bred to frame regal scorn. Except for the hairline white running down one cheek, he was nearly perfect. One of the handsomest men Takeshi had ever seen. Even if a lot more heavyset than he used to be, when as a princeling he still cared how he looked and seemed to others. Before his severe mother, the imposing Dowager Empress, died mysteriously, and conveniently for his ascent to the Jade Throne. Back when she was still alive and he went every night into the dark city looking for kliba of either or any kind. '*The jade eyes he gets from his paternal Oetkert side. The coal oil skin from his maternal Shaka ancestors. It's quite an imperial blend. An easy turn to murder is in both his blood lines.*'

Takeshi smelled a whiff of bitter almonds coming off Pyotr. Was it just a hint of cyanide cynicism to match his own, deeper scent of poison threat? The odor of faked belief in the 'Purity' movement that roils the empire and may yet rock the Jade Throne? Either that or someone in the royal kitchen was slow poisoning the Tennō with a little extra bitter in the mockfish oil or sauce.

Takeshi is right about Pyotr's long bloodlines of murderous forebears, but wrong about the sauces and the cyanide. The faint almond odor Pyotr gives off comes from little cascades of spiced black snuff that he's constantly snorting, sniffling and spilling. He uses it much more now that he no longer goes into the city for hard sex. He stopped his bisexual romps on the very eve his mother the Dowager died, his lust sated by power that fell to him that night. And by rich foods and wine and snuff. He stopped reckless, raunch adventures in the barrios because they no longer provoked her anger and goaded her into error. Later, he found it harder to stop a snuff habit he picked up in imitation of her murdered husband, his assassinated and much missed father.

Pyotr rules as ancient thinkers admired, with an eye to state and throne alone and above all things. Alert to constant threats to his power, he courts the needy Rikugun, his Imperial Army, and the greedy Kaigun, his Imperial Navy. They're the essential instruments of state and dynastic interest, twin pillars of all politics and power in the Imperium, though other players are secretly on the board. Yet he is so much more than the ideal tyrant of the old theorists who preferred fear to love, soldiers to subjects, policies to people. He always was, even as a lad whose every act seemed to please his father but make his sterner mother crack criticism and throw punishment at his head. He was a complex prodigy from his first spoken day, who grew into an enigma for the Ages. He's a rococo composer of genuine talent. He's a writer of learned treatises on politics and philosophy, and even on cosmological speculation. He's also a trenchant critic of all the finer arts, except architecture. He has curiously vulgar tastes and a blind spot there, tending toward ugly gigantism. You can see it in the Waldstätte Palast he built over top the old, more beautiful, graceful palace of his ancestors by the great salt lake of Kestino. He tore that one down in a week, then rebuilt his new monstrosity over ten years.

He's patron of arts and letters and founder of libraries, who also burns books. And just as in ancient fires of religious Inquisition, wherever one burns books one eventually burns people. He has made that crime already, with worse to come in the war he started. Casual and cruel and sure. He calls himself an "enlightened despot," yet he has conventionally misogynist views that are common across the Imperium. Despite claims to profound new thinking, he seldom departs from older ways and ancient traditions rooted in the founding legacy and alliance of Shakas, Oetkerts, and the vile monks of the Broderbund. He promised reform and rebuilt infrastructure, but only so he could make better war, which he has planned from the start. He does nothing to adjust the hard social contract between the Jade Throne, the three ruling citizen castes and the vast majority of noncitizens who sustain his Imperium. He does less than nothing about *dāsa* slavery or exploitation by the high castes of all outcastes.

At the fateful meeting where they started the Krevan War, Takeshi watched Pyotr shove a glazed yam into his full mouth, then push away his half-finished and heavily burdened plate to reach inside his robe for his snuff tin. He took a stiff pinch. Too stiff. Some dribbled on him. '*All his appetites are too large. Which lust does he need me to feed this night? His stomach is full, so it must be his vanity, his pride, or perhaps his bed.*'

In the two decades since the Dowager passed, Pyotr has grown so far above his people and beyond public reproach that he now dresses monotonously, a reversal of wilder and more libertine attire in his youth. There's every royal opportunity for excess, yet on most days a wider if not wiser Pyotr wears the same blue, ermine robe. Sometimes even at the Jade Court. Always in private chambers. Its top is stained darkly with dribbled snuff and spots of fish oil. *'He speaks with literati and glitterati beyond our worlds. Why is he so adored by cultural farfolk elites? It's a clever trick, ruling as a wolf yet admired by the very best sheep.*'

Pyotr is a master of flattery of fops and fools, farfolk or not. Second tier intellectuals he buys so cheaply by a turn of royal praise, he doesn't even need to slip them credits or do high favors. He has admirers and apologists sprinkled across the republican Calmar Union, too, though very few in the Neutral states where skepticism is a skill that survives because it's essential to their survival. '*Not so among aloof and too secure elites on the Calmar twin capital worlds, Kars and Caspia. There, suspicion is atrophied even within the main intelligence services. Powerful but inert armies grow moss parked in the woods, so to speak, while fleets and flotillas sit idle in the shade of moons.*'

Pyotr appeared not to even notice Takeshi, rubbing the back of his right hand under his nose three times to catch a little drop of spiced royal snot that was leaking out. He smeared what he collected on his ermine robe. Takeshi watched his every small motion, searching for revealed meaning. '*He's quite short, and self-conscious about it too. Beneath his ermine they say he wears only heels. So high they threaten to topple him in strong winds. Or so the old joke runs in Cour*t.' It's not so bad as that, but his heels are higher than most men wear. Even those obsessed with the latest Jade Court fashion, which is very high heeled right now. So, too, the powdered wig he wears on his depilated head is taller than any other worn at Court, and his chair always set higher than any other at the banquet table.

And his praetorians are all shorter. No tall man is allowed to serve in his elite household guard lest he stand over and embarrass Pyotr. The cruel bantams of the Palast Wache are captained by a proud little rooster, a short man who worked to his position all his life by studying Oetkert and Shaka history, to anticipate Pyotr's ceremonial wants and needs. One day soon he'll pay for that devotion with his life, without ever seeing Takeshi's knife at his throat.

'*Does he do it as a kind of private joke? Why does he dress his household guard in bright canary yellow, not the green-and-black of the Washi or Eagle Corps barracked all around Novaya Uda? Or the sleek gray of SAC? Does he do it to mock them and the whole Jade Court, his dead mother above all?*' Takeshi *isn't* short. It's one more thing that The Admitted squirm over and whisper about, given his rare access to the Tennō. There are vulgar suggestions about what they do in private chambers. Pyotr laughed when Takeshi reported this to him, hoping to bring down a rival and superior by spreading the tale back to its target.

Pyotr knew. It was a cover story *he* set in motion and allowed to spread to hide the truth of their private talks. He knew courtiers and generals would more easily accept that Takeshi was just a boy toy, latest fancy of the infamous rake who has sat on the Jade Throne for 20 years. "Let their tongues wag about our wagging tongues! We have more intimate business to consummate behind sealed doors, my pretty young colonel. Better that they fear your mouth than your mind, which is the real threat to their influence at Court."

Takeshi usually prefers women, yet he would do Pyotr if the favors of his mouth raised his own purposes. The hint of it is always in the air between them. But beyond suggestive talk, the Tennō never shows any interest in him, makes no advances and invites none. He's too careful and too practiced a schemer to mix his pleasure with his politics. There will always be other golden boys to bed. Pyotr brought Takeshi back to his chambers because he teetered on the cusp of war, but still fumbled for a cause to start it and sustain it. For even an Autocrat sitting the Jade Throne must take account of the opinion of folk, if only so that he may lead them from behind. And he wanted more than that.

"My worlds are too quiet, too content in their long lethargy. I cannot wait for hate to grow from war. I need passion and rage now, cries for blood and iron howling in war's nebula. I need a cause my people will follow, and fight for."

"Do you not fear that an aroused public might pull in its own direction, go farther in rage than the little war you and I discussed starting, that they may turn their anger on you and the high castes, if your war goes sour?"

"Little war? You surprise me with your misunderstanding of my intentions and of the nature of politics in Orion. A great star empire can have no such thing as a little war."

"But we have only spoken to date of war with Krevo, a minor power."

"The United Planets, as those border neutrals style themselves, will be only the prologue to my wider war."

"I understand sire." Takeshi said it, though he didn't. Not yet. Or at least, not all of it. "I see that my lord is a man of war, and would make his name Warlord."

"And I see that whenever you stumble, yes I noticed that you did, you resort to clever words borrowed from dead scholars. Is there anything more beneath that killer's gray you wear as tightly as a condom on my cock?"

"Sire?"

"Do you have the wit and skills to serve me as I need in my coming war? Have you a solution to my dilemma? I need a *cause!* We spoke of it last time, and yet you have delivered me nothing. Do you come here to my private chambers empty mouthed again? It's a dangerous game you play, if you do." He thinks: '*Should I call the captain of my household guard? Should I have this pretty, clever boy taken away in chains to be whipped for insolence? It would be a pity to rip that perfect skin and muscle from the bone, but a hard whipping might garner his attention and focus that exceptional mind of his, on service to me.*'

Takeshi flirted with full on insolence: "That is for the Lord of War to judge. But yes, my lord and warlord, I have considered since we spoke and I can give you the cause you need." '*I see more than you know, and I play a deeper game. I see that you lead an unsteady and sclerotic empire, at once eager for expansion to distract your trodden masses yet wracked by doubts about the stability of what you already hold, and whether you can hold on. I see also that the Jade Court is full of traitors. That this Green polity is inherently unstable and out of balance. It's an old story. One of the oldest. You know it, too. That's why you're so afraid.*'

What Takeshi sees more clearly than Pyotr's white scar, more clearly than his superiors in the General Curia in SAC Main HQ, is that 'Purity' is an even greater threat than is feared by the old elites and upper castes. When the mad doctrine escaped the labs and lounges of Pusan University to slither into the slums and barrios of Daegu, thence to worlds beyond, it morphed into a demand for real revolution. A cry more dangerous to the status quo than Imperator Pyotr or anyone at the top intends to permit. And yet Pyotr more than most plays with Purity's green fire, flirting with its ideas for 20 years. He is trapped by commitment, so that now he makes secret plans with Purity's leaders to launch a new war, the first in Orion in almost 300 years.

Purity for the masses mixes a cult of youth with faux genetics. Yet it's never far from the surface of public life anymore. Ideologues and activists have hitched their doctrine to demands for revival of ancient greatness. It's clever. Instead of opposing Pyotr and the old elites, the rising revolutionaries propose to coopt them to Purity. They want Pyotr to fulfil broken mystical promises made by every one of his ancestors, made as political ritual of a geriatric dynasty to a frozen empire. A rising demand by Purity to live up to the oldest ideals poses a grave threat to the social order, and to the Jade Throne. It's why Pyotr has already officially endorsed Purity. It's why he's going to war. '*Pyotr thinks that he can ride the back of this hungry bengal tiger without falling off to be eaten in his turn. Does he only pose as Purity's champion? Could he be sincere? Is he a genius or a fool? He intends to ride this striped revolution to war or cage it by the same means.*'

Takeshi thinks Pyotr is as cynical as he is, but on some days he's not so sure. The growing threat to the Jade Throne coming from the spread of the Purity faith, for it's that more than the reasoned bioscience it claims to be, is also why Pyotr groomed Takeshi from afar for five years. He sped up the younger man's career, accelerating it like a comet falling sunward, falling to orbit around *him*, sitting on the Jade Throne. And now they meet in secret, to plan war among the stars. Are they in sync, if only in this moment? How long can that last, when each man has murder and betrayal laid inside the other man's plans?

Pyotr is no Jahandar. He understands, as the Tyrant of Nalchik never will, that he needs someone outside his inner circle to bring him ideas he can't reach for on his own. The despot knows that he's too removed from his people to read them rightly. He knows that the Jade Court is so effete in its elitism it's out of touch with deeper currents flowing underneath the power structures of an aging empire, threatening to wash away its class and caste foundations. He cannot rely on advice from courtiers, cactus-like succulents who prick him daily. No spiny aristocrat will do. He needs Takeshi's hard youth, his amoral ruthlessness and useful origins in the common classes. He needs his insight into the Broderbund, which raised Takeshi on Fates. He needs his connections to Purity, which Takeshi cynically joined. Most of all Pyotr needs his high ambition and intellect. Pyotr trusts a man who shows he might assassinate him, more than one who conceals it but not well.

"What cause do you have to serve my war need? You had none last time. What do you think will move the lower orders to support the high castes and the Jade Throne in this war?"

"The Lost Children."

"That old myth?"

"Yes. It's a myth that will rouse your people, hot their blood in service to you as leader of *their* cause. How to make an old, fireside longing into fires of war."

"How?"

"Traditionalists will support your claims to the lost border systems that lie across from the western borders. You need but say the words 'Lost Children' and the old hates will rise from history's embers into tomorrow's flames and war. Even some in the high castes will volunteer for *that* core belief, for a new Oetkert crusade to return lost border worlds to the Old Imperium."

"*Phaah!* This is nothing new! I have thought the same, that we must link fresh hate to the old hates of the last war in ways to make my people want to fight anew.

The issue is only how to do it? What do you bring me that I do not have? Do I appeal to the growing devotion to Purity by turning it outward?"

"I would be careful there, Tennō. I know you have publically declared. I do not question your sincerity, even in these private chambers. Yet, I submit that Purity is more ferocious than you think, and more likely to escape your control than to serve your ends. Be careful, if you mount, how you ride. And remember that dismounting the tiger is hardest of all."

"Are you not an officer in SAC, which has declared itself to be Purity's sword and shield?"

"I am. I wear the gray, but I serve only you, Tennō."

"You serve yourself above all others, as does every man." Still, the flattery works. Pyotr is more corrupt and less immune to it than he believes. He's always decrying and waiving off flattery, yet surrounds himself with insincere courtiers and surrenders to flatterers too often. His mother saw the flaw in him early, and despised him for it. Even though she married the man who passed it to her son.

"True enough, sire. Selfishness is a Law of Nature, after all, as you often say."

"Go on."

"Purity's most fanatic adherents say that they believe in one great thing, in restoration of the origin gene bank to core Grün worlds, and later across all Orion. They say that want a genetist revolution to 'purify' and eliminate AI terraformer changes, especially the alien bacterium gene splices the AIs made."

"These fool ideas have no basis. Worse, they would expose all the billions of Orion to new rounds of the Great Plague that devastated the Dauran stars, and other long since cured mass diseases. Yet they fill the heads of lesser courtiers, and too many of my top officers. Tell me something new. My patience thins."

'*So, he does not believe. It's as I suspected.*' Out loud, he says: "Geneticism is an excuse and cover, mostly to Purist leaders themselves. A rare few are sincere, and hence dangerous. But it's not genes that in the end interest the fanatics of this rising secular faith. What they truly believe in is Death and Purgatory."

"Death I comprehend, but Purgatory? Why do you cite me this tall tale of the Old Believers? Have you nothing more to fill my dinner plate than dead myths from the larder of history's and Orion's losers?"

"It *is* a myth sire, yes. But a powerful one. A place of purging prior to eternal salvation, of cleansing impurities with holy fire, the second greatest gift of the gods. But only through and after death, which is their greatest gift."

"How do you know this?"

"I learned it first on Fates, where the monks of the Broderbund brood still on the role played by Purity and SAC in their expulsion from the Jade Court by your mother, after they killed your father and tried also to kill you and your siblings. And they think on the terrible price: massacre of tens of millions across the Imperium by your mother the Dowager, in the Red Purge of the Brethren."

"I know, I was there." It's one of the truly terrifying memories of Pyotr's boyhood, a dark and terrible place he does not like to visit but returns to unbidden almost every night. There was real threat in his visage when Takeshi spoke of it. "And the other place? You implied a second origin site."

"The Faculty Lounge at Pusan University on Daegu, where the whole idiotic idea of 'biopolitical science' was conceived, like a brat in a whorehouse. From the monks on Fates I learned Purity as its victims do. As the losers see it. From the virtuous mediocrities on the faculty at Pusan, I learned to see it as the winners do. And more important, I learned irony."

"What? Do you play with me?"

"No sire. It was there that I learned just how powerful a truly shallow idea can be, when it escapes the lounges to trouble real worlds."

"*Ha*! Alright, I'll accept that provenance. Now tell me, how does the old myth of 'purge fire' that you say is the true belief of inner sanctum Purity a danger to my dynasty? How can it threaten the Jade Throne?"

"Purity's thinkers and leaders, fools though they are, have been searching for a flammable cause. Any cause will do as they look for worlds to burn, to purify the genome with genetist fire and sword."

"Why do you use that word, and not 'genetics'?"

"Because it's not genetics. It's false science that venerates a passing genome, a DNA moment in evolution upheld as a Golden Calf to be worshipped as a false and eternal god."

"False Gods? Golden Calves? You sound like that twisted monk, Brother Maximillian Kahn, when you talk this way."

"He was my teacher, back on Fates. But how is that you know…?"

"Never mind that."

Takeshi is startled. *'I slipped, and I shall pay for the error. But I also learned something from the fall, that Pyotr meets with the devil, Maximillian Kahn. That they talk on a level and of things beyond the mad monk's role as Broderbund Ambassador.'* He recovers quickly. "Purity's home is the Imperium, as you know sire. It has very few followers among farfolk, not even those living among us. Its followers would sooner burn out your worlds than make external jihad, to crusade to far off countries of which they know little and care less."

"Again, I know this."

"I know that you do. That's why you brought me to SAC on Novaya Uda five years ago. That's why you bring me down to these chambers to juggle a different kind of fire with you, the fire of war. That's why you intend to hand the evermore angry mob clamoring for reform outside your palace door a torch of war, then point the mob to burn down your sleeping neighbor's house instead."

"Not bad, colonel."

"Purity is shaking billions out of a torpor into which they sank even under the Oetkerts during the Long Peace, if you'll pardon me that truth. That was before you mounted the Jade Throne in your youth and virility, to revive your family name and the fortunes of your dynasty."

"That's thrice. Enough flattery! Speak what you think you know."

"Grünen vaguely pine for the Lost Children worlds. Purity demands far more than that. It wants all those worlds restored to a purified Imperium, and for that it needs you to make a big war, to take and hold Amasia."

“That’s a Calmari world! Not one of the Lost Children of the Imperium. It would require a vast war to take and a long war to hold. You and I have spoken only of borderlands Neutrals before tonight, of Krevans, Threes and Helvetics. Not about war with the most advanced of all the Great Powers of Orion.”

“And yet, no great star nation may have a little war. You say so yourself.” ‘*Besides, I know that in private you speak to the General Curia and the Sakura-kai of a far bigger war, that you have promised them Amasia to save yourself.*’

“Make your main point, now!”

“You must link old outrage over your Lost Children to the Peace of Orion. Overthrow it. All of it. The whole settlement. Link your war to the lost worlds and you’ll bring a third of Grünen with you. Link it to the demand of Purists for control of Amasia, last and purest source of the Old Earth genome, and all of Purity will enlist in your wider war. They’ll volunteer for it by tens of millions, by hundreds of millions. They’ll fight for you, thinking that by doing so they’re fighting for their god. They’ll wage unholy war for *you*, as their warlord.”

Pyotr didn’t tell Takeshi that he had other conspiracies boiling fast on other burners, that he already intended to lead the Imperium into an immense war to engage all Orion. Takeshi knew that, but not the rest. He didn’t know that Pyotr had thought since before the Dowager died that he would need strong allies to take on the Calmar Union, to overcome the weight of the Imperium’s past defeats. The logic was inexorable, for there was only one other power who could help him fight and defeat the Calmar Union. It’s the last great secret he keeps from Takeshi, who did not know back then that the Green Ships that sailed once a year between Kestino and Nalchik did so with their holds full of conspiracies and secret plots. Or that plans for war were already in motion between the two great eastern tyrants that were almost ten years matured as he met with Pyotr to plan Bad Camberg.

“One war at a time my very pretty, coppery colonel. First I need a quick war with Krevo. Then we shall see about fighting the Calmar Union. There'll be time enough for more war later. For the moment, there will be no more talk of this.”

“As you say, Imperator.”

“So, we are agreed on target and cause, but not the act to start it in motion.”

***

It happened quickly, hardened suddenly as all conspiracies do. Like a slow poured but fast catalytic reaction. A question was quickly asked and answered, an understanding reached, a pact agreed. Then secret plots flowed, silent plans unfolded, a call for war and murder floated up from Pyotr's chambers, wanting to escape into Orion like odorless poison gas spreading outward on open air.

"You need a story, sire."

"A story?"

"A tickle not a torment. Too tall a tale will be exposed. You need a very small story for which your people will fight, believing that it touches deeper truths and righteousness. A story a child can stand behind. You need to supply a small, just cause to make war work for Grünen."

"What grievance have they suffered to provoke my somnolent people to awake and want the war I give them? What cause will rouse such sleepers as they, to make mayhem in Orion?"

"A lie. Covertly done and thus deniable. A tale to put your enemies in the death ground and your people under arms and in racing warships, raging for justice against all farfolk stars."

"A lie can do all that?"

"Yes, if it's well told and full of woes and wrongs. A tale of '*battle hate and battle joy by the old windy walls of Troy, and how the fight begins again and calls out the old war joy.*'"

"Stop speaking in riddles and ancient verse! What lie?"

"The oldest lie in war: that you cross your borders reluctantly, in self-defense, solely to protect what is righteously yours."

"Impossible! So small a power as Krevo won't attack me, no matter how I may provoke and prod at their border worlds. Yet, if I attack them in any way it will start a war that must leave my people cold to the cause I proclaim, even whilst rousing other powers in Orion against me." He said nothing of his knowledge of Jahandar's preparations for war. '*How can I trust the Tyrant not to betray me, to let me start a war in south Orion that draws all foreign forces here, away from his borders. What the Tyrant says and what he does could be as different as a star that suddenly flips its magnetic field.'*

"I have thought of these things as well. A terror bombing by some fool fifth columnist in a Krevan border world is easily done. Or maybe a mine attached by one of my phantoms to one of their warships, then blamed on saboteurs. What then? Aral will *never* retaliate with force."

"No, it will respond in a measured way and appeal for aid from the Calmar Union, that self-righteous shit bag empire calling itself a modest and moderate republic. It's what Krevo has always done in the past, in each of the first three Orion Wars. They call it the 'Auld Alliance."

"I can escalate, but then we arrive at the same conundrum: I have no cause to rouse my people to a righteous anger they will need to fight for the first time in three centuries. While I risk a great war of Blue against Green that must go long and bloody. A war of fatal attrition."

"Your people will support you if the lie is planned as carefully as a royal birth, to trick them into believing that they consented to the conception and delivery. They'll let it rule them."

"*Harrumph!*" Pyotr let the offense pass, then inhaled a clutch of spiced black snuff. He saw Takeshi watch him do it. "It's best after dining well and before a hunt. And war is the most royal of all hunts, the sport of kings."

'*Yes, even of fat emperors.*'

"I need this lie to hurt Krevan honor, so that they are provoked to violence. But how? I go round and round on this and cannot see a way."

"With respect, that's wrong. You must supply an outrage against *your* honor not Krevo's. A bloody deed that provokes no attack, for you're right about that. Krevans are so small and weak a people they will defend only, never assault across your border. They are like mice protecting the den from inside, never coming out to fight the snapping stoat that intends to eat them."

"How can you force the mice to come out? How can you make mice outrage my honor?"

"Not by any overt, violent act. But by compelling them to name you a liar. Krevo's denial of what they never did, but you say they did, will give your people a just cause. Their denial will most surely seal the truth of your lie. Your people will rise to defend your honor, and their own."

"You have this magic lie ready, a story to both provoke my enemy and bewitch my people?" As their subterranean conspiracy deepened, Takeshi stopped saying 'sire' or giving Pyotr his titles. He had a rising sense of equality, a surging feeling that destiny wanted him to sit the Jade Throne and make policy for hundreds of billions, not play the *eminence noir* to a fat despot draped in blue ermine.

"I do. A lie hot and bloody. For your people's blood must run hot whenever the tale is told, then retold at firesides and bedsides to children ardent for your war and eager to wear the green."

"Very well, cheeky one. I give you a fortnight to come to me with an action plan, to give wings to the lie that I must cross my borders in self-defense against angry mice."

"I don't need so long as that. I can tell you now how to start your war, how to make murder and massacre respectable to your people. To give gale force to the winds of your deceit."

"Be careful with your haste, *taisa*. There's no forgiving failure in this matter. Fail me and I will have you disappeared, but only after much torment. Then all that will remain of you, all that the gossips in all the worlds will say about your silent passing, *puto,* is that your lips failed to please my cock. It has happened before. So know before you speak again that I make politics as coldly as I intend to make war hotly. I win and my enemies lose. I will permit no middle ground."

Takeshi ignored the vulgar insult and too common threat, then bet everything on one roll of iron dice. "That is the Autocrat's prerogative. I only ask that you consider which will be harder in the end, my death or your cock." Takeshi waited in the umbra of Pyotr's silence.

'*This young man has raw courage and rare skill, though too much audacity to serve mine own words back to my face like this. Patience lordship, patience. The time will come to teach this golden boy what true power is and where it lies. Under my crown and in my person, as Autocrat and Imperator. For now...*'

"You have wit as well as cheek, to play with my words as you do, and with my royal cock. Speak then, little tan rooster. How does your own cock crow?"

"Fake a Krevan attack against one of your own frontier outposts. Fly a false flag of their unprovoked aggression to enrage your people and remind them of the beloved *Verloren Kinder*."

"Attack my own outpost? Speak of Lost Children as I do it? What will this serve? Who will believe such a thing?"

"Only those you need. For it will excite your people, raise the yellow bile of their folk memory. Urge them to join your legions and serve a holy cause."

"Excite the lower orders, you mean? The noncitizen classes, the plebs. Not the three high castes?"

"Yes. The three highest castes, the elites, will follow you for other reasons."

"Which are?"

"Their own reasons."

"Agreed." Pyotr recalled in the moment why he had pushed the young SAC colonel's career. When all is said and done, they understand each other at a primal level, and in their hard, brutal politics. "Continue."

"Portray the invasion to the rest of Orion as self-defense. Say you pursue only justice across the borders, that you seek to find, arrest and try the attackers. It will fool no one in the end, but it will confuse enough on Kars and Caspia who do not want *any* war with you to give your forces the time they need to win a small border war quickly. And once it's done, it's done."

"Intriguing. You have more?"

"Proclaim your war with trumpets, not whispers. Announce it. Broadcast it across Orion. Declare that you mount only a limited, punitive expedition to repay an unprovoked violation of your borders. Say you'll withdraw if Krevans will only make restitution. They won't."

"No, indeed they will not."

"You'll win before the other powers can react, if they do at all. For who will want to sacrifice their own worlds to recover Krevo's? Who in all Orion will want to 'die for Krevo'? Their politicians will ask it before your agents say it. Once your armies stand on smoldering worlds and your navies overfly farfolk skies, the other powers will stand down and let your conquests stand."

"Can you really pin my guilt for war on Aral?"

"Yes. In the beginning, at least for most Grünen."

"But only to start. What then?"

"The start is all that matters."

Pyotr saw the truth of the lie right away. '*Once the shooting starts it won't matter how credible is the beginning lie. And there'll be chance aplenty to make fresh deceits! My lies shall walk in long files, each inside the first one's steps, marching off to war along a narrow path though vale and mountain pass before widening on the broad star plains into an unstoppable phalanx.*'

"I will need proofs beyond mere words."

"You'll have hard proofs to take before the Great Law Courts of Orion, should you want to parade justification before such farfolk fools. While the wigged lawyers and witless diplomats talk, I shall act to make truth the first casualty of this war. I will give us warm bodies and hotter pictures to throw at their feet, in righteous repudiation of the great lie that we started the war."

'*Us? We? He elevates himself to my equal in policy and war. As valuable as he is, I shall have to humble him sooner and harder than I thought necessary.*'

"The proof must be irrefutable. I need a true lie my people will believe."

"You'll have it. If you lead, the people will follow you as the 'Father of All the Nation' who calls them to arms to rescue long suffering sibling worlds, your and their Lost Children. They'll march merrily onto your transports."

"You have so little faith that the people can discern the truth?"

"Truth is tribal. Orion will hesitate. Your people will not. Later, if you must, you will force farfolk to listen to the sound of reason speaking from the mouths of your biggest guns."

"*Ultima ratio regis*. Cannon are always the final argument of kings. The great proclamation that the founder of the dynasty and Imperium, the Jade Eye himself, engraved on his greatest cannons."

"Exactly."

"So be it. My armies and fleets shall gather for the invasions. Deliver me this chance and all the Thousand Worlds will hold their breath at my audacity!" Pyotr smiled a cold, predator grin at the naked and open cynicism of the plan they made. He reached out his left hand. "Take this with you."

It was a letter composed in Pyotr's own hand, authorizing any action Takeshi undertook or order he gave. He also handed over the Jade Seal, a shimmering and famed electronic jewel inlaid in molded platinum. Holding it pardoned in advance any crime Takeshi might commit. It couldn't be challenged by anyone, not even his superiors in the SAC General Curia. Not by governors of far off worlds or Rikugun generals or Kaigun admirals. It was a first step toward the true, absolute power Takeshi Watanabe had always craved. Holding such a thing of power in his hand intoxicated him, a commoner boy who ran away from Fates.

Before leaving, Takeshi bowed low as he chanted a 1,600 year old oath of featly to the Jade Throne, first made by his soldiers to Karl Ferdinand Oetkert, warlord and founder of the Imperium. It was more old form, archaic manners in the presence of the *blood royale*, but laid on far too thickly between men such as them. Takeshi thought there was something solemn about sordid conspiracy that rendered his choice of archaic speech a little less absurd than the words sounded on their own. Pyotr disagreed. '*This young man is much too proud of his Fates education, by the Brethren he professes to despise. If he quotes at me or flatters one more time I shall stand up and slap his face, pretty as it is.*'

Pyotr didn't stand. It was hard to stand after so large a meal and so much fine drink. But that was not the real reason. Both men knew that such rituals of absolutism demanded obeisance in the royal presence, even in private chambers. Even between conspirators about to commit murder on a grand scale, ready to unfurl the Jade Eye's war banners. So Pyotr sat as Takeshi bowed low. "Proceed, *taisa*. Move in all careful haste. We are starting the great game of war for Orion. There will be no substitute for our victory and nothing so bitter as their defeat."

And so, easily and quickly, it was agreed. That's all it takes to start a war. You don't need a slow buildup of tectonic forces to shatter the crusts of worlds, you just decide one day to smash them. War needs no deep cause to wreck peace with feral ferocity, just the will to do it. Then other men will run to help you. Wars can begin easily, as the Krevan War did, in a private chamber where just two men of ruthless will decided for war over a grilled mockfish resting in thin wine sauce, followed by a pinch of spiced snuff. Or it can start as the Fourth Orion War will soon start, in a wider conspiracy born of vanity and treachery and plots of despots.

No matter who starts it or how, blood changes all. Once blood is spilled, a war becomes a thing unto itself. It rouses and commits whole peoples beyond where their leaders ever wanted to go or thought they could control events that shape and push and pull at war. Blood demands more blood, to justify the first spilling, to ennoble that first death with claims of honor and sacrifice and redemption.

Takeshi understands that. He is on his way to spill just enough blood for Pyotr to guarantee that the star nations of Orion will rise against each other in anger, that war must come, then spread across the whole Orion spur. This war will begin with a calculated crime, as maybe all wars do. A crime will change the course of all the histories, and the lives of every person across a Thousand Worlds at war.

Ikebana

Alone.

Driven.

Gifted.

Lethal.

Takeshi Watanabe graduated top of his class from Pusan University, but he found his true calling in the Special Action Commando. His raw talent was so obvious and rare there was competition among senior officers in inner circles within inner circles to win his loyalty and clientship. He lent out both as his career required, but gave true loyalty to no one but himself. He's his own singularity.

Not even the ultra secret *Sakura-kai*, or 'Cherry Blossoms Society,' won him wholly. He committed easily and cynically, mouthing its slogans, parroting its claims in public, but disdaining its beliefs. *Sakura-kai* is dedicated to advancing Purity inside SAC, then via SAC to all the Imperium. Membership is by invitation, and is the holy-of-holies for all ambitious officers. The clique is playing the long game, plotting to take over a graying Curia and displace its Old Imperium values.

Not for Takeshi. For him, the Cherry Blossom Society is the mere vestibule of his high ambition. He was a very young captain when *Sakura-kai* initiated him, excited that a graduate of Pusan University itself, birthplace of Purity, pledged "selfless dedication to the cause of Pure genetic rejuvenation." He took the ridiculous secret oath under a mental reservation, concealing a cynical smile. He had another agenda. He always does.

Higher ups in the Curia thought they could infiltrate *Sakura-kai* through Takeshi, asked him to spy on and help control a rising and dangerous clique. They were wrong, too. He took their warrants, learned their secrets and motives, and filed it all away for future use while he fed them careful information that removed *his* rivals inside the flower clique, not theirs. SAC's proposed revolution came at just the right time for a young man of supreme talent and ambition. Takeshi joined up not because he believed SAC's revolutionary ideology of 'new genetics' and 'biopolitical science' was real science, or that the wider 'Purity' movement was a righteous cause or likely to work. He was too intelligent to accept arrant nonsense as either science or politics.

He joined because he saw sooner than most others that SAC would lead the immense changes sweeping over the star systems of the Imperium, whatever the demerits of its crude, rough doctrines. While still on Daegu, he concluded with clinically cold reasoning that SAC was exactly the right place at exactly the right time for a young man of his talents, and his ambition to pursue a path to power. He saw early, as others did not, that a Purity Revolution was coming. In a closed social and political order, he rode the rising tide to heights that men of his low origins never dared imagine, no matter the greatness of their talent. For he matched his talent to a cynical iron will and supreme intellect. Then he found a secret patron outside the Curia and *Sakura-kai*, in Pyotr himself.

In private, he holds *Sakura-kai* in contempt. He despises its heroic aesthetic of a cherry blossom as symbol of the pure life of the true warrior, resplendent in beauty yet doomed to fall while retaining a Narcissus-like perfection, still pure and unwilted. He knows that a fresh fallen blossom is just as dead as any flower lying on the ground and rotten for a week, or a month or a year. He has no intention of dying young, or stupidly, or heroically. Dying is what lesser men are for. Yet, his *Sakura-kai* connections boost him high and fast inside SAC, so that he makes colonel by the early age of 32, remarkable in an era of expanded Youthspan and peacetime years in a military where no combat or command failures served to clear out higher ranks above him. No one else in SAC or the Rikugun or Kaigun achieved so high a rank and position so quickly.

Takeshi acquired riches along the way. Although he doesn't lust for material goods, his role as SAC liaison to Pyotr brought him wealth that made him even more handsome, as riches always do. Beautiful women fluttered around, pleading for notice and the favor of his bed. He's more mature now, yet a tight, almost boyish figure and especially his wickedly intelligent eyes dazzle all the ladies of the Jade Court. And the maids and kitchen helpers, and the old dowagers too. He finds that sexual conquest is so effortless it has become mostly boring. Opulence is another accoutrement of his only lust, for power over everyone around him. Only power has allure for him, makes him want to come back for more, excites him with its hot caresses of aroused ambition. He suspected early that it was all Pyotr's doing. He took the promotions, of course. Took the easy wealth and easy women, too. Yet, he felt cribbed by any constraint of hierarchy or patronage.

He chose the Curia and *Sakura-kai* as wings of his ascent to power, letting each think that they chose him. Now he's beyond the reach of either in an aerie all his own. He's the closest confidant of Pyotr Shaka, the Imperator, the Tennō himself. More, he's coconspirator in the boldest plot of the Age, author of the big lie, secret partner with the fat despot in framing a war to change the face of all Orion, starting with the Neutrals. And he carries a passport to let him do murder.

Some in *Sakura-kai* still want him as the future leader of their ideological vanguard, to wield the 'Sword of the Revolution.' Officers of the General Curia have grown more wary, unsure of his loyalties. Suspecting that his talents serve no master past himself. Maybe not even Pyotr. '*Should I go rōnin? Is it time to move onto my own path to power, separate even from the Tennō? No, not yet. There's use still in Sakura-kai and opportunity with the General Curia and alongside Pyotr. My time will come.*'

Everyone agrees that Takeshi is a man who bears close watching. SAC spies and Pyotr's spies watch him closely. General Curia spies follow wherever he goes. Others watch who are more secret, with yet higher ambition for him, and through him for themselves. Maximilian Kahn charts his old pupil's every move and word, hoping to use him to return the Broderbund to its rightful place in the Jade Court. And yet, no one is watching closely enough. He moves like a spider, weaving webs of deceit inside larger webs of treachery. Already events are starting to stick.

***

Readying to leave on his covert war mission, Takeshi knows that Pyotr was right. That all Grün power and politics comes down to who is the biggest fish and whether he has the will and stamina to hunt down and eat all the rest. High statecraft means ruling the Imperium cruelly and from fear and threat, though with calculated means and restraint that won't provoke open revolt.

'*More like a snake than a fish, really. Like a rock python chooses and swallows its prey.*' In the end, he believes the food chain of power always leads back to a dominant carnivore, a single appetite and will. All the rest is the distraction of fools. And however vain, proud and wicked Colonel Takeshi Watanabe is no fool. He despises gross illusions of superiority and authority in others, the kind that suffuse mediocre men who wear silver filaments on SAC gray uniforms and hold rank high above his own. He chafes under rules made for those of lesser talent, enforced by second rate intellects with third rate personalities. He yearns for release into perfect freedom of action.

He looks down at the *lettre de puissance* resting on a Toruń redwood table beside his small, solitary packed bag. It glows electronic jade in a burnished platinum rollup scroll. '*This will suffice, for now. I have no more need to be polite or professional. Pyotr's passport lets me kill nearly anyone I meet, if I must or if*

I choose. What it must be to hold such power as Pyotr's in one's hands, to so easily pass this power over life and death to another!' Takeshi wears the formal steel grays of a SAC *taisa*. As he stands in his private quarters for the last time, a single black bag waiting on his red Toruń table, he has one thing left to do before taking the main elevator and rising offworld. It's hard, so he has left it to last.

He caresses a delicate Ikebana he shaped into form and flower for 19 years, pruning it in the ancient *rikka* or standing style of Ikenobo table art. His floral craft is self-taught, yet it perfectly emulates the skilled devotees of Rokkakudo Temple, still thriving on Nagoya nearly 1,700 years after that colony's founding. Takeshi visited Rokkakudo during his wandering time, after running from Fates. His keen intellect easily absorbed the special skills and insights of the cloister. Like unspeaking devotees of *rikka,* he's comfortable in silence as cold as space. '*Pyotr thinks and plots more than he reveals, even to me. Is he a different kind of monarch or like all other Oetkerts who came before? The man's so transparent he's damned hard to read!'*

Pioneers of one of the first lightsail colonies, Rokkakudo monks still rule that first wave world. Their martial energy courses through the Grün Imperium, as migrating kinsfolk like Takeshi mingle with its dominant black elites, injecting ancient Nagoyan genes and cultural patterns and isolated traditions into a tightly protected ruling bloodline of the top three castes. Political union of Nagoya with Waldstätte core worlds makes strong, elite hybrids with each new cycle: melding ruling castes, inspiring generations of young men with promises of glory and revived martial supremacy. Nagoyan women are equal on the homeworld but play almost no role offworld: Nagoyan men centuries ago accepted Oetkert and Broderbund misogyny as part of the brutal pact they made. Their wives and daughters suffered, but the men thrived in partnership with the Imperium, taking more than their share of officer commissions and governorships.

Takeshi's growing art assiduously cultivated seven delicate branches as living images of the hills, valleys and waterways of his boyhood home of Fates. He drifts there in his mind's eye whenever he strokes the flowers. He pauses now at the extremity of a petal, then suddenly he crushes the brilliant pink into pulp and snaps a delicate stem into two. A bitter green odor rises to reach his nostrils, tart and raw and hurt, mocking and accusatory. It dissipates as he burns his oldest petalled companion to dry ash inside a hanging brazier, venting it out a small window.

SAC's leaders have long made the same wild urgings that Pyotr now turns to as his *casus belli*. They call for return of claimed border worlds given up 300 years ago upon defeat in the Third Orion War, when the Peace of Orion sapped the martial vigor of Grünen and hemmed in their ambition. Takeshi knows the Curia also mixes cynicism and belief, fear of revolution with exciting lust for violence. '*There's salt in the air, and not just on winds from the Isis Basin. The tide is changing in the affairs of Kestino and Orion. Will we all be "taken at the flood," or will the rising waters lead me to high fortune in this war?*'

He yearns for war's coming, feels it in his bones, thrusts at it with his loins. He wants all that it is, whatever that costs him or SAC or his Tennō or all the Thousand Worlds. Stroking the second of his fragile Ikebana he recalls a verse his teachers chanted at matins when he was a boy, trapped in their pews. It was all mystic and prophetic, full of the usual superstitions and pieties of the old Order. He revises it to make even the Broderbund complicit in the war he brings.

The ocean of Fates is brimming its shore.
A surging tsunami rises in Purity's name.
Broderbund holy men will rally once more.
The players are legion, for war is the game.

He breaks the second Ikebana between his fingertips and places it carefully into the red hot brazier. He watches oily smoke rise out the little window. It was exquisite. It was elegant and cultivated, and was precious to him. And it's gone forever. He picks up the last flower of his youth. He contemplates it in silence. '*The monks on Fates preached that a man's character is destiny, but now all men's fates are in my hands and bald Pyotr's, including the mad monks on Fates and all the scattered Broderbund.*'

Standing over the smoldering brazier with his proudest flower held helpless in his hand, he considers the last living link to his past. It's the finest Ikebana he ever grew or shaped, a monarch of his art and its kind. He holds it still and with care. Almost with tenderness. Caresses it as he caresses no lover. Lusts overs its lines and meaning, then breaks and tosses it into the brazier. He turns and walks away. He never looks back as the last curl of smoke wisps out the window into a dust dark sky. '*I climbed the greasy pole one funeral at a time. Now war is coming and the killing will be in bushels. I have no regrets. Life is good. War is good.*'

***

Over the next three months, rumint that Takeshi devises spreads wildly over all Grün civilian memexes, spilling over the frontier into Krevo as well, ploughing worlds to make them ready for war's seeding. Witnesses he hires accuse Krevans of spying and sabotage on six Grün border worlds. In the second wave, there's talk of terrorism and targeted assassinations, and sure enough bombs go off that kill hundreds of innocents. Seven mayors and two royal governors, along with a dozen of their bodyguards, are murdered by unknown assailants. A third wave of disinformation pours acid on the building crisis, claiming there's a campaign of desecration of Black Faith meeting houses on Krevan border worlds, where ethnic Grün communities are said to huddle in fear of persecution of their faith.

Pyotr makes formal protests to a bewildered ambassador, then directly to Aral officials, pleading that the "terrorism and religious persecutions stop." Aral denies everything but agrees to investigate whether nativist groups opposed to the ethnic enclaves might be going rogue. Frontier naval patrols are put on high alert. Border world mobilizations begin belatedly on agro planets like Genève, where it's still springtime and there's plenty of farm work to be done. Reserve companies like Madjenik are called up by Toruń City and start to train with more urgency under activated but inexperienced officers. Mobilization is more thorough on the capital world Aral, where reinforcements are sent in secret to the ice moons. Just in case.

"Surely this terrible misunderstanding will clear up before summer comes?" Genèvens say. On other worlds or hemispheres where it's not yet springtime and fall plantings do not press with urgency, they say: "I can't imagine what's going on. I don't hold no truk for the Black Faith, but them Greens on the border worlds is free to worship how they please, far as I's care. It's the Life Temple for me, bies, when my due time comes! But not yet! Now bies, who wants another drink?"

It doesn't clear up. An artificial crisis is building a case for punishment of the United Planets. Few yet think it can or will lead to war. Instead, sanctions and reparations are being discussed "at the highest levels." Aral is resisting, but the Calmar Union government on the twin capitals is pushing Krevo hard to agree to a formal apology and a peaceful resolution mediated by the Calmari. All other Neutrals are worried by this policy. They, too, start to mobilize. The long frontiers of the Dauran Commons stay utterly dark, saying nothing at all to anyone. No one thinks anything especially sinister in that. Daura's vast space and many hundreds of stars have been silent to the rest of Orion for 50 years under the mad isolation of the Great Tyrant, Jahandar. Only Pyotr knows that Jahandar, too, is restless. Knows that he, too, has been arming for renewed war for over a decade.

There are a few odd reports of Kaigun phantoms trying to get inside space docks over the Calmar Union frontier. All stories of naval incursions and clashes are denied by Pyotr, and by top MoD sources on Caspia and by the PM to the Lok Sabra, or Great Parliament, on Kars. No one wants war over what seems a local quarrel with the United Planets of Krevo. So the Great Powers lie to their peoples.

They both deny that phantoms were spotted or engaged, while all naval deaths are covered up. Families of a lost NCU crew are told the ship blew from a micro crack in its fusion reactor. Families of a missing Kaigun ship are told a dodger failed while entering an unexpected dust cloud, while moving much too fast.

Now Pyotr's forces stand ready to pour into five Krevan border worlds when war comes. The invaders will fall from the skies in cascades. Wave after wave of irresistible force in overwhelming numbers, with new speed tactics on the ground to overwhelm all local resistance long before the diffident Calmari understand the threat or bring themselves to act. If they choose to act at all. For who indeed will want to die for Krevo, once Krevans start to die on all their invaded worlds?

Pyotr preemptively, and in deepest secret, offers peace talks to Prime Minister Robert Hoare's government on the twin capital world of Kars, home of the Lok Sabra or Great Parliament. He does it via an ultrasecret contact his Kempeitai have via MoD on Caspia, with liaison through a stunningly beautiful double agent who plies the high society set and scene on Kestino. *Lasalle Five* simultaneously sends desperate secret communiqués to her boss, Sanjay Pradip, who reads them in his *All Secure* cubicle in the sixth MoD tower in Lowestoft-on-Stamos. He ignores every warning. He's working with the PM to avoid war, so he suppresses all agent reports that say it is likely coming anyway.

So far, all seems to be going according to Pyotr's plan. The pieces on the board are moving all at once, about to change the history of Orion. The diplomats are all talking still, even as fleets and armies are assembling. Pyotr tells his generals and admirals to mobilize cohort reserves and hasten raising entire new legions. More legions are assembling across the Dauran frontier, but not even Pyotr knows how many or where they will strike, or when.

Takeshi leaves Kestino to handpick disposable men who will soon dispose of others. War is just four months away. When he sends the first code word back, Pyotr's order will go out to massive fleets and armies: "*Position at the invasion jump points.*" When his covert mission to the Bad Camberg moonlet succeeds he will send back a second code, a signal that will unleash hellhounds of war into the Thousand Worlds of Orion. Time's Arrow is in arcing flight, its spine straight, its fletches straining, its barbed tip eager to penetrate history rushing up to meet it.

***

Novaya Uda is a vast sprawl of a city, the largest in Orion. It hosts four billion Grünen and 150 million more farfolk, crammed into a huge bowl shaped valley surrounded by a dozen extinct volcanoes. Its soil is white and acidic from salt of the ancient sea bed on which it's built. Its immense food needs must all be met by offworld supply. That primal need drove its people to export war and to import tribute over many centuries, after the Oetkerts came to Kestino to build their palace and capital on the edge of the great salt flats of the Isis Basin.

The city is immense because it's low built and sprawling. No towers reach into the twinkling sky as they do on most cities in Orion, but it hosts thousands of squat towers and walled off, class and caste segregated commanderies. They were once the personal military bases of the exiled Broderbund, a system of connected forts from which the armed order of monks occupied so many worlds. The walled compounds are mostly empty now, shuttered by the Dowager Empress after her Red Purge that slaughtered most Brethren. Only a few show odd lights at night, raising gossip at Court about potential shifts in Pyotr's policy and politics.

Novaya Uda is hot and dry, dotted with tens of thousands of blue lagoons and hundreds of larger reservoirs. It's poor and miserable, and fabulously rich, built and kept by theft of labor and the lash. It's heavily garrisoned and policed. It stinks of half-treated sewage and smells wondrously of open air cooking, of spiced foods and burning incense on every hectic, bustling street corner. It's impressive and oppressive all at once. It's Pyotr's capital, and his greatest burden and fear.

It's the royal seat of the Grün Imperium, packed with military resources and reserves, riddled with spies and farfolk agents and plotters from all across Orion. Excepting, as always, the silent brown stars of Daura. No one comes from there, except one Green Ship each year. Its huge barrios and slave quarters are watched by ubiquitous police in steel barracks. Just outside its Old City Walls are the broad salt flats of the Isis Basin, home to a thousand SAC prisons and forced labor camps, and more ordinary jails for common criminals and migrants and hill people. At its core is Jade Center, a complex of heavily fortified buildings that include SAC HQ, the General Curia, the Main Barracks of the Eagle Watch, and of course the Waldstätte Palast, the largest building in Orion since Pyotr rebuilt it, to mark his coronation and encase his vanity.

Novaya Uda *is* the arrogant majesty of the Imperium; second historic home of the Oetkerts, who moved to Kestino from the original Waldstätte core 973 years ago. It's the great anchor to the tethered ambition of Pyotr Shaka Oetkert III, Grün Imperator and Splendor of the Ages. Or that's what he's called when he dresses like an ancient Zulu war chief, and stands barefoot and uncomfortable on cold marble, an *iklwa* in his right hand, a rawhide shield braced by his left. It's always hard for his courtiers to hide smirks and sniggers behind fans, and feigned coughs.

The city spreads like a worn out blotter under Takeshi's maglev ascent, 2,000 klics below and falling. His cab slows effortlessly as it nears the upper terminus of the main elevator. Silver filament trims the inner door of an extraordinarily luxurious cabin, made of ancient wall ceramics warmed by Toruń teak panels and floors and furniture, with blue ermine throws so thickly spread under his feet he finds it hard to walk. Priceless art is hung all around. Some he recognizes, from the usual cultural and art history texts. Each piece is over a 1,000 years old. Gold and jade inlaid monograms in all furniture borders on the vulgar, and the interior smells faintly of fish oils and bitter almond. For this is Pyotr Shaka's royal skycab.

It's deceptively shaped. Clumsy looking from outside, like an ancient streetcar or silver tube diner, all rounded and grub-like, obese and obsolete. Kestino's main elevator is one of the oldest in Orion, dating nearly to the founding over 1,800 years ago. Yet the ceramic grub glides easily up along a carbon fiber guide cable to reach the top of the God's Lift, out of sight of an oversize base below that's as distant as the ceiling anchor rock, bola whirling out another 1,000 klics in space.

He doesn't look down one last time though the transparent cabin scuttle to see the curve of Kestino. He doesn't gaze in admiration at Novaya Uda's deep volcano valley, looking like it's full of diamonds, with natural light glinting off its thousand interior lakes by day or electric blues sparking like a swarm of frantic fireflies from tens of thousand of elite residence towers at night. He's not a bloody tourist after all. He's rising above the termite city below on the most important covert mission undertaken by anyone anywhere in Orion in at least 300 years. At this moment, he's the single most important man in all the teeming hundreds of billions who inhabit the Thousand Worlds. For silent, cruel, Takeshi Watanabe rides up to start a war among and for the stars.

Even if he looked down, on this day he'd see very little. An all planet blow is moving in, obscuring everything in impenetrable tawny haze. It's already crossed over twin salt oceans from a desert continent, smallest of three, that powers it with parched thermals that rise ten thousand meters high. It has already crossed the coast, readying to flow down into the deep volcano valley bowl hosting Novaya Uda. When it gets there it will swirl around the elevator base, until only the top of its ultrasteel spire escapes into space. The whole city is battening down to ride out the howling, which will attack it like a horde of screeching banshees. Nothing and no one can prevent or stop a wild blow this big, not even the very best planetary engineers. This is a gathering storm that could last a long time.

It's a monster, the biggest storm to leave the desert continent in 300 years. At ground level it's already turning everything monochrome. Even elite restricted zones look the same as squat factory parks and the barrios. Red-brown sand the consistency of fine flower swaddles walled off, private towers and covered lakes of First, Second, and Third Class areas. Everywhere else it chokes water and air filters and bites at any exposed flesh with a trillion swirling, sand grain midges. It happens twice a year. Storms cross the narrow ocean gap laden with red-brown sand whipped up over the desert continent, the one reserved to the military and SAC that anchors a military only elevator. It's the newest, most spartan of three God's Lifts rising from anchors on Kestino. The one Takeshi rides is the oldest.

Takeshi got out before the blow began. He rises indifferent to it, along cables of the main elevator anchored in the elite zone, reaching upward for a cluster of elite orbital hotels and High Caste playground getaways. Atop them all, of course, is Pyotr's heavily protected private retreat. The Waldstätte Palast is close to the elevator base. Even so, as he fattens, Pyotr likes to travel less these days. A third, heavy industry and cargo lift is out of Takeshi's sight on the farside, sited between two other large and flat urban sprawls. Worker and lower caste cities.

Most of the planet's surface is hidden from unaided sight, not just because he set the cabin floor and walls to *opaque* instead of *transparent*. You can't do that on the basic lift he rode down when he first arrived on Kestino 20 years ago, a talented vagabond but also just another refugee kid, wandering as far away from an unlovely life with the Brethren on Fates as he could get. A country mouse come big eyed to see the great city for the first time. That day, he marveled at Kestino. Today, most of what's below is hidden by immense brackish clouds of sandstorm dust. He's immune to the burgeoning storm as the cab slows and docks. The stars where he's headed are bright, free, and recklessly indifferent to anything below. They care nothing for such minor storms of nature or of human conflict, for dead art or hosts of termites scurrying to make ready to fight over the rocks they claim.

Takeshi stands in confident anticipation as silent magnetic brakes smoothly slow then stop the ride. He strides briskly through wheezing auto doors, not noticing a tiny puff of red dust is making a miniature dirt devil behind him, inside the cabin. It was carried in there on his high black boots, disturbed into movement by a micro difference in air pressure as the doors swoosh open and departure platform scrubbers go into action. He glides across gentle floor magnets holding onto iron filaments in his military boots, resisting yet not resisting his muscles and footfalls just enough to simulate gravity for the brief time he'll be on the departure platform. It's utterly deserted, as Pyotr ordered. No canary guards are there to protect or observe. The place is entirely empty, even of terminus teks.

Takeshi strides across to another airlock, entering and taking position in the pilot's chair of a sleek, stealth, bohr jumper. He pulls away from the dock under gentle steamjet steering, the fusion reactor barely turning over. At 10 klics out he turns on camo and warms in-system fusion engines to *hot*. There's a slight kick of acceleration before dampeners compensate when he engages the main drive.

Novaya Uda recedes over the horizon, its glowing dome hugging the surface already half under the storm, the rest disappearing behind a darkening curve as he boosts away. He kicks hard for the targeted bohr zone, unseen and unheard as his little ship pushes past one of Kestino's dead moons with a steady, routine *hum* of the fusion drive the only sound inside other than his calm, regular breathing.

He will plant Pyotr's lie on Bad Camberg, and change Orion forever. Troops and warships are waiting to gather at jump off bohr points. Waiting on his word. As soon as he receives a success code from the airless moonlet and passes it back by direct link to Pyotr, they'll swarm over the Krevan frontiers to launch the first multisystem war in three centuries. *'It's war at last! Gods, I do love it so!'*

Naujock

"Alright, we're done with preliminaries. Get ready to go dark for the next three months. You're going to lead the offworld training for my operation." Takeshi doesn't *ask* Albert Naujock to do it. Nor does the crooked *gunsō* think about refusing. He knows this *taisa* well, and that he'll kill him if he shows hesitation. Basic security protocol, but also his personal and always lethal style. Naujock is the first man Takeshi handpicks for Bad Camberg. He's a veteran sergeant with loads of covert experience and wet work. His virtue is primal, an instinct for blunt violent action over thought. His vices are coarse, but that will help in this mission.

"Ya boss. Yuh jus tell me when an' wheh ta go, an' I'll do it." Naujock's crude speech pattern is partly his Aral dialect, part coarse family accent, and about a third mangled nose from a street fight he lost badly. But mostly it's just sloppy, lazy speech. He grew up slummy in an ethnic enclave, dropping out of school at 14-years old to day labor. He never had much ambition to fix his nose after it got broke, let alone his speech. But he's not without special talents.

They're both in mufti, sitting in an alcove of a barrio bar in Pusan on Daegu. The room is full of off duty SAC and Rikugun, the latter from Kolno Barracks outside the city. Most of those in pale green uniforms are kids. They're already badly drunk and oblivious to the meeting of two casual civvies in the back of the bar that will change all their lives, and kill a good many of them.

Takeshi shoves a jar across the table filled with fine *shochu*, a milky sweet potato liquor distilled over a base of *koji*, or mold rice. It smells of sour cheese and curds. He tosses an even rarer prize to Naujock, a pouch of Sachi blue chaw tobacco. It's either pre-Grim Revolution from Daura and pulled from a hidden horde in a SAC cellar. No way it was smuggled over the closed Dauran frontier. It's the way they always seal these deals, with coarse liquor and rare chaw and open threats. Naujock gulps the *shochu* greedily, drawing a disdainful look from Takeshi over his display of uncouth haste and sloppy noise. He grins back and stuffs a large blue chaw under his lower lip. A tart odor of dark plant juice and oils mixed with saliva reaches for Watanabe's nose.

"After tonight, until the delivery is complete, until I receive your first confirm code, your *double* confirm code, you're on your own. Got it?"

"Ya, ya."

"I expect twice daily reports and biweekly vids. You have full access to my terminal via the military neb cut out. Get on-and-off fast, but use it."

"Wight boss. All dat's wight hiyah," he taps his head," "da call'in sked'jewel an' codes."

"Are you sure you can handle command?"

"I kinda like it, boss. Ya know, bein' in chawge 'an doin' offic'ah link shit."

"Thought you might."

Three quarters thug and one quarter butcher, Naujock adored Takeshi from the first time they met, three years ago. He's done lots of covert work, not always for the Curia or *Sakura-kai*. He's a loyal if mangy and raggedy cur. His bite is sharp and deep and quick. He has been at Takeshi's exclusive beck and command for over a year now. He knows how to keep secrets, too, cutting a throat quickly with a titanium street shiv if that's what's needed.

Or two or three throats, like the border governor's he sliced last week after he knifed two startled bodyguards who fought back only weakly and went down fast, because they were retired peacetime Rikugun and badly out-of-shape. For this mission, Naujock prefers a military issue Q-carbon blade to the usual titanium shiv. He has one tight to his jackboot, holstered with a magnetic clip.

"I've already stored the funds and main supplies. Over *here*, look at the damn holomap *gunsō!* This is where you'll train. A scaled mockup is waiting for you, crated but ready."

Naujock looks surprised, then skeptical. "*Thehya*, boss?

"Yes, *there*. It's under full spectrum camo, a trapped rainbow. It cost a large fortune to hide it that way. But no expenses spared on this mission."

Naujock pulls his unspoken question back inside, curling his tongue around his juicy blue chaw instead. '*Ya, sure, but it's a helluva ob'vi'us place ta hide a black ops camp, all da same.*'

Takeshi reads his face and hence his thoughts. It's one of his key skills. "It's hidden in plain sight. It's a very old trick. And who would think to look for a rainbow in the desert?"

Naujock has no idea what that means and doesn't care. He trusts this man. It's an error that may one day cost him his life. "You'll set up the scale model before the others arrive. Just give the blueprint to the constructor bots. Any issues with equipment or timing and you get in touch, but only via the designated cut out."

"An da men?"

"I'll send men to you in batches as I find and hire them. No one will notice so few, traveling alone or in twos and threes. They'll start arriving in a fortnight. Any problems, you take care of it yourself. On the spot. Leave no traces. Understood?"

"I gotta couple aw names might do faw ya, if ya wan' 'em. Caw'pwals, bohd ah 'dem."

"How do you know them?"

"We wus t'gether on twee ops in da last two yee'ahs. Gud men wid masahs owh knives. Owh whadevah. An' dey'll keep dey godsdamn mouds shut."

"I'll check them out. Paper only. No e-trails on this mission, ever. Security protocols *at all times*."

"Ya boss, pwoto'call."

"Do it now." Takeshi watches ham fisted Naujock awkwardly draw more than handwrite raggedy-jaggery names on a small piece of flash paper. Clearly, he seldom uses anything other than thought-text, and not even that too often. The list looks like it's written by a drunken goat, all cloven and streaked.

"Gud men, boss," he repeats eagerly. Takeshi takes the note with a look of disdain, commits the names and contacts to memory, and ignites the flash paper with a quick twist of his fingers. It's gone in a white puff instant.

"No promises. On this mission it'll be better if the men don't know each other before they meet at base camp. They'll be mission secured after that."

"Wight. Pwoto'call!" He just discovered that he likes to say the word. Thinks it sounds official and real important.

"It may serve to have two old hands who you know can help you put down any trouble, and who can take your place if necessary." They both know what he means by that. Still, Naujock nods confirmation. "And who can be relied on to do right when it ends. Are these names up for *that,* too?"

"Yas' boss! Gud men, like I say. Ya ken depend. Dese awh not da type who pick da wong winnah in a one nag wace. Dey'll git da job dun wight."

"I'm not talking just about the action on the moonlet. What about afterward, when the op is done? Are your corporals up for *that*?" The white of Takeshi's jet black eyes shows red flecks that flit over from his pupils. A corrosive zinc-and-nitric acid scent rises along with wisps of anger, reaches into the closed air system and across the table. Naujock knows Takeshi's anger smell. He doesn't flinch.

Next table over there's a skinny, totally bald kid in green RIK uniform with a shoulder flash that reads Gross Imperium. No, not just bald. He's depilated, head-to-toe. He turns his handsome head, sniffing the air, puzzled at a strange and bitter odor. He's too drunk to do more. Or to ever imagine that he'll die screaming under ultrasteel tracks of an ACU assault armtrak on Glarus a year from now. The two kids with him came down on the civvy maglev from Lentvaris to see their school friend. The black-haired one looks most like a native Pusan. He's in Rikugun 21st Infantry, a basic outfit. The blond is in the worst unit on Daegu, the scrubeen 32nd Supply. The difference hardly matters. They'll both die on Amasia in 18 months, one from a frag grenade that he fumbles into his own slit trench while trying to hook it to his weaves. The other one will be roasted alive by a 'Goldie' skycraft that takes out his ski troika, leaving him trapped in the cab while it burns.

"Yas' boss! I ken vouch. An' if not, leave dat and dem ta me, boss." Naujock has his own plans for afterward, that not even his favorite SAC colonel needs to know right now. He grins as he chews blue sachi and thinks about how clever he is. Takeshi looks at him with suspicion, then shrugs. He doesn't give a shit about what happens to Naujock after. Only the mission matters.

"Alright, last chance for hard questions before you go hot and silent." Naujock tries to look thoughtful, squeezing furrows into his thick brows and squinting out one eye, the way he believes all smart people do while thinking. He looks like a bloody pirate instead. He knows that this special *taisa,* this sleek and lethal SAC colonel, thinks of every contingency. That 'the boss' anticipates all plan flaws and follies, foresees errors and preempts them. He knows he doesn't have to think up any questions, that all are asked and answered. He *loves* working for this man!

"I said, any questions? Spit out that chaw and answer me right now, or I'll make you swallow it!" Naujock spits away nothing. He's not about to waste a good blue chaw to satisfy this *taisa's* odd sense of dark humor. Still, he aims to appease, just in case. He's seen Takeshi kill for less. He knows that he carries Pyotr's passport and the Jade Seal, excusing any crime or murder. Like the two governors they killed.

"All gud boss. Ya got it cov'ahd." He saw the Jade Seal right after he knifed the second border governor a month ago, and the dying man's guards tried to hold him. He couldn't believe the looks on their faces when they saw his colonel flash that electronic jade at them. They positively groveled, and released Naujock immediately. That was just before they took Takeshi's diamond blade *snick!* into their guts, real fast and three times each.

"No witnesses. Or *you'll* never see it coming, either." That's all this colonel said to his devoted dog as they walked away from the murder scene to a sleek, needlenosed hover, all black with the SAC erect bear stencil glowering on its side.

"Looks gud boss, da plan. Weal top dwawah, I hav'ta say. Ev'ah'tins fust'wate, not lak my last thwee ops. Not dat I'm complainin' mind, I'm jus' sayin' dat I cud get usd' ta dis' way a' do'in 'tings. All fus class, lak."

***

Naujock is happy, and not just about all the extra pay for wet work and all the topnotch stuff he gets to play with. He loves the target of this mission. He hates his native Krevo and all Krevans. The United Planets is a harmless, small republic of just 24.5 billion citizens occupying some two dozen planets and moons in 12 systems. It abuts the northern Imperium right where the last of Pyotr's green star systems reach toward the first brown border stars of the lower fringe of dark, silent Daura to the north. But Albert Naujock hates "each fookin' plah'net and eva fookin' one a dah bill'yons." He hates Krevo because it's part of him. He was born there, spent the first 23 years of his brutish life there. Then, twelve years go, in the capital Yalto on Aral, Naujock got into one too many brawls in a local bar.

It was a lopsided fight and he lost badly. Oddly, it was with three student locals, all tough farmers' sons underneath their books. It started as a typical one-on-one in an end-of-the-week watering hole in the student quarter. He went there to argue politics so that he could provoke the smart boys, show them up and showoff to impress pretty Krevan girls who always fluttered like moths around the Old Quarter bars. And around him, a gruffly virile, worker class tough.

The fight spilled into the street where the three students gave him the beating of his life. They left him unconscious in a gutter with half his face mashed in by a cobblestone. He came to covered in blood and badly concussed, his lower lip split apart and bleeding profusely, his right eye totally swollen shut, his nose unnaturally mashed and flattened right up against his cheek. His lip he sewed himself, so that it's jagged still. The broken nose he unbent after first downing a liter of straight corn liquor. Between the pain and the fog of hard booze he didn't get it all the way back to dead center.

Afterward, he liked to boast: "It's cwooked'ness is a wee'min'dah ta me and a waw'nin' ta youse of ma loyalty ta dah *heimat*, ta ma Faw'dah'land." That's what he called the Imperium. His *heimat*, an ancestral homeland he had never seen except in some Dark Memex agitprop piped in to the Krevan border worlds. The kind of heavy ethnic lies always delivered in the "Voice of God" documentary style that made him long to embrace oddity, like a specialist whore. It was the trigger that started the brawl. What earned him the severe beating in the street and nearly cost him his life was shouting out the ugly motto of the Purity movement even while throwing and taking far more punches. "*Sonnō jōi!* Wee'vee'yah dah Emp'eh'woh! Expel faw'folk!"

"You're the fucking farfolk here!" one of the Yalto student brawlers yelled back at him, not understanding that barbarians like Naujock never know they're the barbarians. Then he caved his face with a cobblestone prised from the curb, muddying an excellent debating point just a little bit.

Naujock shouted the Purity slogan again, then spat a broken tooth at the boy with the brick. So he bashed him a second time, and a third, flattening his nose and breaking his lip and cracking his skull. "Get out of Yalto!" Another slamming blow with the brick. "Get off Aral or we'll kill you, you fuckin' swine!" Punch to face, again. And another. Albert's face started to look rather squashed.

"Go suck Pyotr's cock." Yeah, I know. Not very elevated language or tolerant viewpoint for a Yalto college boy, but that mattered less to Albert than the fact the slur came with a kick that broke two of his lower ribs. Then all three boys piled on. They knocked young Albert senseless, left him bleeding out and pretty much for dead, lying semiconscious in a red-yellow puddle of blood and bitter smelling piss. Yalto police arrived conveniently late to the brawl scene, but found only a bloody brick and a square hole in the curb. He was a half sector away, having gone to another bar where he downed a liter of corn liquor then roughly readjusted his nose. When they caught up to him he was outside, sitting on a curb, humming a cheap, ethnic Grün patriotic song he learned on the dark memex. So they hauled him in for "public troublemaking."

He shouted "Puwity faw Owion, awh Downfall!" and "Det ta aw faw'folk" a third time. That won him another hard beating, this one from the police, with fists and black truncheons. After that he fell unconscious for two days. He woke up in a pile of his own piss and vomit, then spent a month in Yalto's common jail. Then a judge ordered him deported from Krevan space under close police escort. No appeal. He was dumped on the first cargo transport headed to the nearest Grün frontier system and told: "Never come back, or we'll do you permanent." He spat back onto the dock from the cargo ship's ramp as it withdrew into the ship.

He spent a year working in a winery in a backwoods town on Zug before he was scouted, after three more bar brawls, by a *Sakura-kai* recruiter looking for someone to do wet work. He joined a covert ops unit as an unblinking adherent of Purity and a useful thug. An unclean dog who did only a few simple tricks with knives and knuckledusters, but did them very well.

He bit and mauled for *Sakura-kai* on demand. For nine years he made a hard living as a street enforcer and occasional assassin, rising to master sergeant, the highest rank open to a man of his off-*heimat* birth and low caste. That's when Takeshi met him. Now, he's in charge of the greatest mission of his thug's and murderer's career. One so black, so off-the-books, it's not even classified. One with death all over it, going in and coming out. And real good merc pay to match.

Privately, Takeshi enjoys seeing this crude *gunsō* decked out in SAC's elite grays: a certified Purity man, a would be "human vessel original" with a smashed in face, the manners of a hog, and little brain. Sitting in a civvy offworld bar and both wearing mufti, it's obvious who's in charge and wears a uniform effortlessly and naturally, and who's the hired man. Although almost anyone looking at the two of them would surely mistake which one is the more casual and skillful killer.

Takeshi knows that Naujock is a good man to have in a fight, and that he'll do anything he's told and shut up about it afterward. Those are exactly the qualities needed for the Bad Camberg op. They part at the bar door, then move down the street in opposite directions. The next communication they have will start a war.

Phantom

A month recruiting offworld sends 200 reliable, discardable men to Naujock's base camp. Most are just like him, ethnics born into outsider minority settlements that coexisted for the last three centuries in fairish peace on border worlds of the United Planets. The majority hail from three frontier systems jutting like a gallery of Krevan worlds into claimed Imperium space. They speak fluent Krevan as well as Standard, with local Genèven or Katowice or Brno accents. They know and like the local beers and hotly spiced dishes, and understand Krevan townie slang. They're perfect. Should anything go wrong they are disownable as rogue ethnics making an unsanctioned bandit run, for reasons all their own. Maybe they are *agents provocateurs* from KRA intelligence? Maybe they're Calmari plants? Anything but Pyotr's handpicked men on a mission to attack one of his own border outposts. Full deniability is built into this plan at every level.

Takeshi gives the mission the codename *Truant*. The triple *entendre* appeals to him: starting a war over truant systems of the old Imperium, using truant mercs to do it, with himself truant from SAC and Kestino, beyond recall authority of any superior even in the General Curia. He dresses them in old Sendai Garrison gear, stolen in a lighting raid on that backwater Rikugun base on Tohoku. To cover the trail, he orders the base commander executed by garroting for "theft of goods and black market sales." He strips off Sendai Garrison flashes, substituting a generic RIK flash of a unit that doesn't exist anywhere in the enormous Rikugun order-of-battle. No one will ever check that. Not once the shooting starts as the invasion fleets fall on five Krevan worlds with fire and fury, and dropships open bowels full of invaders urgent for release into the foul pit of war.

Using older utes taken from Rikugun storehouses gives plausibility to the mission, and extra deniability. The KRA has uniforms just like Sendai Garrison in storage, taken off Grün prisoners during the last Orion War. If the mission goes badly, the story will change, identifying and hunting down Naujock's men as mercs hired by Aral, not Kestino. It also tickles Takeshi's humor to deflect blame onto RIK and away from SAC, should the whole affair go badly wrong.

On the other hand, he dresses his own perfect body perfectly. It's his one outward vanity, to always sport sharp creases and wear jackboots shiny and new, not blackened by polish rubbed over hard wearings but not covering all wear. Nothing like the scarred boots and baggy ceramic armor weaves two centuries out of style that he ships down to Naujock. His vanity is going to hate Genève when he gets there. It's going to get horseshit, mud and brains all over his shiny boots.

Takeshi keeps the pilfered weapons and gear separate from uniforms he steals from deep vaults of SAC. He orders that special equipment packed in cargo crates and guarded nonstop by reliable men with instant *shoot-to-kill* orders. He visits the out-of-the-way storage facility just once, approving the consciously gruff and dirty look of all the guards and their cultivated air of carelessness. No one will look twice at such rough and slovenly men or think anything of real importance could possibly be guarded by them. Unless you're fool enough to look too close and see a vacuum cold killer looking back with fish eyes. Then you're dead.

Naujock sets up the secret base camp to train arriving mercs at an abandoned prison deep inside the desert continent of Kestino, an uninhabited wasteland even the ancient AI nanny bots could do little with. The old stalag was empty for 200 years except for the clanking of basic maintenance bots. Its silence was broken by living things only when quick sounds of desert rats scurried behind cracked walls, followed by quicker blue snakes that hunted them through secret holes. Takeshi had the abandoned old prison concealed with the most expensive camo in all the Imperium, 'rainbowing' it a full month before Naujock got there. Now it fills with mercs and *hums* with malice and his and Pyotr's lethal design and purpose. It will empty again as *Truant* rises to meet three phantom class ships, then heads to barren Bad Camberg and a rendezvous with murder.

***

Naujock gets the Stage I *go code* from Takeshi: *Tennō chūshin*, "Emperor at the Center." He orders everyone except three NCOs into shackles. It's Takeshi's idea and order. *Truant* will avoid the military elevator rising out of the central desert. It'll board instead on an old shuttle disguised as a fat and slow prison transport, with the mercs in chains and dressed like convicts. A lot of men don't like it, having worn leg locks for real before. They shut up and put on chains after Naujock shoots the two loudest complainers. Their semi-roasted bodies curl smoke from raw chest cavities as the shuttle lifts off. They lie on the desert sand outside the load bay, now just rat food, no longer men. Scurrying sounds say something is coming out from behind the walls to eat. Something awful crawls up one of the dead men's sleeve. It's going to nest in flesh.

The old crate strains hard off the surface, struggling for orbit on worn fusion boosters. Its ship's ID is broadcasting an old but genuine prison code. No ground agent or station pays it any attention, while Kaigun orbital patrols ignore it completely as it breaks Kestino's gravity barrier and enters a high holding orbit. A lot higher than normal for a cargo or prison ship. Two stealth boats, phantom class, take onboard 200 mercs who are now out of their chains and prison getup, wearing Sendai Garrison utilities or 'utes.' They divide evenly. Special cargo is loaded into the bays of a third S-boat. All three phantoms immediately go *all-silent-running* to make the two hour trip to the closest bohr zone. They glide in hot and wink out cold, without anyone noticing.

The little flotilla dodges and feints, to be sure. It makes four misdirection jumps away from the frontier, then nine straight-and-hard to the border, all in stealth mode, before arriving at Koblenz. Thirteen jumps in five days is real hard on the crews, who go through 'the vapors' or 'bohr effect' way too many times in so short a time. One man doesn't come back out. He's bound to a cot in Sick Bay. He's done for, synapses permanently scrambled by the spacetime fold his ship passed through (or under, or over, or…). It's harder on land huggers crammed in loading bays designed only for cargo. But none of them are in the 0.012% of folks who just never come back from 'bohr effect.' Besides, this lot is expendable.

Final destination looms into view as three phantoms glide out of the Koblenz L3, heading toward the small moonlet known to locals as Bad Camberg. It's three hours in normal spacetime at cruising speed from the farside LP to the moonlet. Time enough for everyone to recover from bohr effect. Time enough to check in with mission command via the near instantaneous 'bohr telegraph' that leaps from LP to LP in a quantum instant, before resuming mere lightspeed travel in-system.

Naujock sends '*Truant in position*' by bohr relay. Ten minutes later a laconic Stage II confirmation code arrives from a Kestino outer system LP where Takeshi is parked, to reduce signal lag time. There's no delay on his end because he's already positioned in the bohr zone, but more at Naujock's end where the message slows to mere lightspeed and has to chase down and catch up with the phantoms, to finally arrive in Naujock's HUD: '*Grandmother Dead.*'

"Mission's a 'go,' boys!" Naujock shouts over the full company command link, flashing it to all HUDs as well. Curses and cheers echo inside the two ersatz troopships. *Truant* has long since dropped the prison suits and shackles out an airlock. Now its teams pull on vacuum glide suits over the old and mismarked RIK 'utes.' The vacuum suits are also vintage and unidentifiable.

"Aw'wight, shaddup! Load up an' set'tell down. Check yaw gewah an' suits an' all weps. Not lon' now, boys." The phantoms are fast approaching the sterile moonlet orbiting Koblenz, primary planet in the Sankt Goar system. Koblenz is a quiet world, tucked right up against the Krevan frontier. Not much happens here, ever. Not in the last three centuries, or ten more before that. Not 'till now. Bad Camberg is an oversized rock orbiting Koblenz in a long ellipse. It has a minor defense post to guard the stretched Lagrangian area made by the moonlet's oblong orbit. The S-boats are slowing to low sublight as they near the big rock. It's at the near end during this stage of its bolo orbit, as close as it ever gets to Koblenz. So close, that this is the perfect time and access point for a surprise KRA attack on the moonlet, the planet, and the Sank Goar system. Or so memex propagandists will say, emphasizing how devious Krevans are: "*As shown to all the worlds of Orion by their criminal sabotage and assassinations, and vicious persecution of our innocent faithful trapped on the other other side of the border! Kept prisoner on their own rightful planets, on the Imperium's own Lost Children worlds!*"

Bad Camberg is airless. Its firebase has one small battery of old fusion cannon served by a bored, sleepy crew. Its carbyne shields aren't there to protect from plasma bombardment, since that hasn't happened in almost 300 years of peace. They're there to stop micrometeorite impacts capable of shredding an exposed base worker or bot, like paper maché. If any foolishly go out during one of the regular dust showers as the moonlet plows through a stranded tail of a long dead comet. Koblenz passes though it as well, but its thick atmosphere ensures that it gets only a pretty biannual light show in the night sky.

Takeshi evacuated most of the gun crews a week before, bewildering a young lieutenant who couldn't figure why an anonymous SAC *taisa* flashed a Jade Seal of authority from the Tennō himself, then ordered the guns stripped down and all but 22 young teks sent to retrain in long range fire on far off Glarus. He saw Jade authority glimmer, saluted and obeyed. But he didn't understand at all. A rising crisis was reported over civilian memex channels, growing more shrill daily in anticipation of armed conflict. The novice *shōi* didn't believe overexcited civilian reports that spilled onto the Koblenz memex like a school of cuttlefish spurting black ink into warm blue water. But chatter on the military neb?

That was a lot more serious. It got his attention well before the sleek colonel arrived at his base. A lethal looking SAC colonel, with no unit or personal ID except for rank insignia. But he brooked no questions. His form hugging gray uniform was intimidating, tapering to a narrow waist above perfect black boots before continuing to his chin. Most of all, there was a real killer's look in his red flecked eyes and a very odd scent of nitric acid on the air inside the tiny OP. The young lieutenant is still on the moonlet as the *Truant* phantoms descend into drop position. He's a full blooded, eager Rikugun officer. Obedience is bred in his bones, maybe even in his genes. So it's grossly unfair that as *Truant* swings silent and invisible in the blackness over his garrison outpost he has no idea that the only reward for his total obedience and unquestioning loyalty to Pyotr Shaka III is that he has less than half-an-hour to live.

The base is perfectly quiet as the little flotilla arrives, with here and there only a maintenance bot moving and a bored trooper sleeping guard. No sound comes from the domes of the battery, its gun tubes poking pointlessly upward into the vacuum of the Peace of Orion, like abandoned ancient telescopes.

The phantoms stay cloaked on the final approach. They're *beautiful.* Sleek, silvery cannula. "The only true space design," say chauvinists of the Phantom Arm. Others make vulgar jokes about the cigar tube little ships. But it's hard not to agree with the silent service on this one, arrogant as those asses are. Not when gracefully sheered hulls camber into sawed off fore-and-aft points that give the overall look a perfect symmetry. They're so beautiful that most phantoms are left unpainted, pure silver against the starry, starry night. On the other hand, forced spin means any scuttle is useless, so phantom class ships don't have any. All external viewing is by vidscreen while spinning or free floating when stationary, as is usual when in planetary orbit or making a cargo drop, like now.

It's the only small ship design where tube form is dictated by the need to spin fast to produce minimal gravity. Spinning isn't required on bigger warships, not even ones as small as a *Köln*-class frigate. Even most civilian cargo ships have room for large artificial gravity assists. But you can't stuff one of those into a phantom. The trade off is an exquisite beauty of spinning tube vs. bulky ugliness. Without gravity spin discipline driving design, most escorts and capital warships look pretty much like piles of randomly discarded boxes on a surface dock. Whenever engineers are freed from physical constraints like gravity spin or atmospheric drag, most indulge their crassest functional instincts, indifferent to aesthetics. They confirm why they're engineers, not artists.

***

The three phantoms slow, shifting from a basic 'vic' to an even simpler line or 'trail.' Mercs trudge to the airlocks, 100 pairs of jump boots clunking down the spine on each of the two trail boats. No commandos are on the lead phantom, though. KGN *Bowman* carries special cargo.

Truant is claustrophobically packed into small cargo bays converted for this mission, at 25 commandos per Lock Room times four, 100 jumpers each on the two trail boats. Well, minus two dead men left behind in smoldering clumps on the desert floor outside a stalag on Kestino. And one lost en route to the vapors. Airlock seals are manual, to prevent premature release by crew or a careless thought via quantum dot implants over a command HUD from Naujock or the Bridge. Men wait for the jump order crammed like vacuum packaged mockfish, to within a meter of the outer access rim. Lock Rooms on a phantom were never designed to handle a drop like this, of so many commandos. Or even to hold so many. Phantoms are open space attack boats, not designed as marine assault ships.

A gilded voice glides over the captain's relay from *Bowman*, piped into every combat helmet. It belongs to Captain Rory Atsu. He's under strict orders to obey all mission specific instructions from the land bound, clearly noncommissioned and rough trade looking Naujock. '*A gunsō, a mere sergeant telling me what to do on my ship!*' He stewed over it for days. It's the first thought to arrive clearly in his head each time he comes out of vapors: '*Orders from a fucking gunsō!*"

He balked and flew into a rage when he read a flash paper authority handed to him by that stupidly grinning ape man, who came onboard his immaculate silver ship wearing an old, dirty, half-buttoned uniform that looked oddly out-of-date. It said he had to do a month of training with the covert group, and that Naujock would tell him when and what, but that he couldn't ask why or where. He snatched the grubby paper out of Naujock's gorilla hand and stomped into his wardroom to vid protest to his Kaigun superiors. But only after Naujock snatched it back, rubbing it quickly between finger and thumb to ignite it.

"Who told that primate idiot he's in charge? And on what authority am I sent to do secret practice runs over a dead moon? Where is it again? Yes, one of the outer moons of Manmō!"

"On *my* authority, *daisa*."

"Yours? What..?" It took him that long to realize his coms were hijacked, that he wasn't talking to Kaigun. Instead of a senior admiral he was talking to a trim, tanned colonel wearing SAC grays. Atsu pushed out his chest with all the dignity that navy dark greens and a double row of e-ribbons afforded him and barked back at this unforgivable affront to his office as captain and his ship's security.

"Why, an officer of my 45 years experience in active command cannot, should not, and godsdamn *will not* take orders from a scruffy *gunsō*, a garrulous bully with a crooked nose and the manners of a rutting sow to boot. I don't care what authority you say you gave him, colonel! Who the hell is he? Who the damn hell are *you* to be giving a Kaigun *daisa* any orders at all?" '*How did this golden puppy get my naval command codes? He's clearly a Nagoyan. Those bastards think they run the whole godsdamn Imperium. Well they don't run me! Or my ships.*'

He lies, since he just got the order and hasn't spoken to the other two *daisas* yet: "The other mission captains feel the same way I do. We serve in the Kaigun, the Imperial Navy. Not on some blasted Rikugun cargo boat."

'*He thinks this is a Rikugun operation. Good.*' Takeshi was pleased the stolen Sendai Garrison utes were doing their job of covering the mission's genesis even from the Kaigun captains and crews needed to practice drops then carry the kill team to Bad Camberg.

Atsu recognized the Imperial seal atop the graphene scroll framing Pyotr's face, but only in the back of his mind. The personal emblem of Pyotr Shaka did not deter his protest or deflect his pride. Royal emblems are on everything in the Imperium. Pyotr's face is everywhere, too. Beneath his umbrage he was thinking at an unconscious level: '*Where would the Imperial family be without the Kaigun? Pyotr is an Oetkert brat. He reigns, but we in the professional military, especially the Imperial Navy, it's we who rule the Imperium.*' He's quite wrong about that.

It wasn't until he said several impolitic things about illegal usurpation of the Kaigun chain-of-command, then hinted at gaps in Takeshi's parentage, that Atsu finally noticed the feared *Erect Bear* insignia on the colonel's stiff collar board. He blanched. His guts gurgled a little and his sphincter tightened protectively in response. He made a sharp course correction. "On the other hand, sir, this mission is clearly special. It requires special circumstances and a flexible approach to command. Therefore it will be my honor to serve with your man..."

"*Under* my man."

"*Umm*, yes. *Under* your man. My honor. The mission comes first, always." Then Atsu shut up, feeling white fear fill up his thalamus, then reach for his cortex. He could be a pompous bore at the best of times, but he wasn't reckless or stupid or suicidal. So he launched no protest to his superiors.

Instead, he dutifully spent four weeks in orbit over a small moon in a deep interior and backwater system, making three mock runs daily. Then five weeks waiting in stealth orbit, living off the ship's stores above Kestino while *Truant* finished its desert training. And he took orders without any question from *Gunsō* Albert Naujock, who grinned viciously every time he gave one.

The mysterious colonel never dressed down Atsu or made him apologize. No need for that. They understood each other. SAC's elite *Erect Bear* insignia and reputation had that clarifying effect on people, even senior captains with decades of absolute authority aboard ship. He hadn't even pulled out or shown Atsu the Jade Seal. Didn't need to: the captain submitted quickly and easily, especially so for a Kaigun *daisa* of 45 years service.

***

Still, it chafes. It really does. Here he is, skimming low a dozen klics above a barren, desiccated moonlet. '*To drop god-knows-what out my cargo airlocks*.' Carrying unknown freight he's not allowed to inspect, blocked from his own hold by a crooked baboon of a sergeant who's enjoying every second in command!

"All boats, cease spin ... move to no gravity protocols ... bring airlock doors to 180° ... I want a dead drop to the surface, on my mark, like we practiced."

"*Mark!*"

Three phantoms short burst retro nozzles to counter spin as Captain Atsu looses a flow of boat-to-boat, skipper-to-skipper orders. Unlike on a KRN or NCU warship, his XO and Station Officers simply execute orders; they don't confirm each command, as farfolk naval crews all do. It's a cultural difference. Imperial and imperious. Stiff and hierarchical. It will prove lethal for some Kaigun ships and crew in the war that's coming, that's going to be triggered by a silent lie acted out below Atsu about 20 minutes from now. Kaigun will adjust, but losses will have to be suffered before it does. Everyone is going to learn war the hard way.

"Trail boats *Venita* and *Meteor*, maintain precise spacing."

"All boats, stay in the lane … 27,000 klics to drop."

"Commence final approach run."

"Open Lock Bay doors"

"Release cargo harnesses."

"Trail boats, tighten spacing."

"Drop lane optimum in six seconds."

"Drop ensign, be ready ... *Drop!*"

"Cargo is away, *daisa.*"

He thinks it's just another covert training mission. After all, this is a Grün moon base, not some farfolk world over the Krevan or Calmari border. He can't imagine it'll affect him once it's over. He plans a few more years in a *daisa*'s chair, to finish his lucrative, comfortable, peacetime naval career. Then he'll retire back home to Lucerne and drift into fatness and toward Final Age.

Instead, tomorrow he'll hear shocking news blared over civilian memexes about what happens on the moonlet below. Within hours, the commissions of all Kaigun officers will be extended indefinitely by Pyotr's emergency decree. In a fortnight, *Bowman* will be part of a combat squadron of phantoms desperately hunting and being hunted by KRN escorts, dodging fast *seeker* missiles and avoiding smart mines in heavy fighting around the ice moons of Aral. It will happen so fast he'll not be able to tell his wife the truth of what he did at Bad Camberg. Tell her about the unwitting role he played in the sordid event that will call both their sons to war, and get her youngest killed inside a year. He can't tell her what he and *Bowman* did because of a second interview with the mysterious SAC colonel he'll have as he's flying to the escape LP. It will be made clear to him that the lives of Atsu's whole family are forfeit if he talks.

In six months Captain Rory Atsu will be in the fight of his life against more KRN escorts protecting an *Exodus* flotilla fleeing the burning capital world Aral, to bring the War Government into exile at Harsa moon in the Nova Cincinnatus system, inside Calmari space. He'll barely survive a plasma cannon near miss. He'll think the war is over and he survived it. That Pyotr and the Kaigun have won, with the flight of the Krevan government from Aral. Now he can go home to his wife. Now he can see his fine sons. Then he'll be told to take *Bowman, Venita* and *Meteor* in stealth mode over the Calmari frontier, on a key black ops mission to penetrate the heavily guarded NCU space yard at Narym.

"Get past the electronic net, get into the yards. Find a corner and squat there in stealth mode and wait for further orders. When they come, and they *will* come, you hit 'em fast and hard. Wreck the yards and any ships still parked there. Then drop all mines out your ass end and run."

"Attack an NCU base, sir? Engage the navies of the Calmar Union?"

"If orders arrive while you wait in stealth, yes. You *will* follow orders, captain. We all have to follow orders now. It's wartime. There's no wriggle room left."

The odor of Captain Rory Atsu's life is fast turning red. So, too, is the scent and color of space where hang the glimmering Thousand Worlds of Orion. All around, a hundred billion stars are coldly indifferent to anything ants or people like him might do on or above a thousand discarded chunks of stellar waste.

Still, for ants and flies and people, something larger begins today. It starts on the airless moonlet that will soon be fast receding in Rory Atsu's rear viewscreen. It all starts on this lifeless, useless bit of stellar afterbirth that's about to become the most infamous piece of rock in the Orion spur.

Moonlet

Backed up tight against the rear seal and fiddley of the last airlock on *Meteor*, Albert Naujock smirks as he listens to Captain Rory Atsu on *Bowman* order the start of the cargo run-and-drop. He doesn't give a fig-leaf-in-a-gale for anything that undyed navy *daisa*, that martinet, thinks about him or says about the *Truant* mission. He answers to his *taisa* and no one else. '*Dat fool Atsoo don know a damn ting anyways. He's jus da fookin' dwiver.*'

Naujock smiles, remembering what his favorite colonel told him to call the secret cargo crates if some pushy, unauthorized Kaigun or customs officer ordered him to open them in port during the mission loading phase. "Call them 'special packages' or maybe 'canned goods.' You decide, sergeant." Takeshi exhaled a small laugh at his own cruel and cynical joke.

'Pwetty godsdamn funny, too.' The boss has a wicked sense of humor that his squat nosed gunsō admires, though he doesn't always understand. '*We'se gonna open up dem cans taday, dats faw shore.*'

More crisp messages flow over command links across the flotilla as it loops gracefully upward from a near surface passby of the moon. Maintaining perfect trail formation after the cargo drops, the invisible line of evenly spaced boats pulls up, over and down, then back around to level position to make a second pass. This one will put *Truant*'s jumpers on top of the pods.

"Drop officer reporting: first ground contact 90 seconds."

"More contacts, five second intervals."

"Containers are on target."

"1st pod contact ... 2nd pod down ... 3rd pod contact ... 4th pod contact."

"All cargo pods down and in correct position, captain."

"*Venita* and *Meteor*, follow me on your last pass ... maintain spacing."

Naujock's two handpicked corporals have restricted command link access to *Truant*. They confirm pod ground contact via relay link in their helmets. Like all combat suits, theirs mount transparent armor HUDs. Both are street toughs, for hire corporals-of-murder glad to have this job. Old friends of Naujock, or so they think. They'll be shocked when he betrays them, too.

Command activates via a brainwave channel, controlled by quantum dots air injected into Naujock's dull black eyes just before mission liftoff. Photosensitive silicon flakes enable command-and-control at the speed of thought, which is real damn fast even for Naujock. He only needs one dot. The second is redundant, for use only in the event of failure of the first, say by loss of an eye in combat. Or so everyone is told. Smart officers assume that it stores all their thoughts and actions for download. They're not wrong.

It's uncommon for an NCO to have full access to a command link, let alone control one. Naujock's dot protocols are mission specific, far more limited than a trained officer can access. Takeshi insisted. It's a sensible restraint, since none of the NCOs went to Officer's Basic, none know the full dot command manual or dropdowns. Keep it simple and they can't screw it up.

'*Whad dah fook? Wads dat aw'full smell? Is da ship leek'in?*' Naujock smells something acid and bitter inside his sealed helmet and realizes it's his own bad breath. He chewed so much blue tobacco before dressing for combat not even his suit filters can get rid of all the sour gases he exhales. A thin blue mist is forming on his HUD, slimy and foul. Before he can think how to wipe it off, Atsu's voice is inside his helmet again.

"One hundred seconds to venting."

"Forty seconds."

"Ten seconds."

"Depressurizing all Lock Rooms, *now*."

The rapid vacuum seems to pull at Naujock's chest, as if trying to suck his heart from its cavity. It's an illusion, of course. Purely psychological. His light-weight, flexible vacuum suit is old but secure, a space and battletested technology dating back at least a hundred generations. Not as far back as the First Age of Exploration when Humanity left the origin system, but surely back to the First Orion War, however long ago that was.

'*A towsund yeyahs awh moh? Ahh, who cayahs.*' He checks his jump suit's forearm monitor. *All Normal,* it blinks in *blue* reassurance. He lets *Truant* loose.

“Jumpas, unlock yaw hawnesses. Make weady faw fwee fall.” Naujock thinks the orders but also growls them out loud, mostly from old habit. Then he readies a suited fist to hit down hard on a bright red *Open Airlock* button. The same bright red button familiar to marines for over a thousand years, and just as obvious in its function then as now. “If it ain’t broke why jerk with it?” is the KG Engineering Corps longtime and entirely sensible approach. Same reason no one bothered to alter combat jump suits in so many centuries.

He’s waiting for Atsu to signal from *Bowman* that the boat trail formation is finished its 360° loop-and-back, and is now poised to drop his jumpers right above the cargo pods. Right on cue, Atsu’s voice bores into his ears.

“Drop lane approach.”

“Slowing to minimal.

“Commence jump protocol in 30 seconds.”

“Ten seconds.”

“Open drop doors!”

Naujock thumps the scarlet button, hard. An edge of darkness immediately appears at the bottom crease of the outer door as it retracts up and overhead into a recessed holding rack, opening the Lock Room to space. Pitch darkness eats halfway up the side of the no longer rotating ship. Behind him in utter blackness stand four rows of snugly suited jumpers, stuck to the ridges of the cargo floor with magnetized boots. There are no lights, because it’s a cargo hold not intended for jumpers. Why would inert cargo need drop lights? ‘*Forgodd ‘bout dat.*’

Naujock likes most of these SOBs. They remind him of an old memex vid he watched a hundred times. So he calls out in a mock pirate voice: “*Arrwghhh!* Let’s go git us some gold doubloons, boys!” Curiously, he loses all speech impediments while playacting the role. No one knows what he’s talking about, but every man who can see Naujock half-silhouetted against the open door in Sankt Goar’s reddish light understands his nasty grin well enough. They cheer lustily.

“In jump position ... *now!*”

Atsu barks it into all HUDs, linked across the three boat flotilla. Naujock shouts the order as the signal lamp illuminates *green* at last.

"Gween light! Gween light!"

"*Go, go!* By da numbaws, jus' lak we tawt ya'll. Soun' off!"

Each man moves in turn to the outer coaming, turns off his mag boots and dives headlong toward fractured gray-and-white, streaked craters racing to greet him on the moonlet below.

"One, two, three..."

"…twenty-two, twenty-three, twenty-four."

Naujock jumps last. Bending below is his own stick, to his right three more curved lines of tumbling troopers, each a little farther along the flight path of *Meteor* than the one before. He turns his head to see four more sticks falling from invisible *Venita,* each man appearing *ex nihilo* as he dives out the phantom's light camouflaged cargo door and into naked space. The sticks aren't evenly spaced. Some men engage hand jets way too soon, "jagging" the line. The civvy pejorative is in common use by jumpers because a ragged stick looks too much like a police lineup of civvies after a bout of hard drinking or a night of wandering through some filthy barrio, high on somo.

Pinprick white lights flicker on-and-off from steering jets of jumpers, otherwise too far away and invisible to Naujock against the black of space fast rising to meet the moonlet's abrupt horizon. The *gunsō* watches the farthest set of lights start to brake. His divers are slowing their controlled descents after power gliding almost to the dark rock surface.

Already the three S-boats are lost to *Truant*, heading under cloak for the L1 jump zone 60° in front of the moonlet, at the far end of the elongated Lagrange area it makes. They're as stealthy and unremarked on the way out as in their silent arrival. Captain Rory Atsu intends a fast trip home, now that he has heard the one way communiqué from Takeshi threatening to obliterate his family if he talks.

***

Naujock looks right as he falls toward the surface, curving parabolically from the airlock on departed *Meteor*. He's the last of four in the falling stick, each man barely illuminated by the russet twilight of Sankt Goar's main sequence star. Its dull ruby hardly shows the pale green of combat suits worn by the jumpers. Its weak light can't reveal to his unaided gaze anyone gliding farther off. It's so faint a red glow it only hazily warms the dark and looming disk of Koblenz.

He kicks in his own steering jets to control dive to the surface of the moonlet as he looks up toward Koblenz, an occluded blue-green-brown orb filling one-fifth of the sky. It's in a half-crescent phase relative to its star. On the night side, he easily makes out a dozen large cities linked by fine green filaments, multi lanes of maglev tube glowing with bioluminescent overgrowth native to the primitive alien biosphere AI bot terraformers otherwise overgrew with terran invaders. The plants are attracted by artificial warmth rising from the winsome, 4,000 klic long maglev tunnels. Over a hundred glowing lines trace in all directions from each city hub, like lighted cobwebs in a neon jungle.

Arcing, bluish light from the cities creates glowing domes against the planet's curving night side face. They remind Naujock of sweet Aral mushrooms ready to be picked, back when he was a boy and his mother sent him into the woods to scavenge for his dinner. Or are the milky light domes more like plague pustules on diseased faces he remembers from quarantine wards on Zug? He shakes his head, tossing off the foolishly sentimental notion and the putrid image alike.

'*I hav' a job ta do, godsdamn it.*' He chastises himself as he leans forward in a full stretch position, switching on small thrusters attached to rigid cuffs of his combat suit. His arms are winged back along his sides. He doesn't need to do it here, since the ground target is airless. But it's hard to shake basic jump training and best not even to try. The moonlet's stark surface immediately moves closer, not from his aerodynamic pose but from his small thrusters. It rushes toward him with lethal speed.

Anti-fogging mist in his helmet doesn't freeze and flake like it did during one practice run, turning his helmet into an oversized snow globe and his twisted face into a simulacrum of a strange holiday goblin trapped inside. He didn't like the harsh laughter the image induced. He beat one laughing merc unconscious, then swapped helmets. His new one is working properly, circulating thin warm mist throughout without accumulating or freezing on the viewscreen.

He makes out hard rimmed craters with razor sharp edges that are billions of years old. Their unkissed lips never knew the touch of missing gases that failed to circulate over this virgin rock. Bad Camberg was too small to emerge from the soup of this system's creation with an atmosphere, save a few trace molecules no one bothered to measure. Because the stony worldlet is also bereft of any mineral content, almost none of its dusty surface has been disturbed by humans or their machines. Not even thirteen centuries after settlers first arrived on Koblenz.

He has never been within 10 light years of Bad Camberg, yet as he enters full power glide he recognizes exactly where he is and what's passing below him. He knows it even without looking at spooky symbology and hypervisual enrichment of enhanced mapping that glows in his HUD. It's flashing *green* circles to ID his platoon leaders. *Brown* squares indicate structures, rising swiftly over the short horizon. It's the first sign of the gun battery he knows is down there. Nowhere in his vision are there any enemy *red* triangles. Not on this mission.

'*Not yet, anyways.*' He feels a twitch of vicious pleasure as he belches a knot of sour blue gas into his helmet space. Once more he smells a tart admixture of garlic and Sachi tobacco swirling around. He has walked every alley and crater of this moonlet, as a giant striding over a 1:200 emplastrum mockup. That's exactly how it looks to him now as he falls toward its real surface. The only part worked level by machines is a one square klic plate he sees glinting almost directly below him as he nears touchdown. At its center are four huge, antiship gun mounts, long black barrels thrusting straight out of squat domes that protect crews, arc swivel rotator guidance, and the targeting computers. Protect from pelting dust more than enemies, who have not been not seen in this sky in three centuries.

He knows there's a second flat area that he can't yet see, but which must soon rise above the stony rim. He waits for the garrison quarters to appear as a *brown* haze along the edge of his HUD, then more clearly as artificial structures. Ten seconds later, there it is: a thin ribbon of road. Bad Camberg is an airless outpost and thus unable to use either forced air or acoustic levitation hovers. Nor does it warrant more expensive ground transport for such short distances. Instead, its four gun domes are connected to the barracks by a single surface pathway. A road. He sees it no longer as a thin silvery ribbon but as a strong and regular scar widening as it rises to meet him. He steers for the barracks, a sharp neutral *brown* rectangle. Half a minute more and a bright *orange* ground contact signal flashes three times as proximity sensors in his jump boots detect impending impact. Another signal, also *orange* and flashing softly on his HUD, tells him that nearly all *Truant* is landed and deploying. A last few jumpers from *Venita* are in final glide.

It's a three step plan. First, the barebones garrison will die. Next, it'll be time to open Takeshi's crates filled with "canned goods." Then he needs to deliver a message to start Pyotr's war. After that, he has his own plans that not even Takeshi knows in full. There's no place in either design for the disposable men of *Truant*.

***

The skeleton garrison is still in barracks, enduring yet another lecture on base hygiene by its dutiful young lieutenant. *Truant* drops right outside, unheard in the airless silence and camoed against all EM sensors. The unwary barracks is easily surrounded and blast charges put in place. They aren't given a chance to open the locks and surrender. *Truant* blows them in, killing half the boys inside from the concussive wave, exposure to vacuum and cold. Then the mercs charge through the jagged breech and massacre all the rest with masers, grenades and Q-knives.

There's no resistance. Twenty-two innocent men and a loyal, naïve second lieutenant die unarmed and bloody, with shocked and bewildered looks. They have no air left in vacuum exposed lungs to cry out to their betrayer and emperor: "*Why are you shooting your own people? Why do you kill us, Pyotr?*" It's all over in less than a minute.

Naujock's men rearrange the bodies, putting spare masers brought along as props into quickly freezing hands, laying prone corpses in firing lines aiming at the gun domes. A few dead men they drag away. It's all quickly done because they've practiced all this for months, with bodies and body parts of hundreds of condemned men. They were brought out to the desert base on Takeshi's order, transferred from SAC's sprawling prison system in the salt flats of Novaya Uda to instead die hard and anonymously in desert isolation, all for Pyotr's glory.

"Wight, bweak alla da seals. Get 'da canned guds out an' moving. Let's go sold'awhs, we'se on a tight *scheeduuule*." The more excited Naujock grows the more he slips into a rural Aral accent, and the more his crooked nose twist his words. Still, his men understand their orders.

Four containers crack open, allowing gusts of trapped air to escape widening crevices. Gas stirs the regolith, lifting small puffs of achingly dry and ancient dirt above the surface. The dust behaves oddly. It ascends wherever a container opens or men stir it, hanging in slow swirls and spirals above the surface far longer than can be explained by weak gravity alone. It creeps into the weave of vacuum suits and seems to seek out tiny cracks in every weapon and tool they carry. It clings to all it touches, more like a gray adhesive or ghost than any normal dirt. They soon stop trying to brush it off. That only seems to agitate it and make things worse.

"Damn stuff almost seems alive."

"I heard Koblenz is one of them colony worlds where the shittier AI bots let some original life forms live, mixed in some alien DNA with what they brung here for us. Ya don't think..?"

"Shaddup ya Puwity shit! Ain't no dee'an'ay! It ain't awive! Get back to da crate. Faw'get aboud da fookin' dirt!" Easier said than done, even by Naujock. It's hard to ignore. When pod lights hit the dirt puffs, the dust sparkles like a host of excited imps. It's full of infinitesimal glass bubbles, microbeads of ethereal green, orange and red, products of eons of superheated melting and cooling from uncounted micrometeor impacts. The bubbles are oddly porous, tiny packets of nanoparticles ensnared like fairy snow in a child's shaken, mantelpiece sphere. It's so mesmerizing that Naujock doesn't take his own best advice about ignoring the sparkling, dancing dirt. '*All dat's missen is a music chip an' a mockup of ma ugly face inside.*' He turns away from the light show. Angry at the distraction and himself, he finds renewed focus and purpose in cruelty.

As each container cracks apart it becomes perfectly clear what Takeshi's "special packages" are. Ninety prisoners are hauled out, all ethnic Krevans from the border camps that sprout like poison toadstools wherever Purity ideology took hold and turned local Grünen against "the farfolk other." The containers spill out the unwanted sweepings of empire, rueful innocents and denounced social failures brushed by a harsh regime into discard camps; shelved with common criminals, the homeless, the insane. They're caught in exquisitely circular law that denies non-Grünen access to paid work, then orders them arrested for the crime of "social parasitism." They're perfect victims, warehoused as unwanted until Takeshi came to find disposable people; a discardable cast for a one off stage show.

They're pulled roughly from the crates by border world thugs. A different kind of disposable people, but currently useful and dressed in old style green weaves. Stupefied men and women are hauled out of broken drop boxes and prodded into two ragged rows. All are heavily drugged. They're all civilians, but are wearing stolen, pale oak commando uniforms of the Krevan Republic Army. They were dressed by Naujock's men that way, then rudely crated.

"Move it, ya fookin KRA bawstads! *Hut, hut, hut!*"

A few are Pyotr's legitimate subjects, ordinary convicts or rare dissenters from despised religious minorities. Subjects of the Imperium but not from the First or Second or Third classes. It's Takeshi's wicked sense of humor at work again. It amuses him to dress up and toss some of the Imperium's own subjects into the bubbling pot, a private garnish of cruel irony for the tough stew that *Truant* is about to serve to Krevans and Orion.

Naujock personally pulls the last man out of the last crate. He's the only one still bound tight around the wrists. The only one not drugged, but wide awake and terrified. He was once a celebrated Kaigun captain, so proud and privileged he commanded the last Green Ship that made the once-a-year permitted voyage to Jahandar's capital world of Nalchik. Captain of the famous Green Ship that was the only connection allowed for a half-century between two eastern despots and empires. Why is he here? To collect his reward for impudence. It's that more than the fact he sold smuggled naval secrets and 15 kidnapped shipwrights to Jahandar. It was what he did after, threatening to extort Pyotr with threats to go public with news he had also carried envoys back-and-forth between the eastern tyrants. Pyotr had him bound and handed over to Takeshi to dispose of, who passed him on to Naujock with orders to take him to Bad Camberg for special treatment.

Alongside the woeful, clumsy rows and ranks in oak stride *Truant* mercs in pastel green, worn under the jump suits they've already stripped off. They have RIK insignia but misidentifying flashes on shoulders and collars. They aim stubby masers with lethal threat at the stumbling, slow moving prisoners. Some carry extra heaps of KRA weapons and commando gear, as well as their own. Prisoners shuffle across the surface under guard, stirring up shimmering regolith in haunting pixie puffs. A glittering cloud accompanies the sad sack procession, moving with half the prisoners along the road between the barracks and gun domes. The rest are held back, moved into and around broken barracks, then ordered to sit and wait, across from frozen dead men dressed in green.

They have no idea where they are or why. Some are hurt, injured when their cargo pods tumbled and crashed across the gray skin of the moonlet even though they were lashed to the padded interior of the crates. Two women have broken arms, one man a badly shattered hip. A stalk of bone is cutting through his skin, held in place and away from the killing vacuum by tough carbyne ceramic of his combat suit. The bone man moans and the women wail in answer.

'*Adds to dah aw'ten'ti'city.*' Naujock smirks. Speaking standard Krevan with his usual Yalto accent, he turns on the universal frequency so that all the prisoners can hear him too. "Hey youse two, at da back awh da line. Ya, youse an' youse. Caw'wee dat lame bawstad. Don't let dat bone cut his suit awh I'll cut yaws."

More prisoners struggle to come awake, growing aware enough to realize that they're going to die in a desolate place under a dim red sun, whose name no one will tell them. Humble by origin, debased by the hard course of broken and outcast lives, they'd be astonished to know that their deaths born in service to a lie will abruptly change all human history. That their dying will disrupt and alter the lives of over 2,000 billion spread across the Thousand Worlds of Orion. They know nothing of the raw accounting of the war that's about to start. Don't know the cold lie that slays them, or that it's buried under deeper lies that will slay billions more like them and far more not like them at all.

But they see the guns and hard looks in the eyes of their killers, and the sadist grins, and know that they're on this barren rock to die. It's why they still shuffle, stumble, do whatever they're told by men they know will kill them. Life holds on to every second it can, so no one tries to rush the guards or run from the fate they now know is coming. They're herded to positions around the silent cannon. Thirty are pushed inside control and targeting rooms, twenty more shoved inside and under the bleak domes. Then all are shot without warning. Or blown apart with frag grenades and high explosive satchels tossed inside.

Naujock watches and directs, letting his hired killers do the rest. Except for one job he does personally and up close. He stands before the hand bound Green Ship captain he brought here under special orders from Takeshi. The man kneels with face raised, begging with his eyes behind a silent HUD. Naujock peers inside to see the fear, then lowers his stub maser and carefully blows the man's face off.

"Leave him on Bad Camberg with the rest, but unrecognizable. Understand?" He remembers Takeshi's explicit order about the face, and gives a crooked smile. He gives the faceless corpse a vicious kick, then gets back to work.

"Wight, get 'em in pos'i'shon." Naujock barks it, pointing to the corpses. His men reposition bodies and detached parts, green on one side, wheat sheave utes on the other. When they're done it really does look like KRA commandos attacked the garrison and were violently repulsed. There's just enough staged truth in the lie to make it believable for those who want to believe it hard enough. Which will be most inside the Imperium, but almost no one else in Orion. This is a psy ops aimed at internal opinion and support. It's not meant to change any farfolk minds.

One of the oddest things about killing a man in vacuum is the total absence of expected smells to accompany the sight of carnage. The brain wants to associate familiar scents with views of bile and blood, with spilled guts, with burned walls and scoring marks of pink crystal maser charges. But there are no odors. Each merc works with broken and ruptured corpses in hermetically sealed oblivion to the reek of spilled life and raw death they would make if any air conveyed death's smells to their indifferent noses.

With the stage set and war's crimson curtain rising, Naujock orders two HUD and all gun cameras turned on. *Truant* will broadcast a fake report live over an unsecured military neb, assuring its pickup and rebroadcast by the memex on Koblenz. From there, the sounds and images will race for a thousand bohrs over hyperspace relays, jumping LPs station-to-station, until they fill every screen, penetrate each brain implanted flake of every memex viewer in the Imperium.

***

Private Minoru Honda is a real good looking *nitōhei,* hand chosen by Takeshi to make the narration. Partly it's because his handsome head will please memexes, but more because the lad is made of the same kidney as himself. Amoral, self-regarding, vain and ruthlessly ambitious. Naujock was animated when he told Minoru the good news back in the desert on Kestino, saying it with faked but convincing enthusiasm. "Boy, youse gonna be fay'moose! Youse got a face made faw da memex. Not lak mine!" They both laughed. Naujock knew it was another of Takeshi's lies. Fame is not what they intend for this boy after Pyotr's farce plays out on the moonlet. Well, at least not any fame that lasts.

Minoru has little experience acting, beyond hamming it up in some student plays. He did a little neb casting on his native Brno, before his rank biopolitical rants and Grün chauvinism got the attention of the local police, and he decided the better half of valor was to leave his Krevan Republic homeworld and head off to find his fortune in the Imperium. He signed up with SAC for the good credits and the cool uniform. Takeshi told him about Operation *Truant*, where exiles like him with the right politics could get triple pay. Told him that he had a special role to play, central and essential and historic. Now that he's here, Minoru doesn't regret for a moment the decision or the bloodshed. '*I'm going to be a star!*'

Minoru is real good at accents. He's told to conceal his native Brno drawl, to speak only classic Grün with a clipped cadence: No contractions. Not like the ethnic exile he is, a castaway from a Krevan border world. He's to sound Second Caste, from one of the core homeworlds. An elite volunteer who helped repulse a dastardly enemy attack on the sacred border. One of the best of Grünen, not some schluck from the provinces and lower orders. He practiced the accent and his lines for weeks. Now his moment to stand up, and stand out, is here at last.

'*My performance will change history!*' Minoru knows this gig is different, that it will change his life. He's finally noticed. Chosen for a crucial role by a *taisa* of the Imperium. He wants to be perfect in the role, and thinks he will be. '*Today, my fortune rises as I deserve. No more losing for me! Carpe diem.*'

He strikes a cheesy pose in dirtied up combat gear carefully smeared with a murdered woman's blood. His right hand caresses a short maser held loosely but ostentatiously against his thigh. His free arm supports a "wounded comrade," a big man with an astonishing shock of jet black hair and artificially colored purple eyes. The big man plays his part extremely badly, leaning hard into Minoru while incongruously grinning far too broadly. Showing no wound pain at all. Rikugun military intelligence will later explain, to the few civilian memex presenters who ask about the oddity of a smiling, yet wounded man: "This true hero of the fight to defend Bad Camberg overcame terrible pain out of loyalty to the Tennō and from Grün honor. Long live Purity and Pyotr!" The presenters will all be shamed and replaced, conscripted and sent to Daegu to join sadsack 32nd Supply Division.

Minoru gets the "*Go*!" hand signal from Naujock and begins broadcasting. He keeps talking for 42 minutes, growing evermore confident in his performance with each repetition. By the end, he's sure that his performance is top drawer.

"RIK Firebase Bad Camberg calling. Firebase Bad Camberg here. Anyone in RIK, please respond. Anyone. We have been attacked by Krevan forces..." *As he speaks the main image moves beyond Honda and his grinning black-haired pal, panning damage and gruesomely staged carnage, pausing over the most grisly scenes.* "Bad Camberg here. HQ acknowledge. We have been attacked by military forces of the Krevan Republic. I repeat, we are under attack."

The camera pans over two green clad bodies from the murdered garrison, one missing half a stomach, another headless, both dragged into position at the cannon. It pans back to Minoru. He looks meaningfully into the cold lens. He warms to its allure, tries to reach through it like a cheap memex star to tug tears from watching billions circling distant stars. He'll melt young girls' hearts with his handsomeness. Warm mothers to his youth. They'll prod and push their own reluctant men to join Pyotr's war.

"In the end," Takeshi told Pyotr when they agreed on this plan, "it's always the women who really choose war." Pyotr *harrumphed*, but didn't disagree.

Minoru keeps repeating the message: "This outpost has been attacked by KRA commandos. The first assault has been repulsed. More attacks are expected. Bad Camberg respectfully requests immediate reinforcement."

He added the respect bit on his own.

He liked the rolling alliteration.

Thought it sounded real core worlds.

Thought it sounded real educated.

Thought it sounded like a toff.

The image shifts over to a second HUD camera, this one looking up at the big guns. The cameraman-merc bounds past two cracked open domes, showing the broken barrel of a plasma cannon lying crookedly to one side.

"Requesting immediate relief and assistance. Firebase Bad Camberg calling. Bad Camberg here. Acknowledge. This outpost has been attacked by KRA forces. We are holding on. I will continue broadcasting until relieved."

Go ahead kid, play the hero. Milk it for all it's worth, 'cause you don't have long to live. And it's going to be a shit awful death in the forest, holding your own handsome face in your red hands, screaming. May as well die a fucking hero.

Women *will* cry over you,

weep for your lost youth and beauty.

Men won't really give a shit about you,

but they'll all be just a little jealous.

Jerky HUD motion ... the image breaks feign damaged orientation control, making it seem like the wearer's high on adrenalin or maybe combat meds. "The attack was sudden and unprovoked, but we repelled it. We have taken casualties, but we're holding our position. We will never surrender ..."

The image flutters, fades, then switches to the first person viewpoint and HUD of another trooper, this one bouncing down the narrow road linking the battery domes to the garrison living quarters. Armed men in proud green combat weaves carry obviously Rikugun gear and weapons, but have unclear flashes. They move in odd slow motion, low gravity leaps and hops. "Bad Camberg here. RIK Main HQ, please respond. Requesting assistance. This base is under Krevan assault."

The view moves over and past dozens of KRA corpses and pieces of several more bodies in various death poses, spread around the smashed control rooms and broke open barracks. "Firebase Bad Camberg calling. Is anyone there? We are holding on, but we need assistance from our brothers. Please, please help us."

One crimson scene in a compact kitchen proves especially memorable. Start with slow caresses of foul damage to ordinary things, of disturbed domesticity: broken food dispensers, scorch marks on the floor, plasma holes in an outer vacuum wall. Then two dead commandos in oak combat weaves and a third, a headless female KRA, half-propped in a back corner...

"By the gods, that's a woman!"

"It's obscene that they let their women fight!"

"We would never permit it!"

The scripted lines are delivered off camera by Naujock's corporals. They will be widely and approvingly quoted, until it becomes the common view across the deeply misogynist Imperium. Until the war bots are mostly gone and casualties among menfolk mount, and mount, as a little Krevan War turns into the immense Fourth Orion War. Then even Rikugun generals may have to contemplate letting women auxiliaries into their reduced divisions, and even into combat.

Linger with the camera on a blood drenched sleeve. From out the jaundiced cuff hangs a half-severed naked hand, a woman's hand. Capillaries are open. Frosted and motionless blood clings to the fingers like a fine cobweb. A miniature pink waterfall reaches toward the shot pitted floor in a fan of frozen arterial splatter, never completing its plunge. Pan up to a raw, exposed arm and erupted shoulder. Close in to make billions cringe, watching live or peering greedily later during a hundred million uncut and recut memex shows. Zoom to a ragged metal ceramic hinge. Below it, a jagged bone juts from scraps of icy skin and blue flesh. Focus on the oddly clean flash and unit badge on the pale, dismembered shoulder.

"Outrage! It's the *Red Parrot* of the Aral Special Commando Brigade!" *That's how an angry RIK narrator will break into a recast and edited montage to explain, sending out the new footage within an hour. Traditional martial music will play as the camera pulls back to a panoramic view of the sharp Bad Camberg horizon, Koblenz rising blue-green behind. Cue a magisterial overlay, the image of Pyotr Shaka III, Imperator, standing half-naked in the full battledress of his Zulu ancestors, iklwa in one hand, nguni in the other. Restart roll. Repeat loop...*

"Ya did well," a crookedly smiling Naujock tells Minoru Honda afterward. "Da *taisa* will be pleased. Hell, da Tennō himself will see an' heah ya! Imagine dat! Ya goin' places, boy. An' wid a face like youse got! *Shee'it*! Ya got it made, kid. Youse gonna be fay'moose!"

***

The Bad Camberg vid spirals the crisis out of control. Ten days later a single word is broadcast over and over from the Waldstätte Palast that sends tens of millions of excited folk into the tense streets of Koblenz's cities, while billions cram into the public squares of Novaya Uda and a thousand other cities on hundreds of Grün worlds. A single word cascading down all the memexes sets Orion on edge. The one word that always changes everything: *War!*

Young men on Grün homeworlds race outside their homes and into the streets, gathering in any public space to leap up-and-down in unison, shouting. "It's war! We're at war! We're all going to war! *Hurrah!!*" Chanting "Pyotr! Pyotr!" and "Purity! Purity!" crowds gather to cheer speakers who urge them to crush Krevo for its audacity, its aggression, and its vile occupation of the Lost Children border worlds. Older boys pound their chests, goading each other to enlist and vowing to "fight for Purity!" Old men watch them and wish they, too, could go off to war, the great unmet test of their faded manhood. Young women lift their skirts and dance in the streets. Old women clap for all the little boys pretending to march like soldiers. Fathers beam approval. Mothers weep silently in worried pride.

Everywhere, SAC General Curia and Kempeitai spies are watching, police and military agents take names, make arrests of any who object to this war or are just less than fully enthusiastic. On the first day alone, tens of millions march off to recruitment stations erected in every city and town. Country boys hike and hitch and beg rides to reach the stations. It's a mad moment of righteous, mindless pride.

***

Three weeks later, Private Minoru Honda's especially handsome face will be sheared off by a Krevan blue maser while he's whooping hot for blood on a hover scout mission in the one of the old forests of Genève. War doesn't respect beauty. It rips and tears all flesh. It blinds and lames and scars the beauteous few as easily as it scores and wounds the ugly many. All the rest of us. Cocky and cruel, Minoru never heard the poet's warning: '*If any question why we died, tell them because our fathers lied.*' Maybe because he was one of the Big Lie's fathers, not its sons?

Nah, it's not that at all. There's no fated justice in his death, let alone in the manner of it. It just happens. He falls in a minor skirmish in a forest locals call the Pilsudski Wood. He dies slowly, in terrible, writhing agony, while trying to push his half torn off face back onto a white, exposed cheekbone. There's no justice in Minoru Honda's wild suffering, which continues until a pretty red haired KRA lieutenant blows his brains all over a giant tree root to stop his howling.

While Minoru is screaming and crying all at once, trying to save his own life Minoru's black-haired friend pleads with a KRA captain to let him betray Minoru as the villain of Bad Camberg. It doesn't work. The captain leans in to slice open the black haired man's throat, then orders that both corpses be left to the tree ants.

It all happens to no higher or just or retributive purpose. To no greater moral end. No judge or god orders it done. Even the captain is just making sure he leaves no one behind while he leads his broken and beaten company into hiding in the woods. It's not even symbolic that Minoru Honda's beautiful face is ripped off in one of the first fights of a war he helped start, hoping that it would make his face known all over the Thousand Worlds.

No, it really isn't. *No,* I said!

It just *happens* that way, the face thing.

Just accept it! Why make up moral shit?

Jeez, you want everything to have some deep moral purpose, don't you? Well it doesn't! It's just a fucking *war*! That's its deeper, motherfucking meaning. It's just the same random shit that happens in every war! No morality! Get over it.

On the other hand, the Honda kid is not the first veteran of the Bad Camberg black op to die on the frontline of the Krevan War that breaks out ten days later. Nor is he the last. None of them expected it, to be sent to Genève to fight. To be cheated out of their merc contracts by Naujock and forced into RIK 10th Armored by order of the sinister colonel they only heard about and never met. They're assigned to four man hover scout teams at the bloody spear tip of attack wedges moving inexorably across that planet's northern continent. It's a surefire way to get killed, taking the point for a whole division marching across Genève.

The conscription and transfer orders arrive while *Truant* is still working Bad Camberg, giving fake interviews to memex and neb reporters. Then the cameras are turned off, all coms go dark. The next thing they know they're jammed in a rough, unmarked cargo ship, heading to a dropship staging orbit to join invasion forces at Genève. There's nothing they can do about it and no one to bitch to. *Truant* was a total black op. So black, they know they're dead if they ever talk. Not ever. To anyone. Not even to each other. They're probably dead anyway.

"Youse jus doo youse fookin' jobs." Naujock warns *Truant* before he leaves them all fuming, attached to 10th Armored. He's going back to HQ to serve as Takeshi Watanabe's personal bodyguard. "Shaddup an maybe youse won't die in a pun'ish'men' bat'al'yon, awh by a godsdamn masah squad." Then he lets them know that "da col'onel" has put *Truant* under an unrevokable *Collective Blackout* order. That's all he calls Takeshi, "da col'onel."

"Dat means if any man'jack'a'ya speaks a single fookin' word ta anybody 'bout Bad Camberg, not one a ya'll live ta see anodder dawn. One talks, an ya'll die. Got it?" Then *Gunsō* Albert Naujock leaves for HQ in a sleek black command hover Takeshi lent him, to close out the *Truant* mission.

They know he fucked them over good.

Fucked them over once and forever.

Stole all their merc back pay, too.

They're deployed with 10th Armored on Genève when it reaches the outer edge of Pilsudski Wood. There's a real war on. A godsdamn shooting war where the other side has skill and masers, too. Again and again they're sent into the dense old growth forest to chase down a nasty bunch of KRA rat bastards. Oak weave 'bandits' who keep moving deeper into the wood, and shoot back whenever you try to murder them. Unlike the drugged 'canned goods' on the moonlet.

Bandits kill the Honda kid, his big friend, too. Or so the dwindling survivors of *Truant* think. They're not really sure. Not one of 80 hover scouts survived a big ambush. They never find the bodies, just leave them inside somewhere, deep under freefall in the old forest. Except one. They find a dead officer lying in a clearing. They take him back for fast freezing and shipment to an offworld RIK Morgue for High Caste citizens. They don't know what's hidden inside him.

Survivors regroup, and are sent back in, again and again. They're ordered to scout a path through towering, 1,400 year old gold and silver trees bioengineered by AI bots that terraformed Genève. Sent in first, to find and kill or capture the bandit leader, known to them only as the 'Ghost of the Woods.' They're told not to come back out until they locate the bandit camp that an angry general knows is hidden deep inside. They move under the looming trees into a dark woods. Silent, fearful, betrayed. Not one survives what the bandits do when they ambush them, again. Neither side in the burgeoning Krevan War knows that every man except one who was on the Bad Camberg covert op is dead within a month. Wait, hold on! One man knows. He's also on Genève, back at HQ with his colonel.

Takeshi doesn't like loose ends. And there's a twisted one dangling still from the moonlet operation. He wonders if he should pull on the string called *Gunsō* Albert Naujock. He's proving useful as a bodyguard and dogsbody in Takeshi's temporary assignment on Genève, after Pyotr sends him to that backwater instead of into much bigger fights at Aral system or at Lwów and on Brno. Pyotr does it ostensibly to give Takeshi combat command experience, but it's really to teach him the unteachable: humility. He intends to make Takeshi bow low before the Jade Throne, to humble him with knowledge of who holds real power on Kestino.

Takeshi' orders are to oversee "all bandit suppression operations." That means getting a lot of horseshit and brains and blood on his shiny black boots. Each night, *Gunsō* Naujock cleans and polishes them like new. Then he lays out a fresh, steel gray SAC colonel's uniform, adding functions of a reasonably competent orderly to his résumé as a stone killer-on-command. Naujock is a useful man to have around in a fight. Or to start one. Or to carry out a quick knifing of Takeshi's lesser enemies. Loyal as a dog, too. Still, there's that witness thing…

Data search: Orion
Result: alien life, Rare Earth
Historia Humana, Volume IV, Part III (e)

As every schoolchild knows, ancient OE astronomers found many hundreds of thousands of rocky worlds. About 11% were potentially habitable, while 2% were found at optimum orbits. Signatures of primitive life were found on several thousand rocky planets, but no instrument or SETI project found advanced life or any evidence of any alien civilization in Orion. Not one technosignature was found anywhere in the Orion spur. Organics detection by itself instead made three things clear about the galactic suburb where Sol system resides.

First, there was primordial life scattered across all Orion, except for one statistically improbable barren area astronomers call the "Dead Zone," still unexplained even today. The existence of primitive yet alternate ecosystems on colonizable planets never posed an impediment to their terraforming for human exploitation. Moral and philosophical respect for the "sanctity of all living things" was mooted by Sol system ethicists and exobiologists, but not accepted by Sol governments even about the several primitive genomes found in the origin system, and never by the general public or any of the then still thriving major religions. Instead, in our celebrated amour propre, we reasserted an ancient claim to unique moral, genetic, and cosmic status. If we were not quite the center and purpose of all creation, we were at least the centerpiece of Orion. And that meant that anything useful we found out there, we claimed as our own.

Second, the 'Rare Earth' hypothesis was confirmed. There was no alien life beyond prokaryotic levels, and no other advanced intelligence in the Orion spur. Fermi's Paradox was unraveled, the 'Great Silence' confirmed and reconfirmed. The numerical value reserved for advanced civilizations in the venerable Drake Equation was finally and definitively entered, as 'one.' A few skeptics still say that the explanation of our uniqueness may be the 'Great Filter,' wherein high tek and star faring civilizations that came before us exterminated themselves, or maybe each other. Some suggest this explains the Dead Zone, which remains unexplored: why spend on archeological exploration of dead worlds with so many exploitable inorganic sites within the thriving, inhabited systems of the Thousand Worlds? The sceptics warn that the same filter lies ahead, waiting for us should Humanity discover a suicidal technology or unsustainable trajectories dominate our social, economic and —the least likely outcome, because most tightly controlled by our proven success at grand terraforming— our thousand environmental futures.

We were alone. Unique. Wondrous. The pinnacle achievement of either cold mathematics or calculated creation. Choose. And that meant it became clear that all inhabitable worlds were ours to take, even those with minor alien life beneath our genetic achievement. Alien genes could be replaced or blended with cradle world genomes to improve our survivability on what would become the Thousand Worlds. Otherwise, the silence in the heavens proved far more welcome than any mooted great discovery that "we are not alone." Instead, we welcomed that no one was out there to block us from interstellar empire, if only waiting habitable worlds could be reached by our colony ships. For if history proves one thing above all others it is that empire is our most natural system of organization, the social-moral norm most desired, most of the time, by most of our peoples.

Unfortunately, we established not one but three great star empires, though one insists still on disguising itself to itself as a republic. Today, outside the unexplained Dead Zone where no life exists or will take hold, the Thousand Worlds of Orion are flush with our civilization. And we have just begun to settle the small clusters that lie between Orion and Perseus. It is a matter of regret only that the scattered children of Old Earth are not united across their new homes. We brought too many of our old hates and differences out to the stars, where we waged several Foundation Wars and three terrible Orion Wars before arriving at our current political configuration. However, all that was long ago.

Today the Peace of Orion, the 'Long Peace,' approaches the start of its fourth century. Scholars say this is because the great star empires —Grün Imperium, Calmar Union, and the Dauran Commons— are committed by treaty and also by custom to avoid grave quarrels between the past and present that might lose us all the future. The powers collectively guarantee security, including for several small Neutrals that lie between, and buffer, them from each other: the United Planets of Krevo, the Helvetic Association, the Three Kingdoms, and a dozen even smaller star states. The youngest star nations, those in more recently settled open and globular clusters, also grow rich and secure in the long shadow of Orion's extended peace. They are not part of the main interstellar treaty system, but live contentedly in its shade nonetheless.

Scholars agree, and history shows, that the Long Peace proves we have finally left our violent childhood and adolescence behind. Mystics and the new religions say that we are blessed to live in the Shōwa Age or 'Great Enlightenment,' or 'Satya Yuga' ('Winning Age of Reason and Order'). By any name, we enjoy a deep peace, mature commercial relations across all borders (except isolated Daura's), cultural intercourse, and prosperity across the Thousand Worlds. Ours is an era of enlightened peace such as never seen before in our long, dark history.

A few still say that whether men and women are born to high office and power, or denied it by lowly stations of their birth, some will always hunger for honor and glory and command over others. Skeptics warn that it remains true, even if not obvious during blessed times such as ours, that a new Kali Age awaits us in the endless cycle of rebirth and redeath; that as one OE philosopher predicted over five millennia ago, it is only the dead who have seen the end of war. That is very much a minority view today, and not a truly serious one. Our most informed and advanced thinkers are optimistic. Our philosophers and legal scholars are confident that the problem of war is a matter that should only concern historians or anthropologists, those whose odd temperaments and antiquarian tastes focus them on errors and sorrows of our sordid past. The rest of us are free to enjoy sweet fruits of perpetual peace, to live and explore deep caverns of the mind, to study the majesty and wonders of the vast heavens free of fear of ancient anarchy and the mass violence that marked the turning of history's pages and the end of civilizations. We are changed and matured. We shall not make war again. We have outgrown it. We renounce it.

Ditch

Jan Wysocki feels a sharp ache pulse down his lower leg, again and again. It's getting stronger with each throb, worming into his consciousness out of a fog of drugged numbness. He tries not to think about the jagged gash in his right calf made by a spinning hunk of hot frag five days ago. The first time he ever went into battle. The first time he saw the face of war.

An insistent throb stabs through his fading combat drug barrier more often and more sharply with each new minute. He tries to shake it off, but he can't. It's a deep wound. '*Well, I'll just have to bear it then. Others are hurt worse.*' As Jan crouches his nose draws nearer to the wound. It smells less of pus than antiseptic and antibiots, and a bit of AI satisfaction from a purring field wrap at a job it knows it's doing well. Some of the pain he should be feeling is held at bay by the lingering effect of the combat modadrene he took before the Grün attack on the Main Defense Line. Five days back.

While the moda assures wakefulness over a five day stretch, the real pain barrier is the suspensor a medic jabbed him with, disconnecting a burned tear in his flesh from registering the agony it wants to communicate to his fertile and suspicious brain. The problem is today is Z+5. His dose is wearing off and his leg and primal brain both know what's coming.

The happy field wrap tightened itself around his wound as soon as the medic slapped it on the jagged tear, just before he stood up and a RIK sniper bot sheared the top off his head with a *blue* maser bolt. It came apart like a rondelle of cheese sliced in half with a cleaver, leaving a raw slash that not even the most confident field wrap could ever hope to fix. Jan left the dead medic where he fell. But he took his med pack as he crawled away from the sniper bot's chosen alley. When he stopped crawling and looked inside he found the pack was empty of moda.

'*Not even our medics were ready for this godsdamn war. None of us were.*' He chides himself yet again, as he has since that first morning when he looked down in surprise at a red gash that somehow opened in his leg. '*You're a damn fool, getting hurt half-a-day into your first fight. Some piss poor company leader you turned out to be. Just like you always knew you would.*' Madjenik Company has been resting for three hours. A much needed rest it is. Even powerful stamina pills can push endurance only so far before the body rebels against stress, fear and fatigue, and simply shuts down to protect core systems. The good news is that all the barking Grünen hounds who've been chasing the company for five days and nights must also be at least half worn out. Weary of pursuing this especially sly and elusive, if badly wounded fox. '*If that counts as good news.*'

Madjenik and the lost puppy strays it collected during its retreat from the broken MDL are surrounded by far more numerous, more heavily armed, and more confident enemies. It's able to rest for a few hours on the fifth day of running only because the enemy feels no fear, knows the hunt is all but over, except for the kill. So pursuing Rikugun also lay down to rest awhile. '*Right over there, just across this sweetgrass meadow.*' Now Genève's sun is rising, pulling apart the curtain of orchard mist that hovers over Jan, shredding it with probing fingers of light, casting first shadows of overhead branches that stretch thinly on the damp ditch where Madjenik hides. The day is waking up, and therefore so is the enemy.

'*We can't stay here.*' Jan knows it, even as he feels engorged with anger at the pack of enemy hounds doing banal morning chores across the field, languidly rising prior to resuming the baying hunt. Sure it will pick up the scent of the wounded fox before the day is done, and kill Madjenik. A surge of newfound hatred pushes away fatigue and the gnawing pain in his leg.

'*We stay, we die. We leave, we die. What do I do?*' The little apple wood behind him is banked by a rough runoff ditch. That's where he draws his lean, tall body into a compact curl, to assess stirrings in the nearby enemy night camp. '*Only one other choice: we attack. Gotta do it right. I've lost too many fighters already. The company can't afford for me to make any more mistakes.*'

He glances back along the low ditch where the survivors of Madjenik lie or crouch under light field camo sheets, waiting on his last recon and for his orders. Waiting to see if he can keep them alive and get them through another day. It's all they ask of him, but it's everything. They're a rough and ragged bunch, a hodgepodge of short war call ups and long service Krevan Republic Army grunts. The old breed of the peacetime KRA mixed up with fresh kids and conscripts. They're all that's left of his company, all that he has. Most are resting, clumped in small groups. Or huddled and whispering in dark blue shadows along the lip of the shallow wet ditch which runs down the edge of a little copse of bright green apple trees. This morning's count in his HUD includes a dozen more vagabonds from other broken companies, lost souls latched onto Jan like sandburs.

The ditch is barely a meter deep. Even so, all his fighters are concealed from electronic probes, spy drones, micro hunters and high circling skycraft. Concealed from enemy Raptors and Jabos as fighters lie, sit or squat under a rough camo tent pegged to the clay sides of the little ditch. The cover is hobbled together from standard issue camo-and-thermal sheets that provide light refract, heat block and *huff duff* motion blurring. From even feet away, the light-and-sound camouflage 'tent' conceals the exhausted fighters resting beneath it. From across the meadow, it must look to his enemies as if only a stand of apple trees is waking to the dawn.

'*Good thing they all paid attention in basic. They linked up combat sheets just in time.*' Jan drags his bad leg and lanky frame, trying to stay small as he inches up the cool, clay sided ditch. A thick clump of yellow tumbles down to rest atop his scuffed combat boot. Smaller bits of dry caked ochre soil cling to his grubby, wheat colored combat weaves. Their 'armored' ceramic cloth is as flexible and soft as cotton but will instantly turn strong and rigid as ultrasteel if hit, alerted filaments lining up in a crystal pattern like iron filings under a strong magnet.

'*Not much time left to decide.*' A thin streak of flattened clay blends with the pale beige of his jacket. It's smeared over a black, double headed eagle crest perched right above his right breast, just beneath his captain's bars. He settles into position and peers through a reed thin field periscope, slyly poking overtop dew coated blades of tall sweetgrass. *Torresia odorata* is abundant in this temperate latitude, familiar and loved by locals like Jan. The sweetgrass was reengineered by pioneer AI bots a hundred generations ago, before the first settlers descended to a preterraformed world, so that under Genève's modest gravity it easily grows over two meters high. Seems the nanny bots also boosted its scent genes.

Vanilla odor from tubular stalks and flat golden leaves fills the air all around. The pungent scent transport Jan to a more carefree day a year earlier, filled with languorous lovemaking in a hot summer field just like this one, where ambrosial perfumes of crushed flat sweetgrass entwined with the sweating body of a pliable and eager brunette, her long legs locked around his waist, her loins thrusting and heaving rhythmically beneath his own. He sees her face again, tastes her salty moistness, pulled from the now by a sweet smell of freshly broken grass blades.

'*No such luck today.*' He presses down as flat as he can across the lip of the damp ditch. It's still oozing worms and moist odors and morning dew. Perfect droplets appear then evaporate, leaving no hint behind that they were ever there. '*Would that we could do the same.*'

He raises the periscope above the stalks and peers out at the enemy on the far side of the meadow. Tall, sweet, unbroken blades wave gently over his head in a light morning breeze. The periscope auto adjusts range and focus, suggesting target selections. He watches a large group of enemy infantry in pale green break up their crude night camp, readying for another day of casual killing. Another day of conquest of Jan's kin and neighbors. The pencil thin periscope is more precise than his HUD, a manifold with much greater magnification because it sacrifices secondary sensory and coms functions to maximize visuals. He sees in detail a double crescent moon patch on a picket's shoulder as the boy turns to face east. His weapon is slung high, to let him piss languidly over the edge of the meadow.

Jan doesn't recognize the flash, but the periscope answers the minor mystery before he even asks: "*172nd Light Infantry, Rikugun. Homeworld: Uri. Status: conscript.*" Jan's memory digs into his youth. '*That's one of their original worlds. With two moons, if I remember my grade school history right. An original Waldstätte planet. These locust bâtards came straight from the Oetkert dynastic home! They probably think we should be honored that they're visiting poor little Genève.*'

"Locusts." That's what everyone calls the Grünen swarming over Genève and four other assaulted Krevan Republic worlds: Brno, Lwów, Rhea and the capital world Aral. Wherever the green swarms land they leave death and deserts behind. They're eating out everything, all that Krevans have built over nearly 300 years of peace, since the last Orion War. Since the last swarming.

"What can the Grün Imperium want with Genève? We have nothing they don't already have. Why are they here?" Everyone asked that when the assault ships fell out of the sky. But none of that matters anymore. Not now, as Jan stares at armed farfolk pulling on green weaves as they break camp, rising and readying to kill again. Bile rises along with hate, burning his throat. Looking at smug Rikugun troopers across the meadow he sees a chance that Madjenik hasn't had since the fighting started. A chance to do more than run and die, day after day after day. '*We can't go, we can't stay. OK then, we'll fight. Today, maybe it'll be different. Today, we'll start the killing, not them. Today, maybe we get some payback.*'

***

Jan knows from his recon that the enemy he'll face in the coming firefight in the next few minutes are conscripts from Uri. Knows that their coms and jammers and weps are standard issue for a RIK light infantry unit. He knows this because his periscope tells him, and because he tells himself. As his moda begins to wear off he's finding he talks to himself much more often, and by name. Which is really kinda odd. He never did it before the war. Not before five days ago.

'*They've got nothing special when it comes to weapons. 'Bout the same as us, though a lot more of it, and they've got numbers on us too. The one big thing they have that we don't is backup. All we have is a chance to surprise them. If we don't hit them hard and deadly right at the start, they'll call for armtrak support and call in a skycraft strike. And that will be the end of your brief and inglorious career, Jan Wysocki.'*

Uri is a fiefdom world of the Grün Imperium ruling family, passing down from Oetkert to Oetkert over fourteen centuries. It's an immensely powerful and populous place, teaming with branded *dāsa* slaves and bonded serfs, all serving the top three classes of Grün citizens. It's part of the Imperium core, a Waldstätte foundation world. One of the most important in all Orion. Genève is different. It's a small, sparsely populated agro world, unnoticed and unimportant in the great doings of the spiral arm. Full of intense pride, nonetheless. Jan loves its odd little byways and hardy and unpretentious people. Offworld, he was told with urban and sophisticate disdain while a student on Aral that he smells a bit like Genève: a little oaky, with more than a touch of its old growth forests.

When he got back after just a year away, after washing out of KRA Officer Academy in Yalto, he fell back into Genève's comfortable ways. It was easier to return to the boy he once was instead of seeking out the man he failed to become. But sometimes he would sit silent and alone for hours, behind his parent's modest farmhouse. He would dig with his toes into black leafy humus in a copse of golden trees that like him waited forever for something that never happened, filling his senses with odd yet so familiar shapes and odors. He lied to himself, saying that he never wanted to leave Genève again, that he wanted to be forever rooted like the trees. Yet he always knew that they, too, had tried but failed to reach the stars.

After he was expelled from OTS he learned the officer trade more slowly. He read tactics and history at night, taking his commission the long and local way, eventually qualifying but only to serve with KRA Homeworld defense on Genève. Even then, it took him nearly 10 years to make captain. Still, they had no choice but to give him a company once he got his bars. Besides, lots of ill-made officers held command. What did that matter in peacetime? Someone had to do the job.

Always his own worst critic, Jan actually read more widely than most fulltime KRA officers, and understood more of what he read. As the crisis built between the Krevan Republic and the Grün Imperium, as war loomed, he knew sooner than most what was coming to Genève. '*Helvetti! Over the Long Peace, KRA became a community college, not a fighting force. A holding place for our local youth before they leave military obligation behind to start real lives as civilians. Only failures like me stayed in for 10 years. That's why we never had a snowball's chance in a desert in this fight. Madjenik wasn't ready and it had me as captain.*'

That first day, his first ever day of war, five days back, waves of green clad infantry poured into ever widening breaches made by Rikugun heavy armored divisions supported by long distance, constantly pounding field guns. Jan stood up and shot back when the infantry arrived, until he smelled panic in the air and realized it was his own. That's when he ran. He didn't mean to do it. But his legs rebelled against his brain, and carried him away from the broken position. What he won't admit to himself even now is that they *all* ran, any who survived to serve under him in Madjenik. They scrambled madly back from forward funk holes, the whole company overcome after just two hours of ferocious, lopsided fighting.

If that was all he remembered he might get to forgiveness, might rationalize his running as tactically necessary, and staying as foolhardy and fatal. But there was more. Jan knows that he loped away not just from the enemy but from fading pleas for help of wounded men, from distant cries for mercy that went unheeded, from wild screams by Genèven youth followed by a sudden *pop, pop* as RIK killed the abandoned and all prisoners. Only those who ran survived that day, as many tens of thousands died all around. Yet the logic of running won't dissolve his guilt.

All forward KRA crumbled, Madjenik survivors tangling and comingling with remnant elements of three other fleeing companies. By nightfall, all the stragglers were badly mixed together, all that remained of 3rd Battalion of Genève's 1st or Gold Division. The youth of Northland was humiliated and broken and on the run, fleeing in disorder from an ancient and hated enemy come again in his pride to kill and burn and plunder harmless Genève. '*He was everywhere. His biker scouts out front. Swarms of hover troops in ATCs. Hordes of heavy armtraks. Main force infantry combat gliding in waves. Mobile assault guns.*' Jan knows that the enemy was too many to do more than run and hide, to try to live another hour or day. But he can't and won't forgive himself. '*You'll never get that day back. Never.*'

The RIK had total drone and skycraft dominance above, and still does. Jan and Madjenik were chased through burning fields and hamlets over days and nights that followed. Sometimes the RIK got there first, blocking the way. Farm dogs barked at the intruders all day and all night long, until maser shots rang out and the dogs went silent, too. Joining their murdered masters. And so it went for five terrible days and through four awful nights, after the breakthrough. Jan didn't lead his defeated company in an approved "advance to the rear," the kind laid out by staff officers in the Aral Academy *Infantry Officer Tactics Manual*. Madjenik just moved wherever extreme violence pushed it and Jan accepted that it must go.

***

A passive HUD scan confirms the periscope. '*OK, they're the 172nd from Uri. Not a main or elite RIK unit like we fought at the MDL that first day, or the other locusts that chased us on Z+2, plus 3, and plus 4. These guys are brand new to this fight, looking like they've never been in combat before. They're acting like it, too, standing around in the open. Well, they'll pay for that.*'

Jan watches his careless enemy milling across the sweetgrass. Looks past the stupid boy pissing casually on his homeworld's violated soil, unaware that he's marked for certain death inside a pencil periscope and command HUD. He's counting, locating strongpoint positions and weakest defense points. Plotting to slaughter men and boys he doesn't know and will never meet, except here in a sweet odor meadow he'll scour black with fire and hate and death.

'*We have to keep moving, to reach Toruń.*' That's where KRA Main HQ is, the fortified and heavily defended forest capital of Genève. It's the only large city. The only place to reach for, even if he knows there's almost no chance of getting there. Not against the long odds this war has stacked against him and Madjenik. '*There's no other place else to go. Not on all Genève. But that oversize company of locust bâtards is in the way, over there across the sweetgrass meadow.*'

Main HQ is gone for all he knows, or at least it went dark on the military neb since Z+2. There's nothing on the emergency backup civilian memex either. Jan is deaf, blind and dumb to the enemy. He can't report in and he can't get intel or new orders. He's cut off and all alone. He suspects that most other KRA units are just as badly off, or worse. He's not wrong about that. '*At least we recovered from first combat shock from five days ago. We're actually becoming something of a real fighting unit now. Why not? Those bâtards taught us to fight by fighting, to survive by stealthy movement, to kill them, too. Silently and without remorse.*'

No one is more surprised at this tactical turn by a band of defeated and raggedy amateurs than Madjenik's worried and wounded captain. '*But it probably won't matter in the end.*' Jan thinks, or rather he knows, that whatever happens in the next hour Madjenik will almost surely die before this day is done. There are just too many locust units out there, waiting to circle back to the sounds of combat, to swarm and descend to consume all that lives and moves.

"If ever there was a hopeless cause, it's ours. Well, at least we can kill a hunter's chance of enemy before we die, if we can take them by surprise." He doesn't realize that he muttered the dismal thought out loud, or that it's overheard by a huge, dark haired sergeant who never leaves his side or takes his gaze off the company commander. The big man doesn't move as Jan's dark words reach him. He looks even more ready and intense. He double checks that his maser is warm.

Jan stirs slightly where he lies on the dirt lip of the ditch, waiting and watching as the periscope tallies and marks the enemy a final time. His wound throbs a little more than before. He shifts his leg ever so slightly. It doesn't help. It only wakes his memory. Back to first combat. To the day he failed as an officer and as a man. To the black day he failed Madjenik and fled from death and worse, from his duty.

***

Jan ran hard for his life that morning, back turned full and flat to a pursuing enemy. Until he felt a spear of white hot metal tear into his weaves and pierce his lower calf. The impact knocked him over even before he felt any pain, taking his wounded leg out from beneath where his brain thought it should be, as if his knee was hit with an industrial hammer. As he registered the blow and began to tumble he felt more astonished than hurt. '*No, no! I can't end like this!*'

A sear of pain traveling both ways inside his calf made him cry out loud. He dropped his main weapon. Crumpled, grabbed uselessly for the wound, glimpsed pursuers closing to finish him as he turtled to the ground. Hot shrapnel from frag grenades just like the 2cm piece that felled him tore and *screeched* past his head, sending his HUD wild with *red* threat warnings. *Poumm, keraaack!* Pulse rounds slammed into hot dirt beside his left shoulder where he landed, spraying him with stinging grains as he clenched his teeth in suppressed pain. The enemy was close. *Click clack, click clack, click clack.* He heard the distinctive charge-and-shoot sound of nearby Rikugun masers, then a sudden *whirr zsuiii-slitt!* of two incoming rounds riving grass and dirt beside his head. He tasted a clod of clay that flew into his mouth, mixed with sweat of his face. A clot of warm, black Genèven soil from whence he came and where he must return one day. Dust unto dust.

Maser bolts from enemy rifles sliced down stalks of nearly ripe golden barley around him. He lay half-revealed by burning stalks, under gray-black smoke. He reached his hand out toward his dropped stub maser, lying just out of his reach, desperate to shoot back at his tormentors just one last time before he died. He was still stretching his arm out when five troopers dropped in a semicircle defensive perimeter around him and returned rapid fire. *Click clack, click clack, click clack,* over and over sounded the telltale double signature of their pink crystal masers, charging and discharging again and again as micro lasers engaged the crystal to release a thousand times more focused energy than put in. These were friendly sounds. Close, clear and loud. Scorching the air with microwaves in his defense.

Rough commands shouted in a high pitched female voice told him who his rescuer was: Lieutenant Zofia Jablonski. The 22-year old redhead was fighting and leading like he had not, with authority beyond her years laced through all her actions and her bearing, stiffening the will of the squad of men she led. Moving toward the enemy, not running away from him. She had real tactical command presence and both of them knew it. It was her squad that came back for *him*, that cut apart a charging and overconfident enemy platoon bent on his murder. Her little unit that laid down counterfire of high kinetic rounds, also hand throwing frags and lobbing rifle grenades at the enemy, while also hurling pulse rifle fire.

'*That was an eternity ago. Five days!*' Jan sees it all again right before him. Then he's suddenly back on the ditch lip at the edge of the apple orchard. He can't shake this odd sense of leaping in-and-out of time. '*It must be a side effect of the moda. Well, maybe and maybe not.*' Jan doesn't know this about himself, but over the fearsome days and nights after Madjenik's ugly 'baptism by fire' he started to put aside shame and focus on fresh results. Most hours of the day anyway. Doesn't get that he's growing into the role of a real combat leader, and a good one. He has no choice. He's the most senior officer alive among the strays of four companies. One of just two. Hundreds of scared young faces look up at him daily with mortal pleading in their eyes, enemies at their heels. So he stopped running from the job.

Turns out, he's pretty good at it. Yes, he lost more fighters to ruthless pursuers during several pell mell, running battles to escape the MDL kill zone. Still more in desperate rearguard firefights where he *ordered* some men to stay behind and to fight to the death to save all the rest. Yes, even counting stragglers that signed on, Madjenik is down to 185 fighters from its prewar complement of 300, and it's still barely 220 klics from the MDL where it first started running. But now Jan is leading the company, really *leading*. And every fighter who keeps pace refuses to quit, won't lie down or sit to wait to be captured by pursuers, hoping only not to be killed and ready to beg for mercy. There's more. Everyone still alive, still in this fight and who won't surrender, has lost his or her combat virginity. They're harder, better, more skilled than before. They're becoming true combat veterans.

'*How is that possible? We have only been out here and at war for five days.*' Yet, it's true. Every fighter is a grim and skilled veteran now. Five days in intense combat like they have all seen is enough for the change to take hold. Hard learned lessons show in their faces and the way they move and conceal, even if each silent nighttime rollcall records fewer names in the company ledger. The change is most marked in Jan, but you can see it even in the most scared and youngest fighters. Each day, the pressures of combat and command squeeze more raw tannins and pomace out of Jan, leaving a maturing wine of determination and command and will to lead and survive. Zofia sees it darkening and aging in him, and approves.

***

'*What brought us to this place and moment? How did it come to this, to groups of frightened strangers facing death and each other across the sweetgrass?*' He knows that cold decisions by some great and distant power led him to this hollow, right to the edge of extinction in a shallow ditch alongside a small apple orchard. Swept all Madjenik, men and women, good and bad, into ferocious murder and mayhem. Fed them all into the gory maw of war. But why? And for whom?

'*For vain farfolk whose cause we don't even know. From malice beyond ken. For oldsters who send young to die because their own life's embers burn dimly, yet they want to play at bellows for another hour. They started this godsdamn war that ripped apart our lives, broke our homes and families, wreaked our worlds. I want them here, right now, to see what I'm about to do. Any bâtard who starts a war should have to look into the glazed eyes of soldiers dying in his name.*'

He fights down rage against the high and mighty councils, against the *Very Great Personages* of vast interstellar empires and star system confederations that dwarf the little, traditionally neutral worlds of the United Planets of Krevo. Those who chose to invade modest and unassuming places, unable or unsatisfied with instead raising up the greatness of their own. '*Pahhh! figuring out how this war got started is way above my pay grade. It doesn't matter anyway. Not anymore. Not now, when it's already here and all around, and rolling over the far horizon. All that matters is what I do in the next few minutes to get us out of this ditch. Then what Madjenik does over the next hours while they chase after us. Then the hours after that. And any moments of light and life left to us on this grim day.*'

He looks back at Madjenik's restless fighters. They're trailing pike, exhausted beyond exhaustion, sustained against bone weariness only by the forced alertness of five-day old moda. Those who can are lightly sleeping. More crouch or sit in awkward poses under the ersatz camo tent. Others kneel, eyes across the meadow, taking their turn at perimeter guard. '*If some of us are still alive at nightfall, well paska! We'll displace and move, and move again. I'll worry tomorrow about what to do on the morrow.*' His moda is receding faster. His exhaustion is returning. He's jerked alert again by his stabbing leg pain. With the fresh pain comes a flash of thought, hard and overwhelming. '*I could have died. I should have died.*'

He's right. By all odds he should be dead. Part of him even wishes that he was. Then he wouldn't recall memories of failure that he can't repress. Shameful and intense, they return despite his best effort to focus on the enemy in the sweetgrass, as guilt and exhaustion compete for his attention. '*Why did she come back for me? What did I do to deserve such loyalty? Nothing. I did nothing! Worse, I ran. They should have left me to die.*' A coward remembers and boasts of his one brave act all his life. A brave man like Jan Wysocki hardly knows that he's brave because it comes to him as in a second nature. Yet he can never forget or forgive the one time that he wasn't, the one time courage failed him. So that he failed others.

His backward gaze lingers on Zofia Jablonski. Her clear green eyes are lightly closed, gauntleted hands resting ready on a maser as she dozes, head sinking and jerking as she drifts asleep then starts awake. Even asleep, she's always more than half alert. Like a wary she wolf sensing approaching danger. '*She's the real leader of this company.*' A short curve of apple red hair is visible under the dirt smeared rim of her dull beige helmet, pushing a red curl, a little intriguing bit of womanly color, into the crisp and tart morning air. Her muddy faceplate is pulled halfway back. It perches on a small but not quite delicate, indeed imperfect nose. Her lips are full, slightly parted. Zofia is also exhausted by five days of killing and running, of leading and hiding and too little sleep. She's trained and marked for combat and mucked over with filth. Yet she takes his every breath away.

She stirs slightly, spilling a second crimson curl from beneath a beige helmet rim. She doesn't wake. It was a hard day's night before the current three-hour rest period, with images of pursuing enemy threats showing *red* on every HUD. Even now a faint, illuminated threat matrix reflects onto Zofia's clear, white face. It flickers soft *blue* symbology for friendlies gathered in the ditch, but dozens more *red* threat markers tag nearby enemy, just rising and starting to stir to the day. The milling locust across the sweetgrass meadow are way too cocky, or dumb. They're carelessly exposing their whole position to passive e-surveillance. Their moving presence dances eerie and electric on her HUD, and hence atop her closed eyelids.

As Jan watches her fitful sleep he remembers more from when he was hit while running away. How she held cover fire while two strong men ran to yank him up by the underarms where he lay wounded and waiting to die. He felt a tsunami of searing pain, an eternity of waiting for a kill shot in the head or back. Felt fear of the Wolf of War pursuing the ungainly five-legged creature the three men made as they hell-bent stumble ran, with Zofia kneeling and giving nipping cover fire. Lurching past burning barley his good leg churned, hardly touching ground past gushing, flashing amber stalks. Confused, temples pounding, jolts of intense pain traveling up his hurt leg, calf torn open and smoking where the white hot fragment was still searing deeper into his flesh.

A third man scooped up his maser, shoved it into his hands as they reached low cover of a natural drain at the edge of the barley field. He said matter-of-factly, without judgment, "I think you might need this, sir," before whirling down into a classic prone shooting position to crack off several plasma rounds at enemies suddenly hesitating, then howling from burning wounds of their own.

'*That's when I saw her, alone and exposed.*' Only then did Zofia race across the field. Zigging then zagging, kinetic rounds and erratic maser pulses snapping never-to-be-harvested barley around her. She dive rolled to a hard stop beside Jan, checked him for hidden wounds. Saying nothing. Doing her job. A consummate professional. Smelling of confidence and competence and lethal surety. '*She was born to command. She's a natural. Not like me at all.*'

Jan reluctantly pulls his gaze away from the young lieutenant's curling, lithe and almost feline form. His eyes are blue and brilliant now, shining hot with hate, startling the big sergeant by reminding him of an unstable star he saw once up close, hovering on the cusp of going nova. The glare of Jan's hate warms the big sergeant with confidence. If his enemies could see Jan's face in this clear moment, look into those hard blue nova eyes, they would surely be very afraid.

'*I vow that I'll not fail these fighters again! Or Zofia.*' He means it. He's fully determined to save Madjenik, to live up to what Zofia sees in him and demands of him. Determined at least to lead the company out of this ditch and across the sweetgrass meadow. To do only that, here and now.

Yet he just can't help the flush of self doubt that follows instantly. '*What if I fail again? What if I make a mistake that gets more fighters killed? Gods, what if I get her killed?*' Doubt and self-loathing returns before he can push it back under cover. Then somehow he manages to wrestle it down, reaffirming inner control, suppressing his paralysis of mind and confidence. It's a fight he has every day, even every hour, ever since his failure at the MDL. He thinks it's the fading moda. It isn't. It's a struggle to admit his better self. A struggle that's going to make him a very good officer. If only he lives through the coming fight in the sweetgrass.

At last, he comes back to the brightening apple orchard to stay, realizing that he was drifting off and cursing himself again for weakness. This time he pushes it down and deep. '*Damn! I need more moda. And real soon. We all do, if we're going to make it. Well, there's sure to be a good supply of it on those boys in green weaves across the meadow. We'll just have to take it from them.*'

Jan looks one last time at the unaware men and boys in pale green, rising to meet their last dawn and hour. Feeling their last pleasure, before their last pain. '*An ancient poet said that each of us bears his own Hell within. Maybe, but it's my turn now to play at damnation. I shall make a new and hotter fire to scorch this swarm of locust!*' This is Jan's other self. The ruthless and efficient combat leader he can be, struggling to emerge. To take charge of him and of Madjenik.

He knows now that in the next few minutes he'll cover the vanilla grass with screams and blood, and spill the offal of sons of a far off world. He'll advance Death's pale flags to plant his poles in the chests of unsuspecting and undeserving youths far from home. How can he do this thing? Even to these careless 'locust' boys swarming across a meadow not their own? '*Am I better than those terrible, distant persons who did this to me these past five days? Disrupting my life and ripping my world apart forever, as I'll now destroy the lives of young strangers? As I forever eclipse the love of their woeful mothers with Death's dark disk?*'

These aren't royal Oetkerts, the ruling dynasty headed by Pyotr Shaka III who started the war. They're not from the upper three castes of the Imperium, who gain from it the most. They're not even regular Rikugun troops, the green legions who bear its brunt and its casualties. They're certainly not an elite unit of Pyotr's political army, the Special Action Commando or SAC. Those gray clad killers are hated as much or maybe more inside the Grün Imperium as outside. Although their reputation for cruelty and capricious murder is growing across Orion, apace with fresh reports of the vicious role they're playing in the Krevan War.

These boys are conscripts from Uri. Rear area scrubs filling out behind the main assault by Rikugun regular divisions. They're tasked with lesser duties, with following and 'mopping up' shattered units like Madjenik. He doesn't know any of them, these farfolk dressed in pale green weaves. Can he kill them just for being here? Just for pissing on his native sweetgrass? Can he give the order to end them forever, as night's darkness crumbles into a new day on Genève? '*Yes, godsdamn it! Because it's different! Genève is my home. Our land, our world. Not theirs. They came to reave our worlds. They started it! Now they die!*'

They didn't start it, really. Not *these* men and boys, anyway. But a child's morality is all that's left Jan as he hugs an ochre ditch lip and contemplates pure bloody murder. Men have had this same argument with themselves ever since creeping out onto the Serengeti plain after they invented war among the trees, and wanted more. It's what war reduces moral reasoning to once we're really in it. We're like troops of monkeys throwing nuts at each other from separate trees. Then rocks. Then clubbing and biting each other to death in a collective frenzy. Then setting fire to the whole forest rather than let the other troop have any of it. "Well, you know," we always say to each other after it's over, "*they* started it."

What matters far more is that Jan's blood is up and hot, and that blood wants blood. He wants vengeance for his damaged world and his lost fighters, but also for his shame and lost self. Maybe after that he can get Madjenik's last survivors out of this soggy, filthy ditch. Away from the little orchard just opening to the rising dawn warming his back and exposing his hidden position.

'*To go where?*' To Toruń, deep inside the far north woods, the last possible refuge left to KRA or civilians running from the Rikugun horde that's advancing across all Genève. If Toruń is even there anymore. If the wondrous Arbor City of the locals' deepest pride is not a blackened ruin.

'*How? I don't know how.*' He only knows that Madjenik can't stay here. Not for one hour more. It's camo won't hold and there's more movement in the enemy camp. More sound, too. Beyond the usual clanky matins and dull breakfasting, his HUD is picking up weapons and *huff duff* warming up. And even his unaided ears hear a sergeant's barked orders rousing the last and laziest sleepers.

'*Now! We must strike now.*' He retracts the periscope. It folds in on itself with a series of soft *clicks*. He drops it into a thin cargo pocket on his thigh. Across an open, sweet smelling field is a careless enemy, his Double Moon flashes glinting in the sharp early morning sunlight. '*A whole company just milling in the open. I've got them, the fools!*'

He swivels his head, looking down to his own ragged company. He's more determined than ever before in his life, about anything. He knows that the same mood fills the ditch behind and all around him. These men and women have faced death, too, these past five days. Many times over. They know now that there are much worse things than death. Their desperation makes Madjenik very dangerous.

Jan rubs his left thumb against the handle of a Q-carbon knife firmly sheathed against his boot. He's certain what he must do next. All hesitation and doubt is gone. Doubt is the enemy of command, of a controlled rage he needs to lead this fight. Gruff resolve alone shows through his HUD as he pulls it down over his face, sending command data streaming through a short range tactical net, enemy symbology sent to glow eerily *red* on morning displays across all Madjenik visors.

"Let's put some hurt on these *mulkku!*" he snarls, sliding to the bottom of the slick sided ditch in a slimy, ochre ooze. His troopers are instantly argus eyed. All of them suddenly look hard and grim, slamming aerographite chargers into open magazines of maser assault rifles. Unclipping knives. Readying grenades.

Meadow

The familiar, soft *click-and-purr* of the charged-and-ready crystal masers brings Zofia to full alert. She sniffs cautiously, breathing in crushed apple and snapped sweetgrass. She checks the command link for fresh data. In seconds she assesses the position and situation. She stays prone, but ready. Only then does she steal a sly glance at Jan. He looks stern and intense but handsome as ever, at least to her. Even more attractive for his fierce resolution and killer look in this moment of decision. It all flashes through his tinted visor. She indulges thoughts of him more than in looming combat, for just a moment. It could be one of her last.

'I told him I went back for him because he's my captain, our leader. But why can't he see that I also went back because it was him? Does he even know that I'm a woman? He used to, before the war. But he never shows it anymore. Not since this all started. Not since the MDL.'

She had this thought before, usually while waking up like this and not fully in control. She always pushes it down and clamps it closed, the same way he fights off and imprisons self doubt. She's a professional, a top graduate of the Aral Academy. She knows how to shake off all such thoughts in a combat zone. She does it now, focusing for a firefight that *humming* masers tell her is coming real soon. Fully alert, she shifts from prone to a tense crouch at the edge of the ditch. The pose makes her look like a young panther readying to spring upon its prey.

The big unshaven sergeant watches Jan intently, slow biting into a fallen apple that's dark red, half-rotten, runny with fermenting juice. He chews methodically, looking at first glance like a sleepy koala. His hard and alert eyes belie his slovenly appearance. '*They're narrow and vaguely fish like. No, more shark like. Yes, that's it! He has a natural killer's eyes. But something else, too. What?*'

The 'Double Moons' are real sloppy soldiers. Their pickets are inattentive, like the one who shouldered his maser to take a piss while Jan watched. As if he was pissing in training camp back on Uri, returned from a night on the town and full of sated lust and cheap ale. Too many of the rest are closely bunched around a field canteen at the center of the camp, showing as a dense smear of entangled *red* light on Jan's HUD. No properly trained or experienced infantry would act like this in a combat zone, not first echelon RIK. Not *any* professional troops.

'*Yet we did it, too, and paid a heavy price for it on the first day.*' Jan wonders why, then answers himself. '*No one in Orion has been to war in nearly 300 years.*

Maybe we overestimate these Grünen? They're just as inexperienced at war as us. And this batch are fresh conscripts, not a SAC or Purity death squad or even RIK regulars. Even so, they shouldn't be here. But here they are, making war on Genève. Well, they've made their choice. We're all making final choices now.'

Jan knows that even these rookie enemies shouldn't be underestimated. Even conscripts are a heavily armed threat the like of which hasn't been seen in the Krevan systems for nearly three centuries. With a silent thought he outlines the crowded canteen with a throbbing *red* rectangle in his HUD, marking it as a top priority on all linked Madjenik target screens. That includes stragglers and strays, who Zofia tapped in to the system as each arrived and was vetted.

What Jan doesn't know is that he's a natural tactician. If he did, he would understand Zofia's approving nod at his targeting choices. Officer training bored him as a young candidate, then shamed him when he failed out of the KRA Academy on Aral. Memory of that lost opportunity kicks at him with life-and-death meaning and purpose now. He gives himself no credit for the past five days. Wounded and hurting, he led a shattered company farther through enemy infested territory than anyone had a right to expect, dodging vastly superior forces. No small feat. Even he might be impressed, if he knew the high odds against it.

Nor does he know that already Madjenik's survivors and even the misfit strays will follow him through fire or high water if he asks. Follow him to the stars, if they ever get off burning Genève. Doesn't know that's why the big sergeant is always close and hard staring. Jan isn't thinking about that yet. He's too busy with a HUD tally of *blue* friendlies and much larger numbers of *red* threats. He opens a direct-to-company relay, while speaking softly out loud for the benefit of those crouching nearby. "Alert! Madjenik attacks in five minutes. Repeat, five minutes. '*Snakes*' go in first, then we make a straight up firing line. Get ready."

Everyone snaps to, focusing on their HUD squad and platoon or specialty orders while screening out every ambient sight or sound. The bearded sergeant stops munching. He's down to the core anyway. A chunk of red peel hangs still from a corner of his half-open mouth, lodged between two dirty and oddly uneven teeth. He stiffens, gaping at his captain like a lovesick girl. His big hands raise up and firmly hold a low *humming* maser. It's warm and ready. "Time to show these *mulkku* how we Krevans fight," Jan again uses a crude anatomical profanity. He says it without really thinking. Even though he never said it out loud before today.

It actually fits, since all Rikugun troops are males. Krevans learned that fact to their great surprise the first time they met this enemy in combat. All boys and men. No women fighters. It's not like that in their own little army, or in any other military in Orion. Women wear the uniform alongside men without anyone giving it a second thought. It has been that way for a millennium, everywhere but in the Grün Imperium with its deep legacy of Broderbund misogyny and *dāsa* slavery.

"We're going to hit 'em fast, and hard. Don't stop shooting 'till I tell you." The small firefight for an empty field Jan's about to start won't decide the fate of this or any Krevan world. It won't win the war, or much delay losing it. Yet he knows that Madjenik will fight when he gives the order, will kill madly with every weapon it has, in gouts of gore. Die if necessary, on his order. As it most likely will be for most of them before all this losing ends.

Why? The larger outcome is already decided. Sparsely populated Southland continent was overwhelmed by the first invasion wave. There's nothing anyone can do to save or win the "Battle for Northland" either, if that's even what people will later call it. That chance is paved over by the brutal realities of clear enemy superiority at all levels of capability, by new combined arms tactics and efficiency that surprised and stunned the KRA. Paved over as well by 420,000 KRA lives surrendered on Genève alone, and two million more civilian dead. A normal year of Death's reaping and Genèvens saying farewell in the Life Temples to those whose Youthspan has waned and failed. Now that many in just five days of war.

How many more dead will there be to wail over before this ends? How many more terribly wounded in body, mind or soul? How many tens or hundreds of millions? Jan has no idea. He only knows that Madjenik won't fight from a false hope of somehow claiming victory out of this calamity. Not beyond maybe reclaiming this one summer meadow for Genève for an hour or two, before abandoning it again. It won't fight for *any* lost hope.

But it *will* fight. To stay alive for another hour or a day, maybe another week. It will fight to defy the enemy's every straining effort to kill it. It will fight until it can fight no more, forever. It will fight for hate's sake. Maybe it can hurt its enemy, too, if only a little. Hit back while it can, before the company dies. For everyone in the orchard knows that Madjenik is done for. That it shouldn't have survived this long. It's all anyone in Madjenik has left. It's *everything*. Hate is everything. "*Mita helvettia!* What the hell, we're all already dead." Jan says it into the com, grinning at a weary clutch of ungentle, bloodyminded fighters. He may yet understand them one day, he hopes. They already think he does.

"You got that right, sir." It's the burly, hairy sergeant crouching beside him. A shock of thick black stubble scrapes against the scored sides of his visor, almost audibly to Jan. He pulls the scrap of apple peel from his teeth and drops it to the bottom of the ditch. A field mouse darts over his boot, snaps up the thin peel and with a whip of its thin, reedy tail, it disappears between two tall vanilla grasses. The sergeant watches the field mouse disappear and grins broadly.

Every man and woman in Jan's line of sight nods at the affirmation and returns their captain's mulish grin. They all understand the merciless nature of an enemy who wastes any stragglers or wounded left behind. For on the third day, biting down so hard he tasted wet iron oozing from his bloody lower lip, Jan held still as he watched three young KRA try to surrender. No one in this company will ever try that again. Not ever. No more surrenders. Not to *them*.

One boy was cut apart by crisscrossing masers swayed back-and-forth by a big, pitiless Grün spandau gunner firing from a hover gunship turret. Worse than the sight of the bisected boy was listening to crunching bone and terrible screeches as a second armtrak dropped its hover controls to become tracked ground assault armor. Just to crush the two other kids into puddles of pink pulp under its carbyne and ultrasteel treads, darkly staining the rich soil of their native land. Everyone in hiding was grateful when the horrid screams abruptly stopped. Jan learned the next day from a straggler who joined Madjenik that it's a common Grün practice to grind prisoners down into smeared clods. It wasn't the forbidden act of a single tanker, the sick pleasure of a lone driver. Of a sadist in an armtrak saddle, his lust unbridled by war's opportunity for cruel freedom.

"I was hiding, sir, staying real quiet like. I even had my safety off, ready to blow out my own brains if they came to do it to me, too. That's when I heard 'em, sir. A spandau loader and the driver, taking a break beside their Mammoth."

"What did you hear?"

"The driver said he likes to switch over to manual so 'I can have fun ironing *Gelben* prisoners.' Sorry to repeat that sir, but it's what he said."

Jan knows that "Yellows" is what RIK mockingly calls its KRA enemies, who wear wheat colored weaves. "What else did he say? Take a breath, and take your time. I want details."

"He was a big bear of a man, captain, near as big as the black bears I seen in Toruń Wood before the war. He said to the other drivers, he said the way to do it was to slam one track brake hard while he hit auto drive on the other side, spinning the whole armtrak right in place, sir. It was real sick, sir, the way he laughed about it after. They all laughed. All of them."

Another straggler confirmed it. "I heard one talking about 'grinding,' too. He said it to the other drivers, with a big belly laugh, captain. He said 'It's the best fuck I ever had!'"

"He said *that?* Exactly that?"

"Yes sir, I know 'cause some other *bâtard* yelled out 'And it's a lot easier on the goats!' That's when they all laughed, sir."

"I heard it, too. They agreed that 'grinding' was the thing to do to all prisoners. A couple of the young ones looked as green as their own weaves, but they had to promise to do it, too."

A third catch-up said he watched an ugly, squat nosed *gunsō* give a similar order. The Grün sergeant was standing beside a sneering *taisa*, a silent, sinister, coppery colonel wearing steel gray weaves to match the callow color of his SAC uniform underneath. That afterward the two gray clad men climbed into a sleek, needle nosed black command hover, last seen heading back to the coast where RIK and SAC HQs were set up behind the now broken MDL.

"Gray weaves, not green? You're sure?"

"Yes sir. They were SAC, not RIK. Special Action Commandos."

Gray, not green. Gray, a cold abnegation of all the rainbow colors of life. A deliberate negation of all color, declaring an absolute power of obliteration. Gray, symbol of moral indifference and pallid death, brought to Genève from Death's home in the Grün Imperium. Gray, steel weaves worn by SAC officers and kill squads out on their deadly, daily business of murder. Jan is an educated man. He knows that SAC promotes crackpot theories of "Original Purity" and pursues a pseudogenetic social engineering project to "reclaim the precolonial genome." He knows that gray death squads are roaming freestyle across the occupied northern plains. And he knows there's nothing he or Madjenik can do about any of it. '*We'll settle with that SAC colonel and his pet toad another day. Just not this day. Right now I have to get us out of this ditch or we're all going to die. It's time to attack.*'

He jumps on the company coms. "Engineers, make ready to deploy SRDs."

Zofia sees his plan unfolding and reminds the engineers that there's no motion detector or AI bot probe patrolling the camp perimeter, at least not one they've detected yet. "Stay off coms when you break from visual camo, when you leave the ditch. Hand signals only. Once you leave the sheet cover, standard dampeners, those digital wonders you all call 'digies' that are built into your combat weaves, will hide you from active search pings for *five minutes*. No more. That's all the time you've got to deploy the snakes and make them do max damage!"

Jan breaks in. "You've got less time than that. I want all SRDs in release position in three minutes. *Go!*" Twenty surviving combat engineers gather at two crates of sleek, silvery tubes humped from the MDL on a small carrier bot. Each *Smart Roboticized Demolition* or SRD or '*snake'* is 10 centimeters in diameter and a half-meter long.

"Spread out and deploy down the flanks." The chief hisses the command to the others, each grasping a pair of *snakes* along with all their other gear. Thumb sized, orange capped detonators are dangerously tucked into webbed tool belts.

Jan sends more orders: "Sergeants, distribute grenades. Everybody double up on assault frags. Mortar squads, set up your tubes here and over there." He points to a flat stretch of ground behind him and the gossamer thin camo tent that's fast coming down. "Load HE and plasma rounds in pairs, but wait for the *snakes* to blow first and for my *fire* command." He turns back to the main body of fighters. With his left hand he holds up an aerographite pink crystal reload pack by his head, standard silent signal to *load ammo*. He order flashes a thought command across all company HUDs, adding a harsh whisper in all helmet auditories. "Lock-and-load. We're gonna smoke these *bâtards*!"

Coiled for combat, her red hair all tucked away inside her helmet, green eyes concealed from outside view by the darkness of her pulled down HUD, ready to sprint into the lead of a charge across the meadow if Jan orders it, Zofia whispers out loud to no one in particular: "Things are about to get sparky!"

***

The engineers are semi-exposed outside the shallow ditch as they shift from under improvised shielding to move down the long flanks. They hug the *snakes* close, the stubby masers of their specialty slung diagonally across chests with safeties still on, their wide belts loaded down with small tools and the detonators. Each pair is guarded by a single sniper with a laser pulse rifle.

The rest of Madjenik readies for a direct assault. "No sonics! Frags only. And set all weps to full power. We want quick cookings," Zofia snaps the order at a fresh kid trying to hook two sonics to her upper weaves. It's one of the stragglers, the scared one who saw the bear-man armtrak driver 'grinding' prisoners behind the smashed MDL. She fumbles for replacement frags. The kid is trembling, struggling badly to hitch the grenades into weave loops on her chest. She looks even more frightened as Zofia lays the timeline on for the whole company.

"Three minutes for the engineers to do their job, to get our show rolling. Then two more for the *snakes* to reach their set targets. After that even passive motion search by any nearby locust will locate all our friends no longer under the camo tent. The rest of you watch your HUD clocks but keep *fucking* still as a dead mouse. Wait for the *shoot* and *move out* orders from the captain!"

All eyes are on Jan as he extends his left arm in a silent deployment signal. Without looking at Zofia, he thought flashes the same order over all HUDs: "*Line abreast. Buddy-buddy pattern.*" Two-by-two, still crouching, little sub units take up position, spreading out a quarter klic from Jan and Zofia at the center. Farther down the wide flanks snipers drop into open spaces between each engineer pair, presighting *whirring* scopes on carelessly exposed boys and men wearing pale green weaves. Making them more sure targets to be kissed by the guns.

Morning haze is clearing quickly under a risen sun. A rich smell of black soil, damp worms and rotting apples and leaves fills the air on radiant heat. It competes for attention with the odor of sweetgrass and sweat. Mortar teams site two medium tubes 20 meters apart, behind where Jan crouches, looking intently across the gold meadow for any sign that Madjenik's movement has been detected. '*Nothing. No response. Just give me another two minutes and we might pull this off.*' Three man mortar crews check passive target displays then lock in their weps, ready to drop high compression HE rounds, co-loaded with plasma, smack onto the enemy's encampment. They'll start with the crowded *red* canteen as the primary target, then work the shelling outward and all around until they meet a second wave of desolation moving inward from the perimeter of blown *snakes*. Done right, the *snakes* and little mortar barrage should sandwich and shatter a good part of the sleepy infantry company gathering over breakfast from just over 100 to about 300 meters away, with a great clot of men still hovering around the field canteen.

All other shooters take up kneeling or standing fire positions on Jan's short flanks, forming a bloc of concentrated infantry firepower facing unsuspecting and unready enemies who are still casually breakfasting or lolling slowly awake across the fragrant field. Unaware that they're about to die in fire and light far from their homeworld, for reasons most of them have hardly considered. '*It doesn't matter. They give consent just by being here.*' "If we time this right they'll never hear it coming." Jan whispers to Zofia over the officer only link, as he hand signals *hurry up!* to the engineers with his left fist, pumping up-and-down repeatedly.

"Then time it right, sir." Her reply is borderline insubordinate, but she's right to say it. She moves 20 meters to his left, to command the other half of the central firing position. Jan waits impatiently for the farthest engineers to hand sign their readiness. A minute more and the most distant waves in a '*two*' signal. All are in position, ready to release the *snakes*. It's going to be close. They've got less than two minutes before they'll be detected by the enemy's active tracking gear.

This spread out and close to the active scan exposure window expiring, Jan avoids even a silent HUD order via his command relay. He fears to lose his only true advantage: total surprise in a sudden, overwhelming firestorm. Instead he makes a crisp slashing motion with his right arm across his chest, a signal seen on battlefields for thousands of years. Receiving the *make ready* order, the shooting line rises, resting maser rifles on small tripods on the ditch edge, shoulder sighting and steadying aim at the nearest unwary Grün picket or exposed officer.

Crouching engineers release latches on the front of silver launch tubes resting over the lip of the ditch, poking partway into the tall sweetgrass. Clamps *snick!* open all at once. Something thin and lissome squirts from each tube. Twenty *snakes* are loose and slithering off to hunt prey. The SRDs scan for environmental colors, flash a mottled yellow-and-brown adaptive camouflage, then slither away. They undulate over ochre dirt under the tall sweetgrass. Micron sized phononic crystals spin underneath, baffling sound. Twenty sidling forms wriggle stealthily toward discrete target coordinates. They move with swift, lethal intent, excited to be free and active and purposive after a dark and tubed and crimped existence.

More mottled movement. It's a follow on wave of 20 eager SRDs auto spread to optimal kill pattern, to maximize blast effect and antipersonnel shrapnel from compact explosive charges. No e-search picks up the sleek, metallic maneuvers. Gentle rustles under waving sweetgrass stalks hardly hint to pickets at an animate presence, so the unmindful guards from Uri miss the swift serpent passings. Thirty seconds more and smart munitions arrive at deadly *maximum detonation insertion points* all around the camp, deep inside the Double Moons' careless perimeter.

They blow all at once. A swirling, tumultuous mess as excited as a living, giant breeding ball of real snakes, exploding in a death mating that is both fulfillment and extinction in a single moment of exquisite, orgasmic evaporation. It's a neat trick of all military AI: it finds greatest fulfillment, a kind of machine happiness, in its own planned and purposeful destruction.

Jan bellows and flashes: "Mortar crews, lay it on them now! Infantry, open fire! Single company volley, shoot! Again, shoot! Again!"

A muffled roar arrives from where 40 snakes willingly died as one ... A thinning blast wave reaches Madjenik, standing up in a shooting line but still inside the ditch, pumping low shots across the singeing sweetgrass ... The shock wave is dissolute and harmless, rocking the shooters gently for a moment before it passes whispering into the apple trees above and behind.

"Lieutenant, volley fire by squad!" Zofia takes over. "First Squad fire! Second Squad fire! Third Squad fire! Fourth Squad fire! Repeat rotation. First Squad fire! Watch the heat on your crystals! Second Squad fire!"

A dozen different screams arrive from all around the perimeter and deep inside the camp, reaching above the whisper of deadly snakes to lament so many snuffed out youth ... Across the meadow, a roiling bank of acrid black-and-gray smoke ... Snipers aside and away from the main firing line are shooting between paired sets of engineers along either flank ... two climb into tall apple trees for better line-of-sight ... Masers volley in squad relays overtop the ditch ... aiming for lower backs, snipping spines, incapacitating legs ... far worse than kill shots.

"Six pickets down!" a spotter calls to Jan. "And two officers!" *Those are head shots ... cocky, lazy RIK captains and majors aren't wearing helmets inside their camp perimeter ... stupid, bloody, brain spattering deaths ... Another four pickets down ... falling, tumbling ... bored through chest or gut ... others spinning, thrashing ... legs not working anymore ... they need more than one shot to die.*

"Shoot 'em again! Make it count!"

More screams race across the meadow. Primal. Hair raising. Coming from a different part of the brain than language, yet speaking to everyone who hears all the same. Like flopping fish in a boat hit in the head with a stiff club, the pickets stop moving. The camp disappears into a giant smoke roll rising above where the snakes just committed suicide. But there's much more fire and smoke and secondary explosions than there should be from the *snakes* alone.

"SRDs hit an ammo dump!" The spotter states the obvious. Jan ignores her. He's scanning for fresh targets.

"Individual firing. Fire at will! Pour it into them! Use your HUDs. Pick a target but keep shooting!" Jan's blood is up, his temples are pounding. Zofia's shouting something else. To him? To the handful of fighters still crouching in the ditch instead of standing to fire? He can't make her out at all. Her urgency alone breaks through. "Use the damn command link!" he yells, hand signaling wildly to her.

Zofia sees him mouth the words, taps her helmet to show it's *his* com link that's off. He engages it with a thought command and hears her clear, bell-like laughter bouncing inside his helmet as she tears off another clip of maser fire across the meadow. Others fire all around and beside him. *Click clack, click clack, click clack ... like a swarm of demented crickets ... blue-electric maser bolts pumping ... burning ... smoking ... coring tunnels through columns of vanilla grass and the exposed torsos of young men ... scorching the dreams of vain distant fathers ... isolated lasers churr like partridges, spitting red and green lights from the wide flanks ... Two real birds flush from the tall grass, making startling runs of flapping wings and screeching ... they end in small explosions of muscle, feathers and brains as fighters hot in blood shoot at all movement.*

"The meadow's on fire!" someone yells, utterly pointlessly. The morning's wet sweetgrass smell is gone. All is acrid, tart, burnt, bitter ash in the nose and eyes. Waves of shocking sudden heat roll over Madjenik's firing line as gusts of hot air push across the tall, burning grass, shortening it to black stubs. Then all the sweetgrass is burnt off and sight lines into the RIK camp are wide open.

Hit by three *red* lasers while rolling on the ground, one body in the burning meadow directly across from Jan erupts like a sheep's bladder with the piss let out of multiple puncture holes at once, little red jets squirting upward after death with the last contained pressure in a dead man's arteries.

"Change out your chargers. Redouble firing! Shoot, godsdamn it!" Zofia's voice rings clear in Jan's helmet. "Second Squad, movement on your left. Volley point 270° on my mark, *mark*! Again, *mark!* Got them! Recommence *fire-at-will*." Madjenik is still standing in the ditch. But they see more Grünen now, with the tall grass burned off. Running. Officerless. Men and boys in a mad panic, reacting to first combat without any order or sane direction.

More shots hit the mark ... an ankle is scored by a full power maser and a foot slices off ... over there, a knee shatters, sinew and bone expelled in an explosion of flesh cooked from the inside-out by intense microwaves ... a scream of surprise and sudden pain ... another ... and another ... and another ... A lone, athletic, half-

dressed boy runs out of the smoke toward the ditch, then stops. Bewildered. Uncertain. Afraid. Like a deer chased by a moving forest fire.

"There's one, on the left. Shoot him! He dropped his weapon! Quick, cut him down before he finds it!" It's the stubbly sergeant yelling.

An electric pulse flashes out and hits the mark, taking off a hand ... click clack, click clack, pssst! pssst! ... maser bolts fly over smoking grass ... goring a thigh where a raw hole's erupting ... something red spurting out ... click clack, click clack ... hmmmm, pssst! pssst! ... gut shot now ... the runner drops ... He'll never leap a college hurdle race again ... he'll not make love, greet an orange dawn, kiss his mother's downy cheek as he leaves for school.

"*Ta mère!*" One shooter who got him shouts the vulgarity out, then again in longhand. "*Nique ta mère!* Fuck your mother!" It's almost as if he *knows*. He keeps yelling at and shooting the dead man, cursing all Grünen to hell. And their whore mothers. And their mothers' whore mothers.

"He's done! Next! Keep firing." Zofia flashes a hard glare at the fixated boy, along with a new HUD target order.

"What's that moving on the right?" someone calls out from 10 meters away, along the ditch firing line. *Fifteen stick figures in green ... more red triangles on HUDs, inside the smoke roll ... so many! ... an arm separates, falls from its shoulder, drops onto hard packed sod with a thud ... now a head explodes ... a lost body crumples straight down like a marionette with its strings suddenly cut ... A few return shots, at last! ... then a lot more, zinging by ... That one was close!*

"We're in a fight now, boys and girls!" It's the master sergeant, face of black stubble and with dull murder in his all-black eyes, like a shark's stare. Merciless. Amoral. Fatal. Behind him a sniper tumbles hard out of a tree and splays dead in the ditch, like a broken toy.

"*Incoming*!" A thin youth standing too tall in the line clutches at a dark wine stain spreading across his chest over his beige weaves. His '*limbs fall slack with chill*,' his arms release his maser, and with a resentful moan his life and spirit slips onto shady ground thence off his mortal coil. No one sees. The fight goes on.

Kinetic rounds join the fray ... whistling, whistling ... smack, smack, thuuudd, craaaaaak! ... A tree splinters behind the mortar crews ... apples falling all around ... the master sergeant picks one up, raises his visor and jams the broken fruit into his mouth, not biting down ... not yet ... holds it clamped between clenched jaws, visor up like a tired welder ... shooting his maser.

"They're firing too high!" Corporal Tom Hipper shouts it out, breaking sound discipline like all the rest of the bellowing, howling, terrified men and women in Madjenik's short firing line, and the others, shouting and dying across the grass. His plain brown eyes are wide with joy for life and joy in this battle, with combat's rushing excitement. Shouting anything and everything gives voice to a rush of adrenalin and combat thrill as he never felt before. He's flush with sex and death, so that his groin swells and throbs. It's no more than a natural physical effect of fast rising blood pressure, of pumping blood and adrenalin pushed out by his brain and body in response to mortal danger. So natural and so sudden Tom is utterly unaware that he has the hardest erection of his life.

Everyone is shouting now. No one listens. No one sees. Senses fill with the sounds and fury of pressing battle, and pounding hearts and a red rage throbbing in veins behind eyes, hammering like a beaten drum in either ear. It's the smells they remember most clearly later: urine and wet clay, crushed sweetgrass, mashed apples, iron and blood, the windborne scent of a late summer mockmeat barbeque.

But not everyone makes noise. Still as a dead cat, about 50 meters ahead and to Zofia's left is the erect body of a large, midnight skinned Grünen. He's a major or maybe even a colonel, in any case an officer from one of the three elite ethnic and citizen classes of the Waldstätte core world of Uri. He's dead, but impaled on a triangular shard of carbyne sent hurtling by the explosion of the *snakes*. Gravity is conspiring with strength of the carbyne splinter to keep him upright, like a propped open cellar door. Every so often some Madjenik shooter forgets the dead man is dead and lops off another piece. Cut red meat lies all around his feet.

"I smell cooked apples." A small brunette says it, crouching low beside Tom Hipper in the firing line. The thought is a total stray. The sticky smell coming out of the burning orchard reminds her of the fresh pies she baked with her mother, then set out on a big wood table to cool. She takes aim at a running Grünen, arms waving wildly in the air over his head, trying to surrender. She shoots him. He crumples like a failed crust. '*Maybe not like mother's kitchen after all.*'

Across the meadow boiling smoke roils sideways and out from where the canteen and most of the enemy stood barely a half-minute before. It's racing toward Madjenik like a line squall pulling angrily over a desert horizon. It's five meters high, and rising. It loosens bowels, a little.

"Heavy mortars, *now*!" Jan orders.

A mortar shoots nearly straight up from the center of the Krevan line, then another. KRUMP, KRUMP ... a dull, thick sound from behind the firing line.

Tom Hipper waits. And waits. Nothing happens. "Why nothing?" He worries out loud, firing his maser randomly and at the level into the darkening storm roll, though which not even his HUD can make out specific targets. Just moving *red* blurs against a *white-gray* background. *The dust squall reaches the ditch, choking shooters and reducing rates of fire and any accuracy. Five seconds pass, then in the distance ... KER-thud! KER-thud! The heavy sounds repeat as the mortar crews behind Jan find the range and open a little barrage.*

"They're landing! I knew it! *Ha ha!*" Tom swells with the joy of battle, with murder and his own vitality throbbing in his veins and in his groin. That's when he notices. "I can't believe it! I have a godsdamn erection!" The small brunette hears and grins up at him. "Die, you *bâtard!*" He feels ashamed of the shouted, common thought as soon as he releases it. The feeling of guilt calms him even as it passes quickly, along with his entirely useless erection.

Orange flames, cries of pain ... wounded and dying men and boys lying inside the dirt-smoke roll ... Still the shooters fire and cut down more figures in green, not looking across the meadow but firing into the cloud at dozens of little marked red threats moving on their HUDs.

Jan has no time for shame. This fight's not over. Too many *red* threats are still firing back, forming a makeshift and moving shooting line. He has to finish this before they call in reinforcements. He whirls to yell the next command directly to the mortar crews. "*Daisy cutters*! Both tubes, right now!" *KER-POOM, whoooosh ... KER-POOM, whoooosh ... Two pencil shots arcing dark against the sky ...* Tom sees them open, then flatten into thick disks, self-stabilizing nozzles spurting.

"Smell the apples? Like my mother's pies. So good."

He looks blankly at the wide eyed brunette still crouched beside him, smiling stupidly up, looking away to fire her maser at ankle height across the meadow before smiling at him again. The only thing he smells is burning wood behind and cooking flesh in front, a scorched meat and cloth odor drifting into the ditch with a hot wind whirling in from the scorched, smoking field.

"Mother and I used to bake pies together."

"What?"

"Do you like apple pie?"

Tom's glad he can't smell the damned apples. He thinks that if he smells such sweetness here instead of a vile, burnt and repulsive stench filling his nostrils, that killing might become a habit he likes. He worries about the earlier tightness in his groin, fears he already likes war far too much. The squall is clearing, he can almost see the meadow farside. But what's happening over there? *Daisy cutters arcing up and up, whirling then turning down ... down is good.*

"Beautiful, look at 'em spin!"

"My crystal's burned out!" *Slam another into the magazine ... the maser hums and blinks ready ... click clack, click clack, shooting again ... plasma rifles add to the dawn chorus, like no morning birdsong heard in these fields before ... burp, burp, burp ... chirp, chirp ... caw, caw ... bruurp, bruurp, bruurp.* Three green figures topple over at once, hit by a squad volley fired from the center block of Madjenik's line. Zofia's over there, directing two squads still using volley fire.

Tom's maser overheats from too enthusiastic firing. As it slowly cools he feels his loins throbbing once again with impatient lust for yet more blood vengeance. '*Oh gods no, not again!*' He glances down at the brunette. She's busy shooting.

"What happened to the *daisy cutters*?"

"Wait for it!"

The big bombs open as they descend, spinning into tori, flattening inside the roiling smoke, ground sensors marking distance to detonation ... then, anticlimax ... a soft 'pop, pop' barely heard above the roar of battle ... then an odd silence. Unexpected, like a child's failed firecrackers. Like damp squibs. Tom's coitus is interrupted. "What the hell was that? Jump charges! They shed their jackets!"

The falling of spreading disks is stopped by proximity explosions ... then main charges blow ... BOOM! BOOM! ... a spreading torus of molten metal and plasma spears spews a meter above each ground zero ... 30 meters outward, then 50, 100 ... perfect kill height ... slicing into hard armor and through soft groins and bellies.

Double concussive waves rock Madjenik shooters where they stand, even this far across the meadow. Tom Hipper can't imagine what they must be doing to the

Double Moons. Yet he knows, at some level of his brain. Knows that ripping death and terrible torment is what they're doing to living flesh, for he's right in the middle of it and a cause of it. Wanting more of it.

Wounds are all waist high ... suckling, slurping hits as energy meets flesh and bone ... hips and buttocks flying ... there goes a detached penis ... bowels and bellies split open ... feces and breakfasts spill out ... and guts, lots of gray and greasy sausages strung out on the ground. "Stop! Get back inside!" One boy is frantically stumbling and tripping over his own guts, pushing at them, unbelieving that they're falling out. Out of *him*! It's not working … *slippery ... fainting.* He falls to his knees, fumbling fists full of red-gray guts. "*Mutter*, help me, *Mutter*."

Ten meters away half a jaw spins off a too tall man as he crouches, but not low enough, only lowering his face into the spreading daisy disk. The jaw skims off like a summer frisbee tossed to an old school pal at the beach. Fifty meters more and a severed torso lands atop its own legs, mockingly crooked like a bent and broken acrobat, a contortionist trying to shock children at a town fair. Stunned, wounded, insensible, dying youths everywhere.

Later, all RIK memexes will speak in somber tones about "the sacrifice of our honored dead" and of parents "serving up the red sweet wine of their sons to the nation." About when "our children gave us rarer gifts than gold or mir," and how "honor of the Imperium is returned, like a newborn emperor." The maudlin lies only fool historians and all governments write, and only the safest, most distant civilians approve and quote with knowing nods of blithe ignorance of real war.

They'll draft ballads and play slow dirges, too. Make solemn speeches and etch letters in cold brass plaques on park benches for mournful mothers to sit and softly stroke, mumbling the embossed name of a never-seen-again child who died in a way she cannot and dare not imagine. It is the pity of war that for those not touched by it, war abhors pity. It is the nature of war, and the nature of most of us, to lack imaginative empathy beyond about 500 meters. Maybe less.

"Death! Amiable, lovely death!" A tall trooper, no more than a boy himself, cries out as he cuts down a running youth in green, exploding his shoulder with a short range maser blast.

"What are you, a fucking poet? Shut up and keep firing!" Zofia struggles to contain their lust and rage, to focus it on controlled tactical killing, to make them fight as a unit not for revenge. She's shouting in their ears and across HUDs, stamping and threatening to do indecent things to their hind parts with her hot maser if they decrease rate-of-fire or show the least hint of mercy.

"What's that? Is someone crying?"

"Poor *bâtards*."

"Ahh, fuck them!"

"Shut up! Maintain rapid fire! That's an order!"

Even after clinical death, brains keep working for awhile, trying to rescue an impossible situation. A final electrical surge courses through nociceptors, frantic neurons signaling mortal hurt to fearful and addled brains, falling like cracked and discarded watermelons into the long meadow grasses. Leaving a real mess on the dampened ground. Mercifully, consciousness is gone by then. Other deaths take much longer, so terrible and long the mind has time to watch the body die.

Such a spectacle in the meadow has a whole squad of Madjenik fighters in its gory grip, and won't let go. They stand mute without firing, ignoring Zofia's loud orders, watching the last minute of agony of a blond *nitōhei*, a young RIK private sliced in half who they can just make out through the clearing grass smoke. His torso has landed upright, severed evenly at the waist. His legs are someplace else. He's looking all around for them. He tries to call out to them but can't. His mind knows he's cleaved. His mouth opens only to release a terrible silent scream.

"He's just a kid." One of Madjenik's sergeants says what most in the paused squad are thinking. A short black man from Southland, he's trying to dip into his diminished store of pity to larder out a useless morsel to a dying farfolk boy.

"At least he's not screaming. Not anymore. Oh good, he's gone."

"Ah, fuck him, too." It's a young private standing alongside the sergeant. He's younger than the dead Grün boy. A callow youth at war. Is he just acting tougher than he feels? Only he knows for sure.

"Shut up! Resume firing!" The lad is puzzled to hear that coming from his rough and hard lieutenant. He flushes and concentrates on his firing. She moves to the next shooter in the line, directing her to the next target across the meadow.

Surprise is complete, destruction of the camp absolute once the *daisy cutters* detonate. Resistance melts like a waxen figurine set atop a heated stove. Sporadic shots still fly a meter or more over upright defenders inside the ditch, harmlessly cutting apart ripe apples, dropping warm juice and a gentle leafy shower onto the orchard floor. Across the meadow all is death.

Zofia's barrel tip is glowing bright *orange* hot from too rapid firing. She has to pause shooting to swap it out. She takes the moment to assess the enemy for her captain. "These boys are *not* frontline fighters." She relays her professional contempt over the officer only com link, for Jan's ears alone. "They shoot like they're still on a training range, back on some heavier gravity planet."

"Yeah," Jan answers. "I know. They're from Uri."

Genève is a small Class A planet with 20% lower gravity than Uri. The raw conscripts shooting from across the meadow should reset kinetic weapons to fire lower velocity rounds, and adjust all aim points to account for gravity difference from their heavier gravity training world. They should know that even a maser will feel lighter and subtly encourage them to shoot higher here than back on Uri. They should be adjusting all aiming down to fit Genève, but they aren't. "Bad officers," Zofia succinctly concludes. "Even laser rounds are pumping high."

"Yeah, they're rookies," Jan agrees. "Not at all like us, huh?" It doesn't really surprise him that he thinks of himself and Zofia and Madjenik as tested veterans, after just five days in combat. Though maybe it should. He doesn't have time to analyze that sudden shift in his perception. He's too excited by a tactical insight he has about the poor Grün shooting. He looks hard over at Zofia and knows that she understands him. In combat they already communicate like familiar lovers. Wordlessly, with strokes, gestures and eyes alone.

Before he finishes the order she's up and out of the ditch, standing in the open in the burned sweetgrass, facing the firing line yet ready to take lead position as it advances across the meadow. "Everyone out of the ditch! Reform the line!"

"*Advance*! Shoot straight ahead, firing off the march!" Jan simultaneously sends the order thought to all HUDs, using his command and dot channel implant. He also yells it out, knowing from hard experience gained over the past five days not to rely on HUD battle tek alone. Also because yelling out orders or shouting wild nothings to release one's fear or stress in combat is a very human thing to do. The air is filling with wild shouts from both sides, cries of war and fear.

"Still shooting too high, the fools!"

"Let's take full advantage. Everyone except the mortars, into the meadow!"

Madjenik's fighters scramble up and over the clay ditch, standing erect for a moment on its lip at the edge of the smoldering meadow. They advance at arms length apart, in a close order line, shooting maser bolts into dark folds of soil and smoke still churning on the far side of the field. Changing out blackened maser chargers as they move, ejecting burned crystals, slapping in new ones. Return fire from the other side sails overhead, just as Jan and Zofia expected.

The main phalanx is caught up by combat engineers and snipers pulling even along both flanks, making the whole advance a half-klic wide. Snipers shoulder their precision laser pulse rifles, switching to short assault masers with a wider, more wicked short range beam. Engineers shoot even shorter, stubby masers pulled from chest belts. It's the signature weapon of their craft that sets them off from regular infantry on any battlefield, in any army, across all the worlds. The mortar teams hold in original position, in front of the now burning apple orchard. They're not firing short kinetic bombs anymore. They're readying plasma rounds, electronic 'smoke' and precision EMPs, to be used only in the event of a sudden change of fortune or a command from Jan to retreat. Two scouts scan in all other directions except the battle, watching for RIK armor or Jabos that might suddenly appear. Either one would be a game changer.

Nothing goes wrong. No hovering armor or Jabo fighter-bombers show up to save the Double Moons. Besides, the networked *snakes* and *daisy cutters* did the hard work of killing or maiming most of the surprised enemy already, tearing open green armor weaves like ration foil packs during a meal stop on a training march, disemboweling young Grün boys and men inside. They find 200+ curling, fetal dead on the ground, weaves and bodies ripped apart. Some look to Jan like burned and smoking potatoes pulled from a campfire on a summer night, foil peeled back and tossed on the grass to cool down and await buttering. Others are carelessly mashed, faceless and shapeless.

Another 100+ enemy are wounded, or merely stunned. Some heave in place, with broken or torn or missing limbs. Others crawl weakly to nowhere, like salted, helpless, dying grubs. Dozens are completely unmarked in intact green weaves, looking up stupidly at arriving troops in tan, brains addled by the concussive wave from precision *snakes* blowing as one. Or knocked flat and giddy by the *daisy cutter* blast wave. Or seeking ground before they blew, staying down out of primal fear during the entire fight with Madjenik. They're the lucky ones. Stunned flat or diving prone, preserved from waist high plasma spears of the *daisy cutter* tori that passed over where they lay.

Madjenik's line arrives where the wounded and fearful wait, and completes the grim work *snakes* and mortars started. Zofia's in the lead, as always, but she doesn't come with bandages, water or sponge as she moves straight and swift to the first wounded man. She gives no kill order. She simply kneels on hinged knees over the first befuddled *nitōhei* she comes to, pulls his faceplate back to expose a pulsing artery, and slices open his throat with a diamond blade taken from her boot. She wipes the wetted knife on the gasping private's arm then slides it slickly back into a mockleather sleeve atop her muddy boot. Spurting blood fountains in a meter high arc, splashing Tom Hipper and the brunette as they pause to watch.

A week ago Jan would have ordered Zofia arrested. Would have charged her with war crimes. Maybe shot her after a courts martial. Before the war, whenever he thought about combat ethics he always thought he knew the "right thing" and that he would do it. Yet he's much older and far harder than he was just five days ago. Five terrible, unbelievable days ago. He's the leader of a little band that's like a cut flower in a vase, fair to see yet bound to die. And he has met the enemy.

So he says nothing as his fighters follow Zofia's lead, moving systematically over the smoldering breakfast camp, leaving no man or boy alive. He stands in silence, gazing over the melancholy battlefield as Madjenik systematically polices the smoking meadow, gathering maser chargers, food and weapons. Stripping all moda and suspend off dead medics. The field is rich in odors of nature and battle. Broken sweetgrass juices seem sweeter than when inside healthy stalks. Ruptured black soil, where the *snakes* blew neat round holes, gives off wild scents of humus, roots and worms, mixed with harsher chemicals from the high explosives. Bitter bile leaks dark and tart out of puncture wounds made by *daisy cutters* in sprawling dead youths. A warm sweetness rises sticky and thick from red throats cut gaping open, little pink bubbles forming at the corners of each gash, popping too quietly to hear above the summer breeze and tramping feet. Madjenik sweeps the overrun camp one last time, looking for the very last survivors.

So ends the battle in the sweetgrass.

So ends Madjenik's combat innocence.

So ends the bloody business of the day.

***

Madjenik doesn't have time to bury its own dead from the firefight. Not time even to say the full Common Prayer over the bodies. Those who look down on fallen comrades make only a traditional promise to family who survive the loss of a child: "You will not sorrow alone, dear mother, dear father, over an early grave."

They're gathered in clumps of three or four or ten fighters or more, after killing off the last wounded. They're dead if a high Jabo breaks cloud cover overhead. So Zofia lets them have it. "Spread out, damn it. Corporal Hipper, get them moving and dispersed before a spy drone or ground patrol stumbles over this mess and we have Jabos climbing all up our asses."

"Yes sir, lieutenant. You heard the order, let's move Second Squad. Spread yourselves out, godsdamn it. *Hut, hut.* You, 'Pie Girl,' move your fat ass." All other NCOs join the droving.

Jan connects to Zofia over the officer link. He hesitates, unsure what to say after what he saw her do. He doesn't want any kind of personal conversation. Not yet. Not until he can think about her without seeing a red dripping, Q-carbon knife in her hand. If that day ever comes, after today. But she's his best combat leader and only other officer. He has decided what to do next but he's not sure it will work. He needs her. He must tell her, but he'll keep it real tight.

"Lieutenant, we'll head due west for Pilsudski Wood. It juts out hundreds of klics from the main forest zone at this latitude. We can get to cover fastest there. From Pilsudski we'll go off road, the long way northwest through the old forests to Toruń. At least that'll give us a fighting chance. We have to keep moving. We can't stay out here in the open. Not after this." He cuts her off and switches back to the full company channel before she can reply. "Madjenik, this was a real good day! But we're still cut off and alone. We have to keep our heads down. They'll be coming after us heavy and hard once they find what we did here."

He doesn't look at Zofia. "We'll head for Toruń, via Pilsudski Wood. Off road, using the deep forests for cover." There's a murmur of relief, even a laugh or two of pleasant surprise that they're going to Toruń. Jan decides to squash that reaction fast. Hope is dangerous where he's taking them next. "Some of you won't make it. Maybe most of you. We'll be chased and hunted and hounded all the way by a more numerous and more mobile enemy." They look grimly at him, and he finally looks over at Zofia. He sees it in her face. '*I've gone too far. They need a little hope after all.*' He makes a quick course adjustment, but now too far in the other direction. Finding the right words is hard. He's not there yet as a leader.

"I promise I'll get us to Toruń! Once there, we'll get fresh supplies and orders. More than that, we'll load up on weps and ammo and I'll lead you back out past the great city berm to kick these *saatana* off Genève. Send them direct to whatever *helvetti* they believe in." It's a stiff little speech, way past corny at the end. As soon as he stops talking he knows no one believes the last bit about being heroes and winning the war and saving Genève and all that shit he just made up, like he's talking to small children during a power outage huddled inside a loud and dark storm. It helps them anyway. It's closer to what Madjenik needs in this moment.

Zofia flashes an approving grin. He misunderstands and recoils from her warm smile. She's innocent to the mental shudder he feels when she looks at him now and he recalls her slick knife work in the burnt grass. '*How can someone so pretty be so cold, so morally indurate?*'

Madjenik is in a good mood for the first time in five days. It moves off jauntily in spread formation, observing strict coms silence and electronic discipline. Only now does Jan remember that his leg is aching. He forgot during the fighting in the ditch and across the meadow. It's over 60 klics to Pilsudski Wood, a thousand more from the edge of the forest zone to far off Toruń. '*And when we get there, if we get there, what then? Will the Arbor City be waiting to greet us, or will it be a smoldering pile of ash and corpses? I can't think that far ahead. Take another step, that's all. My job is to get us out of this burned meadow, into the somber night. Then to the forest. After that? Well, let's make cover first and we'll see...*'

The morning larks flit swiftly overhead, dropping snatches of birdsong on the marching column. The sounds arrive like falling bombs. Did he think of that, or did he read it somewhere? He's not sure. He glances slyly at Zofia, walking 20 paces in front of him. He does know she's a woman. He's keenly aware of her. In a moment of weary weakness he lets his mind wander all over her petite form, imagining as he did before the war what her taut body might look like beneath her now hopelessly grubby, oak colored weaves. How the pert curve of her breasts must meet a hard belly, descending to... Then he sees in his mind's eye a bloody blade held in her clenched fist, slicing black-and-red across a gasping boy's throat.

'*No. I can't think about that Zofia anymore, dammit. Not now, anyway. Maybe not ever again.*' He moves one foot ahead of the other, dragging his aching leg along more with his will than with torn, protesting muscles. He tries not to limp, thinking that if he shows any weakness Madjenik will lose its recent and, to him, seriously misplaced confidence in his leadership. '*Right now, their blind faith in me is all that's holding the company together. So keep walking, Jan! Head up. Do it for them. Gods know, you owe them. Show them no pain, or it all will end.*'

An indifferently learned, half-remembered schoolboy rhyme repeats in his head, as hard stabbing as the rhythmic throbbing in his ripped calf. It's ancient, translated into a hundred old and modern tongues, fragments lost and newly added over two millennia. He can't remember all of it, or remember much of it clearly. Yet just trying to recall it keeps his mind off the pain in his leg.

Actually, he garbles it pretty badly. Perhaps unconsciously. For the verse as he recalls it chides him out of the storied past, its mockery keeping time with each footfall he makes. His confusing of old lines with personal doubt haunts each painful stride, echoing first in a teacher's voice, then more harshly in his father's stern and unforgiving tones, then most oddly in his own.

On the first red day our hero ran,
our brave commander, our Captain Jan.
He turned and ran to save his life,
dropped his maser and carbyne knife.

Another step, more pain. Another and another. Five klics from the meadow. Ten klics. He's drenched in shame and guilt. '*How many more will I kill? What new mistakes will I make? How many must die because I'm not good enough, not ready for command?*' Mixed up and ill-recalled verses and voices censor him again, blame him, mock him through his pain and worry.

All of his fighters knew that
their captain had blundered.
Theirs not to question why,
theirs but to follow him, and die.

He's one bad decision from disaster, from a failure that will cost more fighters their limbs or lives. Death is all around as more old verses come back to him, mangled by exhaustion, fragmenting images of war badly learned in boyhood and now shifted to fit his drooping exhaustion and fear of ultimate failure.

Enemy to the right of them,
pursuit to the left of them,
rumbled and thundered.
Into the jaws of Death,
he led the six hundred!

'*Well, at least I shan't kill as many as him, whoever he was. I had 300 fighters to start. Down to 167 at the last check in.*' He laughs out loud at the relentless, black arithmetic whirling through his receding moda barrier and an emerging, combat exhaustion fog. He doesn't notice the effect this has on the others.

Nearby fighters hear him and smile. His short laugh lifts their spirits. They think it means their captain is in a fine mood after his brilliant victory over the Double Moons in the sweetgrass meadow. They think it means he has a plan. They'll follow their captain wherever he leads. What the hell else can they do?

Rout

"We just weren't ready for this fight," Jan admits. "Not by a country klic. They put us in the death ground too soon, forced us to fight on their terms on Southland and again at the MDL."

It's two days after the fight in the sweetgrass meadow and Jan is talking in low whispers with Corporal Tom Hipper, one of three NCO strays who joined Madjenik after his own company was shattered back at the MDL. They're huddled inside a two man camo tent, during a longer than usual rest stop. The corporal wants to know why the KRA has lost the war. For they both know it has, even if the killing and the dying is not over with. They're talking it through, starting before the shattering defeat on "Breakthrough Day," as they've started to call the rout of the main KRA defenses at the MDL. It's a neutral sounding term that's actually soaked in shared bitterness and personal shame and defeat.

They talk in low whispers, further masked by sound baffles woven into the camo sheets they're squatting under. They've started to buddy up like this during rest periods. Partly, it's to continue piecing together what happened. Also, though neither man will admit it, it's so Jan can avoid facing Zofia for a bit and Tom can get away from the nonstop chatter of "Pie Girl."

Madjenik has been under field camo for over three hours, waiting out passing flocks of drones it was damn lucky to identify at a far distance. Well, maybe not so much lucky as good. One of the Southland strays attached to Madjenik, a rustic, simple brown-haired kid who spent a lot of time outdoors, noticed something odd about the flight patterns of the approaching flocks.

"Ain't no snow geese fly'yeen dis faw nord dis time of yar, sah," he informed Zofia, pointing out a series of slow moving, V-shaped passive radar signatures on his scout screen, slowly coming at them from the south.

She immediately brought him to the head of the column to speak to Jan. "Repeat to the captain what you told me about the geese, private."

"Yas, sah. Well, cp'tin sah, dese ain't no snow geese, is all I ken say. De geese is all s'posed ta go da udder way, go soud by now, cp'tin, whad wid winta comin' to Nord'land in a couple mons." He pauses, then adds confidently to both officers. "Dey gotta be drones, sahs."

On a distant world, RIK engineers who designed and built the spy bots to mimic Genève snow geese got the timing all wrong, putting them on the wrong continent, migrating the wrong way in the wrong season. A typical bureaucratic fuck up. And a lucky break for Madjenik. "So, their MI geeks got too clever by half? Well done, kid. Keep your eyes peeled for any other anomalies you see. You just got promoted to lead scout, private."

"Yas sah, tank yu, sah, *err*, I tink."

Madjenik went to ground 15 klics shy of the eastern edge of Pilsudski Wood, waiting as two more faux flocks passed the wrong way overhead, along with a mountain eagle that was way too far out from any mountain to be real or alive. Animal ground scouts and insect drones that must be out there are a greater worry. Madjenik has intermediate range camo even on the move, and Jan deploys laser snipers on its march flanks with orders to take out any rabbit or cat or dog or fox or other small animal they spot on infrared or by line-of-sight. Swarming midges and other insect drones are short range only. The teks have good short jammers.

"Where the RIK always thought in terms of aggressive war and built oversize weps systems to that end," Jan explains to Tom, "the prewar KRA thought only about defense and protection. The difference in style and plans is showing up now. We're pretty good at hiding."

"Yeah, but it showed in a different way on Southland and again on Breakthrough Day, back at the Northland MDL." Tom sounds bitter.

"When their fleets arrived we weren't ready for how good and powerful they were, how well planned and truly massive their assaults would be, how closely integrated from orbit to our upper skies down to the surface."

"No more than our politicians were ready for the speed and brutality of Pyotr's lightning diplomatic offensive and the ferocity of his propaganda."

"The Bad Camberg lie that started the war raced up and down Orion while the truth was clambering out the airlock and gasping for breath," Jan glumly states. He remembers how the United Planets government on Aral was still readying a repudiation of the shocking charge coming from the Jade Court on Kestino, that KRA commandos had raided a minor Grün moonlet without provocation. That's when, without warning, huge invasion fleets arrived at four border systems and a fifth attacked the asteroid belts and ice moons of Aral itself.

Tom didn't pay much attention to news or politics before the war. He's still angry at himself for that. "Why weren't we ready, sir?"

"Here on Genève, probably everywhere, the KRA was still mobilizing," Jan explains. "We were training hasty recruits in makeshift bases when the Kaigun fleets and dropships arrived in system. They hit us too fast and real hard."

Once Grün ships blew past Genève Squadron their well protected flotilla of high orbit transports couldn't be touched by ground defensive batteries, all sited to protect the capital of Toruń on Northland. There were none to stop a landing on rural Southland. So that's where the invaders came down, scudding onto the only other significant landmass on Genève beside a few scattered islands. KRA ground guns were hit by precision fire from Zerstörers making such low orbit attacks that two skimmed hard and hot against the upper atmosphere and spun out.

"Our ground positions were wiped out by hypervelocity unpiloted gliders or just by dumb 'gougers' dropped from untouchable battleships and cruisers. And we had no navy left." Both men recall gougers coming down white-hot and utterly unstoppable at Mach 30 or more, plunging into hidden or buried KRA targets like a vast shower of untracked meteors. Thousands of gougers left long, precise lines of smoldering craters where woeful defense batteries and exposed barracks and whole towns once stood. Smokes rose tens of klics high over waffled Southland.

"Once our ground batteries stopped firing back, Silver Division never stood a chance." It's Jan, thinking out loud to Tom.

Southland's towns and defenses were reduced to ruins and hot fresh craters. Then RIK ground assault waves rode to the surface of a long peaceful world, disgorging from immense armtrak carriers and squat infantry boats that looked like bakery boxes. The ground fight that followed was a constant emergency for the overwhelmed KRA with action exploding from one point to another. Dumb kinetics, *whizz bangs*, self-guiding shells, and clever mini plasma '*streakers'* to pummel bunkers, coms lines, and supply and support bases. It stunned defenders of an overmatched and unready force holding the southern continent, a simple land of tree farms and ranches, lacking any major city. Those not killed by gougers or shells faced a massive infantry assault, once the dropships fell to ground.

"Neither of us was there, thank the gods."

"Yeah, it must've been awful. They had *no* chance."

"Over quick, at least."

KRA armor was a small undergunned and underpowered type dubbed 'Rhino' in mockery of its almost comical, stubby main gun. Back when there was time for jokes, countryfolk said that a Rhino "looks like a Toruń bachelor, poorly equipped but always ready for his wedding night." The generals rushed them forward pell-mell, trying to patch gaping holes. They were no match for the enemy's heavy armtraks. There were only a few hundred Rhinos on all Genève, in any case.

The few Rhinos available on Southland rushed forward three hours into the fight, trying and failing to close yawning gaps in broken perimeters and shifting defense lines. They were smashed by precision drops from Raptors overhead, or swooping Jabo streakers that almost never missed the rumbling, stubby little tanks. Silver Division infantry was pushed aside by waves of armtraks and hover grenadiers in acoustic levitation ATCs, rushing into rear areas like an elemental torrent through a broken dam. Leg infantry followed, leaping on glider boots.

The inexperience of KRA generals and Silver Division, the locally raised and nearly exclusively infantry defense force on Southland, was revealed in desperate flank battles. In just hours, all the ill-used Rhinos were blackened hulks, burning amidst many tens of thousands of dead youths and long columns of stunned and surrendered infantry. All over Genève a shorter form of the Common Prayer for Dead Youth was hastily said: "*You will not sorrow alone*."

The fight for the sparse southern continent was lost in a day. Silver Division was surrounded and sundered, or dead or missing or captured. Only 50,000 KRA got out, fleeing across the intercontinental gap in speed boat shuttles pursued by taloned sky fighters swooping down to strafe anything moving on the water.

In desperation, Main HQ at Toruń on Northland sent every cruise and ballistic missile it had over the gap to hit the RIK before it dug in. Every missile and attack drone hurled southward, wasting reserve strike power. The limited prewar supply of missiles and pilotless drones also ran out after barely 200 minutes of heavy launches. No one prewar conceived that an air battle could consume skycraft supplies at such rates, but it did. Everyone has a lot to learn about how this new war will be fought, it has been so long since the last one.

"Then came the awful retaliations," Jan says to Tom. He means the 'Death bird' missiles that skimmed and dodged sketchy ground fire to obliterate targets in deep rear areas across more broken positions, reaching far across Northland.

“That’s when my unit came under fire, while marching to the MDL. You too?”

“Yeah,” Jan confirms. “First time we got hit was while on the road, by Jabos. Madjenik was lucky, though. Most of the smart shells and big missiles just flew over our heads, carrying that destruction farther inland. Guess we weren’t enough of a threat to get targeted by missiles.”

On just the third day RIK set up its Main HQ and assault base on Southland. It was protected from orbit by heavy warships out of reach by Toruń City’s ground batteries, parked unimpeded in geostationary supply and reinforcement circuits behind the arc of the planetary horizon. The ground buildup continued until RIK generals were ready to jump an assault subatmospheric over the sea gap, to force a fresh lodgment on the larger and more important continent. That’s where the bulk of Krevan troops waited, in a shore Main Defense Line. There was a pause in fighting as Rikugun readied to cross a flat ocean, on most days calm and vivid blue under sunlight reflecting as bright as glare from a polished mirror. It was just enough time to give Gold Division HQ in Toruń the illusion that it was prepared for the assault. Yet foreknowledge hardly counted when the attack came.

A second landing jumped directly continent-to-continent, with additional orbital drops and fire support on either flank of the landing zone. It gave RIK generals a toehold on the eastern lip of Northland. The larger, more temperate, more heavily populated of Genève’s continents was still nearly as agrarian as its austral counterpart. Its rolling terrain hosted neat fruit and grain farms, sprinkled with ten thousand villages, a few bigger towns, and a single forest city in Toruń.

Thirteen RIK divisions disembarked. Four were armored, each centered on 1,000 burley Mammoths and huge mobile artillery tubes. Four were mechanized infantry, supported by herds of armtrak Mastodons and ATC hover troops. The rest were regular RIK leg infantry or barely trained conscripts. Mop up grunts and cannon fodder, but RIK Tactical Skyforce was almost unimpeded. KRA Main HQ was still moving ground forces to the coast when the RIK lodgment was secured, wide enough to allow a second buildup prior to breach assaults against the MDL.

“Our generals made another mistake,” Jan tells Tom. “They pushed all our reserves into a hasty new defense line they drew 200 klics inland, digging in to wait under the hard pounding by more enemy missiles and gougers. We should’ve counterattacked them at the coast.”

“You think?”

“Yeah, I do. Better to disrupt their plans. Instead we let them come at us like a storm of steel, a fury that rolled over all our defenders along the sea rim. Our MDL was way too brittle.”

“I remember. We’d pulled into our so called strongpoint and dug in when they hit us, harder than I ever imagined possible. We broke in just two hours.”

“So did we.”

“You did, sir? Hard to believe.”

“True all the same. We were just one of hundreds of companies in place or still en route when they hit us. HQ was still moving to the second line, trying to defend-in-depth but getting to it too late. That left us spread out, not strong enough to hold either defense position or to counterattack.” It’s a pretty damn accurate operational conclusion, based on only minimal tactical information. Jan has a real good military mind, though you could never convince him that was true. Thinks of himself as a failure, a washout from Aral Academy.

RIK controlled the skies that day, unchallenged since it first met outclassed fighters of Genève Sky Defense on Southland, burning skycraft on the ground or shooting them out of the summer air with superior human and AI pilots flying in greater numbers inside better machines. Next came flocks of ultrafast, unpiloted tactical suicide drones, wave after wave plunging down. “We had nothing to shoot down the drones,” Tom laments, remembering directing his platoon in ineffective ground fire turned skyward, that hit maybe one in 50 incoming drones.

V-wings of human piloted Raptors and Jabos swirled high overhead, picking off short distance targets or suddenly diving to pound explosive smart ordnance low-and-tight atop an unlucky or decamouflaged unit. Jabo dive bombers strafed wildly, uncaring of civilian losses, shooting pulse maser cannons into buildings before pulling up and away in screaming climbs, safer even than the drones from interception by feeble ground fire that rose almost lazily behind them, passing kinetic ordinance harmlessly through widening vapor trails and wake turbulence.

“Then their heavy armor came at us in ‘V’ wedges. Couldn’t do anything to stop it, not with the light weapons we had. Their machines were all too big, too fast, too powerful. Rhinos failed, too.” Mass shock came in form of a series of hard punches by RIK Mammoths and Mastodons, multi turreted hoverships forming the mailed fist of the assault. Three big ones came straight for Madjenik, rapid firing two plasma cannon and four spandaus each. AI targeting bots slaved to the guns spit *red* light in gatling cycles from M-8cm and M-10cm masers. They ripped high energy rounds into strongpoints and flew right past Jan's troopers.

Underpowered, undergunned and underarmored, Rhinos just had no chance against RIK armtraks built for just this kind of mass assault. A few took out an enemy vehicle by ramming, but most were blasted apart in just minutes. Any left were destroyed by the Rikugun's planetside Skyforce. The deadly Jabos raced in at Mach-plus speeds from hasty bases a continent away, strafing and bombing anything that moved. Wrecking exposed infantry trying to muck to the front to help. Or running the other way.

"Why does RIK call their big armtrak Mammoths?" Tom asks. "They don't look like that at all. They looked to me more like a passing maglev train, long and straight, fast and lethal."

"Dunno. We call ours Rhinos, even though they fight like warthogs. Sorry, I shouldn't have said that. A lot of fighters died horribly inside our lost Rhinos."

The big armtraks had magnetic rail kinetics down their long sides, used mainly to batter buildings and smoke out infantry. They shifted from hover to tracks when they neared Krevan infantry or strongpoints, taking on a shockingly low profile to avoid local surface-to-surface missiles. Madjenik scored only glancing hits as the heavy armor roared through its position and past, racing into the interior. Then came smaller Mastodons, Elephants, and assault infantry. "They were worse than the heavy Mammoths, those small tanks. They were so damn fast."

Elite hover grenadiers supported the leviathans, acting as remoras cleaning off any KRA attackers. The crack assault troops rode in armored hovers and smaller, darting ATCs. They shot up soft targets the rule governed bot guns left alone as nonpriority threats: crawling or sitting wounded; men lying gashed open with pink lungs heaving like bellows; women running in mortal fear; teens dropping weps to stand with hands raised high, crying while vainly trying to surrender.

RIK generals never paused. Not even to finish bleeding, broken and smashed units scattering and running from all the MDL breakthrough points. The RIK did supreme damage at lightening speed then raced its armor and assault guns through each shattered Krevan position, speeding past or right over stunned defenders to bring death ever deeper into the panicking rear. Jan and Tom remember heavy armtraks and hover grenadiers shooting *red* spandaus and *blue* masers at anything wearing beige, slicing KRA fighters in half, cutting them down by cooking them inside their own combat suits whether they stood or ran. Sonic and frag grenades, delayed action mines, all spectrum guided missiles showered into dugouts on pre-sited trajectories. And many more terrors in a cacophony of hurtling fear, piss and panic, and fast moving death. The last Jan saw or heard of the heavy armtraks was a rising mushroom glow of pulse cannon blasts and a distant, *click clack* of heavy pink crystal guns on the far side of a tree covered hill, about three klics back of his smashed and abandoned original position and MDL 'strongpoint.'

Racing ATCs followed the heavy armor, spraying medium pink crystal maser bolts as they sped through the rigid, cracked open line, gunners jeering the dead and the dying. Hand fired masers from hover grenadiers atop the carriers kept defenders' heads down. Piercing hot light scorched any flesh it found, erupting limbs into a fine spray of red spittle and bone. The extreme fury of the elite hover grenadier attack was unbelievable to those it met. Nothing they trained for or dreamed about before the war prepared them for such violent malevolence.

"Bad day, bad day," Tom says, for both of them.

"Yeah, real bad day," Jan concurs out loud. Privately, he remembers: '*The day I ran away. The day I failed Madjenik.*'

The second day was nearly as bad as the first. Regular infantry struck at dawn, crushing the last MDL resistance. RIK troopers rushed through more breaches, fanning out behind ragged holes punched through the rear side of the broke open line. Lean gatling bots and squat ground crawlers, crusher bots and automated spandau platforms supported the fresh leg infantry leaping ahead on power glide combat boots, jumping five or seven meters with every stride, shooting on the move. They came out of hover Armored Troop Carriers flying alongside the assault wave, gunners laughing and shooting even small animals that dared show a black nose or darting tail. Stragglers from broken sectors along the shattered front told Jan that heavy columns of RIK Mammoths, Mastodons, Elephants and hover grenadiers blasted multiple corridors through the two line frontier defense of pillboxes, firing pits and forward shooting stations. The second, rear line of the MDL stood for less than a day, barely defended by overwhelmed KRA infantry.

"Yeah," says Jan, visibly struggling to return from his shame, from his dark, personal reminiscence. "But the biggest surprise of all was that once they busted through our perimeter they should have spun all that armored force around to trap us between two grips of a vice. But they didn't."

"Why not?"

"Because they didn't have to. We weren't a threat anymore, with so many companies and battalions broken and scattered by the first assault, and ... running. So they kept moving farther inland, leaving units like ours to lesser mop up troops, like the Double Moons. Seems to me it was always their plan." He's right. It was.

"Damn, captain! The Double Moons were just reservists? You mean that we haven't beaten their best, and nearly half the fighters in Madjenik already gone?"

"Sorry, Tom. Their best smashed right through us on the first day, like we weren't even there. Madjenik took on and took out their scrub second eleven in the meadow, no more."

"Godsdamn, in that case I want to meet up with their elite units one day. We'll show them! We'll pay them back for the MDL, and after."

Jan lets the foolish boast pass. "Maybe. You gotta think that no one in our HQ ever expected our main forces to be left behind by an invading enemy that moved that fast, so that the battle swept right over the coast and moved too fast inland." That was the core tactic, on Genève and the other four Krevan worlds where invading armies struck without warning and simultaneously. Hit and move, then hit again. Wave after wave, not pausing or even slowing attack momentum, never relenting. Keeping the defenders stunned and off balance, until collapse came and everyone in beige weaves reeled backward in panicked flight.

Follow on attacks overwhelmed with firepower and bewildering maneuver, hitting the Krevans hard then moving quickly to strike fresh targets ever farther to the rear. Leaving frontline survivors in smashed formations to be dealt with by a third wave, then a fourth. Cascading attacks left more broken bunkers and dead Krevans behind, and isolated clots of stunned stragglers like Madjenik Company, dodging and running and trying to hide from 'growlers and grinders' and conscript leg infantry humping after them in cocky mop up units.

"Sure as hell worked," Jan concludes, "as far as I can tell from campaign info we picked up before Main HQ went dark. The signals were pretty chaotic, but always said the same thing. 'How can they be *here* already?' 'What happened to my reserve?' 'Where's my support?'"

"They must've taken out every one of our military satellites, including all the deep space stealthy ones, to blind our HQ like that after just two days."

"For sure. I think Genève Squadron mush have seen some tough fighting, too." Jan has several old friends in the local naval squadron, dating to his school days.

"We lost to them everywhere."

"We positioned in a hard crust defense," Tom concludes, seeing the big picture now for the first time, closely following Jan's brutally honest teaching. "Once they pushed armor holes through that crust they were unstoppable, eating right through the soft middle like into a warm apple pie."

Jan smiles to think that Tom has summed up the whole campaign in an image he has been trying to get away from ever since the meadow fight. A hard pie crust with a soft apple interior. Now full to the rim with wriggling green worms. But he says only: "Yeah, you've got it."

"Could we have done it different, sir? Was there a better way to defend than the way we tried?"

"We would've been better off defending ground in depth, layer after layer receiving the penetration thrusts but shaving off some of their attack momentum, attriting their forces."

Tom nods, hesitates for a moment, then asks. "Do you think that would've stopped them?"

Jan says what he really thinks. "No, surely not. We might've held out a bit longer, and sure, we would've killed a lot more of their men and machines before we broke. That would've been something. But no, we never had even a puncher's chance to win this prize fight."

"No chance at *all*, captain?"

"*Mita helvettia!* We're two local divisions of the KRA! The whole Krevan Republic is just 24 worlds. They're the vast Grün Imperium. They *invented* war! No, no chance at all." Each man falls into deep silence, almost mournful in its heaviness, sitting under a shroud of military camo. Then their thoughts drift from the big strategic down to the merely personal. '*Why crush his hopes like that? What the hell do I know?*' Jan chides himself, as he often does. '*I'm just a washed out officer who would've run from my first fight no matter where it took place.*'

Jan Wysocki is the most self-unforgiving man on Genève. Tom is younger and he has no burden of command, so his thoughts aren't so darkly personal. He likes himself far more, too. Still, he goes quiet, thinking about family and a hometown now deep inside the Occupation Zone. Both men are also thinking about other things seen on and after Breakthrough Day. How too many enemy laughed as they cut down scared children in beige uniforms with Silver or Gold division shoulder flashes, standing stiffly as if at school, without weapons and arms raised in futile submission before they were killed. Lots of civilians met the same grim ethic.

Tom saw up close how ordinary Grünen wearing uniforms enjoyed the violent freedom gifted to them by war. Heard elite troopers from Yokohama shout the dread and ancient Rikugun battle cry "*sonnō jōi!*" Yell "revere the Emperor, kill the barbarians!" Watched them pump masers into upturned, childish faces.

Jan tells Tom that he heard other elite troops, from the Waldstätte, shout "*Todt, Todt!*" as they dealt out "Death, Death!" in fact to prisoners, to wounded, and to harmless civilians. The week old memory is as clear in his mind's eye as Tom's face is in his real eyes. It shakes him physically, not with fear but with deep rage. It's clear to everyone under the temporary camo that terror killing and atrocity is to be the Imperium's conquest and occupation style, even if they don't know yet that the order comes straight from Pyotr sitting on the Jade Throne in Novaya Uda on Kestino. Jan decides then and there that he'll pay back this enemy like with like, blood for blood, death for death.

Zofia breaks into his coms, startling Jan back to the present. "The last 'V' of bot geese is passing overhead, honking to each other as if they're real. Time to get moving again, captain." Five minutes later Jan and Tom stand up and gather their camo sheets into march packs. Tom heads back to his squad and Pie Girl. Jan moves to the head of the reforming, forlorn little column, careful to walk beside his new head scout rather than his second in command. Zofia throws a secret look at him, and scowls to herself. "Right, move out, Madjenik. Fifteen klics to reach forest cover." He thinks: '*Then it's turn north, and the long trek to Toruń.*'

***

Even as Madjenik is breaking camo and making ready to move at last into Pilsudski Wood, follow on waves of enemy are also moving. RIK 10th Armored has hover scouts out, looking for hidden pockets of KRA in what is now its rear area. They find a burnt field with 300 dead conscripts from Uri, a third with cut throats who must have been alive when the *Gelben* shits found and finished them. But the attack plan can't be altered, not even to find who committed this atrocity.

Scouts will come back later. Oetkert vengeance will be had. After all, where is there left to run on Genève when Rikugun has taken Southland, broken the MDL on Northland, and is marching methodically across the plains toward the northern forest zone that wraps around the only major city, Toruń inside the deep woods?

For now, 10th Armored's infantry must plow the sea in the parting wake of its advancing armtraks, its robo *gatlers* and heavy fighting bots still plentiful in these first days. Complex prewar machines aren't yet used up by daily attrition, not yet worn out and proven too expensive to replace in the numbers with which this little local war in central Orion begins. That will change as war cascades up and down the spiral arm, sooner than realized. There are signs of it already.

Tek planners should've known better about the combat bots. After all, from the first hour of the war masses of human fighters are engaged. Flesh-and-blood fighters are far more plentiful than smart silicon and steel war bots, a fact that will only grow in importance as the Krevan War broadens and continues. As a planned short war goes long instead, gulping industry and finances, billions of lives and the futures of whole worlds and systems. The war bots will run out on every side.

Besides, flesh is cheaper, more adaptable and more easily replaced. That brutal truth will grow truer as expensive war machines become harder to build or restore, reducing armies to more basic weapons carried by infantry and armored vehicles. Only as many fighting bots will roll off straining assembly lines as sphinctered wartime budgets will permit. There won't be enough, not once this war expands. Smug RIK generals and everybody in senior tek and military leadership across all the militaries and governments of Orion will only learn this the hard way. Learn the only way any army ever does. Not by books of old histories and doctrines and close study of so called "lessons learned" in prior wars, but by fighting the new one. As war spreads to more systems, the toll in flesh will mount as autonomous fighting machines clash, fail and fall. Things are going to fall apart, for everyone.

All that lies ahead, on other worlds than Genève. For now, heavy armtraks, AI bot *walkers* and squat *armadillos* and *crocs*, and mobile *gatling* guns abound on one side only, creating an illusion of permanent invincibility of the Imperium. The speed and modernity of the swift advance across the face of Genève swells Grün civilians with pride in empire and in their military, as they watch official war vids of green clad boys marching and trumpeting over the memex.

Hardly anyone notices that the Imperium is already suppressing casualty lists, contacting each bereaved family directly with the news, but also warnings to keep its loss and grief private and contained. No memorial services are allowed. Only victory celebrations. For not all is going smoothly for Rikugun and Kaigun in the opening invasions. Errors and indiscipline affect the flow of ground fights beyond the shattered MDL, grating against the advance, slowing it here, separating it over there. It doesn't help that orders are ignored by imprudent and insubordinate corps commanders eager for a too personal glory. Instead of concentrating all armor into tight spear tips to plunge deep into Genève's exposed belly, they make an arrogant broad front advance, too confidently attacking all points at once.

Sudden flash fights disrupt RIK's grand marching schemes with little battles Main HQ doesn't want, as its armies pursue strategic envelopment of the running Krevans. In division and corps sized assaults made against isolated battalions or just companies of harder resisting fighters, senior generals launch oldfashioned attacks taken from faded storybooks or military fables learned in boyhood. Or in some hoary prewar tactical class. It's *their* first war, too. After three centuries of peace no one really knows what to do. So attacks made into desperately defended strongpoints bring Rikugun casualties to alarming levels, even for so indifferent an officer corps as the Imperium's.

Krevans can't win, but they are losing far more effectively. They dig in behind outdated, loopholed walls of ultrasteel forts centuries old, where maser troops once stood and held off dead Grün kings and crusaders of the Black Faith. They're eventually blasted out by superior and heavier Rikugun weapons, but they serve as breakwaters to the advancing assault waves, letting stragglers move westward and leaving tens of thousands of boys in green lying still on invaded soil, or in the streets of burned out towns and flattened villages across Northland's plains. The count of the dead includes a whole company of Double Moons from Uri, wiped out by the shattered remnants of Madjenik and its handfuls of gathered strays.

KRA snipers and skirmishers and half-battalions on Genève take cover in extended ditches fanning away from the old forts, in low trenches and along any high ground. Too many eager volunteers wearing pale green weaves, and far more green clad conscript lads not so keen for battle, are killed or grievously wounded by defensive fire that rakes their upright ranks as they're recklessly sent forward across presighted killing zones around the old forts. Tens of thousands are laid prone by crescendos of maser fire and a rapid *"crack-crack-crack-crack"* of wall mounted or hidden KRA rapidos. Tumbling *blue* pulses come out faster and at greater range than green clad infantry can match, struggling uphill with outclassed and outranged stubby masers. RIK planners put so many resources into AI bot and armored forces over the prior 50 years they didn't upgrade infantry weapons. The price of neglect is now paid in hosts of lost fathers and sons, and keening mothers.

KRA rapidos make gaping red holes in the staggering bodies of men and burning armtrak hulks. Rikugun is already calling this weapon "Hell machine," for the ripping lethal impact its far heavier caliber pulses punch through flesh and armor. What saves the day for the generals is a standing practice in Rikugun of concentrating directly off the march, as soon as contact is made with any enemy. Each time a firefight breaks out more divisions and corps hasten to the sound of distant masers, and screams and explosions as the terrible fury of battle grows nearer and louder. Massive RIK numbers win these small encounter battles each and every time, but at rising cost in lost lives and wounded and in confidence of the troops. Grünen know now that they face defenders who will fight hard and well and to the death for every inch of their violated and cherished soil. It makes volunteers and raw conscripts alike hesitate, then halt. RIK generals are going to have to do something to clean up the rear areas after all. Toruń must wait.

It happens on four other Krevan worlds as well, until the brashest RIK generals are removed from command or summarily shot for failure, on distant Pyotr's order. Their successors don't make the same mistake. Instead, they adjust, and make entirely new errors. They pullback, regroup, hesitate and delay. They avoid casualties by not attacking, sending probes ahead that succumb to ambushes that bring casualties anyway. Kaigun does it, too. The advances are all slowing, letting more KRA units slip away. Others regroup and turn back to fight some more. The Genève Flotilla was nearly wiped out right at the start of the invasion, but KRN is putting up especially fierce and effective resistance over Aral, at the ice moons.

KRA officers are also new to this game of combat. So they leave their infantry over bunched, to take terrible punishment from RIK assault artillery that's always vigorously pushed forward, across rivers and canals and burning fields atop low flying hover rafts. KRA is outnumbered and outmaneuvered by the end of each day's fighting. Its generals also fail to reinforce initial strong positions at the forts, or to countermaneuver around the attackers while they retain some advantage of firepower over Rikugun numbers. Content to rely on the stationary rapidos as their ancestors did in the last war, they fail to spread support infantry to maximize the defense. Some isolated KRA units show foolhardy courage in doomed last stands that repeat a hundred times or more across five invaded worlds. In one bloody field on Brno, a 'Forlorn Hope' of ragged fighters charges massed ultrasteel guns and infantry ten times their number, attaining in red defeat only piles of mangled youth. And brain-and-blood splattered memories of a useless slaughter smeared over medics' long white aprons. Not one fighter reaches the enemy line, or lives.

Outnumbered or outflanked by each day's end, despite fighting hard and well, the KRA on Genève is forced to withdraw from its pummeled forts and retreat along the north plains roads leading to the forest zone. Forced out into the open, it pays a heavy price as RIK skycraft swoop and strafe and bomb the ragged and retreating columns, shorn of long since destroyed sky cover.

This is what defeat looks like. Raggedy and roughhewn, pouring over the land as chaotic as a torrent from a broken dam in a wild hurricane. It smells like burning flesh and acid melt. It tastes like iron in the mouth and of dark and bitter bile. It sounds like primal howls and mortal screams and harsh laughter of conquerors. It leaves corpses as detritus in its wash and wake. There's no mistaking defeat.

Before the war, Gold Division was standard bearer of a proudly independent agro planet. Its 'sheaves of wheat' cap flash gained wearers instant respect. And free rounds of beer or shots of corn liquor or rye whiskey. And back patting and tales by fat, middle aged men and white haired old men and women of their own youth. It was almost worth three years compulsory service every Genèven youth undertook, all that free drinking and free food in any of tens of thousands of simple village pubs. Or lying naked with an athletic KRA girl or boy in some reserved military hotel room, while on extended leave in sweet smelling Toruń.

Parents, grandparents and great grandparents of the children's brigades who now wear the venerated golden sheaves in this real and raw new war all wore the same proud symbol in decades past. Though no elder grumbling over onrushing defeat ever went to war themselves. They never faced an armtrak skimming at terrifying speed over a wavering cornfield, the lost crop ablaze and buffeted by explosions, lights and swirling smokes. They never stood before a plasma cannon in an onrushing turret blasting holes in dirt, while heavy side masers sheared a childhood friend in two a meter or so away, spattering her proud Gold flash with blood and brains. Or bored an instantly seared and smoking 10cm hole through his torso or head or gut or groin.

Beyond the burning edge of the Grün advance, blue and orange fields of abandoned crops undulate over Northland's valleys. Farmlands slowly turn into unplanted meadows as the terrain rises to meet far off mountains, where colder and more fallow valleys are covered in delicate purple flowers, in millions of *aster alpinus*. Slow creeks and wandering rivers border with summer sweetgrass, with tall elephant grasses and long rows of wild black bulrushes. All resisting death among ugly gouges where some RIK missile or bombardment pattern landed amid KRA gunpits and hasty rally points, murdering the huddled, frightened, defeated youth of sad Genève. There are no natural defense lines or basins. No large lines of hills or ridges or broad or raging rivers cutting through the flat landscape of Northland. Only far off Toruń, awaiting its doom.

The 'Golden City of Wood' is famed even among the roughest of marching Grünen, known for its unique, all wooden architecture. It was a favorite site of offworld cruises made by Imperium Upper Castes, before the war. It's the only urban prize on all Genève, with its huge granaries that supplied the farfolk trade and KRN repair pits and docks and heavily defended shipyard. Everyone knows that the invasion must climax at its berm, and end there in only one way.

Toruń lies far from the battered coast where RIK landed, 2,000 klics inland and more than 300 deep inside a vast old growth forest covering the high third of the boreal continent. It waits past the winter line where shorter crops and even poor farmers finally quit, surrendering to acidic soils and the cold northern climate and winds. Deep woodlands surround it, rising upward to the north and west to meet then climb a range of high mountains that continue all the way to the ice pole, before marching down the other side of the world into another hemisphere. There's no more forest or farmland over the top of the world. Only rocky heads of the tallest peaks wearing pack ice all up their broad shoulders, with snow topped peaked hats poking above the permanent cap.

A terrible enemy is heading for the five Old Forest Roads that lead to Toruń. He plans to overleap the city's great earthen berm to bring fire to its amber streets, crowded with defeated fighters and desperate throngs of refugees. Toruń waits on the coming onslaught. The mountains and ice don't know or care at all. Whatever happens, on their slopes and in the valleys they'll hold steady in long, indifferent rest. So, too, the silent, indifferent stars that flicker and blink and sleep far above.

Data search: expansion
Result: terraforming; ascent; DNA arks
Historia Humana, Volume I, Part II (a)

After tens of thousands of years of futile wonderment at far off stars, Humanity finally reached up from Old Earth to grasp them. It girded for space and slowly rose off the planet of its genesis and evolution to settle the home system. Though not as one. Even in this enlightened era, our Shōwa Age, we do not act with unity of effort or purpose. Our ascent to the stars began as our residence among them continues: divided, fragmented, uneven, unwilling to share them or the future. Two ancient motivations finally moved us into space to stay: greed and fear. Greed for new wealth from moon and asteroid mining operations, and fear that planetside rivals would acquire first access to these untapped resources and use them in wars of domination. Results were more spectacular than hoped, streaming enormous resources into dozens of Luna and Mars settlements. A magnetic shield (artificial dipole) built at the L1 protected Mars from Sol's deadly wind, inside a spreading magnetotail that shielded from radiation and protected the thin natural atmosphere. Rapid warming from the equator outward to both poles regenerated atmosphere from frozen CO2, to reach stabilized air pressure at 50% Old Earth Standard. Water generators added O2 and trace gases until the magnetic shield and greenhouse effect together released vast stores of Martian subsurface water ice, recreating rivers feeding into a 1/7th surface ocean not seen in three billion years. With a stable and breathable atmosphere, system trade, population growth and food production took off. In 2218 (OEY) the first of four Mars colonies finally attained self-sufficiency, after seven failed and were cannibalized. Terraforming worked. We had done it! We were off the origin world, and on the way to empire.

Humanity reached next for the large moons of Jupiter and Saturn. Specialized colonies were set up on Callisto (2273) and Ganymede (2295), supported by water and volatiles surface mining. Ice mining of the Jovian moons was supplemented by subsurface mining of the largest Greek and Trojan objects (2315). Cheap outer system water supplied rising demand from dry Martian cities, ultimately allowing hydroforming of two small, freshwater seas. Several older, domed Luna cities also expanded significantly at that time. Thus the system entered the doldrums of the first Satya Yuga, a Winning Age of widespread contentment that greatly slowed tek and cultural advances. Historians also point to the 'suspensor revolution' in private life as contributing to a general slowing of our ascent offworld. By greatly lengthening average lifespans and far more importantly, Youthspans, suspensor caused us to once again postpone reaching for extra-Sol habitable worlds. Our purpose faded, our ascent stalled, and the First Age of Expansion died of success.

The key change leading to the Second Age of Exploration and Expansion, to interstellar settlement, was realization that the future lay in our DNA, not atomics or metamaterials. Success came not from a new tek revolution but from a cultural shift that built on incremental but unrelated tek shifts once our capacity to reach the stars matched a growing desire to go there. The change led to abandonment of large colony ship and fast drive ambitions in favor of lightsail nanocraft and DNA arks. The first ships were AIs only, nanobot explorers with small mass and thus achievable energy velocity thresholds. Their job was to map targeted planets and ready optimum landing and cultivation sites for the second type, the DNA arks that followed only decades or centuries later and began basic terraforming.

Some 120,000 nanocraft launched, powered by light sails that dwarfed the AI packages, riding Solar wind with gossamer sheets many square klics wide. Light sails were assembled by AI 'spiders' printing fabric from over 10,000 spinnerets, assembly line fashion. The little ships the spiders wove soon passed beyond the heliopause in both directions down the plane of Orion, riding pulse 'assists' from solar power generators parked in L1 gravity free orbits. Thus boosted, the first nanoships reached 15% lightspeed. The stars drew ever closer, some actually coming within Humanity's reach. But it all still took too long, so that most of us lost patience yet again with the idea of leaving. Most nanoships were abandoned, assists turned off to save costs, or lost in jealous system wars or to indifference.

Interest in the explorers finally renewed as surviving nanoships were tied to civic projects or scientific or investment ventures, notably in exoscience research. This combination led to a renaissance in exploration interest, and great advances in bioeconomics, exoengineering, terraforming, holistic ecosystem and climate management, and other developing exosciences that was spurred at first by minor alien genome discoveries on Titan, Europa, Ganymede, Callisto, and Enceladus. At last, DNA arks went out to follow the original nanocraft, host ships for genetic molecules programmed to interact directly with organic material, one of the boon ideas of the new exoengineering industries that came to dominate Second Age economics. The pods seeded alien soils with our own cradle DNA, self-assembling bacteria, then simple plants and lower form animals, all guided by great AI bots that we all still honor and admire today [Editor's Note: See *Purity*, Vol. XXXVII, for a recent exception to this statement]. *The pod infusion terraforming method eliminated life support and other gigantism issues in older colony ship design.*

DNA arks served as coded databases of all human knowledge. DNA turned out to be the ultimate compact storage medium for any forms of information, not just building diagrams of trillions of exported life forms. A single gram of DNA dedicated to information storage held 500 billion gigabytes of data, capable of access by the AI bots and all future colonists. As the first colonies were mapped then bioseeded by teams of AI bots in dozens of distant systems, Humanity shared a rare moment of unity, peaceful conviction, and near universal public support of exoplanetary exploration. It is widely agreed by historians that this was the single greatest achievement of the Heroic Age, an unfolding era of peaceful expansion. Yet, not all DNA ark or colony sponsors were properly screened. Some turned out to be fronts for ethnic or religious isolationists, ranging from harmless Inuit who settled unwanted and icy Nunavut to intolerant sects of ascetic renunciants and fanatics such as the Broderbund. That opened the door to grave error leading to greater sorrows, to deep historical regrets, and to the reinvention of war...

Scouts

The massive teaks, maples and oaks of Pilsudski Wood remain gold leaved, for it is just past midsummer. AI bot bioengineered for Genève's lower than standard gravity, the smallest of the wondrous trees stretch up over 125 meters. The greatest grow tens of meters higher. Wide root spreads, huge base girth, and vast canopies spread out to match these great trunk heights.

Inside the ocean of gold deciduous trees are pointy islands of silver firs, rising to top out at 60 meters. They're protected from root and canopy competition by acidic needles shorn onto and hence changing the soil far below. They, too, were bioengineered by nanobots before any settlers arrived, only in brilliant silver pine rather than deciduous gold. No one knows why the AI terra bots did it, since they weren't programmed for bioaesthetics like this. All agree the result is spectacular. The Old Forests of Genève are famed not just within Krevo but across all Orion.

On the forest floor, puddles of shining needle rain merge into shimmering silver lakes bordered by golden shores of undisturbed windfall. The leafy bedding is plush and comfortable, home to many hundreds of species of fauna from tiny shrews to rabbit and raccoon, deer, elk, moose, quick red fox, black bear and solitary gray timber wolves. The animals of Genève were also made by AI terra bots that carefully tended spore, seed and fauna gene banks carried on DNA ark ships from Old Earth. The AI bots reworked alien soil and air for more than two full centuries before the first quantum drive colonists arrived to found Toruń, sited at the base of the northern mountains and optimum location for the planet's only elevator. The bots are all gone now. No one knows how or where, only that they're revered on Genève as makers and shepherds of the great forests. The elevator is gone, too, its ancient bola asteroid tether blasted apart by a Kaigun Zerstörer.

***

"You were right, captain." Tom Hipper says on their next break. "The pursuit is ferocious and unrelenting. I'm still not sorry for what we did in the meadow."

They have finally reached the forest edge, far from the burned sweetgrass they left carpeted with spent crystals and scorch marks, and enemy dead. With boys blasted open by the satisfied *snakes*, scythed in half by the big *daisy cutters*, bored through an eye or chest by a sniper's laser, cooked inside-out and burst into messy red clumps by assault masers fired at intimate ranges. Madjenik left no wounded behind, no witnesses to its tactics or spies to its direction. Only dead men in green, gaping skyward with throats cut ear-to-ear by carbyne blades. And fifteen of their own dead, laid in a respectful long row inside the ditch in front of the apple trees. No one expects that Rikugun will leave them there when its own men were left by Madjenik scattered over the burnt sweetgrass, but it seemed important to do.

Just 107 survivors make it to Pilsudski Wood. Sixty were lost by threes or fives, or twos or tens, along the way. Some fell from a careless camo accident that exposed scouts to a sudden, strafing Jabo. A few more to unseen *hunter-killer* mini drones or undetected mines left by retreating KRA Some fell in sharp firefights as suicide rearguards Jan formed at the start of each day, staying 3 klics back to ward off pursuit as long as their lives and ammo lasted. Sixty dead out of 167 who survived the tart ambush at the apple orchard and in a burned meadow.

Madjenik swells past its original size once it gets inside the forest, joined by nearly 300 stragglers from other broken units already there. Without officers, they fled individually or in small groups under the golden canopy, to stumble into or be drawn to Jan and Madjenik beneath the boughs.

One older fighter pleads with Jan: "Please sir! We gots no place ta go an' no one ta folla. Just gives us some ammo an' water. Gives us a chance ta fit back."

A young woman with a cut hand: "I never even fired my maser, captain."

A rare Silver veteran says: "Ya' gotta let me join Gold, sir, an' fight. All the bies I joins up with is dead awready."

Jan is senior officer and Madjenik the strongest single unit among the forlorn inside Pilsudski Wood, so he assumes command. Zofia is the only other officer and remains his second. Among the strays, there are good NCOs he assigns to leaderless squads. For three days everyone hides among the tall trees, recovering strength for the arduous trek to Toruń to come. Then it gets sparky again.

***

Madjenik is having a shit load of trouble with an aggressive unit of RIK 10th Armored hover scouts, probing in repeatedly from along the forest edge. The scouts are so cocksure they make no effort to hide their presence or movements or intentions. The arrogant asses even sing smutty Grün songs at the tops of their voices as they come into the woods, like they're drunk or on leave and heading to a cathouse instead of toward mortal combat.

It's a long way to Kestino, to the best whores I know,
right behind the Palace, where slave girls love to blow.
When I've fucked all Genève's women, it'll be time to go,
way back to my homeworld, to the Purest girl I know!

One scout shouts as he mounts up: "I shall redden my sword in bandit blood!" He turns red faced as his mates collapse in laughter at such mock medieval posing. Then they remount and scoot over the forest edge on compact hovers, boasting:

"We're going to kill the bandits!"

"We're going to kill *Gelben*!"

"Death to all KRA!"

***

"Alright, I've had enough of these *bâtards*." After the fourth scout raid Jan organizes an ambush of the whole brigade group of 80 hover scouts. He briefs Madjenik overnight. "We'll lure these careless *mulkku* deep inside the trees. I need ten volunteers for a special mission. A onetime unit." A hundred hands snap up. "Right, thank you all. Lieutenant Jablonski will make the selection."

That's quickly done, in a HUD flash. "You'll use our last hover bikes, feign like you're in trouble, pull the scouts into the woods after you. Let's call the unit the 'limping squad.' You'll..."

Zofia interjects: "Seriously, sir?"

"Well, what would you call it?"

"How about 'wounded rabbits'?"

"OK, now *you're* serious? How is that an upgrade?"

"Let the volunteers decide."

"Wounded rabbits! Wounded rabbits!"

Seven men and three women shout over and over, until Jan hushes them. They stand grinning insolently at him while stealing looks over at Zofia, who grins at them from behind Jan's back. An hour later the plan is set and the order is given.

"Mount up, rabbits!"

They clamber onto five untippable carbon fiber, two-fighter speed bikes, the last transport left to Madjenik besides a few small cargo carrier bots loaded down with ammo, food and water. And with wounded. Zofia winks at the rabbits, then says whorishly: "Flash your tits and some cottony tail at the arrogant enemy! Bring him to us with his cocks all hard. We'll show him a real good time."

Jan doesn't know how to rejoin to that, so he wisely says nothing. '*What a thing to say to men going into battle! She's always a surprise*.'

The hover scouts are breaking camp outside the tree line, a thin morning mist hanging low over the first spreading light of day, when five two-rider bikes break cover and enter a too loosely guarded perimeter. The bikes scud to a stop and quickly reverse, riders feigning panic and surprise. Shouts of "Bandits! bandits!" and "After them!" rise down a half-klic of forest edge. Several carelessly snapped off pistol shots ring out. Making certain they're followed, the "wounded rabbits" swerve back under cover of the thick forest, seemingly bounding away without leadership or purposeful direction. Fleeing wildly, as frightened rabbits should.

Excited shouts ring across the scout camp, not an alarm so much as a call to an easy kill and quick murder of what is assumed is a bandit scavenger party out looking for food. A short company from 10th Armored takes Jan's baited hook, swiftly mounting 20 four-rider, softskin hovers. They zip away and yell and shoot wildly as they pull in behind the darting, hip-hoppity bikers. Trying not to pull too far in front of the pursuit, a short brace of "wounded rabbits" is hit right away, scored in the back by hover mounted masers. Four men fall fatally hard off their bikes, crashing and tumbling into huge tree roots and heavy undergrowth, broken and burning bikes setting small fires left behind that the damp morning forest easily contains and soon snuffs out.

Success urges imprudence on the 10th Armored scouts, hot on a blood trail. Whooping and shooting wildly, they weave their slower, heavier four-rider hovers over huge root loops or under thick, down hanging vines and branches. In minutes they leave all artillery support and the rest of their company behind, and any hope of rescue or reinforcement. That's all left outside the dim woods that close around.

Two more rabbits tumble. The scouts want the rest, forgetting the warren must be near. Four klics inside and four surviving bikers whir into a natural clearing, then whirl to stop at a preset shooting line, no longer rabbits but now acting the cornered worm who turns at last to face its tormentor. It's Jan's preset, narrow-V kill zone, over 200 guns waiting down each long side in a tangle of high roots and low branches, silent under field camo and heavy oak canopy.

"Shoot!"

Madjenik fires as one, slicing down scouts in a quick and efficient slaughter. Surrenders are offered by fallen and wounded men with frantic waves and shouted pleas. None are accepted. It's over in just minutes, leaving the clearing smelling of smoking wood and burnt soil, of bike oil and bile, scored metal, burned out hovers and scorched hubris.

A wounded scout is hauled over to Jan. He's a very big man with a mashed in shoulder and panic in his artificially colored purple eyes. He pleads for his life all the way over, imploring the grim KRA fighters prodding and dragging him across the clearing. He keeps offering to trade secret info on the Bad Camberg special op, a false flag attack on a Grün moonlet that Pyotr used as an excuse to start the war. His premise for invading the blameless United Planets of Krevo.

The scout looks up dumbly at Jan, repeating: "I was there! I was there!" He smells of old barroom piss and new forest-and-fear shit weighing heavily inside his lower weaves. Two surviving 'rabbits' force him to his feet. "Please, please. I'll tell you all the details of what we did there!" He begs again, then offers the Judas kiss to his only friend in the hover scout unit, even in the whole RIK. "That boy over there, the one screaming by that huge tree, he was the one who made the broadcast. He was the one, not me. I was only..."

Jan interrupts, coldly refusing the trade. "We all know what happened at Bad Camberg. Your filthy trick fooled no one. But it's good to know we have as our guest one of the murderers who started this fucking war. Welcome to Genève."

He reaches out and slits the big man's throat ear-to-ear, with a single broad stroke of his black diamond knife. A young, thoughtful fighter holds the startled man's head up by a fistful of his shockingly thick black hair as his knees slowly buckle and he slides down. She does it so he won't spurt jugular blood onto Jan's already filthy, oak colored weaves. The dark ejaculate spurting to the forest floor smells of iron and thick proteins, of lipids and severed lymph and last betrayal.

Jan looks to see who it is who's holding up the half-severed head. It's the small straggler girl who reported the 'grinding' of KRA prisoners by Grün armtraks, the rookie soldier who fumbled with sonics at the meadow before correctly mounting frags. She has a hard fistful of black hair, tilting the man's neck back to widen the gash and speed release. She waits until the body stops spurting and jerking, then lets go. It collapses into a dark, spreading pool of escaping fluids.

Tramp! tramp! tramp!

Advance scouts from a colony of tree ants has already found the sticky red treasure. Soon a long supply column will stream down a broad trunk to collect and gather it to the nest, guided in by chemical messaging. Soon, Madjenik's finest mini drone sensors will pick up their grating formation moving down the hard bark to reach the forest floor. Already, a miniature army is following a blood trail into gore and to the spoils of war. It marches to gather up a winter's feast into heavy mandibles. To collect manna from heaven, if you're an ant.

Tramp! tramp! tramp!

Jan nods acknowledgment of the straggler youth's thoughtful act, then orders: "Leave them to the forest. Bury their hovers in the deep hollows, under a century of windfall. Cover the bodies with their own camo sheets, but strip off their weaves! Leave flesh hidden but exposed for Genève tree rats to gnaw. Let their dead converse bone-to-bone and feed our forest saplings."

So they toss the black-haired man with a newly sliced throat awkwardly down beside a naked, once handsome kid whose face is half sheared off. He was seared by a maser right at the outset of the fight in the clearing. The boy flopped and howled in terrible agony all through the quick forest battle. Before he died, his screams made him sound more like an animal than a man.

Why? Because men and boys *are* animals, and scream like it when half their face is carved to fall like this most fetching boy's did into astonished hands that trembled as he tried to stick flesh back onto an exposed white cheekbone.

Or when they know they've been stuck like a pig, vitally in the gut in hand-to-hand combat, and the ripping blade is about to sneak in again, *snick! snick!* to spill their bile and blood onto the forest floor, where ants await the sweet red rain.

Or neat laser holes appear in weaves and the red spurts out, even though they feel no pain. Not yet, though it's coming, like a freight train loaded with fire on hot tracks running into their mind and soul, already up-to-speed and unstoppable.

Or a calf or thigh erupts from the inside-out as a maser cooks marrow inside thick bones, exploding the limb like a July firecracker stuffed in a holiday hotdog by a naughty child, who afterward carelessly tosses the damaged and unwanted mockmeat onto the campfire.

The dead boy slumped against the tree screamed about his missing face and far more primally, until the fight was over and Zofia finished him with a quick head shot. But only after the black haired man flung his weapon down and his arms into the air, crying and pleading for his own life while offering to betray his dying and only friend. Like all the other dead scouts, the faceless kid's shoulder flash says: *RIK 10th Armored*, then right below: *1st Scout Company*. That's not what pisses off everyone in Madjenik. It's an ID holo they find tucked deep inside an inner pocket, a party card that boasts: *Minoru Honda, Brno Purity Volunteers.* Brno is a Krevan border world, but with a large Grün ethnic minority.

"The kid's a godsdamn native born Krevan!" The grinder girl shouts it as she finds the tag. She turns ice sheet white at her discovery, then lava red with rage.

Tom Hipper gives the body a hard kick. His dark mane of hair tosses from the blow. "Fucking traitor! Rot in *helvetti*, you son of *saatana!* You whoreson!"

One RIK officer they leave fully dressed, but boobytrapped with poison gas injected up his anus, loaded into a dead man's stomach. Then they shove a fleshy butt plug deep inside him. They lift his corpse 400 meters from the clearing and battle site but don't camo it. They want him found. He'll be taken to a field morgue where a Rikugun mortician will surely puncture the anal plug and stomach lining with a long trocar. When he does, the erupting dead man will surrender his lethal toxins and kill anyone within 5-10 meters. If the clever little trick works, a small cloud of deadly gas might kill three or five or ten more of Madjenik's enemies.

Medical workers, probably. It's better if it's field medics. Or maybe they'll freeze dry the corpse temporarily and ship him home to be embalmed, prepped and set up for a grand ceremonial disposal, as all dead RIK officers are. He's the perfect carrier of the poison. A sharp trocar will surely find and release it, either here in a Genève camp or on his Grün homeworld. There's no point fixing up enlisted dead the same way. RIK burns non-officer corpses, usually right on site. So Madjenik strips and camos those, leaves them to army ants and rats and tree snakes. Besides, a poison "booty trap" is a onetime only trick. A ripple of coarse laughter moves down the ranks as Madjenik marches deeper into Pilsudski Wood.

"Hey Corporal Hipper! Hey Tom, that's some killer fart we left behind!"

"You would know, sergeant. You've let loose some of your own."

"Got that right. Best way to get a camo tent all to myself!"

They're happy to have killed so many hated scouts, sad to have lost six good men among the 'rabbits' when they did it, but mostly mad as unholy hell about the dead Brno kid. And there's one more thing. After the ambush and slaughter of the scouts no distinctions are made or accepted between Madjenik "originals" and an engorgement of straggler "newbies." Everyone is in the same shit and thus the same outfit now, which they start calling "Wysocki's Wreckers."

The name sticks, no matter how vehemently or often the captain objects when he overhears it. Not least because, behind his back and sporting a big grin as she does it, fiery haired Lieutenant Zofia Jablonski endorses and encourages the fierce new combat moniker. Jan would be mortified if he knew. All he can think of is how he just got six 'wounded rabbits' killed.

Ghost

The ambush of the hover scouts severely embarrasses General Nikita Brusilov, Rikugun *taishō* and senior officer in charge of 10th Armored Division. He's yet another royal "blooder," a distant cousin to Pyotr Shaka III, but definitely part of the Oetkert clan and dynasty. He has the signature jade eyes that all Oetkerts have, while his midnight skin shades closest to the maternal or Shaka side of the family.

Across his fat right cheek is a careful "dueling scar" he claims dates to a test of honor during his High Akademy days on Kestino. It's almost a requirement of his rank in RIK, to wear a white dueling scar. In fact, he had it surgically added while getting repairs to a vicious gouge in his cheek made by steel fingernails of a Kestino whore he was roughing up more than usual. A week later the girl was "disappeared" offworld, a nameless throwaway from the slums. It's what Oetkerts do. Just because they can. Because no one dares say "no" to the *blood royale*.

Brusilov is connected and very much a political general. He's unnoticed on the military nebs and not consulted by Main HQ, but he's prominent in civilian propaganda. Not least because he appointed a captain to his staff whose only job is to make vids boasting about the progress and mightiness of 10th Division and its general's extraordinary brilliance. The volume of boasts is rising with surprised realization that he's stuck fighting 'bandits' on a backwards world, on dull and rustic Genève. He knows the really big battles are underway on Brno, Lwów, and the ice moons at Aral. Still, he's an Oetkert. He can always command attention.

His enemies know it, too. News about his lost scout unit somehow leaked from the milneb to the civvy memex. It's embarrassing, not just to him but to Pyotr and the whole Oetkert clan. That's why Nikita Brusilov is raging mad, shouting about "bringing unholy hell down on all stinking, *Gelben*." He gives the order to kill all "the rat bastards skulking as filthy bandits" inside the woodland sanctuary. That's why he has rashly sent in three battalions with simple orders to "clear the yellow fuckers out! Use any means, but do it *today!*"

Brusilov's arrogant ineptitude flows downhill, through his staff into poor field training and ill-preparedness of the whole division. 10th Armored is better at killing and raping civvies in open villages, better at flaming temples than fighting armed KRA. That's why Jan and Zofia catch the *taishō* and his ops staff in a clumsy and hasty penetration, made without adequate intel or proper arti support or the critical sky cover 10th Division enjoyed on the rolling Northland plain. Instead of moving inside the woods in basic echelon, Brusilov sends his battalions in serially, one after the other. So Jan and Zofia and the Wreckers isolate, fix and beat living hell out of them, one after the other.

"Who told the bandits we were coming? There are traitors on my staff!" Five officers are arrested and shot, *pour encourages les autres.* They join 1,500+ dead of 10th Armored from a series of intense battles fought over three days and nights. Jan's 'Wreckers' suffer 100+ casualties, more than 25% of all Madjenik fighters inside Pilsudski Wood. But in exchange, they slice up two RIK battalions.

A third waits its turn to file into the woods on the general's orders, but its officers see the carnage of the first two unfold on farscopes. They retreat the whole battalion well outside the forest edge. Madjenik doesn't pursue, but its alert and aroused fighters kill any wounded or stragglers left behind by the two withdrawn battalions. The close hunting lasts fifty hours. Jan and Zofia are methodical, the determined fighters of Madjenik are ruthless. No one found alive is left alive. Not even the dead are entirely safe.

It's done without Jan's or Zofia's knowledge, but most of their fighters know what happened. They know that the corpse of one man who managed to kill two Madjenik fighters, before a third masered him in the back, was skinned. Then his slippery hide, an underside of yellow-white fat brilliant in the sun, was spiked to the trunk of a huge sycamore, the last great tree where the forest edge met the perimeter of 10th Armored's base camp. As the morning sun revealed the human hide, the sight terrified all those in 10th Armored who saw what their enemy did.

Stymied by the dense forest and Jan's and Zofia's hit-and-run tactics, *Taishō* Brusilov readies to go in again, and again. What does he care for the lives under his command? Each time, he does it in more or less the same brutally stupid way. Each time, his ill-led battalions are met by Wysocki's Wreckers in more or less the same deadly fashion. Casualties mount, and 10th Armored's will starts to wilt.

Brusilov is not a doubter. Not a learner. Too arrogant. Too royal. Too much like his more famous and powerful cousin Pyotr, the Grün Tennō who rules a vast but brittle empire from far off Kestino. Too much the Oetkert. Too much a prewar general. Too much a fool playing at war. Over a large camp meal of mocksteak and freshly dug potatoes, wood roasted in gee while brushed with cut parsley and dusted with coriander, he pushes aside tactical objections from more competent officers. One still offers him last minute words of caution: "Sir, I fear we may be heading into a trap." The major is no fool. He's careful to use the plural.

"What kind of trap?"

"This bandit captain is a special kind of leader, sir."

"So am I, *shōsa*." He pushes another glazed potato into his full mouth.

"Indeed you are, sir. I only mean, *umm*, that he's done it to us twice already, thrice if you count the scouts we lost."

"Done what?"

"He's lured our men into the woods, cut off our columns as they strung out in the density of the forest, then beat each battalion column separately and in detail."

"They were badly led." Brusilov takes another bite of steak, hot juices leaking over his teeth onto his double chin. He dabs at the dribble with a lace napkin.

"No, sir. They were well led, but they met a superior foe deep in the woods."

"*Superior?* How dare you! Must I do everything myself?"

The major hesitates, then he says what Rikugun Security Unit, the division's intel staff or RSU, concluded but has so far feared to tell the *taishō*: "The local kids say that he's using a child's game to trick us, my general."

"What are you talking about? A *child's* game?"

"Yes, *taishō*. They call it 'Box the Fox.'"

"Box the what?"

"Fox. It's a local game of distraction and maneuver."

"I am no mere fox! I am a wolf of war!"

"You are indeed, sir," the staff officer judiciously lies. "Yet, it seems that this bandit leader has a rare and natural gift for tactics almost as great as yours. He has lifted his method not from the KRA manual but from a kid's game that he and the other bandits all played before the war." It's an ancient game on Genève, where some children distract local farmers while others steal apples or pears right from under their noses. Most farmers don't really mind them doing it, having done it themselves when young. Some even play along. The more foolish get red faced mad and chase after the nearest taunting kids, returning to find even more apples are missing.

"You are children yourselves, to believe this tale. Or are you traitors?" The bold officer knows he's gone too far. His life is at stake in these next minutes. This is a prince and *taishō* with his commission to High Command of the Division granted by birth and affirmed by the Jade Court. He backs down.

"One thing, sir." It's the division RSU officer, finally bringing the latest intel to his commander. "A captured bandit told us, after experiencing one of our more persuasive methods, sir, so we know it's true, that more stragglers are joining the bandit group as it moves about the woods. The bandit leader again has over 400 fighters. He has therefore recovered all his recent losses."

"I have 40,000 men. And a covey of scared and incompetent staff officers! I can believe this of *them*, sniveling Third Casters, all of them. But you're a Second Caster and RSU man. You're supposed to have iron in your soul. I see only rust."

Another major finally dares to offer an opinion, his first ever. It's perfectly timed, calculated to go directly against the advice of his fellow staff officers: "We should go in exactly as you say, sir, but with massive firepower and overwhelming strength. The whole division all at once!"

A third finds rare courage in a quick negative inspiration, and says: "Or maybe not at all. Just let them starve in there. They are weak, they pose no threat to our operations or supply lines." The Calculator is upset at being so easily and quickly preempted in his *shōshō*'s attention by the Opportunist.

"*What?!* You fear this 'Ghost of the Wood?' Yes, I heard that you idiots call him that. Are you such utter cowards, to fear this criminal lurking in the trees, a bandit who fights without honor or rules?"

"Sir, I must protest! We are *not* cowards! We only say..."

"Silence! Do as you are ordered! Send my march columns in again! I will hang this 'Ghost' and all his filthy bandits, or I'll hang all of you! Choose!" He pushes away his unfinished meal and stabs his clear diamond, royal dirk into the wood table, where it quivers with lethal threat. It's a theatrical gesture he used before with servants and *dāsa* back on his hereditary estate. But that was peacetime.

Incompetencc is a common problem at the start of all wars, usually on every side, until the white heat of combat burns away prewar illusions and burns down undeserved commands. It's a problem hugely aggravated in Rikugun and Kaigun by hoary Grün traditions of royal appointment. Brusilov is strictly a peacetime and political general. Not as bad as some, but much worse than many. He's more experienced at pushing peas around his plate with a flat breadknife than pushing forward a blood-and-fire advance against an intelligent and desperate enemy. He's a man of the *blood royale*, a distant cousin of Pyotr Shaka. That makes him an intimate member of the extended ruling clan, which Pyotr is already beginning to lament occupies far too many positions in Rikugun and Kaigun, resting solely on royal blood connections. Because that's what peacetime royals do, wear uniforms with unearned medals glowing over their breast, pretending to be warlords in the grand tradition of the founder of the Oetkert-Shaka dynasty and Grün Imperium.

Their collective ignorance is already lethally combining with clan entitlement, elite laziness and tactical ineptitude. The problem is disguised so far on Genève and elsewhere in initial fighting by Rikugun's massive superiorities in firepower, numbers and matériel. But incompetence will out, especially in battle. If Kaigun and Rikugun go up against the armies and navies of the Calmar Union they cannot hope to win as easily as they are against the Krevan Republic. And it's not even so easy anymore against Krevans.

Struggling in his first ever combat command, Brusilov resorts to brute force. Just as he did back in his civilian governorship when he routinely sent in police and troops to crack heads of bread rioters and arrest and shoot any ringleaders. So he sends in 4,000 men on foot, noisily crashing into Pilsudski Wood in two widely separated columns. Orders are to penetrate 60 klics straight ahead before bending inward, to close enveloping pincers that must "trap and annihilate the bandits." Years ago he read in a military text that pincer tactics were very clever in war.

Why go in on foot? Four-rider scout hovers are one thing, but the big ATCs are unable to move through dense, massively rooted, dark and drooping woods. Not even shifted down to lowest hover mode. They're just too big. So the infantry gets out and advances clumsily into the forest, on combat glide boots designed for open field assaults. Trained in fast advances made over open plains, too many of Brusilov's men over accelerate, banging into looping roots thicker than a man and twice or thrice as tall, bashing into huge low level branches that reach down to the underbrush on the forest floor. It's dark, it's frustrating, and it's slow going.

They're tactically blind. Their best scouts are dead and 20 destroyed hovers have yet to be replaced. Men curse the forced shift to glide mode, trip over loose undergrowth and misstep into leaf fall many centuries thick, unlike anything on any of their homeworlds. It covers deeper hollows and gullies, trapping stumblers in natural tiger pits, muffling their coms and lost cries for help. Some of those who fall into too deep hollows are hurt and lost. They join with the forest forever.

Listening to the crashing, dismounted infantry from 10th Armored are Jan and Zofia and all of Madjenik. They're waiting in deep ambush positions that start 25 klics inside forest cover, well sited at the edge of exhaustion and morale for the incoming enemy. Only a handful of quick scouts on the wide flanks of the advance report back on the slow progress made, and where and when the best ambushes might be laid in. The columns soon feel as if *they* are the hunted ones. Blown up by mines at the head of the march or picked off by snipers at the rear. Stalked and killed silently in ones or threes or fives should they wander off the trail or straggle behind the main body, put down with diamond knives or wire or root garrotes. Caught by the throat in small snares if they stay on the path. Men look around and the man beside them is just gone. It's like they're in an Andean jungle and sly and stealthy panthers or drooping, silent pythons are taking them out one after another. Hauling them off to some terrible, unimaginable agony and slow, crushing death.

Jan gives orders to the snipers to wound rather than kill. "Wound 'em bad. I want them so hurt they can't crawl or walk, but don't kill them. No head shots." It's not misplaced mercy. It's a sound tactical decision. A dead man is stripped of weapons and equipment but left behind by advancing RIK. Good, one down. A wounded man howling for help means two or four more drop from the column to carry him back on a stretcher to the waiting evac bots. That's three-to-five down or out of the fight with a single well-placed laser snipe. "Except for their medics," Jan amends his sniping order. "Kill all their medics outright." Fighters love their unit's medics best. Killing them will really hurt morale.

Tramp, tramp, stumble, tramp. "Shoot!"

Tramp, tramp, trip, fall, stand up. "Sniper!"

Run, stumble, fall, get up, get hit. "Stretcher!"

Some snipers use their own initiative, blending his orders. First they spot and wound a medic, drawing out several Rikugun who take more chances breaking cover to help a medic than for anyone else. After shooting all the newly exposed runners the sniper turns back to plant a kill shot to the head of the downed medic. When Jan hears of this, he appoints the man who thought of it as his head sniper.

Displace and repeat! "Keep them reeling!"

Cry, scream, crawl off to hide. "No Mercy!"

Fall down, look up. "No, please don't kill me!"

Box the Fox. Zofia leads a quarter of Madjenik in darting, diversionary attacks on the long righthand column, hitting it hard to draw it farther right while pulling reinforcements from the lefthand column, for when the main Wrecker attack hits the hardest. Jan leads a quick attack into the flank of the strung out and reduced leftward column as it passes hidden positions, cutting it into segments like a worm caught by wrens, devouring each helpless wiggling part in its turn. Forest hollows fill with muffled sounds of rout, smells of burning wood and tree fall, sights of a screaming slaughter of maser scorched youths. The columns turn to flee, leaving 1,137 dead and 385 wounded behind when they limp back out. Madjenik loses 65 dead and wounded all told, a heavy price but still a trade of 23:1

Wounded are quickly knifed. No one is left alive, no matter how they plead and cry or implore the gods or pity's sake or their children's. It's not done on Zofia's word or example this time. Jan stands over the wounded and prisoners and gives the explicit order to all Madjenik. "No masers. Knives only. And make it quick." He kills two himself, to show that it must be done and that he means for them all to do it. He understands now. '*Zofia was right, back at the meadow. We have to kill all prisoners. I was wrong to judge her, to think that I was somehow above necessity and her. She's a better officer than me.*'

"You'll make their mothers weep." She says it to him as he's walking back, wiping black blood off his knife with a large, damp oak leaf. She says it without malice, as a statement of fact. There just aren't enough oak clad fighters to guard prisoners. And they'd consume vital food and water, and slow Madjenik down as it runs. It's too dangerous to leave even bound and disarmed enemy behind as Madjenik moves camp peripatetically around Pilsudski. As for the order to use knives only, no charger packs can be spared to maser captured men. Then there's the other thing, that Jan and Zofia don't speak about but all Madjenik knows is true: not one of them would be left alive if taken prisoner by Rikugun, or at least not after they're tortured for any information they might have about the 'Ghost.'

"Strip all dead of anything we can carry. No covering them up this time. Let their Rikugun mates come back into the woods to find and collect them. Let them see what Madjenik can and will do to anyone who pursues us."

"Yes captain." It's Corporal Tom Hipper. "Fourth squad here, to me. Police this clearing. Take everything useful that we can carry." They collect food packs, water canteens, all medicines, and vital crystal aerographite chargers for masers, loading as much as they can onto two captured carry bots. They will have to hump all the rest, along with their own heavy gear and weapons, food and water.

Jan can tell himself that killing prisoners is a military necessity, because it is. But there's something more to it, much more. For both sides the fight is hardening, shifting past the old prewar rules, moving beyond mercy or pity. Far past even the most basic law of "kill or be killed." It's *personal* now. Vital, coarse and full of hot red rage, vengeance and bloody murder. With plenty more to come. For this war is going to spread, first across all 24 inhabited Krevan worlds, then across the Thousand Worlds of the Orion spur. Pyotr and Rikugun have no idea what rough beast they have unleashed into the stars. If they did, they would shudder and hide.

"We're a vile and a noble species." Jan confides the thought to Zofia in a rare moment of down time. An even less frequent moment of direct talk between them, of honest reflection. It comes during another forced march, after he orders quick dispatch by carbyne knife of another brace of eight prisoners picked up wandering in the deep woods. They hardly even converse anymore, except about command decisions. It's not just because they must fend off Brusilov's columns. A darkness dropped between them at the sweetgrass meadow. Jan can't say why it is he pulls back when *he* now routinely orders prisoner kills. Zofia doesn't understand at all.

"Yeah? So be it!" She doesn't like these fleeting, brooding dark moods of his. She squints angrily at Jan, startling and confusing him. Like she astonishes him at least twice each day.

"What? Why? ... What, *umm*, what do you mean, 'so be it'?"

"I mean be as vile as you must so that we can live to be as noble as we like."

"I don't understand."

"You need to, sir. You're our leader. We need you clear eyed, not mopey and distracted. Your nobility, and ours, must wait until this hard fight is over. Captain, this is a time for iron."

In his mind's eye he sees her in the meadow, holding a Q-carbon blade slick with fresh drawn neck blood, a gasping and clutching youth bleeding out, his open throat gushing color onto her dirty oak uniform. The boy's blood was thick and dark ruby, not crimson like the brilliant red dress she wore that night before the war, when he fell for her hard and forever. When he first met this remarkable, pretty young officer four months ago.

'*Is that all it was? It seems more like two years since Gold Division was doing routine training, back when we thought the pols and diplomats were still on top of things. Before the final crisis and war came. Before that bunco black op the bâtard locusts pulled on Bad Camberg to set up their aggression.*'

He remembers that he thought she had eyes to die for. And what she smelled like before the war began, before the fighting and killing, before their unwashed trekking over Northland. Before he saw her use a sleek combat knife to slit a boy's throat. She smelled back then like wanton sex, all musty and warm and wet. A faint odor of woman's musk arose even from the hidden curves of her clean, tight uniform. Strong, earthy, warm, deeply inviting. No military starch or regs stopped it reaching out to his senses. Not even those regs that said no one in uniform could wear perfumes or jewelry. She never did. She didn't have to. No damn regs could suppress the natural perfumes or allure of her taut body. She knew it, too.

The first time he saw her off duty and not in her lieutenant's uniform was at a dance in the dumpy Officer's Club just off base. He went there that night looking to get loaded. The OC had the best bar in town, and it was considered OK to drink to get drunk there since it was off base. He didn't go to dance or for anyone's or any woman's damn company. He was pissed off that night about something that typically, he can no longer remember. He was pissed off a lot. He wasn't looking for female company or coitus. Certainly not with one of his officers. Especially, he wasn't looking for *her*, for he knew even back then that Zofia Jablonski was a terrible, dark and smoky danger to him. If he touched her event horizon he would be forever lost inside her, fall into her eyes forever and a day, never to return. So he held back, not knowing or daring to reach out to her singularity.

None of the other women in the Officer's Club interested him. '*They all look like experts on the ceilings of rich men's bedrooms*.' The disdainful and unfair thought occurred to him as he surveyed the dance floor, casually checking out each woman in turn. Undressing, imagining, and rejecting each in turn. Although he told himself that he didn't go there for that. Sure, he would sleep even with women he disdained from time to time. But he never went looking for the other thing, the vital flame that burned him so badly when he was a student on Aral that he failed out of the Academy, returned to Genève in disgrace to face a worried mother and permanently disappointed father.

Until he saw Zofia in a red dress.

She held him in a forever gaze.

She enthralled him with her presence.

She stopped his breath inside his throat.

Somehow they ended up drinking over soft talk. Until she left his side, invited to dance by a young officer who couldn't stop gawping at her breasts. While she spun around on the dance floor in another man's arms their eyes met. It was like watching the beacon of a lighthouse as she swirled, the light of her eyes circling ever back to him, calling him to safety onshore. Then her look became a prairie fire leaping over the grasslands of the room, robbing him of air and will and power and resistance, until he found himself standing tall beside her once again. He could never remember how he got there, with no words to say as he stared into emerald eyes that throbbed with physical longing as they looked straight up at him, liquid and green as a surging sea tide. He felt dizzy, unsure if he was on land or on water.

That night she wore a coy perfume atop her native musk that smelled of amber and gentle dogwood, amplifying her own unaided musty scent, teasing him with erotica both natural and assisted by the best seducers civilian chemistry provided. It intoxicated him. It aroused him. He breathed in her scent, deep and rhythmical, leaning down and in toward her as they whispered to each other about nothing at all, oblivious to all others in the noisy room. He never wanted the moment to end.

But it did. Inept as always, he watched her move away on the arm of another man, a senior officer with ridiculous gray swatches arcing back from each temple into jet black, too virile hair. Jan sulked as he watched her sway on the dance floor in that thigh high, slit red dress and black, high heeled evening shoes, tiny blue ice diamond earrings culled from a gem comet sparkling as they caught the light of the room and her laughing eyes. She twirled in the older man's strong arms as lightly as fresh froth atop a tropical surf. She knew that she was the most beautiful woman there. She saw him drowning in her, from across the room. For Jan, from that moment Zofia became the most wondrous and unreachable thing in all the Universe. And he also to her, though he never knew it or could think or believe it.

She looked coyly back as she dipped low, and caught his gaze brooding on a matching blue ice diamond pendant sparkling in the V-curve of her half-naked breasts. She looked to him like the Milky Way, gossamer and sparkling on a warm summer's eve. She stole his breath again with every twist and swirl, made him feel flushed and fifteen and all fumbly inside, yet also hard with a grown man's arrested desire. She saw that, too. And laughed. Later, out in the field at the MDL and since then on the march, he often thinks of her wearing that low cut red dress, twirling like a madding dervish into his open arms as she never did on that far off night when he missed his one and only chance to cross the dance floor and kiss her. Now, sitting in the woods after another killing of hapless prisoners, he knows that she's right. The time for red dresses and lovemaking is passed, as is the time for mercy. The time of iron is come, to them all. And upon him, most of all.

For the Wolf is on Genève, his sharp incisors running wet with gore and grief. He pads behind Madjenik through the deep floored woods, drooling with red want from his gaping maw. He has no love in him. He's empty of all but raw, red rage. He pants and hungers for more death as he circles around Madjenik, restless and sleepless under sheet camo in its daytime camp. He pads outside the Toruń berm, clawing at the sloped wall, eager to get inside. Red eyed, he never sleeps. He circles the wooden city, sniffling and digging with steel claws, looking for a way to get inside. But the way is barred. No one and nothing can enter Toruń.

Data search: terraforming
Result: nanobots, Purity
Historia Humana, Volume II, Part IV (b)

Most early terraforming projects failed, but 12% were successful. Enough to reshape over 1,100 transiently habitable planets to our will and in our image. The first brave new world remade by our godlike genius, by direct artifice and our AI bot's skill and patience, was a midsized Class A in the habitable zone of a nearby K-range orange star. It was called Terra Nova back in Sol system, but renamed Rodinia by its settlers. Today it is a quiet, thriving member of the Calmar Union...

Terraforming began from the floating biosphere of open sky, as soon as the DNA arks arrived. Microbial rain was initially seeded from low orbiting pods, leading to accelerated reproduction of anaerobic bacteria in air, soils, lakes, and oceans. With the biocarpet laid, the first furnishings were reengineered Old Earth keystone species: algaes, planktons, mosses, corals, simple plants, hardy grasses. A uniquely helpful addition were echidnas, short-beaked spiny monotremes that greatly accelerated bioturbation with their endless digging, mixing nutrients and species diversity in soils they disturbed in great volume. AI nanobots, inevitably dubbed 'nanny bots,' nurtured and managed all ecosystem development. They modified genes where necessary to produce plant or animal features specially adapted to unique exoplanetary conditions, such as lower or higher temperature or gravity than the Old Earth Standard (OES). That gave all the new worlds we inherited and inhabit today greater coloration and biodiversity, though confined to a standard range arising from DNA limits even with modified alien splicing.

On some worlds, nanobots added varied generations of flowering plants and supporting insects. Advanced animals included worms, grubs, aphids, ants, and other ground dwelling insects and their specialized predators. Small birds were added as conditions permitted and insect control demanded. Next came modified shrubs, long grasses and flowering fruit trees, working up to full land-and-sea forest ecosystems in colors that ranged across the visible spectrum. Land ecology saw interrelated additions of rodents, snakes, larger birds, feral cats, and other smaller predators closely matched to prey species.

When the first settlers finally stepped onto the new worlds they breathed in cleaned air brushing over lakes and inland seas green or orange or blue with aerobic algaes and plants. Fresh turned dirt of first gardens smelled like home, for it was filled with familiar humus made of generations of molds, ferns, mosses, grasses and shrubs from Old Earth. Soils were saturated with beneficial bacteria, aerated by trillions of worms and ants and grubs. In the air buzzed common insects, pollinating hosts of flowered species. More and more flora and fauna were introduced with each passing year and decade after first settlement. Skies filled with song birds and continents overgrew with the first green shoots of what became vast savannas or temperate or tropical forests. Except on lucky Genève, where great golden woods were already planted by AI bots of singular aesthetic imagination, roamed by varied strata of higher fauna.

Today many of the Thousand Worlds boast vivid oceans and freshwater lakes abundant with OE species: planktons, corals, fish and sharks, crustaceans and amphibians. River systems, long sterile or more recently sterilized of primitive native life forms, became homes to red or blue frogs, golden salamanders and bright green gators. On favored planets, AI bots dipped into data banks that led them to the highest fauna, usually on large islands or small detached continents. Vast herds of herbivores thrive there now: gazelle, impala, water buffalo, bullock with pendulous dewlaps and overlarge pizzles, migratory reindeer, forest elk, moose and bison, and restored herds of eohippus. Also their native predators: lions, panthers, tigers, coyotes and roving packs of wolves. Slower big breeders fill our savannahs and tundra plains: African and Asian elephants and two pygmy species of pachyderm, as well as revived great and lesser wooly mammoths and other prehistoric reclamations long tried and successful on Old Earth.

It is often said that "God made the Cosmos, but nanny bots made the Thousand Worlds." Of these, all agree that their masterpiece was Amasia. The exceptional range of bioseeding on its oceans and the supercontinent Lemuria was the most complete and successful transfer of OE genes. Amazonian and arctic ecosystems flourish there, alongside vast deserts, savannah and tundra, deep forest zones, fragile alpine meadows, even a very large marsupial enclave rife with bandicoot, quoll, kangaroos and tree possums. Amasia hosts many tens of thousands of specialized microbial, insect, fish and bird species found no place else in Orion, not even on Old Earth. Amasia is a shared treasure of all Humanity. Orion's genome vault. A great DNA reserve bank of and for us all.

Humanity is content with its history of terraforming, universally agreed as the most impressive achievement in all the histories of the Thousand Worlds. Or most of us were, until a few decades ago. Now there are dissenters from our history. They are mostly Grünen and ecoreligious in inspiration, with very few adherents outside the old Imperium. The movement has a pseudo intellectual wing known as 'biopolitical science' by the Grün intellectuals who founded it, but more often as 'Purity' among commonfolk, who embrace it almost like a new mass religion.

It argues that Orion's imported ecosystems are not wondrous but corrupted, pale copies of the pure OE form. It says that we must return to a restored OE genome, and that the Imperium will lead the way on this enlightened path to the past. Some analysts say that this idea is gaining dangerous influence among key Imperium elites and power bases, notably within the Special Action Commando and across parts of the Jade Court of Imperator Pyotr III. Others refuse to believe that an idea so clearly preposterous and antimodern in origin and outlook could move decisions in council chambers of one of the great star empires of Orion; that 'Purity' is only a matter of court posing and fashion. That it is an intellectual fetish of the passing moment, not a concern for the rest of Orion.

A few suspect a more sinister explanation, that Purity is a cover story for traditional Grün aggression. That it has a core purpose of readying the masses of the Imperium to return to war, by giving them a new crusading idea to replace the defeated Black Faith of the old Broderbund. This is not a widely shared view among the major intelligence services of the western star states. They assure us that the Satya Yuga holds, that the gilded peace of the Shōwa Age still rules. That is inconceivable that a major civilization like the Imperium could ever be taken over by so transparently false a doctrine, or its elites would again resort to war.

Forest

For two more weeks the Wreckers hit noisy Rikugun pursuers and patrols hard and often and brutally, as both pursued and pursuers move roughly south-by-southwest in jagged bounds. Jan orders all dead Rikugun stripped naked and strung over tall root loops as a warning against further pursuit. They're fed upon by scavenger animals and hordes of insects. Some are gnawed raw by gray bears.

It works. Patrols stop coming into Pilsudski as more officers flatly refuse to lead their commands too deeply into the forest. Instead, they stop after penetrating no more than three or four klics, waiting for a few hours before turning back. One aggressive major tries to go further, but his men conduct a sitting strike, feigning injuries and exhaustion. When he threatens them with severe punishment they put their hands atop trigger guards in an implied threat of mutiny. He agrees to return to base camp. Then he puts in for a transfer to another division.

The souring mood forces 10th Armored's tactical staff to lie to Brusilov, as well as to a horde of RSU intelligence officers back at Main HQ. They report to their angry general and to RSU that only a handful of bandits are still alive.

"We got 'em all, *taishō*. All the bandits."

"All of them?"

"All but a few scattered stragglers. They're starving and alone in there. They pose no threat to *anything* we want to do on Genève. The coming winter will kill the very last ones off. You won, general."

But even the last reported stragglers are wanted dead or alive by the enraged *taishō*. Maybe even more by a civilian memex on the homeworlds that's hungry for better lies to be told about the war. "I want *them*, too, do you understand? No waiting for winter. Go in there and bring them out."

Brusilov insists on daily briefings about his coverage on the civilian memexes. He seems more concerned with the public than the tactical advice delivered by his staff. So the briefer makes a quick adjustment: "We can send in swarms of HK drones to hunt them down. The rest will then come out, to resupply or to surrender. We'll scoop them up at the forest edge as they emerge, like fish in your net."

"What of this so called Ghost? I want the specter's head. Bring it to me on a silver dinner plate, so that I may gift it to my cousin Pyotr."

"That'll be harder, sir. Maybe impossible."

"Why?"

"Our reports confirm that he's dead, evaporated by one of our big spandaus. Nothing left of him to bring to you, *taishō*. Not even a jawbone."

"A pity. But just so he's a real ghost at last!" Brusilov laughs, thinking that he's a wit. It almost works, too. He briefly backs off more aggressive tactics and tells RIK Main HQ on the coast that he's won the fight for the lower forest. He makes it sound like he's a world conqueror, especially in memex interviews. The ruse lasts until Jan and Zofia come out to set up night hit-and-run raids to kill his troopers where they camp, outside the forest edge.

They drop his pickets dead where they stand, catch them in infrared scopes by snipers who kill with focused ultrasound, raising brain pressure until membranes simply burst apart. Surprised by stealthy death, the dead pickets have eyes with astonished, bulging looks. They're cursed and kicked by other Grünen, for letting bandit infiltrators pass them to reach the camp interior. Wreckers creep catlike into field huts pitched too close to the woodland line, cutting any sleeper's carotid that wants slicing. Sleepers take care too little, and so are quickly slain. After, the slain care not at all as they sleep forever. Wrecker squads set up boobytraps for drunk and late returning bunk mates, men staggering back from RIK portable vid brothels and the gin stills. They leave them all in spreading ruby pools, then pad silently back under leafy cover. Moving like panthers on paths they know best.

One raid carries off four enemy 'suspends,' lightly wounded and 'frozen' RIK waiting on med evac. They awake under stimulants back to the pain of unfrozen wounds stinking of pus and pain and smart gauze, then move right into quick and brutal interrogations. After that they're quickly knifed. Killing all prisoners is now SOP in Wysocki's Wreckers. Before Jan orders the murder of the last prisoner in Pilsudski, the badly beaten yet defiant officer says that Toruń will be surrounded by ground forces and fall under daily attack by Rikugun arti and Jabos. Good news and bad. It means that Toruń still holds out, but that there's likely no way in.

'*Where else to go? All of Genève is under occupation. It's Toruń or no place. Toruń or death.*' Jan means to link with the last standing garrison, and not just to save Madjenik. He wants almost more to spare himself. Each night he dreams: '*A superior officer will relieve me of this burden, take over command of the company, knowing that I'm not fit. They'll let me fight but not insist that I am in command.'*

He always wakes to find himself inside a dark forest surrounded by desperate young fighters looking to him, and to him alone, as guide and savior. It worries him sorely. He thinks all fighters under his command must perish, that only the timing of his next error evades foresight. The old lines from the sweetgrass march, increasingly garbled from when he learned them in far distant school days, stride back into his thoughts. They filter through his doubt, pain and fatigue:

All of my fighters know
Their captain has blundered.
Ghosts follow me like a sigh,
all those whom I left to die.
I'll soon kill all four hundred.

He pushes the thought away, bending to his task, misleading RIK pursuers as to where Madjenik is headed. His voice is calm in command, deeper and leavened with a tactical confidence he displays always, but doesn't always feel. He doesn't understand that his self-doubt is redoubling his quality as an officer, forcing him to check and correct every decision he makes without causing him to fall into command paralysis. Only Zofia sees it. But they're not talking anymore. At least, not outside shared command responsibilities to preserve Madjenik.

"Lieutenant Jablonski, send four two-scout units south, then southeast. Tell them to make sure they're followed and to make it look like we're heading for the south coast river delta. They should leave small, but not too small, tracking clues behind in hasty camp sites. Pick our best, most skilled woodsfolk for this job."

"Yes sir. They'll leave two hours before dawn, one hour before we move out and turn north-by-northwest. How long do they go out?"

"Five days, no more. Then they're to double back the long way around. They are few and we are many. They'll catch us up in time."

"Yes sir. Should I lead them?"

"No. You're needed here, lieutenant. Send out Corporal Hipper. He's all hard for a command of his own, and to get away for a bit from Pie Girl. Let's see what he can do out there."

Jan orders a last feint to the southeast, then doubles back in a wide westward loop before turning the main body of the company silently north-by-northwest. Tom Hipper's little first command moves the other way. Noisy as a wounded bear.

Tom leaps to the job of deceit, and he's good at it. Every few klics the small diversion group leaves careful bits of carelessly dropped rubbish: tears of ration foil, a broken hardtack biscuit, burned out pink crystals, an empty water bottle. It makes gashes in the roots that rise in arching loops three times higher than the tallest man. It leaves odd rifle gouges at shoulder height in tree trunks five or so klics apart. It disturbs deep leaf fall on the shores of silver pine lakes, impressing dozens of knee marks in the mud so that it looks like a hundred men collected water there. It makes subtle paths, but not too subtle, in grayed teak windfall that litters the deep forest floor where it has lain soft and unmoved for centuries. Forest creatures watch and wonder at the noisy bear's passing, then hide from hundreds of lumbering RIK pursuers who are never more than an hour or two behind.

The deceivers are native to Genève and so are raised to woodcraft, unlike the crashing, grunting RIK pursuit. Before the scouts circle back to rejoin Madjenik far to the northwest, they go quiet. They leave behind a whole backpack worth of tiny crawler bots and recce tree snakes. The decoys scatter in all directions, giving off false locator beeps and blips. The split up bots lead inept pursuers even farther southeast, before finally going dark and still. RSU is left utterly baffled.

The main body of Madjenik moves more like a single squad, with woodcraft of a quality only native Genèvens can pull off. Raised to it from childhood. Raised to respect and familiarity with the old growth woods. They turn off and baffle all electronics, leave no fresh marks or green gouges, make no impression in deep windfall or new leaves, hide their shadows in the shade. Once Jan is certain the ground pursuit has been blunted by his ambushes and quick strikes, then gone off chasing Tom Hipper's ursine deceits in several wrong directions all at once, it's a straight trek for the Wreckers through the ancient forests. Northwest to the Toruń berm, to a great and golden city of wood under a fiery siege. Will it still be there?

Wary, scared, cautious Rikugun trackers delay for several critical days before reporting to 10th Armored HQ that they just can't say where or when Madjenik is. Nor can befuddled RSU officers explain the escape to an enraged Brusilov.

"The bandit trail has disappeared, *taishō*."

"What? Impossible!"

"The bandits are gone sir. We looked everywhere."

"I want all officers who led the southeast search arrested! Today! Do you hear me? I want them in irons by sunset! The incompetent fools!"

"It will be done, *taishō*."

"Then burn it!"

"Sir?"

"Burn the forest. All of it, if you have to. I want those bandits dead."

***

The only creatures who see reunited Madjenik move are forest foxes who sit still and hidden in balls of golden fur, blending into thick leaf fall. Or a lone kestrel hovering over a small pine clearing by day to spot a careless mouse who dares leave ground cover. Or small owls with big round eyes like infrared searchlights that pierce the blackest night to track prey moving quickly among the windfall.

At the feet of gentle hills Madjenik avoids all small ponds and lakes. It stays away from the still water, not wanting to leave footfalls in thick guano beside tiny inland shores. But it can't help startling nervous loons whose long, plaintive calls hang in cooling summer air like air raid warnings. That worries Jan, who fears that a listening drone far overhead will notice and vector down. Finally, hanging calls of unquiet loons settle hauntingly behind the walkers as they move on and deeper into the woods. Under ever older oak and teak canopy, slyly sliding north.

Little owls screech down from dark trees at night, angry at a clumsy movement below that keeps mice and other small rodents too scared to come out where they might hunt them. Fighters hear animals scooting overhead along high branches or burrowing under huge roots that rise like arches above the forest floor. They don't know what the creatures are, unable to be sure what's moving in canopy even with night vision, so careful is the timid fauna to keep distance from a troop of humans moving through long forbidden, undisturbed, ancient woods. For most of the deep woodland creatures, these are the first humans they've ever seen.

Sometimes troopers do see the noisemaker, coming upon a startled black bear or a small herd of forest elk or a family of small red deer. Then deterrent roars or braying trumpets of fright rise up, crashing sounds of mortal fear and flight that tear apart the deep stillness of the thick woods until the terrified animals get away, always protecting their precious young the way humans in Orion have forgotten to do. Instead, hurling them in tens of millions into danger, death and war.

Madjenik walks under a cathedral canopy of engineered gold oaks and teaks, birch and maple, and mightiest of all, towering redwoods. They move soundlessly across a spongy floor meters thick with undisturbed leaf and branch fall from a thousand autumns. The old windfall smells of new mold and long centuries past, since lost to time and seasonal repetition, to the eternal rhythm of the woods. For Madjenik is in the deepest forest on Genève, and even in all Orion, growth no cutter or tourist saw in more than ten centuries. Only a lonely warden or two ever comes this way, every few decades. Approves, admires, and passes on.

***

Then it all changes. Officially, the swarm of strike bombers that arrives over the southern forests is there to give 10th Armored tactical support, with orders to make precision attacks following "reliable sightings of bandit movement." Main HQ even tries to restrict General Brusilov's use of incendiaries. His orders are: "*Exercise great care not to damage valued export property of the Imperium. After each precision strike is made, Jabos must drop fire retardants on affected areas. Fire containment is priority outside approved target areas. Confirm.*"

Off-the-record, pilots are given verbal orders by the humiliated and furious *taishō* of 10th Armored, enraged to learn of the Ghost's escape. For he has heard fresh rumors that the man is not dead, whoever he is. He almost screams the new orders to the pilots, in a private briefing. "Set the forest ablaze, north to south. Burn it *all* down if you have to. I don't care what Fourth Army HQ told you or what it costs my cousin in lost lumber. Fucking trees! Burn them all if you must, but kill everyone in there! Roast every rat bandit alive! Kill the Ghost! No more excuses! No more limits! As an Oetkert prince and *taishō*, I order you to do this."

Madjenik barely stays ahead of the falling fires that enraged Brusilov sets to chase them. Jabos are dropping incendiaries at random to literally smoke any last Wreckers out. Skycraft and pilots divert from bombing the Toruń berm perimeter. Most pilots are quite happy to leave a combat zone over a city where they meet deadly *streak* missiles and heavy anti-skycraft fire. "Archie" is what they call it.

"Shit, it's a lot easier bombing trees!"

"Yeah, they don't shoot back."

"Look at that forest burn!"

"The whole area is glowing orange as far as the eye can see, even this far up."

"Beautiful, isn't it? And surely nothing can live in *that?*"

The forest bombing mission is far more to their liking than the ongoing fight in the sky over Toruń. It's closer to the original "Happy Time," as pilots call their great plains campaign when Jabos and Raptors strafed targets, unmolested across the prairie. When they dove at will, ripping up the long columns of woe, pounding retreating KRA and refugees who scattered like ants but couldn't get away.

"Taxi war. Lining up to wait to take turns strafing slow ground targets."

"Still fun to pull the trigger over these trees, to feel pulse cannon pound the airframe when you fire."

"Well, you bet! No better feeling outside a Kestino whorehouse."

"You mean outside your sister's bedroom."

"Shut the fuck up Kat! I'll pay you back for that when we land at base."

"Shut up, of all of you." It's the bomber group commander. "Stay on target, drop incendiaries, fire six pulse rounds, then go back to reload all racks." He's not really angry at his pilots. This mission *is* too easy.

Almost as easy as the "Second Happy Time" that lies just ahead, when Jabos will make unopposed strafing runs along five Old Forest Roads where there's no archie at all, to roast the endless civilian columns trying to flee to Toruń. Madjenik doesn't know about the Old Forest Roads. It's not far enough north yet to know. Not far enough north or ahead in time to yet smell the vast ash and death zone that will soon replace the ancient woods. Madjenik is still in the deep south, inside the preserved, roadless oldest forests farthest from Toruń. They're now on fire, too.

The first night of the fire bombing, 130 Wreckers are trapped inside a towering ring of intense flame and heat, unable to strike back at an incorporeal enemy. Or hurt its sinister master, wreathed in flames of hubris, laughing at their dilemma of an impassible barrier of fire he has set all around. They prepare to die, praying to old gods or new ones, calling back to mind parents or lovers or children, all while huddling in a compact circle of primal fear. Some turn trigger locks off, holding their armed and *humming* masers to their temples. Or clutch frag grenades to their chests, ready to end themselves and each other before a flame wind reaches in to lick them insane with pain beyond imagination.

An hour passes as the canopy turns from dark living green to screaming red. Scorched and hairless, angry trees stand groaning and smoking all around. Then the sky clears and the lost platoons are saved. By sheer bloody and unadulterated luck, a gusty wind has carried the high blaze skipping over the vaulted roof of the great forest without ever clambering down to braise cowering platoons hunching fetally on its carpeted floor. Zofia is right in the middle of it, driving Jan mad with helpless worry. She laughs as she steps out, dubbing it "the fickle fortune of war."

Fickle and fortunate, yes. But not for everyone. Five men die screaming in a secondary fire, beyond any reach or hope or help. After that, Jan breaks Madjenik into smaller march groups, fearing to lose the whole company in a single unlucky blaze. Smaller groups can also move more quickly across the forest floor, darting from burn patch to burn patch, reasoning that Jabos will not burn the same trees twice. Always, the movement is north-by-northwest, heading to Toruń.

***

Curls of billowing smoke from the fires are welcome in a different way. They conceal Madjenik from thousands of mini drones curving and flying above the canopy, where the smoke clings like cotton bolls still hanging on the stems. The intense heat confuses thermal drones and scorches e-sniffers mounted on crawling or slithering bots. Madjenik is undetectable. Protected by the surviving canopy from any visual observation, hidden by smoldering fires from infrared, concealed from normal movement and e-surveillance by captured RIK equipment and codes.

It was easy for a company tek wizard to reverse pilfered detectors so that they jam all RIK search channels instead of assisting them. But where did Madjenik get RIK *huff duff* gear? Zofia took it from a Grün engineering squad her platoon blundered into just one klic shy of Pilsudski Wood on the first day, as they reached and probed the forest edge. That was way back when, as she scouted ahead of the main body of the company. The reversed *huff duff* has helped keep them hidden and alive ever since. They probably would have been found by now without it.

The skirmish with the engineers took place four mornings after the sweetgrass ambush of the "Double Moons." That's what Madjenik's veterans call the dead conscripts from Uri with twin moon flashes, the ones they assaulted from a wet orchard ditch, attacking with suicide *snakes*, short masers and mortars. Madjenik means it more cruelly, knowing that it left 100+ boys in a gore soaked meadow grinning not just out of dead mouths but also smiling from crescent throats.

Some thirty-odd RIK Skyforce engineers were taking a break from setting up a tac station for circling Jabos and Raptors, most of which were high above the northern plain or shooting civvies heading to the five forest roads. They stood in a confident group. Talking, eating, lounging overlong in the shade of three idling acoustic hovers. They were cocky and content, eating cold sandwiches with mugs of hot field coffee when Zofia spotted them. She instantly ordered her squad to low crawl into a semicircle ambush position.

"Kinda odd we're setting up way out here, along the southern forests. Ain't no real targets worth bombing that I can tell."

"That's OK with me," says a second engineer. "Just means we're also too far away from the fighting front to be targets for any KRA fuckers, either."

"You're right. So let's lose these damn useless helmets. It's way too hot under this too blue sky." His homeworld's sky is pink. Blue seems very odd to him.

Dropped helmets and HUDs, leaning stub masers with safeties on, and a dozen shiny foil sandwich wrappers carelessly littering the torn ground around the ATC hovers. All of it glinting white under a bright sun, like freshwater fish flashing in a shallow stream as they come up for dragonflies dipping too close to the surface. The engineers were way too confident in themselves and even more in their detect gear, especially the thermal camogel suits they were quite sure must hide them from all Krevan HUDs. It never occurred to them that they could be under direct eyes contact and observation. Besides, they were certain there were no KRA left who weren't dead, captured, or running scared inside the woods.

So it was a short fight, pretty much onesided as Zofia gave the *shoot!* order via HUD platoon relay to Madjenik troopers who silently low crawled to within 50 meters of their over bunched targets. In thirty seconds of mayhem 14 engineers lay dead, or scorched inside-and-out and dying hard. Zofia stood up and advanced alone into the smoking work site. She spent a minute observing the dead and dying enemy then hand signaled *come* to the scout platoon, with a circling left arm raised over her head. The whole platoon was around her in an instant. Half pointed their weapons outward in a compact perimeter defense, the rest waited on fresh orders.

"Burn the ATCs. But only after the rest of Madjenik gets here. Get 'em ready to burn, with delay action incendiaries. But hold off firing until we're all away or you get further orders from me or the captain."

"Yes sir. Prep for burning, but hold for additional orders."

Six fighters forming First Squad in this compact half-platoon readied the too biggest, most ungainly ATCs for destruction. They were directed by the kind black sergeant who pitied the severed half-boy at the meadow, thinking of his own young son now lost to his knowledge somewhere on occupied Genève.

"Spare the bikes. We can use those. And get those three cargo bots humming," Zofia ordered. "Load all *huff duff* onto one, ammo and food and potable water on another. Move them into the forest now." Another short squad of fighters hurried to reload the squat cargo carts. "Sergeant, take the hover bikes and two cargo bots with you and scout three klics over the edge of the woods, then set up tonight's camp site and send back a guide to this rally point." It's the burly, apple eating sergeant she gave the order. The shorter, black sergeant and all First Squad were still busy stripping weps off the ATCs and readying the hulks for burning.

"On it. Second Squad: you're now lead scout. Get on those bikes and loaded cargo bots and be ready to move out with me in five minutes!"

Zofia again: "Corporal, empty all RIK shit off that third bot, yeah, the flat one. Shift anything useful to the other two. Send this one back the way we came, to the captain, with the main body. He'll know to use it to carry the most badly wounded. Keep your men here. The bot can go back on its own. Just reset its orders to KRA codes. I'll flash the captain that it's on the way."

"What about the bodies, lieutenant?"

"Stuff 'em into their own ATCs and halftracks and let 'em burn, too."

Troopers started carrying corpses to the waiting cremation pyres. But not all of them. One engineer Zofia found dead, sitting up with a partly eaten sandwich in his mouth. Because the top of his head went missing all in a moment, there was no way for the bit of brain left in the half bowl of his skull to tell his mouth to chew or his legs to run. Zofia ordered him left exactly as he died. Except that she returned a fallen coffee cup to his stiffening dead hand, hooking the handle over his extended thumb. Then she tapped a message into the vidscroll she found in his pocket. It said: "*Catering courtesy of Madjenik Company, KRA*."

The rest of Madjenik moved through the scene some 15 minutes later, grateful wounded packed in gauzy rows atop the flatbed bot, riding for the first time since the sweetgrass meadow fight. More critical equipment that Zofia ordered stacked and left behind was collected and humped under nearby trees, then into the forest.

***

General Brusilov continues to send heavy patrols into the woods, not knowing how few of his combat leaders ever dare to cross the forest's edge anymore. Senior officers probe just a few klics, ordering wildly noisy searches meant to warn off bandits who might be hiding nearby. Then they file false combat reports. Better a lie to HQ than lose one's brigade to the Ghost, and one's life to Brusilov's rage. Finally, an exasperated Lieutenant Colonel, who is certain Madjenik is long gone and doesn't care if it's still somewhere inside the forest, puts in his After Action Report: "*Today's patrol killed bushels of bandits. No more resistance is possible or expected. Mopping up operations commencing. Banditry is crime, punishable by immediate execution, No prisoners anticipated. None will be taken.*"

The *taishō* doesn't believe it. Brusilov wants hard proof of his victory. So the clever colonel recycles refrigerated RIK officer corpses, dressing them in bloody KRA weaves to fool the suspicious general. He thaws them out and sets them up in forest ambush poses, before flying him in to view the faked and staged carnage. The colonel wasn't at Bad Camberg and doesn't know that he squared the circle of deception with the use of KRA uniforms on dead RIK men. If Pyotr ever hears he did it, the man will roast, be revived, and roast again in a Waldstätte dungeon.

Instead, General Nikita Brusilov Shaka Oetkert is satisfied at last. He declares victory in a personal message of self-congratulation and tactical boasting that's hand delivered to HQ, with a copy sent directly to his cousin Pyotr. A third copy is broadcast copiously over the memex. The last Jabos are released to resume their northern missions. Now is when they fire the Old Forest Roads leading to Toruń.

Madjenik puts any pursuit far behind after it fords a shallow, meandering river marking the border between Pilsudski Wood and the Gold Oak Forest, a second vastness of untouched ancient woodland. Three weeks after the ambush of the hover scouts Madjenik is 700 klics away, moving stealthily through roadless oak woods, creeping across the grain of old growth laid out centuries before by AI nanobot bioengineers. Far from the fuming, fumbling, boasting General Brusilov.

As fighters brush past the ancient trees they invariably shake huge wheels of delicate silver threads, giant webs sparkling with tiny droplets of morning dew that tremble with their softest footfalls. Tom Hipper thinks they look like range finders made by the giant, lurking spiders. Jan thinks of them instead as targets, knowing that he's pulling the image out of some forgotten and ancient verse. The swift passing of Madjenik sends the sullen spider architects fleeing, then back to work reinventing fresh web wheels to replace a life's work carelessly destroyed by war's indifferent passing. Ants and flies and midges are more happy to see the thumping human columns pass; they welcome war, if it means destruction of their ancient enemies and masters. They smirk at the angry spiders, and dart past them at daringly close distances. Briefly, the natural order ends in the disturbed forest.

Wreckers see fewer drones and micro hunters, hear fewer circling skycraft as they move. Once, a whole week passes quietly after reconfigured detectors pick up the last faint signals from RIK air bots, and none whatever from ground probes. It's late summer now and stately snow geese honk as they migrate high overhead. These are going south, in less uniform 'Vs' than the faux geese that went north.

The head scout with a keen eye for drones reports in to Jan. "Deys real wons, c'ptain. Deys goin' da right way."

"Very good, lead scout. Now, back on point."

Early whooping cranes, calling out with never ending voices, are also heading south, indifferent to, or at least uninvolved in, the desperate war below. Jan listens to a feathered 'vic' pass *honking* and *hooting* onward, envying white geese and whooping cranes their freedom and the power of flight. *'I wonder if they know something I don't? A thousand klics still to Toruń. I promised to get Madjenik there, and I will. After that, we shall see.'* His mind wanders back to a red dress.

Madjenik has shaken all pursuit but it's completely out of touch, cut off from any coms with military or even civilian higher ups. If any are out there still. All satellites are down and old frequencies carry only dead static. Jan and Zofia and Madjenik don't know if they're the last free Krevans on Genève; whether Toruń holds out or is a smoldering ruin under the Jabos' reign of fire; what became of the rest of Silver and Gold Divisions; if their families are alive or gone forever. They don't even know whether the damn war on Genève or for the other Krevan worlds is lost and over or just beginning.

"Where are we going on today's march, sirs? Will there be more trees when we get there?" It's a cocky question asked during a rest break, but Jan answers it.

"We'll keep moving northwest, heading for Toruń."

"Do you think it's still there, sir?"

"We'll find out what's happening at Toruń and across Genève when we get to the berm that rings the Arbor City. One day at a time 'till then."

"You heard the captain." Zofia interrupts. "On your feet, Madjenik."

***

'*The woods are lovely, dark and deep.*' And they're utterly sick of them. Sick of the verdant dark, thick moisture, strange animal and bird calls, a heavy smell of old vegetative rot beneath their feet and in the stagnant, unmoving air. They hate every leaf and root and sagging golden bough. They'll regret feeling this. They'll want to return to the mighty golden oaks carpeted in a millennia of musty windfall, hear the woodcock's call and finches, smell living wood and leaves and old roots and fresh droppings of kite hawks, tree squirrels, bear and elk. They'll long to walk silent and sad in the leafy, feather pillowed, protected womb of the southern woods. Once they learn what awaits them on the pitiless path ahead.

Data search: lifespan
Result: suspensor
Historia Humana, Volume X, Part V(a)

A key contributor to the Second Age of Exploration and Expansion, epigenetic intervention extended life expectancy as degenerative diseases were eliminated at the DNA source. But the critical jump came from adaptation of military thought-command tek: the quantum dot. Medics adapted a photosensitive silicon flake implant used to link HUDs, to instead treat brain injuries, migrating from radical combat trauma to relief of ordinary epilepsy and other brain disorders in civilian populations. A com dot's databank infuses new information directly into affected and targeted brain tissue, bypassing damaged sites, correcting synaptic misfires, reordering biologic communication failures. Civilian dots eliminated dementia and other brain diseases related to aging, making a long stride toward extending what medical professionals still call "negligible senescence." In sum, quantum dot tek led to a revolution in quality of extended life, an indefinite prolongation of a healthy mind past what our ancestors ever hoped. This period of protracted vigor is popularly known as "Youthspan," a multi decades extension of the period of life that is most alert, active, and desirable.

A historic connection of military research to human longevity is usually noted as ironic but is easily explained. As much as any military wants efficient means to inflict wounds or death on enemies, it wants to save the limbs and lives of its own personnel more. The first step toward "immortality" was this mix of motives and a fortuitous discovery during an OE conflict called the Great War, as an early bio arms race led to poison gases that forced research into antidotes. One poison was a weak, weaponized derivative of hydrogen sulphide (H2S), a foul smelling but naturally occurring gas found in most sulfur pools, decomposition by anaerobic digestion, human and animal emissions and sewage. Researchers concentrating H2S to inflict mass death by aerosol and shell delivery instead noticed that in low doses it had the exact opposite effect, producing reversible metabolic hibernation in lab animals. Low concentrations of H2S, about 50 parts per million in normal room air, increased nematode and mice life spans up to eight times normal.

It was realized that there was more than just superstition in a long history of prescientific humans seeking natural H2S as a cure in sulfur springs and similarly "healthful waters." There was real empirical experience and medical wisdom in worldwide hot spring rites, for hydrogen-sulfide indeed regulates rates at which a human body consumes oxygen. That discovery led to a long search for a H2S catholicon to slow, then to suspend metabolism. A refined, artificial compound was finally made with enzymes from decapod crustaceans, long lived species of remarkably slow senescence. Another key ingredient was artificial resveratrol, found in natural form in red wine.

At sufficient levels, the synthetic H2S-decapod-resveratrol compound, known simply as "suspensor" or "suspend," lowers oxygen burn rate until a heart stops beating, cells cease to die, DNA stops synthesizing, and all bio-movement ceases. All without causing cell or brain death. Suspensor places living creatures into an effective state of living suspension long thought merely fictional and impossible. The final key was an established and simple med technology: hydrogel nanobots. These permitted delivery of suspend solution nearly simultaneously at the micron level, to every cell in an entire body (hence making possible GDM sleeper ships), or to any targeted and damaged body part, say of a soldier wounded in battle. "Freeze and bag 'em' was a military medic's watchword. Repair came later.

Other research advanced basic bioprinting, copying genes from stem cells to make printouts of living tissue on demand: skin, muscle, marrow, even whole joints, bones and organs (except the brain). Bioprinting became cheap, effective, and universally available to the civilian population. Together with suspensor, bioprinting extended average lifespans even of the very poorest citizens until they approached those of the socially privileged. That's when all the trouble started...

Roads

The same day Madjenik attacks the Double Moons in the sweetgrass, 600 klics to the north and 200 farther west a short column of badly shaken and even worse beaten KRA soldiers retreat ahead of the relentless RIK advance. As they draw alongside a simple cottage standing just off the roadway they are met by an old woman in a blue checkered headscarf.

"The locusts are back the other way!" she accuses. "Where are you going? Running, are you? And you wear the golden sheaves? Shame! Shame on you! If I was still in Gold you'd not see *me* running away! What cowards you all are!"

They know it's her fear that hurls hurtful words at them, her mortal fright over sheer helplessness and their abandoning her to the oncoming swarm. They resent her anyway. "Say it to all my dead friends, mother!"

It's a too stocky private, shouting as he suddenly breaks ranks and turns back toward the old woman. He steps menacingly at her, with red faced threat. Until his weary corporal orders him back into line. Unable to take her with them, the battered remnants of 2nd Battalion, Genève Gold Division, tread silently past her remarkably tidy little cottage. They are not the first, but they are the last retreating troops to do so. Their shoulders droop, their faces are dour with foreknowledge that Rikugun following close behind will surely burn the little cottage down.

The old woman knows it, too. She sobs as she tosses small stones after the passing troops, loose ends of her checkered headscarf flapping in a gust of wind, the slack of her ancient breasts sagging as her shift opens when she stoops to grope for more stones. They ignore her, too proud and too ashamed to object to this last indignity, shifting their heavy gear and shuffling onward. A few pebbles clatter harmlessly on the cobbled lane behind them. Then the last soldiers are gone.

***

Groups of discombobulated fighters from Gold Division retreat across the plains, avoiding roads wherever that's possible, speeding along them whenever they can. Everywhere along the byways there are burning hulks of abandoned military hovers and acoustic ATCs that prove too vulnerable to use as transports, with RIK Tactical Skyforce flying over from bases on the austral continent.

"Some traitor must have given our camo codes to RIK, or they couldn't have picked us off like that, so easily." It's a bitterly angry Special Branch officer, limping down a back road a day after his intel unit was shattered by a diving Jabo.

"Not traitors, not in the KRA. It was all the damn politicians. They did nothing to prepare for this." She's the sole survivor of a company smashed at the MDL.

"How could anyone prepare us to face the mighty Grün Imperium?" He's an older veteran. "How do you prepare for *this*? How could we ever hope to defend Genève from *them*?"

"That's defeatist talk!" He's a very young soldier, screaming red faced at the others. "I'll report you when we get to Toruń!" No one pays the beardless lad any mind. Most of them don't think they'll ever see Toruń again. Most others are too stunned to have opinions. They only have stories, of fleeing villages, of strafings on country roads, of dead friends or family, ruined lives and hearths and homes.

"They came from the air. They flew, we ran. They bombed, we died." He says it in a whisper, head bent low, a rare survivor of Silver Division who made it all the way over the water from Southland. Only to be bombed again, beaten again, and have to run all over again once the Northland MDL collapsed.

A young woman says out loud, though mostly to herself: "The awful smell ... burning hovers, roasting flesh. Everywhere the sweet, sickly smell of day old death." She has a vacant look in her eyes. So do many in the forlorn crowds that file ever westward, away from the guns behind.

A few stragglers get away on rugged carbon fiber motorbikes, the untippable type with multiple gyros that stay upright at high speeds, around hard corners.

Or bouncing offroad over rough fields.

Or down a mid channel of a gravely creek.

Or along the sloppy banks of a cold and fast river.

Or zagging like wounded rabbits in a forest.

Some units form ad hoc defense rings after the breakthroughs of the first week of fighting on Northland, setting up weak pockets of resistance to hold up RIK ground attacks for a little while, here and there. Men and women fight to the last, empty crystal chargers fighting at the old ultrasteel forts of the Third Orion War;

are overrun at the end of the day, shot down where they stand with cold, empty masers. Or they stand alone or in small groups against a stone wall to be executed.

"Long live Krevo!"

"*Vive la Genève!*"

"Firing squad, in volley … *fire!*"

Click clack, click clack, click clack.

Sizzle.

Slump.

Silence.

The rest move haltingly, like the unkempt survivors of 2nd Battalion passing the old woman's doomed cottage. Jerkily heading northwest toward hoped for shelter inside the great forests that rise to meet the high mountains. Pushed by enormous violence hither and yon more at the whim of enemy commanders than with purpose by their own officers, most of whom are dead or missing. A handful of refugees move southeast, soldiers and civilians looking to hole up in brackish marshes and swamps of the Toruń River delta. Delaying the inevitable, at best.

North or south, it doesn't really matter. All oakish fighters want to live another hour or to fight another day, but no one thinks on victory. They know the KRA is a beaten army, pursued by hard youths in pale green for whom the war is still fun. Who fire merry masers to burn down farms and cut down farmers' sons. Kill their daughters, too, as if they are only shooting water guns in a child's backyard or in a town fair game. Then they scythe the fruity tops off orchards with hot spandaus.

Bigger columns of retreating KRA break up, smashed and harried by diving Jabos who strafe and bomb everything that moves on the northern plain. Any who survive sky attacks to make the great trek inland from the coast do so because they move alone or in pairs or small groups, or are widely spread out. Concentration at even battalion level brings down massive long range missile or arti bombardment, and skyfall fire from diving Jabos. And real hot ground pursuit, right behind.

Only the lucky or skilled, and not all of them, infiltrate a bushy copse in groups of three or five or ten, hide in muck up to their necks in a thick and sloppy slough before sliding a few more klics north, hiding and slipping away again tomorrow. They're hunted by tens of thousands of mini drones with full spectrum detection gear. They lie under superceramic fiber screens and other adaptive camo, standard issue gossamer sheets doubling as thermal insulation blankets. It's just enough to conceal electromagnetic signatures and body heat and movement from ground patrols, mini drones, insect-like micro hunters, and the ever circling Jabos.

Swallows wheel overhead, flying overtop the fray and slaughter, seemingly singing dirges to the dead below. Thinking themselves more noble and pridefully poetic than these dire ways of men. They fly slow and low over the panic, above all the parched pain of wounded too hurt to walk or crawl, abandoned by unhurt men now too tired to carry their stretchers any farther. The songful swallows avoid the longest trails of fresh made corpses, undeceived of all cares by a maser shot or spandau ball of *blue* electric fire. They leave those carrion trails for white tailed eagles who circle in pairs, and murders of black ravens that *caw caw* with delight at the unexpected harvest of dead flesh. The swallows sing instead, even into the silence that settles everywhere once the armies pass by. Not so the carrion eaters. They swoop down to tear with beaks and talons at the unbidden larder that war always lays out in fresh abundance for such creatures as them. The raven's portion is neither victory nor defeat. He feasts indifferently, and alike, on dead meat and offal that spills from open wrappings, whether they be green or oak in color.

***

A tight drum tattoo *rat-at-tat-tats* in the prairie distance. Do you hear it? Now a heavier drumbeat sounds, *thumping* on the hard summer soil. It's the sound of marching columns of death's battalions, of Rikugun's divisions and corps. *Listen!* Do you hear ten times a hundred thousand black boots stomping and tramping on the tarmac roads in unison? What's that? *Ahh*, rough martial songs sung coarsely into a summer wind! March ballads from the last war. Bold songs of old victories and past glories. Bliss it is in this summer of war to be still alive. But to be young and wear the victory green of Rikugun? Why it's very heaven!

Underneath the fateful tromping in the distance there again rises that lighter sound, a tinny parade *rat-at-tat-tat* of a snare drum here, another one beating over there, tapping out time for the green clad marchers of destiny, of Purity's sacred army and of Pyotr's pettiest vanity. Luring them into war, the *"drum's discordant sound,"* the same that lured so many generations down four score of centuries.

Nitōhei Lars Knut is keeping perfect time. As he does, he recalls an ancient warning dully learned at school but understood fully for the first time only now, as the brand new volunteer RIK private marches over Genève's scorched fields. He and his friends all had two years prewar training, of course. It was mandatory for all Grün males from age 16. Now they finally have the chance to use it, to find real life meaning and transcendent purpose in the greatest adventure of their lives.

His mind wanders back to when he heard the announcement of his and Pyotr's war over the homeworld memex, piped into his classroom just a month before his 18th birthday: "*Hear this, all subjects of Pyotr Shaka III. The Imperium's honor and dignity has being insulted. Our borders have been violated. Foreigners have done murder to our people, on our land. Pyotr knows that you are with him, as he is with you in this dark hour of need. Onward to Victory! Onward to liberate all our Lost Children worlds! Long live the Empire and its Emperor!*"

Lars and every lad in his age cohort cheered and rushed from school, running all the way to the nearest recruiting station. He got there without even his hat, on the proudest day of his life. He has had regrets every day since then. He doesn't know why he's here. He wishes he wasn't. The other boys in pale green marching with him over Northland can hear only the snare drums as they parade to war, and inside war. They're still too virgin not to strut, not to think they cut a fine jib as they keep time with the march drum. They're the discordant proud, the many, the great majority who eagerly embrace Pyotr's war, out on his and Death's anointed rounds. They have no regrets. It's too exciting. They want to be in no other place.

RIK ground vehicles course down cobble streets in empty towns littered with unburied corpses from the last bombing run by Jabos, or swarming drones. They lead charnel columns across hundreds of klics of burned out farmland, destroyed hamlets and butchered villages. Thousands of black smokers rise behind the corps, stretching far back over a golden horizon hidden by haze. The long trails of black smokers are victory spires to the marching columns, marking their advance. To refugees, to survivors running for the forest edge, they are wispy monuments to shattered lives, homey dreams destroyed forever, families scattered and broken.

One RIK officer reporting in to HQ recalls rolling over the northern plain to reach this point, the outer fringe of the forest zone. "It was gruesome. We had to force our halftracks and armtraks through endless rows of corpses. I remember the sound of skulls cracking beneath wheels and the dull *thump* of arms and legs caught in our treads as we rolled on, never stopping. All cohesion in our column was lost as some of our drivers frantically shied, like frightened horses trying to find some other way around the dead."

"What did you do?" His debriefer asks him not from horror but in mild, polite disinterest. He has lots of other *After Action Reports* to fill out and this emotional rubbish just gets in the way. Yet the slow talking man is a *shōsa*, a promotable major gaining his combat badge with a quick tour in the Rikugun before he heads back to Corps or Army HQ, or maybe even as an adjutant with the Great General Staff on Kestino. So the debriefer has to listen for a minute or so, at least.

"I ordered everyone to get off manual drive and back on auto. That way we rolled steady and true right through the burning towns. The crunching of skulls and *thumping* limbs accompanied us everywhere. I don't think I'll ever forget the sound. Sometimes I think I hear it in the falling rain."

"That so? Interesting. I've made a note. See? Right here. Look ... *umm*, well, thank you *shōsa*. I think I have everything I need from you for now. *Sonnō jōi!* And good hunting!"

Hardly a barn or crop or shed stands after the columns pass. Where once spring horses nickered in neat enclosures, red mounds and lumps of exploded hair and horseflesh now lie inert, mare and foal together. Whole fields of unharvested, sun ripened corn burn like paper maché as rows of dry stalks, heavy with ripe bursting, yellow ears, flare up in a flash fire then burn low to the ground for hours.

Abandoned fields left untouched by Rikugun are fired anyway, by stray sparks from passing nailed boots or radiant heat from burning crops and buildings one field over, or two or three. Until all the spreading plain is dead and gray and smells of scorched crops and splayed out corpses. Of burned and primal carbon.

The land layers over with ash fall that looks like dirty snow, covering fields and villages and ruined towns with warm gray blankets. Once sweet country air fills with blown cinders and the smells of burning vegetation and roasting flesh. Flames *crackle* and *snap* hotter and higher wherever melting fat of footloose herds feeds the fires, as deranged gates swing crazily open, hanging from madly bent fences. Human corpses mingle with dead pigs, goats, and silent herds of cattle.

As Madjenik treks over the great eastward bulge of Pilsudski Wood its fighters don't know that five wide rivers of refugees are flowing toward Toruń. The sight is pitiful even amidst all other suffering on Genève and four other burning Krevan worlds. Civilian innocence of combat makes it worse somehow, matching naïve befuddlement to anger, fear and uncertainty. Refugees move singly or in family groups, until caught by stronger currents that carry them to places they don't know because they can't resist. Can't reach a safe or sheltered shore against so powerful a force of nature as war, whose mighty undertow pulls them from their old lives and carries them out to sea to drown. They know not where or why or when or how they go, only that they must. It has all come down to this.

Forty klics beyond the old woman's cottage, now burning on the horizon, an incoherent and floundering cacophony of refugees is trying to squeeze into a gap between towering trees at the start of one of five Old Forest Roads that cut through Toruń Wood to Arbor City. Modified for size, color, growth rate and longevity, the great trees of the famed golden woods of Genève command full luxury prices. Wood carvings by Toruń's craftsmen are specially valued offworld for soft, subtle hues of exposed grains, each artifact injected with an embedded nano flake ID to guarantee authenticity. Export to closed Dauran worlds was stopped decades ago, after the Grim Revolution closed off that largest of Orion polities. But fine flutes and violas and many other wood instruments, aromatic frankincense and delicate carvings, are always in export demand by the wealthy of the Calmar Union and even among the cloistered elites of the Imperium.

Before the war, even roughhewn, raw lumber of the lowest grades was avidly sought, gifting premium credits to cutters and exporters. Genèvens managed the tree crop wisely, fast growing export trees in tall rows a thousand klics long on sparsely populated and rural Southland, while keeping pristine the old growth forests of Northland. All wholly free from timber gatherers and poachers, guarded by watchers and wardens and local pride. Old gold-and-silver forests around Toruń were preserved for tourists and the pleasure of Genèvens. The spectacular and much older southern woods were left untouched, even unvisited, valued solely for their wondrousness. Until General Brusilov ordered half the southern forests burned to nubs, setting fire to a thousand years of old growth, leaf and windfall.

Now, along five narrow, serene roads built for offworld tourists to travel through parts of the northern preserves that fan away from Toruń, huge crowds of terrified refugees are surging. They're all trying to get off the open plains where Jabos swoop and hordes of RIK in black boots tramp ever closer. They're trying to reach the woodland edge, and thence move under forest cover to Toruń, the amber city that lies 300 klics to the northwest. Dogs jump and bark and nip at ankles and hanging finger tips, harrying anyone who dares touch hard pressed masters. Larger breeds run away, or turn in foolish barking circles, keeping people wary and at bay. Cats are nowhere to be seen. Perhaps they're in the trees hunting chipmunks and unsuspecting tomtits? Being cats, they have their own agenda.

The worst jam starts two score klics from the old woman's burning cottage, where a mob is heaving and shoving into the arched entrance of one of five Old

Forest Roads. Yet the column is barely moving. Curses, exhortations and hard pressing come from the rear and sides of the fleshy funnel, as those still exposed and frantic to get ahead push pitilessly on the backs of those they think must be stupid fortunates moving too slowly, with an RIK column closing behind.

A red faced man curses: "Damn all locusts! I don't deserve this misfortune befalling me and my family. Why is my life taking this hard turn?" Perhaps it's his fate? There is a war on.

"Get out of my way!" *Thump! slap, slap.* A fat woman hits an oldster and two children she accuses of blocking her way. The oldster looks startled and confused. The kids start to cry.

"Don't you be hittin' people, you fat cow!" *Thump! Thump! Thump!* She takes several blows to the back of her head from the children's separated and terrified mother. "Here's another for you!" *Smack!*

A red headed child and a small woman faint inside the close and sweaty crush but are jostled forward regardless, heads bobbing insensibly as their limp bodies are held upright and in place by the hermetic indifference of the billowing crowd of desperate refugees. No one even notices as they float along like leaves or wood chips in a narrow, languid Great Plains stream. The tailback becomes less dense and agitated just inside the forest, where the funnel shaped snarl forms a cannula slow flowing between massive arboreal pillars. No human will or pushing or hard cursing or prayer can hope to budge the great trees. They stretch in two endless, even columns. A living Parthenon. But there are no gods alive among the ruins.

Are there ever?

Flowing like treacle onto a darkly shaded road are 'townees' in pastel colored shirts and light summer frocks, and farm families in rougher working clothes, many wearing dirty old hats. Weary teachers herd clutches of small children still wearing school uniforms and chittering like sparrows, or crying for their mamas. Heavily pregnant young mothers are being pulled or pushed in simple carts by older women, or by widower grandfathers. Gray and withered oldsters well past 120 years shuffle along, aided by middle aged offspring still in their spry eighties or nineties. More dogs walk beside the compact family groups, tails between legs, ears down, eyes furtive and suspicious, wary of the dark canopy high overhead.

One banker is thinking about large ledgers filled with now worthless credits: '*Is this the accounting of my life? All my diligence only to end up here, stuck on the road with this rabble?*'

A factory worker thinks about his missing daughter, now fighting somewhere with Gold Division farther south, as far as he knows. '*Oh my sweet Sophia, to see you one last time. To touch your dear face, so like your mother's. Only once more. It is all I ask of this failing world.*'

A worried woman of fading beauty asks: "Has anyone seen my gray mother? She's old and not fully with us anymore. We were going to take her to the Life Temple next month. Have you seen her? Her name is Golda. *Ma mere, ma mere?*"

Many on the Old Forest Roads are frightened youths, male and female. Still too young to enlist or fight in the KRA, they're old enough to know they might yet be raped by advancing RIK marauders. Or executed as accused *tirailleurs* by roving SAC or Purity death squads. Or deported offworld to slave for Pyotr.

It has been three months since Kaigun broke into Genève system space. On that dark day a vanguard wedge of Zerstörers flashed in from the outer system to cut the "God's Lift" cables, loosing the Toruń space elevator bola asteroid. It spun away on a trajectory and escape velocity that will take it out of the system in about ten years. With the bola gone, they dropped Genève's archaic elevator onto the northern forest, severing the cable 900 klics above the first landing dock. The highest quays and platforms tossed away from the planet, outward from a spinning world to which they were no longer tethered, beyond hope of rescue or recovery by anyone on a smoke obscured and war pummeled world below. As lower cab ascents aborted, cabs full of lumber, grain and people, fell back from tens of klics high, crashing into the quiet forest west of Toruń, setting patchy fires. A thousand klics of tattered nanocarbon ribbon snaked gracefully down over several weeks.

More enemy ships jumped into the L1 on the windward side of the system's largest planet, a cold and orange-blue gas giant. Kaigun capital warships bashed through Genève Flotilla to reach the inner moons, in a short battle Kaigun calls *Genève Obliteration*. Then more Zerstörers swooped across the sky to detonate 50 EMPs in the upper atmosphere, knocking out the civilian memex and nearly all military coms. All that came a full week before the first planetside landing on Southland, and a month before KRA started its cascading ground collapse at the MDL and retreat across Northland to the forest zone.

All hovers and skycraft, military and civilian, are demolished or abandoned. Shot down or forced to ground by thousands of RIK falcons that hunted the sky clean of native birds. Raptor fighters caught outdated KRA fighters parked in long files on the first day, killing most in their nests before they could rise to challenge for supremacy of the sky, making it a domain of unimpeded RIK supremacy. Then the Jabos came, sleek skim-and-dive bombers free to hunt and strafe all targets.

Millions of civilians are fleeing the war as best they can in private vehicles of all types. Running from the pursuit, from the barking guns, away from a strangely orange glowing horizon that holds its flickering color even at midday. In the first days the Jabos were preoccupied with attacking military traffic as priority targets and let civvies run, or indifferently strafed raggedy refugee columns. But now that all KRA targets are dealt with, the Jabos and Raptors are looking for fresh prey.

Hodgepodge traffic collides and chokes into five Old Forest Roads, impassible tailbacks have formed, the like of which Genèvens never saw in their 1,200 year history. After reaching the forest, refugees abandon all useless ground transport, leaving tens of thousands of vehicles impossibly tangled at five tunneled entrances to the deep woods. The crowded, unruly parking lots invite air attack. Burning of abandoned vehicles has already begun, raising towering clouds of acrid black.

"Don't bunch up!" someone cries. There's no authority in the words or in the woods, so the warning goes unheard and unheeded. The danger is real enough, however. It makes no sense to bunch. People do it anyway, instinctively huddling together against the breaking storm of war. Raptors see the jams and skim to just above the treetops, making strafing runs parallel to the five roads that cut through the immense northern forests. Pilots hungry for targets since denuding the great plains turn toward the packed forest roads, through woods less sacred and thus more traveled than Pilsudski or the Gold Oak Forest, yet nearly as thick and tall.

Panicked refugees block each others' way, like stumbling jams of logs from high mountain streams feeding into the broad Toruń River. They push as if they, too, were cut in high crest line woods and cast direct into rushing white waters to make a jumbled way down jagged mountainsides, jostling pell-mell to sawmills and great booms and docks below. There to tumble and turn, to be claimed and pulled out, reshaped as artisanal treasures or disposed as waste if too damaged by rushing down the mountain. Only the jams of refugees are trying to go the wrong way, up the boreal mountains at whose feet gentle Toruń lies. The last safe harbor.

Long, stretched crowds pressing through the narrow, pillared roads are calmer than broad and rowdy mobs frantically pushing into closing funnels where Toruń

Wood meets the plain, where marching and singing Rikugun heave into view. They trudge along tall, shaded defiles through immense dark forests that fan out for hundreds of klics from the hub of Toruń City, vital heart of all Genève. Five arboreal canyons spoking away from a frosty northern city to reach warm plains and rich farms of lower Northland. Beautiful and calm. In peacetime.

The rivers of woe flow toward Toruń as if they're glaciers, hardly moving to naked vision. All five Old Forest Roads are clogged tight with human detritus, like pent up *jökulhlaup* pushing under an ice dam or melting glacier. Nowhere is the slow river of flowing flesh able to breach blocking canyons of groaning trees that tower on both sides of each road, all along the way. No one can force a path through to the last defended site and garrison on Genève, the last sliding chance to maybe board a transport and flee a devastated and soon-to-be conquered world.

Wanderers are made mad, wilded by suffering. After the bombing starts only the healthy young and unusually lucky will somehow trickle through or squeeze out the top of each frozen column, gaining room to lope to Toruń's berm. The rest move as slowly as a hard glacier or not at all, jamming together in rising despair at a pace so halting it might make a Galapagos tortoise rage.

At first the bombers track unshielded lines of bodies with infrared scans that peer through the naturally buttressed canopy, reaching out and interwoven from either side. Like the roof of a medieval cathedral, the highest boughs cover and shade tightly crammed crowds standing or kneeling to pray far below. The green rooves frame canalized tangles of stopped vehicles and forlorn pedestrians that surge with panic after hearing thrusters overhead. In minutes, the canopy above, thinnest right over the Old Forest Roads, is ablaze. Along with the bombs, burning timbers fall onto screaming refugees beneath.

Wave after wave of skim bombers swoop down low over the five logjams. Soldiers mixed up among civilian refugees shoot hand masers and a few pulse cannon skyward, in hopeless protest against the enemy's dominance of the sky. Anyone on the ground close to the tree line dives toward the great roots and trunks, seeking any sort of cover. Those too closely jammed together to move, trapped by the multitude and weight of flesh, fill the middle of the road. All they can do is embrace for final comfort or in prayer. Or despair, and scream and die in fire.

Out on the plains, Rikugun infantry advance ever closer, snare drums beating all around as great marching columns draw toward the forest edge and redeploy into line, in long semicircles around the mouths of the five Old Forest Roads. The sight of so many guns and men in green pushes civilian panic in waves before the redeploying troops. The crowds stampede, trampling hundreds to death without gaining any distance on the men in green. Always, more refugees block the way.

There's no escape from the singing marchers or *snapping* snare drums or wide firing lines that now array for volley fire, front row prone, second row kneeling, third row standing. More divisions arrive in the rear and down the flanks, ordered to stand with arms shouldered to witness the greatness of the Imperium in action.

"Battalion, ready masers."

A dull *humm* rises as weapons come off safety and tiny lasers warm the pink crystals. The terror peaks. Women in the back files of the crowd scream and cover their children's eyes. Men plead for their lives. Children clutch at a praying parent's leg and look up, bewildered.

"Battalion, present arms."

The order is repeated all down the volley lines, until ten thousand maser barrels present toward the heaving crowds at each of five blocked forest entrances.

"Fire by volley!"

"Front rank, *fire!*"

"Second rank, *fire!*"

"Third rank, *fire!*"

"Again. First rank, *fire!*"

It continues until crystals burn out, after 20 shots. Men and women push at each other like penned cattle in jammed chutes of a Dauran slaughterhouse, bellowing fear in wild animal voices unrecognizable even to themselves. Others rush like bullied bison heading over a bluff, falling into a Sioux blood kettle waiting below.

A few try to turn, to stand and die with dignity while facing their murderers. They're not permitted any grace. They're pulled away by the madding crowd or down by a death grip of a stranger tearing at their clothes or arms or faces. One old man does manage to stand alone and unafraid, wearing a neat suit and tie while surrounded by a mound of dead, and by heaving wounded waiting for follow on troops to deliver their kill shots. The battalion colonel walks over, pulls out his pistol, places it square against the old man's white head and pulls the trigger. He falls, lying still across the body of his dead wife.

"Advance 100 paces and reload. You, boy. Step over that woman. She's dead. Keep pace with your company. Don't hold up the firing line. Move it!" *Nitōhei* Lars Knut has no idea what's going on. Only that he never signed up for this. He vomits onto the next man he kills, then wipes the bile off his mouth. His training is all he has to fall back on. So he puts one shaky foot ahead of the other. He keeps in line. He follows orders.

"All halt."

"Reform ranks."

"Front rank, *fire!*"

"Second rank, *fire!*"

"Third rank, *fire.*"

It's just like they all practiced in basic training, right out of the RIK infantry tactics manual. It's so close to basic weapons and march practice that many men don't realize right away that they're scorching flesh when they fire their masers. Not until they have to advance, and step over the smoking dead.

Nitōhei Lars Knut knows. He cries wet tears with every shot he fires. But he still shoots when he's told to, reloads when ordered, advances and does it all over again. He's lost count of how many lives he's taken in the last 15 minutes. He can't afford to know. It could drive him mad.

"Advance 100 paces and halt."

"Reform firing ranks.

"Commence fire at will."

"All ranks, *fire at will!*"

Now the *click clack, click clack* sound truly does resemble a host of crickets. Or maybe a swarm of locusts, moving methodically across a wheat field. Consuming everything living before advancing again. So oldfashioned is the firing drill, so bunched up are the mass of shooters, that if there was a real army on the other side a helluva lot of RIK would die, too. Main HQ back on Kestino knows this to be true. It's scrambling hard to change the basic infantry manual, which dates back 300 years to the last Orion War.

Why change? Because on Lwów another rigid prewar general tries the same godsdamn parade ground tactic, but not against unarmed civilians. He goes in against determined KRA resistance and gets an entire Rikugun division shredded. Over 50,000 dead. A one off? No. It also happens on one of the ice moons of Aral, where 350,000 RIK are already gone in a fight just now getting started. Says one cynical but honest staff officer, just before they arrest him for it: "That's a lot of hidden family losses to censor on our homeworlds."

Back on Genève, there's no running from the swooping skycraft and firing lines. No running from heavy masers shooting *blue* bolts down into the forest from Jabos and Raptors swirling above. Or from rippling *red* plasma that cuts into the roads to rip apart huge trees at will, tattooing with incinerating heat anything and anyone below the swooping skycraft. *Whirr, keraaack*! Lasers slice the canopy, dropping multiple ton flaming branches onto cowering families, crushing them and cremating the corpses. Jabos and Raptors whirl and spin overhead however they choose, their crews doing needless acrobatics to impress watching peers.

Poumm, zzssuiii! Pulse packets slam into dirt along the roadsides, kicking soil and bitter roots over abandoned wounded, tossing more women and children and vehicles high in the air. The enemy skycraft circle high above picking the fattest, slowest targets. They line up like taxis, waiting for a turn to swoop and strafe, to dive bomb the crawling, bleeding columns far below. Rikugun warbirds are as unchallenged as hunting eagles selecting which flashing fish to snatch from a run of salmon packing the tumbling streams below. Crying, screaming, burning, dying civilians back up over hundreds of klics of blazing forest, along each of the five Old Forest Roads. The rooves above them are gone or hang in smoky patches. All five roads are deeply hole, wrecked and impassible. Everywhere one looks there are burned vehicles, upended carts, abandoned wounded and the dying.

Those who can't move die where they stand, too old or too little or too young to shift. Many who are virile and fast also die, pinned in place by the crush of the panicking crowd. Ditches and roadbeds fill with burning bodies, the dead and still dying. Nor is there cover inside the forest edge, away from the center of the fire roads. Not when huge slabs of living lumber cut from the canopy by heavy masers tumble down. Multiple tons of flaming green wood, hissing sap and heated gases and colored smokes and fire, falling and rolling, setting alight the base and roots of the massive trees until pillars of fire rise hundreds of meters into the sky. It's like some great pagan spectacle recalling Hades: the Pillars of Pandemonium.

There's no escape into the woods from the road, either. Not when great roots smash up into exploding pulp, showering splinters from echo blasts, rip apart with flash lightening rounds, upend heavy vehicles to scorch and flay alive anyone inside with balls and bolts of *blue* electric fire. Not when "The Great Fire," as this soon will be called by those huddled inside Toruń, races into the trees and burns out a half-million square klics of forest. No one who makes it into the woods lives.

Agni the Fire God is come from the sky to burn the forests short and gray, uncaring of innocent animals scurrying and scrambling inside: mice and voles, wrens, tree bats, hives of wasps, small green snakes and fleet deer, and stumbling people fleeing in all directions but always forced back into fire. This is the start of the Kali Age.' *Creatures by the thousands scream in terror and are scorched. Everywhere writhing on the ground with burning wings, eyes and paws.'*

Once the huge fires turn outward and move away from the roads, choosing single targets inside the blazing forest becomes pointless. Everyone trapped on the roads is dead or marked for death by fire. Besides, ambient heat columns and rising billows of smoke from the terrible conflagrations play havoc with skycraft thermal targeting and optics. So pilots peel away, heading to base to rest and rearm for the big assault on heavily defended Toruń. They want to raze the 'Golden City of Wood,' a ridiculous place of which backwoods Genèvens are much too proud. They've known only easy victory so far in this war. Only a few pilots know that attacking well shielded Toruń will be a lot tougher than burning out undefended columns of fleeing civvies. They're still having fun, still marveling at their own skill and at the awesome destructive power of their machines. They don't yet know that war is far harder than murder. They have no idea how long it will last.

The ancient forests are ablaze down all five long and winding roads leading from Toruń to the great northern plain. They look that first night like orange-red rivers of lava, for they are in fact smoldering ribbons of terror and torment. Five phoenix serpents consuming everything: teak and redwood, sycamore and maple, vehicles and people, all creatures great and small.

No one is left to pray or to mourn.

No one is coming with water or aid.

Toruń itself will now come under siege.

The woods are ashen, dark and deep. Hundreds of lesser fires leap newborn from great infernos that suck in air and fuel and spit up flames that rise and race along the canopy, then down groaning trunks to start a whole new fire, until it seems half Northland is ablaze. When the last fires flicker out a week later, when it's finally only smoldering inside roasted Toruń Wood, 2.7 million Genèvens are left unmoving along five charred roads. Ash falls for days, fills in clouded over eyes of the dead, covers charcoal remains in a humbug shroud of soft white-gray. The only ones still alive amidst the cooling ashes are the dazed, the dumb, and the dumbfounded. Even the mad god Agni is flown away to set fresh fires.

The Wolf is prowling on Genève. *Listen*!

Hear his pack's mad, midnight howling?

Now he's in the woods, stalking red game.

Now he's at the city gate, pawing to get in.

Temple

"Move it, you cretins! Double time! *Gunsō*, get these *nitōhei* moving!" The *taisa* who barks out the order is the worst sort of martinet. More interested in medals than in motivating troops, more interested in parades than precision.

"Yes sir. You heard the colonel. Move your asses, privates! *Hut, hut, hut!* Double time, march! 3rd Squad is out-of-step! Five circuits around the battalion, full kit. Do it now!"

Tramp, tramp, tramp.

Tramp, tramp, tramp.

Tramp, tramp, tramp.

The rhythms of war have a natural beat all their own. A steady and reliable meter. The cadence of uniformed men and uniform thinking, all acting toward one ascendant and collective purpose. Or so the training manual says. So memex vids tell all the homeworlds. So dull political officers report up the chain-of-command. So all Grün civilians believe. It's a grand illusion, this idea commanding officers have that they, or anyone, is really in control of battle and war. No one understands that this is just beginning. Not even Rikugun is fully ready for this war, and it has been preparing for 20 years. It's troops are just kids, green as their new combat weaves. They only think they're soldiers. Even the Old Breed, the lifetimers who were in Rikugun for years before Bad Camberg, have never been to war.

Yet such is the Grün sense of superiority that RIK armtrak crews think they're invincible, having faced only a few hundred pathetic KRA Rhinos. Sky pilots fly too low, unimpeded by their enemy's already destroyed Skyforce, doing loop-the-loops to impress grinning troops glide marching below. The ground force generals fancy that they're masters of maneuver warfare, of perfect doctrine and orders. All around the burning fields of the Imperium's aggressive war is a soaring song of higher cultural vanity. Maybe it deserves to be sung. Or it may yet prove to be foolhardy hubris of an overreaching, arrogant star nation rising on nova wind that will burn it down, too, before this all ends. That's really what this war is all about.

Most RIK officers openly despise their men. None of the troops come from the same elite castes as officers, or wear honor as a shield to keep out conscience and moral doubt. Status is framed by clear diamond dirks carried in transparent holsters, hooked to tan belts that offset dark olive uniforms with lots of gold and silver trimming. Ordinary RIK rankers wear much paler green weaves. They carry only simple black diamond daggers, strapped against a black combat boot.

Many officers sport dueling scars, *snicked* in a cheek by a quick blade back in a military fraternity on Kestino or one of the Ordensstaat worlds. Or truth be told more often, acquired in an ugly bar fight over some lower class whore or slave girl. Or like General Oetkert, bought from a surgeon who carefully cuts and folds only surface skin, under anesthetic. Variations on a familiar scene play out over many worlds and down the generations, wherever RIK officer cadets gather.

"Do it quickly! Cut me, you damned fool! *Ow!* Thanks."

"Now, cut me, too. Do it now, do it quick as I did. *Owwooo!*"

"How do I look? How do I look?"

After the staged fight cadets agree to lie, claiming they engaged in a trial of honor. Just like their fathers lied. However made, thin scars are left jagged, unrepaired and proudly worn. To be twenty and without one is to be a lesser man, a loser and outlier. If you're from a good, First or Second Caste family in the Grün Imperium. Below that social rank a dueling scar is seen as pretentious, and openly mocked.

The three-tiered elite uses the Imperium Akademy on Kestino as a finishing school for military gentlemen of the highest castes, born to the highest commands. Even the Third Caste does not usually qualify, although it produces most officers who actually accept field commissions instead of HQ staff positions. In combat operations, high rank officers hold back and stay back, only giving orders to lower caste officers and wannabe citizens. Only a fool leads rankers from the front. The higher castes of elite education and character and bloodline must not be exposed to hostile fire. The enemy might ignore their natural superiority.

Rankers come from the vast lower orders, from sprawling barrios across the Imperium. From urban cesspools where the scars a man wears are are far likely acquired from the flashing steel knife of some whore's unpaid pimp. Men like that are fit to fool and send by the tens of millions into combat, with its squalid and brutal and classless ways of death. Fit only for that. This broad officer contempt against the rankers of Rikugun isn't wholly unjustified. Orion's armies, like all armies, reflect the societies that raise them, equip and license them, then ship them out to war. Rikugun thus takes internal caste contempt and class conflict with it into battle. It's mostly a source of strength, giving RIK corps and armies profound discipline and unblinking obedience. It's also a source of early weakness, from inherited rather than earned officer commissions and senior commands, a tradition that puts too many incompetents like General Nikolai Brusilov in leading combat roles. That's why it now uses all the old tricks of the military trades to keep morale up and men marching wherever they're told to go, in long green files.

"Corporal, march music. Get 'em singing."

"Battalion band, strike a tune."

"Which one, *gochō*?"

"Let's make it *Rikugun Forever!*"

Three snare drums start to *rat-at-tat*. A base drum sounds the deeper beat. A dozen flutes and fifes test the smoky air as the ranks move into the forest, heading for Toruń. Then it comes together, as the battalion's superb alto tenor leads off with the first verse of a march song dating back 300 years, to the Third Orion War.

Armtraks moving out in time,
leading our swift advancing line.
The wild boar runs where our eagle flies,
he'll make a grand feast once he dies.
Rikugun, oh Rikugun! To serve is all we ask.

The men need little prompting. They're feeling good today. Flat bellies are full of hot breakfast, victory is in their sights, morning lust and being just eighteen while heavily armed and licensed to kill swells hardening groins and consciences.

Far away from our homes, at war,
we watch the bold black eagle soar.
And when tomorrow's battle comes
We'll trounce our foes to the sound of drums.
Rikugun, oh Rikugun! To serve is all we need.

Well, everybody is feeling good except maybe Three Squad, One Company, Two Battalion of the 4th Imperial Artillery Division. That squad is from Malmö. It's heaving and throwing up, just finishing the third of five times around their home battalion in full kit, masers held double handed overhead.

For most of 'the boys' of RIK, as they commonly call themselves in a uniquely all male army, combat thrills and simple propaganda supplies motivation. At least to start the war. The problems will all come later, if it drags on and expands across Orion. If the war's fortunes shift. If victories don't come so easily. For now, they accept the morality of doing what officers say is their duty. Including dirty tasks like shooting "bandits" and "saboteurs," and making reprisals like burning down whole villages and shooting all males who run. And herding oldsters and women and children into crowded control & occupation camps that reek of fear and feces.

They disembarked from new dropships and landers on Southland then assault hopped a salt sea to reach the hardened coast of Northland, and were glad. They busted through the enemy MDL in a day, glide marched on combat boots over the broad plains with officers barking and bullying from dark green hovers that flew well behind the march columns. They loved every minute of it. Each quick victory and smashing of an opposing KRA position. Loved using their weapons, too.

They only grew more hesitant when "enemy civilians" offered traditional gifts of bread and salt, even after they trampled crops or readied to burn down a cottage or village. Many of 'the boys' grabbed the warm bread greedily, without giving any pay or thanks. Others felt deeply shamed by a familiar, homespun gesture and the sourdough smell. They slunk away, guilty and empty handed. Conscripts are growing ever more disoriented as they advance over the plains, now pushing hard on hordes of refugees who fan out in disturbed pond circles of woe from the first tossed stones of war, spreading tales of shocking destruction and despair that lap across the quiet land. Young men are confused by odd reactions of civilians they meet, those who can't run fast or far enough. Or those too foolish to run, who sit and wait, disregarding or disbelieving the worst tales of rapine told by passing columns of fleeing others. Staying in old and well loved homes, come what may. Until their error blooms into sudden horror and the stench of murder and rot.

Whole units succumb to sudden fears. They shoot up empty houses and into hedgerows, without fire discipline. Officers call this curious, panicky behavior "hedgerow psychosis," and punish it hard. Not to save the civvies caught in the wild shooting but to preserve unit discipline and their own authority. It happens anyway, in village after village. It comes from a rising obsession with being shot at from behind hedges or from inside cottages and shops, even though detection gear precludes simple hiding places as concealed firing points. No one can ever say for sure that he knows anyone who was actually shot this way. Although they all say they know someone, who for sure knows someone who was surely shot at by bandits or partisans or *tirailleurs*.

"There! Over there! I saw a light!"

"It was a muzzle flash!"

"Where? Where?"

"There, there! Inside that open window."

"There's another, behind that big shrub."

"Quick, shoot before they fire again."

Click clack, click clack, click clack. Whirr, brzzzt!

'Hedge fright' means houses and barns and sheds in little villages scorch with maser fire. Rubble and the humblest ruins burn twice over. They're not the ruins of great, lost empires. They're ruins nonetheless.

***

Three Squad finished its penal run an hour ago and is back in march column, but now it's walking point. 'The boys' are smoldering angry at being singled out this way. As they pass through another village, a family huddles in a basement. Two houses down, another family with five kids hiding in a root cellar makes a noise. Three doesn't know who is in there, but 'the boys' don't hesitate when they think they see movement and a flash of light escape the cellar door.

"It's a sniper!"

"Lob two frag grenades down there."

Boom, boom.

A skinny lad is sent down to investigate. He staggers out and vomits on the grass. He asks if it's a crime to kill blindly this way. "It's simple self-defense," the NCO assures him, and all the rest of them. Supply is told to rush more crated frag grenades to infantry units leading the advance, because they're running short.

There are no big cities on Genève except Toruń. So the columns march from hamlet to village to small town, back to hamlet to village to town. Over and over, day after day during the RIK advance. Country folk they meet don't look like the terrible enemy described by their old high form teachers or nervous family back home, those hanging on every memex lie and vid. There are some still who won't believe that Genèvens are their natural or blood inferiors, no matter what they're told. No matter how many old men and women they roust and boss about as if herding dairy cattle. The only difference these honest young men can see amidst the mud and fire is that they have masers and Krevan civvies do not. That makes the folk they bully powerless, not inferior.

"Those two arguing old sods we passed a way back sounded just like my cracked grandparents," one lad from far off Schwyz laughs to a kid recruited from the closer border world of Zug.

"That ginger kid reminds me of my brother on Glarus," says another.

"Hey little girl, where's your momma? Stop crying, it'll be OK."

"That one looks *exactly* like cousin Klara from Uri. Same eyes and hair."

Genèvens don't descend to the levels of evil depicted in daily briefings by the politruks, the politico-priests assigned to each division in a dual command system hated by all RIK officers. Most politruks are minor Purity ideologues who give propaganda lessons on 'biopolitical science' and other regime dogma. They bore most of the men, but tend well enough to morale. So they're tolerated, of some use to officers even if they're also spies reporting to Pyotr or to the General Curia on the loyalty of field commanders. A few over interpret their authority as superior even to operations staff, but they're slapped down hard by RIK generals as soon as the real shooting starts. Still, no politruk can be dismissed outright, even by a general. Not without a real good reason and maybe also a royal permit.

Now the officer class turns to the hated politruks for a different kind of service. They're ordered to spread malicious rumors across the ranks about atrocities committed by lying and cunning civvies. In the first set, old women are accused of giving out envenomed fruit, young women of seducing Grün boys then slicing off their testicles as they sleep. Rumors fly among units, swift lies on gull wings.

"Crushed glass is baked into the bread they offer us!"

"Don't eat anything those filthy bitches give you!"

"And stay out of the root cellars!"

"I heard that, too! They're all mined with nail bombs."

"It's the old women who stay behind who do it."

"They coat the nails in rat poison, too!"

"They put cyanide in salt shakers in abandoned cottages."

"No, that can't be right. I had some today, on my mockmeat ration."

"It's true, I tell ya. My friend smelled bitter almond in one shaker!"

"Gods! I think I'm gonna throw up!"

"Filthy scum!"

"Cunning *teufel*."

"Murderers!"

"Old whores!"

"*Schlampes*!"

Confusion and embarrassment shifts into fear, then to hatred, as rumors spread that civilians in the next village, or the one after that, are spies. Or worse, that they hide guerrilla fighters in every copse or barn, that snipers are lurking around every bend, hiding behind each hedgerow. Or even that children are spotting for KRA snipers concealed under flooring or inside a woodpile. It doesn't matter that few or no *tirailleurs* or enemy snipers hiding in trees ever shoot at them. The accused village is punished anyway, with indiscriminate harshness. With passing days and more sacked villages on their resumes 'the boys' grow ever more used to hard practices and collective punishments, until they come to see such easy brutality as normal and all kindly things as odd and foolhardy.

Other rumors arise more naturally as heavily armed youths bully the weak, the unarmed, the fragile old. It's always thus in war, that nether realm where power comes to youths allowed to drink too soon and deeply of dark pleasures of bossing and breaking the frail and frightened. Where they're confused by fake newsfeeds and unearned armed power over the lives and deaths of innocent farfolk. On five invaded Krevan worlds war dissolves what once held youth in moral check. War drips onto them like fluorosulphuric acid onto glass. They're decentered from any law, isolated from their parents and socially enforced morality, led into brutality by cynical officers, goaded to act more cruelly by politruks and then by each other. The terrible corrosive of combat dissolves softer bindings of restraint holding back the natural barbarism of the young. They become lords of flies and death.

Every rumored atrocity becomes real and then reciprocal. Whether stories of poisoning and castration are true or not, RIK drag Krevan girls and mothers into a field or barn to rape and murder. In a thousand villages, high pitched cries and screams are followed by fatal silences. Parents are shot in front of their children and worse, children are shot in front of their parents. Or all are shot and the corpses burned together in pyres made of household furnishings and bedding.

"You can't run a godsdamn war like it's a charity," a snarling 2nd Division major general snaps when asked about his rough tactics by a concerned journo. She's eager to report home on the liberation of one of the 'Lost Children' worlds, but shaken and shocked by what she sees out there. "Hawks eat doves," the *shōshō* declares matter-of-factly. It's a sentiment that Takeshi Watanabe would approve. It's the ethos of the RIK, even of the Imperium. "Now get the fuck out of my HQ."

Censors cut out his remarks and block the story on the Imperium's nebs and memexes. The journo is arrested and sent home on the next shuttle carrying back wounded, to be met at the space dock by agents of the Kempeitai. She's declared *damnatio memoriae* and never seen again. Never to be spoken of or remembered aloud, not even by family. Mourning her is a severely punishable offense. Then the declaration sentence itself is erased, and she disappears into a memory void.

Taishō Nikita Brusilov orders RIK 10th Armored to shoot all Krevan males it finds. Long before reaching Pilsudski Wood its hover scouts kill hundreds of men and boys, and some women and girls, piling corpses inside their homes to burn. When the edge of darkness moves over the land, the division's line of march is marked back to its day departure points by pyres of burning farms and villages.

One 20-year old private, called "Jacko" by his friends, objects when lads he trained with, fights with, eats alongside, all from his own Fahnlein or 'small flag' tactical group, gang rape and then crucify a 40-year old woman on the door of her own barn, leaving her to hang naked and die in slow agony. '*Are these really my squad mates? 'The boys' can't be this cruel, not to this poor woman. They can't do this! They mustn't do this!*' He blurts out a heartfelt protest. "What are you doing? We're here to defend against Krevan sabotage and aggression, to liberate our Lost Children worlds. These people did nothing to hurt the Imperium! That woman did nothing to deserve this. Stop! Stop it!"

He's arrested, then drumhead courts-martialed for "incitement to mutiny," and sentenced to summary execution. All on the authority of a SAC lieutenant about his own age, a young tough so enraged at Jacko's "sympathy for the enemy" he has to be restrained from shooting the naïf with his pocket maser. The lieutenant angrily jams the pistol back into a low slung hip holster, reluctantly convinced to let an execution party from Jacko's own Fahnlein shoot him instead.

It's not at all unusual. The Purity Revolution executed millions of Grünen before this day, and that was long before imposition of martial law and military discipline inside the field army was applied to Grün civvies as well. It was Takeshi Watanabe's suggestion, made in private to Pyotr, who didn't need encouragement. A year ago, Pyotr personally justified all prewar killings in a secret speech made to top Imperium officials, and to the officer corps. Not one man present protested.

"We execute many people without knowing if they're fully guilty. My regime and the Purity Revolution can't stop progress to conduct investigations. We have the obligation to triumph." He knows it has always been the Oetkert-Shaka way.

All Grünen know it, too.

It's a threat as well as a fact.

It's history. It's the New Order.

It's what's at stake in the war.

Still, the "Jacko affair" causes a stir in 10th Division. A young private, a Grün ethnic from Brno who speaks real good Krevan, gets up early to walk over from the nearby hover scouts unit. He takes along a large, black-haired friend who doesn't say much but is always stupidly grinning, Since the whole division has been ordered to watch the execution, they want to get the very best places. They would make the trip to watch regardless, orders or no orders. The fair faced one thinks he has a reputation to maintain. His companion is just along for the ride.

It's over fast, but not 'till after the division eats a full breakfast of hardtack fried in mockpork grease. Jacko waits bound tight, alone under double guard, watching them eat from his death perch. He's fed nothing and given no water. The Imperium doesn't waste supplies on any "useless mouths" like him. 'The boys' eat quickly, unconsciously eager to see how Jacko will die. The firing squad sits off to one side to eat and to wait, unspeaking and unspoken to by the rest.

The execution is carried out without ceremony. Jacko is made to kneel before the trunk of a wide oak tree, mouth gagged and head bowed low so that his killers don't have to hear his last words or look into his eyes as they cook him with maser rifles from just five meters away. Two wiser, or just more experienced, men in the execution squad plug up their noses with tuft grass so that they won't have to remember Jacko in every burnt roast smell. The squad's *gunsō* gives the order.

"Ready!"

Jacko trembles, a mortal shudder he can't help. '*What's happening to me? To all of us? How did it come to this?*'

"Present!"

He lifts his head as high as he can against the restraints, pleading with eyes alone, unable to spit his gag or cry out. Two camp friends squinting down tubes of stubby masers hesitate, but only for a moment.

"*Fire!*"

A smoking, headless, useless corpse falls forward in front of the oak, then lies still. The great tree rustles briefly in the strange silence that follows, broken only by the sounds of masers checked and shouldered, and by small *crackles* of melting fat rising from the smoldering body. Low branches heavy with summer green are hardly bothered by a merciful breeze that flutters past, to lift the stench of roasting flesh, hair and offal away from the site. But the gust betrays the closest onlookers by curling back around, carrying a small cloud of blue-black and foul smelling smoke over the firing squad, thence to choke front ranks of suddenly frightened boys and men standing stiffly in green combat weaves. Their officers are not happy. They're kept there for a full five minutes before a dispersal order is given.

Minoru Honda of the 10th Armored walks from his prime position to Jacko's lifeless, headless body, his large black haired friend trotting alongside like a loyal hound. Minoru unseals his utes, pulls out his penis and pisses on the corpse. His friend is content to spit, grinning all the while. Minoru looks at Jacko's distraught squad mates still standing in the firing line, his fat penis in his hand, dripping dark yellow on the body. He laughs. "Someone has to put out the fire you started!"

Later that day 10th Division packs up and moves out, heading at last into the great forest with orders to reach and invest Toruń. But first its pale battalions are marched past the gagged head and dead man slumped before the oak tree. They tramp by in silence and crisp parade ground formation, barked at and pummeled by sergeants if anyone tries to look away.

"Eyes right, trooper!"

"You *will* look at the traitor."

"Long live Pyotr! Long live Purity!"

The point is made by the officer corps. There will be no more dissent in this unit. Not without consequences. Holovids of Jacko's execution are dispatched to all other squads and companies and divisions, marked *Mandatory Viewing*. It's not the last such vid the men will see on Genève.

No comet streaks across the sky after the shooters from Jacko's squad put away masers. The heavens don't blaze forth in protest at their friend's passing life or death. His mates aren't struck dumb by his murder, not beyond an hour in any case. They accept the sentence, hard as it is, guilty as they are for provoking it, and for carrying it out. Jacko's fate angers them fatally nonetheless.

Not against the callow SAC *chūi* who ordered the execution, then made certain Jacko's best mates formed the firing party. They're allowed no anger in that direction, toward the thug lieutenant in perfectly creased, suffocating slate gray weaves. As gray as dead Jacko's skin.

No, their rage is directed outward, away from the SAC discipline they can't escape and toward all Krevans, so vulnerable and inferior to them in power and status, unable even to defend their own homes. Especially, they grow angry at the woman they raped and crucified. Their rage moves them from guilt to vengeance, to the only mood allowed to them by the RIK and the only victims permitted them.

"Damned Krevans!"

"Jacko would still be alive if not for them, right?"

"Too right!"

"They're why we're fighting on this shithole planet."

"They started this fuckin' war!"

"They did! Yes!"

"That's why Jacko's dead."

"You're right!"

"They attacked our base at Bad Camberg."

"We'd still be at home if they hadn't."

"Jacko would still be alive!"

"Before that, in the last war, they stole our lost worlds."

"Took all our Lost Children."

"That's why we had to come here, to take them back."

"Bastards!"

"Bitches!"

"*Schlampes*, all of them!"

"We'll show them."

"Let's pay them back for what they did to Jacko."

It's nothing deeper than lines fed to them in basic training and by politruks, about who started the war and why they're here, invading Genève in self-defense. It's more than enough. The enraged Fahnlein seeks "justice for Jacko" in the next village. Over six hundred frail oldsters and women with minor children are herded into the local Life Temple. Doors are bolted, outer walls soaked with incendiary chemicals and the Temple is set on fire. The whole Fahnlein encircles the blaze, shouting and shooting down anyone who tries to escape the leaping flames. That means shooting pointblank at small children lifted up to broken windows by frantic, pleading mothers locked inside. Then they shoot the wailing mothers. Or they push arms and faces back inside the burning building. As it loses integrity and collapses, the Temple emits a choking cloud of smoke that smells of incense and burnt child. They'll quickly forget Jacko, but they'll never forget that smell.

In the weeks that follow anyone who hesitated while Jacko's mates "flamed the Temple" finds it more prudent to volunteer for cleansing squads doing similar work. Or for any other anti-resistance sweeps. Or *any* dirty job they can get to prove they're "on the team." They made Jacko a martyr to their cruelty, now they morph themselves into unjustly, tortured saints of virtue and Purity. When asked about it later one young veteran who took part in flaming the temple shrugs and says: "War does not make people tender." No one in the Fahnlein mentions Jacko or the execution or the burned out Life Temple again. Jacko is another nonperson who disappears into the maw of war, joining tens of millions gone before him.

Billions more will follow them,

from one end of Orion's spur to the other.

This thing could go on for a very long time.

***

Not everyone succumbs to raw circumstance. One reactivated old *gunsō*, a thirty year veteran sergeant who served in the peacetime Rikugun, gray flecks starting to streak his black curls, stops to share his rations with a Krevan refugee mother and three hungry children hunkered at the roadside. Her thick flowing hair and slender, angular face remind him of his daughter. Her little one smiles at him and reaches a tiny hand up for the hard biscuit he offers, like his granddaughter did the morning he left Zug. The day he reported to his old unit to serve in Pyotr's war. "Here you go, poor things. Eat, eat. Madam, take this for your children."

The disheveled, blank faced mother says nothing. She makes no gesture. She doesn't hold out her own hand to receive his offered ration of hardtack biscuits and a squeeze tube of cheese. She was gang raped twice, over four days and nights of screams and pain, of beatings and humiliation. The older kids are scared and blank, too. They huddle beside their mother, without ever touching her or seeking out her comfort. Only the youngest looks up and smiles at him.

When his company captain hears about it the older sergeant is reprimanded, then paraded before his unit and formally charged with "lending aid and comfort to the enemy." He's lucky there's no SAC officer nearby to make it worse. All he gets is four days on half-rations of hardtack and water, then two weeks pulling double perimeter guard duty. Far worse is all the laughter and teasing by younger soldiers in his own unit. It never stops. Women of the attached Auxiliary Corps are the cruelest and most brazen.

"Do I look like your daughter, too, dad?"

"I'm hungry. Can I have your rations, papa?"

"Sure looked like you wanted to give her a fourth kid, granddad."

"You old fool! Don't you know that they're the enemy?"

The old hand lowers his head into the gale of mockery and slogs forward. He does his duty and keeps his mouth shut. He has a family, too. The war has become a bizarre place he no longer understands, where he is rewarded for murder and mayhem yet mocked and punished for feeding another man's hungry daughter.

Takeshi

Takeshi Watanabe is at the center of this war. Hidden hand of Pyotr Shaka III, the *eminence noir* behind the Jade Throne. He's the spider standing on intersecting webs of schemes, plots and lies. He's also in his natural political element, where his unique talents and his fortune and powers must swell. He is Hector's warning embodied, revealed even to himself for what he truly is. There's no chance to win him over to pity's side. He has iron in his breast and bloody murder on his hands.

Only at this moment he's not *exactly* at the center of events, or even near to where he really wants to be. He's far from the Jade Court and inner circle, inside all other inner circles as the most favored of all 'The Admitted.' No, he's stuck in backwater business on Genève, doing low level work on a minor agrarian world already largely overrun by the RIK. '*Why did Pyotr send me to this shithole?*' He holds a middling rank in SAC, yet he has met with the Tennō many times. Both men have been moving toward this moment of war and toward each other for many years. They're near perfect conspirators. They're also paired scorpions, wary yet ready to strike should the other man make the slightest tactical misstep or inadvertently reveal his true long term intentions.

He looks over a smoldering village, out from under the peak of a silver-gray forage cap. Its rim is circled by a green puggaree signifying an active combat command. His jet black eyes are unblinking, unnaturally steady, with a flicker of red flecks in intensely contracted pupils. '*Not for the field experience, as he said.*' A snug, steel gray uniform clings to tight contours of his hard and trim physique. In his black gloved hand he grips an argentine swagger stick, thick at the top. It's the same baton of office carried by all senior commanders. He taps it methodically against his athletic thigh. '*Pyotr sent me here because he thinks I need a little humbling before we continue with our plans, to remind me who is the Tennō and who is his at-will servant. No matter that we both know that I am the greater mind and have by far the superior native talent.*'

He's right, and he's wrong. Yes, Pyotr is jealous of this man of immense will and talent who serves at his whim. But Takeshi was sent to Genève for a smaller reason and a big one. '*It's the Imperium way. I'm an outcaste from Fates, without family or title. Born outside the elite castes originating on the Grün homeworlds, for whom only an Oetkert or Shaka can be to the Waldstätte Palast born.*' True, but he's just feeling sorry for himself. A royal agent deep inside RIK HQ sent a private report to Pyotr detailing the terrible firestorms, one started by his idiot cousin and the other by his general's too blunt assault on the Toruń roads and then against the berm by too eager and cocksure pilots. Pyotr sent Takeshi to Genève because he needs eyes on the ground that he can trust. Not just a buffoon cousin and inept, plotting generals who lie to him daily in their *After Action Reports*.

'*It's my own fault. I admit it.*' Knowing as no one other than Pyotr knew that invasion of the United Planets loomed, Takeshi asked to be assigned to combat duty when war came. The appeal was made during one of their audiences sealed in Pyotr's inner chambers in the Waldstätte Palast, where they planned to take all Orion into war. Calculatingly, ostentatiously, Takeshi pleaded with Pyotr: "Send me where the action is, so that I may serve you in your splendid little war." It wasn't just a pose. At least, not totally. Takeshi wants to be where his rare abilities will bring him notice and influence, on the winding path to power. He just thought that would be on the most important invasion, of Aral. It never occurred to him that Pyotr had a sense of humor, that he'd instead send him to Genève, first to dispose of the *Truant* mercs, then for a second time, for an extended combat tour.

"I'm glad that you believe in service. Or say that you do. I shall think on this awhile." And so he did. Takeshi served him well when he was sent to organize a team of mercs who took down Bad Camberg in a false flag op, framing Krevo so that Pyotr could violate the old borders and have his war. '*He needs a tug on the reins, lest he take the bit in his mouth and run wild in his talent and ambition.*'

Even before he helped the Tennō start the Krevan War, Takeshi's name was whispered in the highest levels in the *Sakura-kai* secret society and more broadly within SAC, and also at the Jade Court. He is marked for command. Everybody says so. Maybe even marked for greatness, though fewer will concede their own vainglory and ambition to his. He's too young, too handsome, too rawly talented. Yet real power is still not coming to him as fast as he wants, as fast as he needs. Even though to all others at Court, and inside The Admitted, the speed of his rise is astonishing. It fills his rivals with the blackest fear and greenest envy.

No one understands the quickness of his rare intimacy with Pyotr. There are ugly rumors, of course. Lots of those. That Takeshi is a mere foil for SAC, whose general officers are said to be secretly running the war and controlling Pyotr. That he's really the bastard son of some great noble house, or even that he's Pyotr's own bastard, born of a whore mother from the barrios of Kestino. Or that he and Pyotr made a pact in blood to serve the Black Faith of the hated monks on Fates, and that the Imperator is planning to restore the banned Broderbund of Takeshi's homeworld to a coveted place behind the Jade Throne. Or most commonly and vulgarly, that he is the Tennō's latest, secret lover. That's the most popular rumor, because if it's true it means Pyotr will discard him soon enough, allowing others to step into yet another dead man's boots and bed.

Takeshi *is* Pyotr's protégé, a coppery colonel in Special Action Commando, but his own man first and always. Yet, his talent is so great that Pyotr kept him at arms length after he returned to Kestino, after he oversaw the Bad Camberg covert op and dispersal of its perpetrators into high risk combat roles on Genève. Pyotr needed credible deniability should his man or the Bad Camberg lie be exposed. So he kept both distant, sending *Truant* to Genève. '*I expected to be well rewarded for my advice and service. These baubles of property and income you give mean nothing. I want and I expect a high command in this war that we started together.*'

As Takeshi stands on the rim of his black command hover in a shitty Northland village he remembers the exchange that brought him to this place and moment. When Pyotr finally readmitted him to his private chambers he said: "This war is supposed to be run at a profit, yet it will not be possible to feast if my generals and relatives burn down the worlds my armies conquer. That is what is happening on Genève." He lamented that so much valuable and rare Toruń wood was lost to the conflagrations, making no mention of charred lives.

Takeshi despises physical weakness. He thought: '*Your larder and your table, Pyotr, like your thick waistline, seems well stocked already. Surely you do not go to bed hungry at night?*' He longed to say it, just for spite, but mouthed only loyal nothings instead. Albeit with a poison sting curling in a tail of keen observation: "There are few among your peacetime generals who see beyond their old books and tactical manuals. And none who understand your long war plans as I do, since I helped you draft and execute them at Bad Camberg."

"Agreed. Yet generals are much like royal relatives, not least because, and too often for the sake of my war, the two are the same thing. Still, both come and go, family and generals I mean. In time I shall replace any man whom the drag of war exposes as unable or unworthy. Or disloyal. After all, the Imperium is brim to full with ambitious young men." Pyotr's jade eyes glinted at Takeshi as he said it.

'*Yes Tennō, I know that you know my ambition. As you know that I know your war plans, for we made them together.*' Yet again he chose prudent silence over speech. As Pyotr's coconspirator, Takeshi has license to speak truth to him on politics and the war as no other man in the Imperium. But even for such as him, there are real and strict limits. Dangerous borders that he may not cross unarmed.

"Good. We understand each other. Then go to Genève."

"Genève? Why there? Why not Lwów or Aral, where the serious fighting is?"

"Genève is where I need you, and more important, where I want you. Find out what can be salvaged from the ineptitude of my cousin and the High Command, who are burning half my new forests looking for this man they call 'The Ghost.' Report to me also on the progress of my armies at the siege of Toruń."

"As you command, Imperator."

"While you are there, take charge of all bandit suppression patrols. Sweep the surface clean, but save my forests from more damage by my generals. Burnish your military credentials, but do it safely, from behind the main fighting lines. If you wish to advise me in this war, you need to see it up close at least once."

'*As do you, Pyotr. A slut in every bedroom but still a virgin king when it comes to making war. Yet, I don't see you shifting your ample ass from the Jade Throne to don adamant, gird your loins, and raise a sword. You would rather sheath the blade that hangs between your legs inside some virile young lover, while better men die for you under burning farfolk stars.*' Takeshi bowed low, saying nothing.

Pyotr was pretty sure he knew what Takeshi was really thinking. He, too, said nothing, but for a far different reason. Pyotr observed no limits or borders in his speech that he did not erect himself. He gave Takeshi vague assurances from Main HQ that the fight would soon be over on Genève, that the fall of besieged Toruń was a matter of when, and not if; that he wanted a first hand report from his most trusted adviser among The Admitted. Both men lied so habitually and brazenly to each other that it would have made them uncomfortable to speak plainer truth.

"It is good to know victory is close, Emperor. Though the news comes more slowly than we expected and hoped the last time we spoke in private."

"I expect nothing but victory from my Rikugun," Pyotr proclaimed stickily, ignoring the subtle jibe of Takeshi's plural, sucking instead on a thick slice of syrupy peach he pulled from a tall white jar on a table beside him.

"Your admirals swept all before them, except for the heavy defenses at the ice moons of Aral, that continues."

"It was a great victory."

"Actually, given how small the Krevan Republic Navy is, or was, it was no great feat for so large a fleet as yours to succeed at Genève, Brno and Lwów. But to get bogged down at Aral? You will need some new admirals soon, I think."

"We grow them by the bushel in the Imperium."

"The real problem, sire, is your generals. They do not deliver victory, do they? Neither swift nor easy or complete, as you rightfully demand. An easy run across the open plains of backward Genève, then a lurch into the forest. Costly progress on Brno, yes, but things do not go so well on Lwów or at the outer moons in Aral system. I hear another of your cousins lost the Light Patrol in a crater fight there?"

"My army shall prevail there, and everywhere. There is plenty of time before the next phase of my war plan unfolds. As for the flames that scour my conquest of Genève, I chastise my cousin and generals but I understand that fire is war and war is fire. Making war without fire is like eating sausages without mustard."

'*Must you phrase everything in metaphors of gluttony?*'

"That is why I send you. There is resistance on Genève, behind the frontlines. A legend is spreading about a bandit leader, a man they call the 'Ghost.' Suppress all resistance, crush this story before it starts. Heroic stories are dangerous things."

"I will have full command authority?"

"In rear area operations, yes. But no more than that. First, show the Jade Court, and me, what you can do. I preauthorize all your actions. As you did before, you again have my passport. Take ten companies of SAC commandos. Clean out the rear areas and any 'bandits' who dare to remain active. Crush the resistance."

'*A limited command, yet an elite one. More important, it's independent of both RIK and SAC. Well, fair enough. That means I'm closer to the center of things than ever. Besides, the moonlet's secret must be kept. It's why I was first sent to Genève, to make sure the Truant mercs were put into lead combat positions, until they were all dead. I'll take Naujock along again. He enjoys this kind of duty.*'

"I please your ambition. No, don't respond." Pyotr sucked noisily on a second slice of honeyed peach, dripping syrup onto the blue ermine gown he always wore when in private chambers. It was stained badly with many prior meals and with drips and dribbles of his favorite spiced black snuff. "Questions, my dear?" '*For I have many I want to ask you, my sweet young killer. Standing there all red and copper and black, coiled to spring like a sonoran coral snake. So very pretty and so very quick and totally lethal. Yes, you are always ready to kill and to feed off lesser snakes. Indeed you are. Do you understand that I am no pretty poisoner? I am a python who can crush your quickness.*'

"Just one. Bandits?"

"It is what my royal cousin calls deserters and stragglers. A useful little term, actually. Rather like my late mother's nightshirt: it covers everything. It will let you do anything you deem necessary, to anyone you say is a resister."

"I see. Yes, that *is* useful. Thank you for this opportunity to make history in your name." Takeshi is not good or practiced at open flattery, on which the Jade Court lives like other men live on air. He still fumbles it more often than not. It's not in his natural skill set. He hasn't the patience for it. He's too eager for power that's independent of all others, including one day free of Pyotr. He's far better at secret manipulation of other men's vanity. And Pyotr is overflowing with vanity.

"It is not so great a chance as that. You are to stay exclusively in the rear areas. Leave the taking of Toruń City to my generals and the main army on Genève. At least for now. They, too, have a righteous role to play. They, too, must feel useful."

"You know that I could handle that mission for you as well."

"Perhaps, but it is too soon. You need this field experience, colonel. It will put some fiber in your bowels. More important, it will put notches on your sword, and that could be useful to me when it comes to dealing with my generals, later. Report to me in one month. Dismissed."

***

'*It has been three weeks. One more and I can leave this backwater. I have been away from the Jade Court for too long. One cannot divine Pyotr's thinking from out here.*' As Takeshi turns to gaze left the bill of his peaked SAC cap slices into a stiff, late afternoon breeze. It carries a strong smell of burning horsehair and roasted animal flesh to his nostrils. He so slightly wrinkles his nose. Otherwise, the *taisa* looks content. Lost in his own sublime presence, absent in excitable thoughts about the vast sum of hate and power and opportunity that war unleashes.

As he swivels his head back to the right he catches a quizzical look from an overweight major standing four meters away. The portly *shōsa* frames the butt end of a line of eight gray men, forming today's execution party. Seven meters ahead, four frightened boys stand in a jagged row before a rustled and unkempt old tool shed. Behind them a small family cottage is burning from its roof. Three are brothers, ages 14, 16, and 12. The oldest is trying to look defiant, The youngest is crying openly. The middle child merely looks blank. A 13-year old school pal stands stiffly apart from the threesome, silently bidding to somehow disassociate from them. In another minute the modest distance he achieves won't matter.

A plump woman and an old man still wearing his hat, mother and grandfather of the three brothers, lie in widening crimson pools where they fell in front of the boys, trying to protect them with their own bodies. The oozing blood is still warm, dark and oily and thick. Takeshi glances down to a lump of horseshit clinging to his polished boot. He stokes it against a rise in the ground. It clings still. '*I want to return to my karesansui. It needs my attention.*' He has tended a miniature Zen garden since boyhood. It's all he has left from his past, the only thing he took with him when he fled from the Broderbund and left his home on Fates forever. Even Takeshi is not sure why so small a thing is so important to him, only that it is.

'*I may be more Nagoyan than the monks considered.*' There are much greater rock gardens deep inside the Waldstätte Palast, the largest built in secret centuries ago by the first Nagoyan advisers to Oetkert-Shaka dynasts, to Pyotr's forebears. He discovered these extraordinary Imperial Gardens after he was anointed one of The Admitted. He prefers his odorless miniature. Takeshi has no discernible scent. He's cold, antiseptic, odorless. Except when in his anger or while killing. Then he exudes a brash, red metallic smell, like nitric acid spilled on zinc. He reeks of red metal at this moment, as he looks down at the dead mother and grandfather.

"Orders, sir?" *Shōsa* Alfonso Gomez asks for the order in an eerie decadence. He has big, wide, artificial yellow eyes that hardly ever blink. "Shall I carry out the execution of the saboteurs?"

Takeshi thinks it odd that he uses such formal military manners in the midst of this filth. He doesn't reply, not right away. He's thinking on his career, as always. He *really* doesn't want to be here, in this stinking, fecal village. '*What's it called? Ahh, it doesn't matter.*'

It looks and smells no different than the last score of villages he 'evacuated' before today. Although this one is farther north, colder and poorer than the others on the rich flatland plains of Genève. It reminds him a little of one of the clusters of *dāsa* slave hovels on his homeworld of Fates, one of the original Ordensstaat worlds still ruled by the broken and exiled Broderbund. Except there are no gelded clones here. No male *dāsa* tethered behind acoustic levitation tractors working the rich fields. No flashing lash tearing slave flesh under a dim blue sun on a grand commandery, outside the sealed monastic compound where he grew up. Nor any female *dāsa* like those who toiled in the barracks of his youth, and also served monks' beds. There is no school of the Black Faith here, either. Nothing like the dull green halls where he spent his childhood, the most brilliant and recalcitrant lad the cruelly hard priests of Fates ever taught. And their greatest disappointment.

For he believed in blasphemy against their core doctrines. Just ten, he yelled at the bent over old Masters, whom he knew he already exceeded in both intellect and wisdom: "Blasphemy is essential to finding truth! Blasphemy *is* truth! Heresy is freedom!" They beat him for that outburst, and many others like it over six more years. They hated his bold skepticism, and feared it. So they beat him with hard, dead scrolls. He wouldn't recant. He stayed defiant, committing every unjust blow they inflected to his perfect memory. Storing each one and the name of the man who delivered it in his vengeance vault.

At 16 years he was allowed to leave the compound on his own for the first time, on an errand for Brother Maximillian Kahn. He hid his *karesansui* under his robes and fled the monks forever. Left behind the monochromatic life of devotions and daily study of the *Corpus Hermeticum* and all the other arcane mysticism they planned for him. They wailed and raged when they discovered he was gone, for they knew he was much greater than he realized. Knew that without him all their plans to return to power on Kestino must falter. Although they did not yet know the true, great secret about him. That was still hidden in the scrolls. Its discovery lay 20 years or more in the future. They weren't even looking for it, back then.

For four years he wandered the Imperium, exploring its greatest cities and exciting worlds beyond the Ordensstaat core. He ended up at Pusan University on Daegu, where he learned of the radical ideals of 'Purity' that then challenged all orthodoxies, from the Black Faith to the *Satya Yuga*, to the old sciences and the Peace of Orion among the star empires. He also learned about SAC's dominant power on Kestino, both over Pyotr and across the Imperium, and a far different tale about the Curia and Pyotr than the gnarled and embittered Brethren told him.

Pusan skimmed the cream off the empire's intellectual life. It was thick, rich stuff that excited young men of talent like Takeshi. Yet it was spotty with flies of mediocrity, only there because of their high caste and their rich fathers. He hated its clotted orthodoxies, as he hated the old lies and fables of the monks on Fates. That independence of mind brought him to the notice of the best professors and of SAC's top recruiters. He was cultivated, groomed. Beautiful young men and women were sent to seduce him, to compromise him, only to report back that he never compromised and could not be seduced. He was prepared in the usual ways for a career in covert ops and intelligence with SAC. In time he found it politic to convert to the new doctrines. In private, he despised Purity's rank pseudoscience as much as he did the ancient superstitions of the Black Faith as taught on Fates.

On the surface he mouths whatever phrases he must, to please Pyotr or his superiors or any useful audience. Within, he indulges an older and crueler wisdom even he must credit to the monks of Fates, reinforced by life experience. It reduces to a Vedic-Brethren meld, a syncretic verse of the Black Faith based on the myth warrior Arjuna: an ancient embodiment of murder, a godly excuser of killing, of feeding off death as the natural order of all things great and small. The image of Arjuna returns to him in this moment, standing in muck and blood and horseshit in a ridiculous village on Genève with a dutiful *shōsa* waiting for his 'kill' order.

'*Creatures live on creatures, the stronger on the weaker. A mouse eats the wheat. A mongoose eats the mouse. A cat eats the mongoose. Dogs devour cats. Wild beasts eat the dogs. Even ascetics or hermits may live only by devouring. The hierarchy of devouring rules all things in, above, and below Orion. This is the central truth of all life, of all thousand histories of the Thousand Worlds.*'

For Takeshi, stripped of the mysticism he has no time for, and no faith in, this is a first order belief. He revels in the moral smoothness of its logic, in its freedom from restraint and in the inevitability of murder on the path to power. Killing has always come easily to him, naturally and without remorse. '*And if murder feels so keen, how much better must be command in war? I must rule an army before this ends. I must feel in my hands the power that Pyotr wields over billions of lives and the fate of worlds. I am not meant to serve in a heaven made by the Brethren or Sakura-kai, and reigned over by Pyotr. It is not my destiny to serve anyone. I am meant to rule. If I cannot rule in the Imperium's heaven because of my low birth, I shall turn it into Hell and rule it then.*'

Takeshi is slick, secretive, cunning and duplicitous. He kills more easily than any true believer in SAC's authority or in Purity ideology, which he despises. Every ruthless, calculated murder he makes must achieve his own interest first and last. Or at least his pleasure. Not some abstract cause. He doesn't care about dull theologies. He won't kill for ideas. He's a natural born killer nonetheless. He has a scientist's focus, a politician's insight, and an assassin's soul. These are rare and useful vices. His superiors are glad of them. Even if no one in SAC's General Curia or any Admitted in the Tennō's inner circle trusts his ascending talent. Trust is less important than his silent, ruthless competence. And he has that in buckets.

That's why Pyotr chose this special *taisa*, this trim and capable and ruthless SAC colonel, to lead the most critical covert operation in over 300 years.

'*Yet for all my talent and ambition, here I am leading a few thousand thugs on filthy Genève.*' He hates standing in the three brothers' village, surrounded by stupid peasant things, with dull thugs like Gomez and the firing squad under his command, always awaiting the next order. And the toad Albert Naujock waiting for him back at base camp, a mockery of an orderly and soldier. '*What was I thinking, asking to leave Kestino, ending up in a fetid village stinking of piss and hay? I'll accept it for another week. I have to accept it. But I don't have to like it.*'

He's standing just in front of his black command hover, barely deigning to descend into the muck and malignity of the sad little hamlet he is come to burn. The whole affair is too small for his swelling ambition. Already, simple murder like this no longer satisfies him. It lacks measure sufficient to his talent. He wants, he needs, to murder on a far grander scale. He's confident that he'll command an army, or more. He wants to appear before all Orion as if he's Death itself, riding a pale horse to make murder on a scale never seen before. '*It's my destiny, my purpose. There is and can be no other.*' His smoldering anger at the mediocrity of murder smells like nitric acid poured on copper. It turns air around him red, bitter and suffocating hot. His men sense it, and even smell it. One man shifts uneasily. The fat major just stares and waits. And waits.

Takeshi looks disgustedly down to his boot a second time, to ensure it's finally clean of the horseshit he stepped in when he hopped the last few centimeters from the lip of his command hover. It isn't. He wipes the soiled toe on a loose turf of grass disturbed from the ground by his hover's air blasting descent brakes. It's a sleek, six-man flyer with full field command-and-control coms. It's coated in all black carbyne sheeting, except for transparent armor scuttles on which reverse images of navigation and piloting symbology glow in subdued blues and greens. **Special Action Commando** is etched in angular, gothic silver letters along each side of its telemetric needlenose. It's one of the forbidding looking, new and top line types favored by SAC officers. It's meant to intimidate.

On the flat right fuselage a gray rectangle breaks the blackness, framing a large bear who rears up on powerful legs, *rot* tongue lolling from its snarling mouth. The claws are bloody, too, as is its painted penis. It's the 'Erect Bear' emblem of the Special Action Commando, famed and feared on all the Imperium worlds for decades before it ever scowled down at huddling farfolk in stinking villages on foreign Genève. Engraved in gold lettering across the bridge of the nose is his personal motto: "*Enemy of Mercy. Enemy of Pity. Enemy of Peace.*"

His thoughts darken as he recalls that his exquisite *Ikebana* flowers are broken and gone, snapped and burned by his own hand before he left to set up the Bad Camberg lie. He broke stems and crushed fine petals so that no one but him could ever know them, ever gaze on the unique shape and fragile beauty that took him over 20 years to cultivate. Only he knows their fineness. He laid them down with more care than he'll leave the discarded vessels of the brothers and their school friend. Four lives waiting on his word, as have so many murders past, present and to come. They mean no more to him than a casual puff of dead leaves surfing on an autumn wind. He looks over to the firing line. "You may shoot when ready, *shōsa*." He says it with just the slightest mocking hint of formal manners.

Major Alfonso Gomez is oblivious to open scorn in his colonel's voice. For there's less and more to the order than unquerying obedience, than a functionary's casual careerism and a moral shrug of *à la guerre comme à la guerre*. There's a rising belief in all those around him in the Power State as new secular deity. All that is, save Takeshi Watanabe. He believes in nothing.

The others think that these dirty little killings are moral because necessary to their higher cause. It's the secret key to Pyotr's power and to his war, and to his cynical embrace of Purity, a quack biopolitical theory he doesn't believe in or care about one whit. Men like Pyotr and Takeshi, men who believe in the permanent imperfectability of Humanity, only kill for personal advantage. They don't make the holocausts that Purity plans. Genocide is always the work of idealists and dull, gray helpers in civil service suits who pass along necessary papers and resources. As long as the order comes from higher up, with triple signatures. As long as other dull gray men in dull gray uniforms, men like Major Gomez, carry it out without question or pause or regret. Idealists and functionaries make genocides.

The *shōsa* gives the first command. "Present arms!"

Out here, in the middle of a war, Takeshi knows what true freedom is. Old moral codes and laws and rules dissolve under his acid will, under the sway of Pyotr's passport. He hears the Wolf of War call him, howl its red lust. He knows that there are billions upon billions of sheep waiting to be slaughtered, all across Orion. And no wolf is ever troubled how or why sheep die. He wants so much more than this. He longs to release his inner wolf straight for his enemy's throat. Which enemy to rip up first? He hasn't yet decided. Ferocity is a cardinal virtue in war and Takeshi knows now what he previously only suspected. He can be the Wolf of War incarnate. '*But will they let me? Will they stop me before I win?*'

"Shoot!"

Eight *click clack* maser shots sound almost as one, so practiced and skilled are these routine killers, so close their range to the boys. All four crumple and fall, chests seared and still smoking, exploded outward from maser burns and instantly cooked and boiling organs. Three die before slumping heads hit the ground, two brothers and a school friend. The 14-year old lies in half-conscious agony a minute from reaching that undiscovered country from which no traveler ever returns, if any even reaches it. His head rolls to the right, once bright eyes semi glazed but open and still alive, filled with surprise and pain and interrupted boyish hopes.

The *shōsa* draws a stubby pistol, walks eight paces to the moaning boy and fires a maser bolt into his temple, exploding brains and bone across the grass. It's no *coup de grace*. No act of fatherly mercy to a dying and suffering boy about the same age as his son. It's a standing operations rule in the anti-bandit campaign, nothing more. "*Field Order #43: All bandit cleansing to be final and certain.*" The rotund major fires single shots into the other three small, unmoving bodies as well. All head shots. Eight men of the kill squad stand watching in a relaxed line, awaiting their next order. "Secure weps and gear. Police the corpses. Get them in the shed and burn it." Gomez isn't upset at all at what he has done. He's hungry and bored and wants to get back to base camp. He'll do it all again tomorrow and the day after that, and sleep soundly each and every night.

Raw ambition brought Takeshi Watanabe to Genève, to this filthy field to lead a SAC death brigade 'purifying' rear areas of stragglers, of soldiers who molted their KRA uniforms to hide among the civvies, or just boys accused of sabotage and tried and executed on-the-spot. Vanity and ambition make him give the order to kill any 'bandits' or other *undesirable persons* among the occupied population. He's utterly confident in his ruthless cunning, certain that he can return to SAC HQ on Kestino to dart and maneuver inside the shark tank, thriving even among the many sleek killers in churning waters filled with swimming treachery, both at the Curia and in the Jade Court. What he doesn't know is how many eyes intently watch him, already keenly interested in his every thought and whimsy and act.

Pyotr, the *Sakura-kai* secret officer society, ever plotting and wizened fanatics of the exiled Broderbund, all see in Takeshi a powerful tool of their political advantage and future monopoly of power. All plan to shape and control him. All misjudge him. He is always and only his own man. More so, now that the moral solvent of war is washing over him and opportunity for mass murder is all around.

'*It's not enough. It's never enough.*' He thinks it as he watches *Shōsa* Gomez's kill squad dispose of the bodies. Vanity courses in him, throbbing on the lip of his command hover before a burning cottage and a shit-and-blood smeared hamlet on unimportant Genève. His vital egoism, his whole being is enthralled by war. He is circling a white hot flame of absolute power, alive to terrible danger yet helpless to turn away from its brilliance. War is the ultimate theater of power. He senses its nova heat of unlimited possibility. He must fly straight to the flame. He must.

Takeshi watches the kill squad dump the limp body of the youngest boy into the gaped open tool shed. Already inside are the other three boys, their mother and grandfather. They were shot five minutes before the four trembling boys were killed. He watches Gomez set the hutch on fire, sniffing warily at rising wisps of wood smoke, searching for hints of melting fat and burned bone. Otherwise, he has no interest in the hamlet or dead 'bandits' anymore. "*Leaves on the wind.*"

"Prepare to move out," he orders, more than ready to lift up from the burning horseflesh reek and *crackling* of melting fat coming from the tool shed. The sound is getting louder every second, flames licking and leaping with oily fuel. "*Shōsa* Gomez, I'll be at 10th Armored HQ for the next three Standard Hours. I'll rejoin your Special Action Squad in the next village, at..." He checks coordinates: "Y7 lateral, B15 vertical at seven hundred hours. Wrap up everything here by then. I want a complete report on the day's business by ten hundred."

"Yes sir, a full report by military midnight. You'll have it, sir." All militaries operate on a 10-hour Universal Standard Day, 100 minutes of 100 seconds in each of ten standard hours. It clashes with local time but keeps things orderly among fleets, distant HQs, and far flung imperial systems. For the same reasons, it's used in all bohr system travel and trade. It's confusing as hell, and absolutely necessary.

Black odors and rolls of smoke from the tool shed are growing heavier. Acrid, harsh, rancid. Full of scorched hair, dank clothes, and melting boys. Takeshi steps into his command hover. It's *humming* with tense expectancy of flight, holding acoustic white noise nozzles steady at 15cm off the ground. With a small flick of the silver tip of his swagger baton, he motions to the pilot. For all his bored and calm exterior, as the sleek flyer ascends and whirtles away Takeshi quivers with excitement. He secretly relishes these daily opportunities for murder that his SAC grays provide. The chance to indulge a callous sadism he first noticed in himself when at age 12 he killed the monks' old guard dog on Fates.

Just to feel what it was like.

Just because he could.

He felt the same cruel pleasure when he shot the boys' mother and grandfather. He was especially amused that the old man's perfectly creased hat stayed atop his head even as his already lifeless body slumped down to the ground, making an unkempt pile of oozing gray and red helplessness. He feels a white flame drawing him ever closer, immensely dangerous and seductive in its flickering allure. As the hover turns to take him back to Main HQ he shudders with orgasmic pleasure. He thinks it, not for the last time: '*War has come to Orion. And war is good.*'

Data search: colonization
Result: sleepers
Historia Humana, Volume III, Part V (a)

Like the DNA arks, sleeper ships used only very primitive lightsails past the initial boost phase, and before braking. Although multigenerational, they were very small by our standards: shorter than a mercury ball pitch and about as wide. Larger mass limited them to 7% lightspeed, forcing one way voyages lasting up to five centuries, the maximum ever attempted by pioneers. Today, most of the Thousand Worlds lie far beyond that era's reach, settled by later quantum drive ships that caught up and passed the original sleepers. It is hard for us to imagine the devotion and toughness needed to spend lifetimes confined in such primitive vessels, even suspended in a stasis pod. Though all were surpassed by faster ships that left decades or even centuries afterward, we owe them honor and respect.

The key tek making sleeper ships possible was 'suspend,' first used to treat catastrophic trauma such as industrial accidents and war wounds. Suspend halts all biofunction at a molecular level. That allowed reduction in ship mass and corresponding increases in speed by eliminating most life support requirements and psychological limitations that had hindered practical colony ship design and operation. Most of the sleepers who volunteered were scientists, but not all. Plain folk went, too. It was a concession demanded by the majority who stayed behind, who argued that Humanity was not comprised solely of technicians. AI nanny bots tended the sleepers and banks of zygotes and unfertilized eggs and sperm, to be used to replace any dead after transit and to make new colonists to rapidly expand settler populations in the fragile period right after new world planetfall.

Colonization of far off worlds already being terraformed by AI bots remained unattractive to most in Sol system until development of the quantum drive. And why not? It was a happy age, the First Satya Yuga in our recorded history. Why leave for harsh, if brave new worlds? Besides, using GDM drives capable of 0.3 lightspeed still meant decades had to be spent between stars. Most folk anticipated greater velocity breakthroughs in their own near futures, or their children's. So they postponed leaving, then never left at all. Only 13 GDM ships ever left Sol.

Kagoshima, Nagoya, *and* Yokohama *were key players in early Orion history. They founded prosperous colonies under those names that ultimately merged into the Grün elite in a cultural-political-military alliance that changed the history of Orion. Their many descendants are a real force in Imperium cultural and military syncretism still, becoming even more prominent after the Great or Red Purge by the Dowager, Mary Oetkert. Eight of the GDM ships settled in what later became*

Dauran space: Idaho, Kashi, Liaotung, Novgorod, Odessa, Rio, Shanghai *and* Vatsa. *Those worlds were soon closed to outsiders by the 'Hermit Empire,' as successor Dauran worlds remain sealed to farfolk today by the tyrant Jahandar, the 'Father of the Grim Revolution.'*

Most infamously, and unfortunately for the chance of peaceful settlement of Orion, the GDM ship Deus ex Machina *carried the austere Sword Brothers (or Broderbund der Ritter) to arid Terra Deus, cursed foundation world of the old Ordensstaat. Its departure was marked by an act of religious violence that shook the whole colony movement, and sent fleets of New Meccans and New Medians chasing futilely after them, into the darkness. All the New Median ships were lost. The New Meccans looked for decades before they gave up the search and settled on a semi desert world, like seeking like as happened across so many of the new Thousand Worlds where settlers seemed to want replicas of what was left behind.*

Worse, Deus ex Machina *carried secret, illegal DNA banks and reserves of human zygotes used to clone concubines and dāsa slaves. Such gross violations of the rules of colonization changed the colony movement and all history. As is well known, the Brethren then built the first interstellar warships, raised the first colony armies, and brought war out to the stars. Later, they allied militarily with the House of Oetkert, to build out the original Grün Imperium while waging two more interstellar wars in the name of their austere Black Faith. By the time the 'Auld Alliance was formed by Daura, the Calmar Union, and the last Neutrals, to wage the Third Orion War, that evil doctrine ruled over a third of the Orion spur.*

The last GDM ship was Baffin, *which settled on icy Nunavut, the only colony established on a near ice planet. No one else wanted it. Its determined and radical, but mostly harmless, Inuit traditionalists kept apart from the politics of Orion for centuries, refusing to join any of the three star empires whose borders they abut at a critical juncture. They finally joined the Calmar Union after coming under direct attack by the bordering Dauran Empire during the Second Orion War. Nunavut's long tradition of independence is preserved in a distinctly traditional culture almost lost before its founding, and the main reason for its founding. Its eventual confederation with the Calmar Union was made on special terms, with a unique exemption from universal meat and other animal husbandry laws that permit certain cultural practices and live meat dietary exemptions that are banned elsewhere. Famous for their winter games and their homeworld's fabled 'Great Snow,' the people of Nunavut also welcome...*

Some sleeper ships were destroyed in collisions with uncharted dust. Others drifted off beam as assists were turned off when Sol's economy dipped or a war broke out. Later, Z-pinch fusion and quantum drives that antiquated light sailing overtook sleepers still in transit. Some were out 400 or 500 years, then caught up by much larger and faster vessels that left decades or centuries later. Once awake, the original sleepers were told that worlds promised to them had been colonized by settlers already there, under an ancient claim right known as terra incognita. *Most sleepers abandoned their old lightsail ships and destinations upon hearing this disagreeable news, agreeing to transship to join already settled worlds.*

A few refused, taking new type engines onboard but declaring that they would continue on to vastly more distant stars. It is not known if they ever got there. We lost all contact as they sailed off in secret, boosting new deuterium-tritium drives to nonterraformed systems at the farthest ends of Orion, or perhaps even beyond. A few are thought to have tried to cross The Gap to the Perseus arm, which is still not possible even today. The worlds of Orion grew indifferent to sleeper fates as decades passed, then centuries. In some cases, knowing the sleeper ships housed drear cults, we were silently glad to see the last OE fanatics leave the Orion spur.

Flowers

Madjenik has left the southern fires behind, moving stealthily through the still standing Gold Oak Forest north of burned out Pilsudski Wood. The company has left all pursuit behind as well, and the Jabos and HK drones that General Brusilov sent after them. It has gone as far west as Jan intends. The whole company cheers when he gives the order: "Turn hard and due north. Head straight for Toruń."

Now they face a more relentless problem than enemy pursuit. The trekkers are running out of supplies. Water they gather from streams as they move, but all food is gone, or gone black. Including ration kits taken from the last RIK dead. Even the last "dicks of death" are gone. That's what Tom Hipper called horrible mini mockmeat sausages Madjenik found in captured RIK ration kits. Everyone pushed off eating the foul things to last. Then they had to eat them, the last ration of any kind taken from the last dead enemy they left under leaf fall in Pilsudski Wood.

Two days later and even Tom admits to his squad during a short rest: "I sure could eat one of those dead dick things now. Don't suppose anybody has one? No? Yeah, thought not."

Four days later and the whole company is trying to live off handfuls of wild berries gathered along the way, but they give everyone the blue runs. Madjenik reaches a crisis point. Too many fighters are too weak from hunger and the runs to go farther. Jan calls the company NCOs and Zofia over to talk it out.

"Zeke, you're a true woodsman. Give it to me straight. Is there any way we can scrounge enough food in these woods for so many fighters?"

"Of course, sir. But there's only one way. You know what it is."

"Is it come to that?"

"You know it has!" Zofia snaps at him. She is impatiently worried about the food problem and has been for many days. She's even more concerned about his inability to see the solution and to act on it as everybody knows they must.

"What? What do you mean?"

"It came to that three days ago, captain." Her criticism of his leadership in front of others always hurts more because he knows she's right, and that all along she has seen right through him and the problem that he's stalled on.

"OK, it's agreed then." Jan concedes the issue that at least three quarters of Madjenik don't want to face, given their native Genèven devotion to conservation. "We have no choice. We hunt."

Tom Hipper says: "I recommend that we camp right here for two days, rest and restock the mockmeat bins. *Err,* with the real thing this time."

"Zeke, we're going to have to rely on you to dress the kills and prepare all live meat for cooking. I don't think any of us know how."

"Not sure *I* do, sir. Never done it before, either."

"At least you know these animals better than any of us, no?"

"Sure. But I was a game warden before the war, never a hunter."

"You still know more than me, or anyone here. Do the best you can."

"Well, once we have meat, it should cook exactly the same as mockmeat."

"Put someone else on the cooking. I want you in charge of the prep work."

"OK, I'll get Third Platoon to rig cooking gear. They've still got engineers. I'll need five or six troopers to dress the kills."

"Pull them from Tom Hipper's platoon, from Dog." Jan turns back to Zofia. "Lieutenant, since you're so keen for this and so sure it's the right thing to do, I'm putting you in charge of the killing. I hear you're pretty good at that."

***

On Genève, conservation of wild fauna is an almost sacred way of life in which all locals take fierce pride, connected to their pride in the old growth forests. Even now, on the lip of genuine hunger, some in Madjenik cleave to a rigid animal rights ethic from well before the war, and resist the idea of a hunt. They still can't understand how ancients managed it, or accepted mass slaughter of herd animals every day. Others feel real nausea when thinking about eating a dead animal. The majority are simply used to cheap synthetic proteins, to mockmeat, so they've never given much thought to a long settled moral and legal issue. Jan orders the NCOs to make sure every fighter eats a share of the fresh meat, once it's ready.

Zofia leads out a hunting party of Madjenik's five best shots. Her snipers bring down a brace of hares, several partridge, five wild turkeys, an elk, and a whitetail deer. They skin and clean and cook the meat with improvised microwave roasters made from spare masers. It's not a lot of food to share among so many, but it'll keep them going. If they can get over being so sick.

It's the first real, natural meat anyone ever eats. Nobody eats real animal flesh in Orion anymore, especially on an agro planet like Genève. Cattle are kept for dairy, sheep are just for sheering, chickens and geese and guinea fowl make eggs. That's it. Otherwise, all flesh-like protein is vat grown. Mockmeat is plentiful and cheap and suits most people just fine. Grown in hanging slabs of insensate protein in industrial vats, it's easily shaped and molded and chemically flavored to taste like beef, fish, pork, chicken, mutton, gazelle, bison, snake or any desired or exotic flavor. Developed for quantum colony ships nearly two millennia ago, mockmeat is a basic industry right across Orion.

Most worlds have banned live meat. It's reduced to a rare, illegal indulgence of bored and wealthy epicureans. Beyond that tiny market there's little demand, since mockmeat is readily grown and available. Larger scale eating of real meat is confined to poorer Dauran 'real meat' worlds where backward people hunt and fish because they must and herd animals are penned and slaughtered as in the past. Outside Daura, it's only allowed on Nunavut in the Calmar Union, where ancient cultural practices are historically and legally indulged and exempt.

Half the Wreckers throw up their first stomach full. It's a physical, not moral reaction. No one ever slaughtered a food animal before, so the elk and deer and birds are unsafely gutted, contaminating the flesh. But they learn quickly. Hunting parties fan out every day as they resume movement through the deep woods, filled with animals. Another few days of no longer dining a graceful distance from the slaughterhouse and everyone in Madjenik gathers around the cooking masers and meat racks to dig dirty fingers into the greasy gore of a large spit roasted moose. They chew its cut flesh with real pleasure. Hunger is worse than complicity.

***

Another 200 klics north-northwest through the Gold Oak Forest and Madjenik stops at the startling edge of a wide meadow. A dark forest canopy and a must of silver pine needles and decomposing oak and maple leaves, and other lichen rotted windfall, has enshrouded them for weeks. Suddenly, the dank gives way to clear air and canopy opens to a vista filled with stars overhead.

Madjenik is standing at an old botanical border planted by the AI nanobots to mark the boundary between separately managed old growth forests. In this case, the borderland between the Gold Oak Forest they're leaving and Toruń Wood, just across the wide clearing. A gentle breeze carries delicate scents from yellow-and-white honeysuckles and hordes of scarlet trumpet-vine blossoms running alongside the meadow. Beyond the line of yellow-and-scarlet stretches a broad and open field full of late summer blossoms. Tens of millions of daisy-like white flowers wave and dance in a gentle breeze. They stop to stare and to breathe it in.

"Those old nanny bots sure had green thumbs, didn't they?" one trooper in the lead platoon remarks as they break out from under the forest canopy.

"You mean green widgets, or whatever."

"Did they even have hands?"

"Who cares?" says a third man, hurrying to pause and look. "Look what they *did!* And smell it! It's like breathing ambrosia."

"You're right. It's sheer bloody *genius*! Yet again! What marvels they were. Master terraformers."

"Do you see them, all the daisies?"

"Actually, they're african moons." It's Jarred Whitmore, interjecting as he rarely does into conversation by others. He knows all these flowers types well, from gardening with his mother before the war.

"Really? OK kid, you would know, I suppose."

Jarred falls silent, embarrassed to seem a know-it-all in front of his mates, but even more because he's lost in a rush of memories of Mother and her wonderfully varied flower garden. He stands there with the rest of his platoon, joined now by all Madjenik. Gawping at the open space, marveling to see stars again.

The youngest natural eyes in the company, and several artificial sets soft *clicking* and *whirring*, narrow to make out a dark tree line to the north, on the far side of the botanical break where the wide meadow worked as a natural fire stop preventing southward spread of the terrible blaze that reduced Toruń Wood. They don't know it yet, but the flowers saved the Gold Oak Forest they leave behind.

"The Great Fire." That's what immense blazes along five Old Forest Roads spoking away from besieged Toruń are being called, though Madjenik doesn't know that yet either, or even that any fire broke out up north. They know only that blotches of Pilsudski Wood geysered pillars of flame and smoke all around them when an angry RIK *taishō* looked for "the filthy bandits" who kept embarrassing him, and so hurled Zeus's electric bolts randomly into the deep woods below.

"A'right," barks an anxious NCO, leaping to disperse the company before Zofia jumps down his throat for letting them stand clustered in the open. "Enough ah yur gawkin.' Space out and reform duh files! Let's move."

They step guiltily through a host of golden, bell shaped flowers. "*Narcissus pseudonarcissus*," Jarred says softly but out loud, thinking that he says it only to himself. They hear him and laugh.

"Jarred Whitmore, you have so much wool in your head it's a wonder you aren't taken away and sheared for being a sheep!"

The spread '*stretches in never ending line along the margin of their day. Ten thousand they see at a glance, tossing golden heads in sprightly dance.*' Jarred hears the familiar verses sonorous in his mother's voice, almost as if she's walking beside him in the open way between two great forests planted over a thousand years ago, managed by wondrous AI who worked so patiently and wisely to raise new life under a skyfall full of stars. '*They flash upon my inward eye, which is the bliss of solitude, then my heart with pleasure fills, and dances with the daffodils.*' He does a little hop step that his mother always gives when she sees the daffodils in a neighbor's meadow close to home, the place she taught him that and many another ancient verse. Battle hardened fighters on either side of the line of march look quizzically at him and then each other, but say nothing. They know he's a bit of an odd duck, but also that he's an OK kid.

It's not just Jarred the flowers surprise with joy. Madjenik breathes in sweet scents of the white-with-black-center african moons and flocks upon flocks of purple disk morning glories, and is revived. Some stoop down to scoop up a blossom or two, better to smell the sweet aroma by pressing soft petals right to their noses. Several women tuck flowers into weave pockets, and one also into the brow of her helmet with her faceplate raised. Some things never change.

Yet they hasten across the firebreak, glancing upward frequently. For after weeks of easy arboreal cover they feel naked under open sky and scudding wisps of nighttime clouds. In their urgency they make good time, moving eight klics north straight across the flowers. As they draw closer to the far shore of the wide meadow and see the dark tree line loom they grow giddy and gay again, like small children let out unexpectedly from school on a bright spring day.

Then everything changes. Dancing white, red, yellow and purple blooms and sprightly green grasses turn to uniform gray as they reach the edge of the ash zone. A lonely, timid coyote bays in the distant desolation, answered at greater distance by a coywolf. A moral chill descends, colder than the gray shrouded night. The north edge of the flower barrier smells of old campfires after a heavy rain sluices down, full of damp rot and frigid mornings, dashed hopes and new hatreds.

The great trees begin again, but they're not living towers of gold oak or silvery pine spires. Underfoot is no deep, musty leaf fall to carpet arboreal cathedrals like Pilsudski Wood or the Gold Oak Forest. The way ahead reeks of ash and death, of malice and murder. It reminds Jan of another landscape, one a dead poet saw in front of an adamantine and ironclad Temple of Mars, its red dome glowing with war, the landscape destroyed all around:

> *"A cake of scurf lies baking on the ground,*
> *and prickly stubs instead of trees are found.*
> *Woods with knots and knares deformed and old;*
> *headless the host, and hideous to behold."*

They move into ashen desolation, all disconsolate with ugly, gouged, mutilated stumps and runty pillars. They walk past verdant lives that burned in agony to half their former height, or less. Charred sentinels stand mute with outstretched, naked limbs, black against a crisply starry night. The trees are raped of rustling leaves and bird song, abandoned even by insects and homeless rodents, left with raw pain and open wounds leaking sap like cankerous sores. Left with solitary hostility to all living things that pass indifferently below.

"There's no eye cover here" Zofia notes to Jan over the command link, ever pragmatic about drones and other surveillance, and the company's well being.

"Right," he agrees. "We'll have to hole up by day, move fast at night. But first we need to move Madjenik quickly out of this field, get under whatever canopy is left in Toruń Wood."

"Yes sir. Also, from the look of that burned out tree line, food and water are going to be problems again. And real soon."

"Right again, lieutenant." It has been a long time since he called her Zofia, not since the sweetgrass meadow. "So conserve our water. Half-rations, starting now. Same with our food supply. Make it happen, Jablonski."

"Yes sir, *captain.*" There's a hurt bite to her use of his rank that even Jan can't miss. It has been like this between them for weeks now. They are pushed apart by taut emotion, forced back together by duty.

"Move out, people! Let's go! Move your lazy asses! That includes you, Private Whitmore!" The boy looks up guiltily at Zofia with pale blue eyes, still lost in thoughts of his old home and mother.

***

Later that night, during a rest break with Madjenik advanced well into the ash zone, Jan looks longingly at Zofia. She's panther-like in the darkness, crouched on guard duty and in command as he takes his ten minute turn at rest. '*Not so long ago I couldn't imagine how such a beautiful creature might engorge with cruelty. Until I saw what she did to boys lying insensate in the burnt sweetgrass.*' Now he no longer shudders when he remembers her knife work on Z+5. He has done too many similar things himself, and he knows it well. '*I've ordered too many hard beatings of prisoners since then, to get intel I needed to keep us alive. I've cut too many throats, to show others that it must be done. I've overseen executions of crying youths. I feel no moral distance from Zofia, from anyone in this filthy war.*'

He was right that worse lay ahead after leaving the meadow, but wrong about why and where the enemy spearheads would push out across Northland. RIK left him and Madjenik far behind, uninterested in so small a prize. '*I wasn't so clever after all. I never dodged and ducked brilliantly around the whole RIK main force to reach Pilsudski Wood, as my troopers think I did. Any straggler bits and pieces like us that got through the drift net into the reef of woods did so because so few RIK commanders paid us any attention. The interrogations told me that. We were minnows wriggling out between net wires that held a whole school of larger KRA dolphins and tuna well enough.*' All bloody and panicking as Rikugun speared and shot and killed all the KRA inside the drift trap, while all around frantic sharks bit and thrashed in a froth of blood frenzy at any little fish that sought escape.

Minnow or not, Jan saw too many of his fighters die no matter what he did.

No matter how clever his tactics of hit-and-hide. Until he finally learned how to fight by fighting, inside Pilsudski Wood. So when he looks over at Lieutenant Jablonski now, red curls whispering softly to him in an ash wind as she crouches alert to potential danger, he sees not a stone killer with no mercy or qualms in her but a highly competent officer. His essential "Number 2" on the trek to Toruń.

Sometimes, and this cooling night is one of those times, he stops being her commanding officer and sees her as any man must. Recognizes a vixenish young woman called Zofia, for whom he has longed since before the war. Since he first saw her stamp across his parade ground in a taut KRA uniform that hardly hid her perfect figure. Since that alluring, red dress evening when he fell into her eyes and personality. Even now he sees under dirt and strain a trim, compact beauty who sometimes shoots him quick looks on the march he doesn't understand, yet craves.

He dwells long and longingly on her curved and feline form. He can't smell her musk anymore, the promise of sex she always gave off before the war. Here, in seared and dead and desecrated woods, she smells like everyone else: of ash and death and dwindling hope, of gray mud, red murder and mad bloody mayhem. Yet, he knows that he desires her more every day. At night he throbs with longing as he dreams of her in red of a different sort, wearing a low cut and slit thigh dress she swirled in to tease and seduce him, once and forever.

Way back when.

Before time ended.

Before the war started.

Before the knives in the sweetgrass.

Before long nights of pursuing fire.

Today he caught a quick look from her flashing green eyes during the dusk march. He lies fitful over the rest period, until at last he surrenders to it, allowing himself to imagine Zofia naked and lying with him. Imagine her beside him, then thrusting under him in sweetgrass bedding on a hot, high summer's day. Just like the time he lay with that lithe brunette three summers back. Only that girl meant nothing. Now, of all places, in the damned ash zone, he dreams of Zofia in a miasma of foggy fantasy sex. Not as she is here in a dead forest, taking turns at watch, ready to kill a man in an instant with a hot maser pistol or a slick, black diamond knife. Not as she is at rest, curled and covered in muck, smelling like death and ash.

Zofia glances over and notes a rare wry smile curling on Jan's lips as he lies still, eyes closed and seemingly asleep. '*Men!*' is all she says to herself, knowing full well what he's dreaming about, because she dreams of him that way, too.

***

"We're getting closer to Toruń, captain," Zofia cautions him five days later.

"Yes, I know." The closer Jan gets to the end, the gloomier he becomes.

"We should expect intensified surveillance. Even if they're not looking for us, they might see us anyway."

"Better slow and safe than dead. We've come so very far."

"Right, captain. When we move we jam, with everything we've still got?"

"Make it so."

Zofia hates these dark, taciturn moods that carry him away from the now more and more often as they draw nearer to Toruń. She knows that she's losing him to the war. Losing him before she ever once had him.

Madjenik is OK on thermals because all around barren, branchless trunks are slow burning and the ground is seared several meters deep, heat traveling along immense, still smoldering roots deep below. Infrared can't pick out their bodies in all that heat. Motion is another matter. So Madjenik uses captured ELMs, which RIK and RSU drones don't detect, because they're not looking for their own side's signals. If they did, a swarm of Jabos would be overhead already.

"Don't assume that the enemy isn't looking for us, or that they've written us off as dead and burned in a reckless general's southern fires."

"Right sir. We mustn't assume that the arrogant *bâtards* in RIK Main HQ on the coast of Northland think that everything in the ash zone is dead, and have yet to stop looking in here, for us and any other survivors."

They're exposed by day to visual spotting by mini drone remotes, disguised as insects and small birds. The damn things stay up forever, as do micro hunters. Superlight aerographite drones are quickly repowered by overflying mobile lasers operated by ground handlers, or by flying into a power beam sent down from picket ships and satellites in geostationary orbit, unmolested by a defeated KRN flotilla long since chased out of the system. Also immune from suppressed ground fire. They've been up there for months already, circling and weaving and looking.

Madjenik moves at night, fighters sleeping fitfully during shortening, cooling days. They lie under a paling, autumnal sun and the blackened trees, covered with dual purpose camo-and-thermal blankets layered with photonic metamaterials that conceal them at nano scales. KRA field blankets keep most warmth in and prying sensors out. They're all safe, but fitful and morose. Especially Jan.

After eight nights of forced marches through desiccated woods every man and woman curses the land and dead trees. They're tired, thirsty, filthy, complaining constantly. Each fighter humps personal weps plus a load of extra gear, their share of captured weapons and equipment, divided proportionate to body weight: tents and blankets coated in deep acoustic muffling, light-bending metamaterials, anti-sound projectors, canteens of water last filled at a quick stream inside the Gold Oak, days before they reached the ash zone of Toruń Wood.

They're crossing a sahara of ash, hot barchan dunes of shifting gray dust. Dry ash blows into artificial or modified eyes and gets into hair down to the scalp. It worries into skin creases on faces and hands, gets inside weaves to burn crotches raw. Slips down boots and into socks to irritate precious spaces between clammy toes that whinge to sore and swollen feet with every leaden step. Water is strictly rationed, and only for drinking. They can't replenish from creeks that no longer flow in this dead land of dry baked beds and little dams of burned branches, of ash clogged streams and dead oases with the gray look and grainy texture of fresh mixed cement. They smell of ash and liquid feces, for they all have the "ash zone runs." There's too much grit in their water, in their food, and in their bowels. It weakens and slows them, grates against physical effort and their spirits.

It's worse when rain gutters down. The gritty, slimy water they capture in their canteens and helmets doesn't really compensate after the first quenching for what it does to the ashen ground. For rain turns deep ash to thick sludge that sucks at combat boots and at their morale like no mud they ever met or saw, slowing and exhausting them and weighing down all the things they carry.

***

Then they reach the southernmost Old Forest Road and all griping stops. The carnage is immense, awesome, and all around. Thousands of vehicles line up like stranded ghosts at a spectral cemetery gate: large commercial types, small private transports, abandoned military hovers, export timber haulers, civilian troikas with skis retracted, even primitive wooden wagons and a few children's toy carts. All tangled and stopped in a colossal traffic snarl of ash and death. Most are reduced to charred frames, evenly spaced along the road, dutifully stopped from colliding by careful auto drivers before controls were incinerated. Passengers still sit stiffly in rows inside stopped buses, as if at attention.

Bodies are no more than porous ash. Touch one and it collapses like a child's castle of dried sand, losing frail shape and any meaning, sifting down into a rough black-and-gray cone. Caught by the next stiff breeze, what was once a kind father or mother or beloved child or wise old grandparent erodes to a dusky stream that glitters damp nostrils of the living, the stunned troopers of Madjenik. Until gritty mucus runs black from their noses, down over caked lips.

Faces are gone. Etched memories of special worries or the odd joys and humor of one unique life after another, after another, after another. All melted to manikin smoothness. Visages look out from darkened hollows where parents' missing eyes searched the last terrible moments of their lives, to gaze helplessly on the final terror of their burning children before also dying. Like terrified hikers overtaken by superheated gas and rock of a pyroclastic flow cascading down a volcano side, whole families are holding hands, huddling for last comfort in odd merry-go-round sculptures of love and soot. Nearby, Jan sees the ash shade of a loyal dog. Over there, Zofia sees lies an inchoate lump of ash once a small child, watches a young mother stretch out to save the infant, destined never to reach him. Beneath his feet, Tom Hipper sees shadows painted upon the ground by ferocious heat, shades of life brushed atop burnt soil. Soulless, sexless, featureless evermore.

It seems forever that Jan lets Madjenik gather and stand and stare, agape and silent. He's shaken, too. This is a hundred times, ten thousand times the death and destruction anyone saw or wrought 'till now. They can do nothing for so many. Not even bury them. For they mustn't tarry. There's no tree cover over the canyon-like road. The canopy is all burned away, leaving only cold, callous and indifferent stars in a cloudless and careless sky. Topless, roofless, burned trees stand in long rows down each roadside, like useless pillars of ancient ruins that once upheld the vanity of gods and empires. Madjenik stands inside a Parthenon of death.

Yet, against tactical rules and wisdom, for Humanity's sake and their own, Jan doesn't object as shaken men and women of Madjenik gather in a circle right out in the open to say a quiet prayer for the departed. Or spit a silent curse against the God of War, as is the favor and belief of many fighters who have no time for the

Common Faith or who lost it in first combat. He fills with silent rage. He has no voice for this. An ancient accusation flies into his mind from a lifetime ago, from his forgotten student days, a verse all out of time adapted to the precious moment: '*Go! Tell Pyotr, you who pass us by, that here, obedient to his will we lie.*'

Out loud he speaks only the ancient promise to parents and grandparents left behind by Krevan youths who die too young: "You will not sorrow alone over an early grave." The Common Prayer that the religious among the fighters say, all bunched up on the road, gives no one comfort. It invokes no sense of divine mercy as they stand in the midst of a crematoria of ash families and isolated, lonely dead. Small consolation comes instead from a most unlikely source, from words quietly spoken by, of all people, woolly headed Jarred Whitmore.

"Please sir, if I may? I don't think we can light a sage smudge stick, but my sweet mother, Janine Whitmore, used to say very old words in times like these."

"Shit, kid!" It's one of the NCOs, as shaken as the rest. "Sorry, but there ain't no such words, 'cause there never was times like these."

"Any time a friend or family member dies is times like these."

"What does that mean?"

"That this terrible place is full of unmourned and dear departed."

"Yeah? So what can we do about it?"

"We owe them words."

"Sure, kid. But let me tell ya, no words can..."

"Quiet," Jan orders. "Let the boy speak. What did your mother say, son?"

Jarred speaks the ancient verse his mother said over the graves of many a lost friend, and once also over the grave of a lost child. No one interrupts, and not just because Jan said not to.

> "*Turn wheresoe'er I may, by night or day,*
> *things which I have seen I can see no more.*
> *Though nothing can bring back the hour*
> *of splendor in the grass, of glory in the flower;*

we will grieve not. Rather find
strength in what remains behind."

"Nice one, kid," the skeptical soldier says quietly to Jarred, and to him alone. Then he pats the lad on the shoulder and walks a few paces away, hand to his face. Those are the last words that anyone in Madjenik speaks for the longest time.

Except for the captain and lieutenant, but they only talk to each other because they have to give the company its march orders. Madjenik hauls north across the cemetery road, moving back among silent, begrimed trees. Nothing more is said as they leave, trailing not clouds of glory but little puffs of ash that rise behind two shambolic lines of grieving fighters shuffling silently in thick combat boots.

Even if the *Chemins des Mort*, as Zofia now dubs the Old Forest Road, wasn't exposed to overflights and hunter probes, not too dangerous to take on the last klics of the trek to Toruń, no one among them could stand to make such a journey. Not emotionally or mentally. They have no moral strength to pick a callous path around the dense crowds of corpses still on a gadarene exodus to nowhere, on a thoroughfare of death that stretches hundreds of klics through an ash forest many remember so much more greenly from childhood days. Childhood's over.

They quietly redeploy five klics deeper inside the dead and decimated trees. They trudge though deeper ash than necessary, over burned and fallen branches, past giant smoking stumps, under arching roots as black and bent and mocking as the Gates of Hell in old stories. They trod on, always paralleling but carefully out of sight of the dread road they know is there. They take turns walking flank, rear or point. They keep watches while their comrades erratically slumber. Try to sleep when ordered. Snatch an hour here or there, lying atop still warm and downy ash, but suffering fits and fevers. They eat shrinking rations sparingly, without interest. Sip tepid, gritty water from quarter full canteens. Stop by a blackened root to pass dark urine whenever needed. Defecate silently at the bases of dead trees.

For eight more nights they make forced marches, stopping every two hours for rest-and-water breaks. More nights of stepping on hidden roots, kicking past sooty clutter on the burned out forest floor, stumbling through a half-meter of choking ash with each dragging step. The dawn breaks into nighttime gloom much later this time of year, this far north. It's two months past a lost harvest interrupted by invasion. The long, cold nights give them several extra hours of dark to trudge in silence. To not be seen. And better, not to see.

It's not just the *Chemin des Mort* they wish not to see, or the drear ashland of a once beloved Old Forest now past saving. Soldiers always hate daylight more than concealing dark. With new light comes new danger, especially exposure to detection by bird and insect mounted drones. They haven't seen any for a while, but two buzz over them as they draw nearer to the Great Berm. Even with *huff duff* blockers and adaptive camo refracting light around sleeping forms, bending it into an illusion of ashen floor and hiding thermal signatures and the rhythmic movement of their breathing chests, scared sentries say afterward it was a damn close thing and some time before the drones moved on. No one cares to repeat the chance, to tempt tiny metal mistresses of the day to alert monstrous Jabo masters who will call death down upon their heads.

On and on they trudge, edging ever closer to Toruń. No one speaks about the hideous spectacle they all know runs alongside their way ahead, a host of ashen ghosts keeping silent company with them along the final klics to the berm wall. As night turns into gray and back into night, again and again as they tramp north, Madjenik dreams silent dreams of bloody reprisal for the murders done to kinfolk on the plains and the Old Forest Road. The next morning, they get their chance.

Berm

The early morning air is cold this far north this time of year, already late into autumn. Especially with the thick foliage of the old forests stripped away, with no canopy to keep the bitter cold out or any warmth in. Gray light falls on a grayer landscape, so that an unaided eye cannot tell ground from sky. Even the dew looks gritty and dull. It's one of the ugliest mornings anyone has ever seen on Genève.

Jan can't access the old *Surface Position System*, the prewar SPS grid, because all KRA and civilian government satellites were knocked out by low swooping Zerstörers during the first days of invasion. He must rely on smaller, portable tek. So he studies a dated, static tactical map traced over his HUD. '*We're here at last. Two klics east and four south of Toruń Gate. So near, yet so far from home.*'

He looks down the short length of a shallow gully where he crouches in a half-circle with Zofia and the NCOs. He's damned and determined not to walk into a trap, let alone run into one. He needs Zofia's tactical counsel. He knows she sees the same intimidating imaging that he does on the officer only command link. So he asks her directly, looking straight into her startling jade eyes. "Should we just make a dash for it? Can we hope to get through that way?"

Zofia is emphatic. "No way, sir. It's far too risky to break cover now, this close to the berm. We shouldn't move the company at all before we fully scout what's waiting for us up ahead."

The NCOs agree with her. Tom Hipper points out a second danger. "Toruń HQ has no idea that we're out here, sirs, assuming it still exists. Not a damned clue. That could be a real problem." Their first concern is stumbling into hordes of RIK lodged in perimeter siege trenches, but a second is triggering friendly fire from the garrison should they just barrel toward the Gate.

"No dash for the Gate, then" Jan confirms. "Not now. Not when we've come so far over so many hard days' nights. Against all odds. Against the Will of God." Defying the gods makes him sound smart and tough. Only he needs to know that he, too, is weary past endurance and worse, uncertain what to do next. That he needs a helluva lot more tactical info and time to think before he decides how to approach the impassible berm wall that surrounds besieged Toruń City. '*And three day's sleep, and 5,000 extra guys in oak weaves on this side of the godsdamn wall. A couple of Rhinos and heavy field mortars as backup wouldn't hurt, either.*'

Jan is not a religious man. He hasn't visited a Life Temple or Common Faith prayer meet since he was a kid, when his mother made him go. Hasn't wanted to meet or needed to pray. He says whenever he's asked that the gods are too fickle, too cruel and capricious to trust or respect. "Just like people, only more so." He has said it so often over the past ten years it comes out of his mouth by rote. That's why even he's a little surprised that he said the last bit out loud, about defiance.

'*Why did I invoke a deity I don't believe in just now? Might be the Old Forest Road ... the old prayers that Madjenik spoke there? Maybe it shook me up worse than I thought. OK, time to get over it.*' Maybe he will. Maybe he won't. Truth is, the charnel smells and ash images didn't stagger him as much as *that*. Not enough to flip him on the religious question. No, there's something more at work that he doesn't want to admit to himself, can't and won't believe about himself.

It's that he's getting real good at this thing called combat command. He knows that even though he thinks no gods have anything to say about Madjenik's fate, a whole helluva lot of his fighters believe that they do. He knows they need to hear about it from him, here on the eve of final combat. So he lies to them. He's a good officer now, a leader who knows his fighters well. Knows that two of the NCOs and many of his troopers *do* believe in a watchful god or gods, even if he does not and never has. Knows that a few words about defying their deity will please rather than offend them, because bone weary troopers about to enter into an impossible fight need their captain to say exactly that. Because even the most religious fighter in Madjenik doubts whose side God is really on these days, after seeing all Genève on fire and so many innocents dead long the Old Forest Road.

Jan refocuses. The fact is, gods or no gods, he doesn't have a clue how he can deploy Madjenik or get it inside the city, or even what tactics to use in the coming fight that awaits. So he stalls. "We'll halt here for now, and scout ahead. Before we move again I need to know how many *bâtards* are between us and the berm. Lieutenant Jablonski, you're up. Pick 30 fighters and get 'em ready."

"Yes sir." Zofia says no more, just crisply salutes, palm out in the traditional KRA way. There's nothing more for her to say to him. Not now. Not yet. Maybe not ever. Zofia is focused solely on the tough job facing Madjenik, knowing that one or both or all of them is unlikely to survive.

Jan looks over his NCOs, five grimy sergeants and seven tattered corporals, most of them brevet promoted after the sweetgrass meadow and Pilsudski Wood. They don't look like much, but they herded sorry survivors through three forests to reach this gully. '*One red, one gold, one gray*.' He knows he could never have made it without them. He wants to thank them. To kiss them.

Instead, he acts how they need, and says only what they need to hear. Wracked with doubt within, to them he seems supremely confident in command. Only Zofia knows what he's really feeling and thinking: "We're gonna hole up here and rest everyone for two hours, then use what's left of the night to creep a little closer. After that, we go into Madjenik's last fight. Neither your gods nor I promise that we'll come out the other side OK, but let's make it our best fight anyway."

They know that Jan still refuses to call the ersatz unit Wysocki's Wreckers. They love him all the more for it, and for his brutal honesty about their long odds and more odd gods. They listen to his last orders, nod agreement, then move off in stealth to resume their due places in the Wrecker line. It's not just Jan who has changed. They're all far better soldiers than when their first war began. There are no combat virgins left in Madjenik. They're all veteran fighters and killers now.

Jan splits the company into five oversized platoons of 50 fighters each. He prosaically dubs them, in the KRA standard way: A-B-C-D-E, or 'Able' through 'Easy.' It's a simple if ancient method, confirmed in its utility over eons of now forgotten military history. All that matters to Jan is that it's quick, it's easy, and it works. He'll order four platoons to move ahead in echelon, staggered at 60 meter intervals. The fifth he'll keep as a last reserve, and to help the walking wounded.

"Pickets, maintain position. Everyone else, rest up!" He knows that he must send Zofia and 30 of his best fighters out as a scout line moving in advance of the main company skirmish line. She'll be his eyes, with passive HUD scanner on. She'll be a tripwire, to warn of looming danger. She'll be a panic siren in the dark. If needs be, she'll stand to fight to hold off the enemy while the rest of Madjenik runs. She's the love of his life and he's going to send her ahead, likely to her death.

It's what he must do.

It's the price of command.

No favors. No flowers.

Jan doesn't think twice about ordering Zofia to lead the scout line. '*She would volunteer anyway, if I didn't give her the order. No stopping her on this mission. Besides, she's the best I've got.*'

Armed with stub masers, frag grenades, and black diamond combat knives, Zofia's "Forlorn Hope" moves out two hours later, followed at 200 meters by the five big platoons, in echelon. Left behind are the three carrier bots and nonlethal gear. There'll be no need of it tomorrow. Coated in clinging ash, the Forlorn Hope disappears from Jan's naked sight in less than a minute. Lost amidst the gray ruin of dead trees and burned off undergrowth, coated in a sickeningly familiar blanket of white-gray. All the trees wear the same dull, ash coating as Madjenik.

Zofia takes center point. She looks like a young lioness prowling at the head of her pride, aware that far more numerous packs of hyenas are lurking all around, occupying the only water hole. Denying it to her thirsty young. She will not have it. She will find a way through for Madjenik, somehow. If she finds the foe without being discovered, the Forlorn Hope will halt, cull tactical intel and await orders. If the enemy makes first contact and a firefight breaks out, her orders are to drop, shoot everything she has, and to "hold in place for three standard minutes." Time enough for Madjenik to move in to help. Or to pull out and run.

Jan never says the last bit. They don't talk about it. No need. Each is familiar with the working of the other's tactical mind, confident as lovers who know each curve and contour of another's body. They both know that his decision to fight or run will rest on just how big a sleeping RIK bear Zofia rouses, and if Jan thinks he can get the rest of the company past its slashing claws and teeth or must flee.

Thirty men and women are asked to give their lives to save something bigger than themselves. Honor? Duty? Madjenik? There'll be three minutes for each one to decide. Just 300 standard seconds of fire, of sound and fury, until Zofia releases any survivors with that ancient cry of honor's duty done heard over ten thousand battlements and battlefields: "*Sauve qui peut!*" Save yourselves, whoever can! Only that last order can set them free. If any still live after three minutes of combat with frags and lethal light. That's why the scout unit is called a Forlorn Hope.

Jan gives the *Advance!* order, flashing a command onto all HUDs. Madjenik is a veteran unit now, and old hands scatter into a wide dispersal pattern and move forward with extreme caution in the suspected presence of hostiles. So Madjenik deploys neatly and without delay or question in four big platoons in echelon across a half-klic frontage, with a fifth in center reserve ready to surge into any gap. Zofia is out front, probing gingerly for the hidden enemy. Fighters are grateful for the first time that dry ash as thick as pillows lies underfoot, muffling every footfall. A good thing, too. At two klics out from the berm a hundred *red* threat warnings of huge enemy numbers, and heavy weps position triangles, suddenly pop up on Zofia's HUD. The info instantly relays to Jan and all NCOs via shared tac display.

Zofia gives the silent command, arm reached back with open palm: *Stop!* Then a raised, tightly clenched fist: *Freeze!* Her tac relay is unclear, but sheer volumes of *red* threat symbology suddenly flashing bright across all HUDs prompts her to hiss: "*Halt all movement!*" Redundant? Maybe. But better than having someone stumble into a Rikugun funk hole or trip over a picket. She scans the multitude of threats. Her HUD can't identify every one or pinpoint exact locations, but the scan IDs elements of two full RIK infantry brigades, at least. The center of the enemy's trench line is barely 400 meters in front of her. She's almost in his camp!

'*Merde! That's over 4,000 men! And they've got five heavy assault guns and four armtraks parked nearby.*' Zofia knows Jan sees and thinks pretty much the same thing she does.

She hears him exclaim "*Jumalauta!*" under his breath, another odd invocation of divine help. He says it with angry, sacrilegious profanity, hurling it into ether in a way he hasn't spoken the word in 20 years. Maybe he *is* more religious than he realizes? No, he's just appalled and uncertain and scared nearly witless. That's why he defaults to local religious curses learned in childhood, ear cuffed by his mother whenever he used them. His doubt is curling back on him, like a dying old man curls fetus like as he reverts just before the end to a child's first fables.

He recovers quickly and sends an urgent flash: *Immediate halt! All units!* It screeches into every HUD in Madjenik, in both visual and auditory. It freezes all five platoons in place, behind the already frozen Forlorn Hope.

"Looks real bad," Zofia agrees, whispering along the officer only channel for his ears alone, excluding even the trusted NCOs this time. '*Don't want to spread panic. Time and enemy enough for that!*'

Jan think-switches to *show contacts*, then filters the order with *threats only*. His HUD instantly presents two full battalions of *red* infantry ranging out 700-900 meters from the berm, betwixt his present position and the heavily defended Gate. Also sitting between Madjenik and Toruń are five plasma cannon pillboxes and a heavy maser battery. It's impassible.

"*Voi paska!*" he curses. It's picked up by the open link to Zofia.

"Yeah, I know," she whispers back. Their shared command link is desperately counting and marking in differently shaped *red* symbols the incredible density of thousands of enemy troops, hundreds of guns, and dozens more waiting armtraks spreading all the way down the berm along both flanks of the locked Gate.

"There are no gods!" Jan wails in a whisper. "And if there are, then godsdamn them all! How in unholy hell are we supposed to get through *that?*"

***

Two first rate combat brigades occupy the critical space between Madjenik and where it wants to go, to the berm and through the Gate, thence over the sole bridge into Toruń. They look rested and heavily armed, with heavy armor and arti support locked in place all around. '*They must have skycraft, too, but flying high over the berm and shields to keep clear of our archie and streak missiles. This close in, at least we don't have to worry about Jabos and Raptor strafers, not so close to their own guys.*' Cold comfort, but the only morsel Jan can find.

Raptors and Jabos are holding back, but not just to avoid friendly fire incidents along the berm. They've taken real losses since they switched from runs over the open northern plain then the five Old Forest Roads. Anti-skycraft fire is so thick around Toruń the bombardment of the city is being left to long range artillery, dug in 500 klics back, far beyond any KRA ability to reply. And to even longer range missiles fired from thousands of klics away on Southland. Some ice kinetics fall from orbit, lobbed from fast destroyers that dart-and-dash low. But the Kaigun is wary of the big Toruń batteries. It has been hurt too badly by them already.

RIK Skyforce took far too many losses in the first cocky days of bombing, as pilots predicting "an easy match" flew too low and way too straight over a fire zone recently cleared extra wide around the outside berm, and bristling with short range *streakers* planted there by General Amiya Constance. They paid a high price for arrogance, in downed Jabos making jellied landings smeared over the forest floor. Pilots were happy to be called down south to pound Pilsudski Wood and the Gold Oak Forest, looking to roast 'bandits' for an angry general while infantry was sent into the burned out berm perimeter to take out the *streaker* launchers. Then the Jabos firebombed five Old Forest Roads, turning a half-million square klics of forest and nearly three million refugees and retreating KRA into ash piles. Ultimately, they were ordered back to Toruń. Again they attacked, again they paid a high price against a determined fortress city with anti-skycraft guns on every rooftop and more *streaker* launchers placed atop the berm. A pair every 50 paces. Suddenly the war was a lot less fun. Fewer pilots returned to barracks for each end-of-day meal. They were replaced by rookies, who crashed even faster.

Otherwise, the siege is going all Rikugun's way. At least if, like the worried generals reporting daily success to Pyotr, you consider as success literally scaling walls and ramparts of your own dead, left behind from a dozen prior attacks. All around the berm the bodies wait in unburied heaps, kept from rotting by suspend but piled with indignity beside larger piles of scorched and broken gear, caved in armtraks, smashed gun tubes and stalled Rikugun ambition.

"Yes, but the next mad rush will surely make the breach," a general promises. Or maybe the one after that? Toruń's fall and burning is inevitable. Only that hope and expectation keeps up morale, as indifferent generals foolhardily leave their own dead exposed for their men to see and worry. The conscripts take it badly.

Madjenik has problems, too. It has 15 walking wounded hobbling along only with aid from a reserve of just 50 fighters. The worst off smell of gauze and scabs and anti-biots, pus and piss and bone weariness. The only thing working on Jan's side at this last hour of the long trek from the MDL is that his worn out, outgunned and wildly outnumbered fighters are as yet undiscovered by a rested enemy. He's trying hard not to admit his doubts about himself or Madjenik's chances, but he's not succeeding. He hasn't felt so utterly helpless, so totally without hope, in three months. Not since the first time he saw combat and ran, wounded and scared and forevermore ashamed. Hauling himself before his own Court of Character to pass merciless sentence on himself, to condemn himself as a coward and a bad leader.

He's not a coward, but he's no fool either. Ahead lies an immovable obstacle in the berm, *and* an irresistible force of RIK besiegers all around the perimeter, as far as his HUD can detect or count. Yet there's no going back. Not into the ashland of Toruń Wood. Jan's fate is a one way street that leads the Wreckers to Toruń or Death. He knows it. He hesitates to step onto the path. '*How the hell do I get us through? It's just not possible. It can't be done. Not with that huge force standing between us and Toruń, and the path to the bridge and the Gate so narrow.*'

It's Jan's worst nightmare coming true. All the proof anyone will need that he's a bad officer, that he should never have been given command of Madjenik. That whenever he's called upon to save his soldiers and lead his company he fails miserably, and everybody dies. '*I'm going to kill all these fighters I led through the forest. How can I not? I'm going to get Zofia killed, too, right here at the feet of Toruń. Right here, outside the berm. With all of Genève and Krevo and Orion watching. Everything has been for naught. This will be my greatest failure yet. If we attack, we'll die. Maybe I should just surrender Madjenik instead, to save it?*'

Zofia almost reads his thoughts as they move across his face. She won't accept them: "Godsdamn it captain! Snap out of it! These fighters followed you here. This was *your* idea, *your* plan. You did it. You got us here when we thought we were going to die in fire and ash. Well fuck you, Jan Wysocki! None of us came this far to watch you falter and fail. So get off your ass and get us into the city."

"Ah hell, Zofia," he says after a long silence follows her outburst. It's the first time since the sweetgrass that he has called her by her name and not her rank. "It's better to die on our feet than to live on our knees. Call the NCOs. Tell them to get Madjenik ready. We're going to attack."

Epilogue

Hundreds upon hundreds of parsecs away an alien Intelligence broods on the outbreak of war in the Orion spiral arm. A thick, grasping organ with long digits and a bright metallic glint reaches down to a gossamer light display, more gaseous than hard or flat. It flicks one digit subtly, and a time delayed image shuts off. The image that dissolves more than fades away is of the Minister of Defense of the Calmar Union, Georges Briand, addressing an overflowing Lok Sabra on Kars. It travelled all this way via superluminal hyperbohr relay. Still, the distance is…

The image from Kars is replaced by a swirling starmap of the Orion spur and Open Clusters, curving in the far distance from where the Intelligence watches on the cusp of the outer, stately and more majestic Perseus spiral arm. More majestic, yes, but also vastly more troubled and troublesome. And yet, the decision is made. A powerful fusion drive engages on a warship unlike any seen in history. At least, not in Orion's history. At least, not in *human* history.

It streaks toward a gas giant L2 in a quiet system in the outer edge of the long Perseus arm, the last three-body bohr system before mostly emptiness and solitary wanderer stars reach out toward the distant Boreads. That starry archipelago floats adjacent to the extreme far Western Gap lying between Orion and the first wispy stars of the main conglomerations of gas clouds and stars that make up Perseus. If the Boreads weren't there the middle passage could not be crossed. But they are there, so a strange warship will hop and leap and jump The Gap to reach Orion. There will be many more to follow. Many, many more.

It's going to be a long trip to reach the human homeworlds. It's over 24,000 trillion klics just to make The Boreads. Yet, it won't be far enough to keep humans unaware of a far more terrible war that has already been raging for 10,000 years across Perseus, an interminable war of attrition between two ancient civilizations. Remarkably, unknown to either of the great, warring alien races, a hidden third civilization secretly watches them, as it watches The Gap between the spiral arms.

The Intelligence sends a final message relaying by bohr jumps back to central Perseus, then it engages an exquisitely refined quantum stadimeter. Not without a touch of wry humor, it thinks: '*Well, aren't you humans in for a real surprise.*'

RIK Ranks

Imperium ranks followed Broderbund practice until the First Orion War, which is to say there were no officer ranks. All commanders were called 'Brothers' or 'Knights' and all soldiers were classed as either basic infantry (*landser*) or cloned military slaves (*dāsa*). Rikugun no longer uses slave soldiers. The term *landser* survives, but not *dāsa*.

Rikugun terminology changed with martial marriage of the original Oetkert-Shaka dynasty with the elites of Nagoya and Yokohama, after the First Orion War. By the time of the Second Orion War, all officer ranks were Nagoyan.

Kaigun (Grün Navy) ranks

vice admiral	*chūjō*
rear admiral	*shōshō*
captain	*daisa*
commander	*chūsa*
lt. commander	*shōsa*
lieutenant	*daii*
ensign	*shōi*
midshipman	*shōi kōhōsei*
warrant officer	*jun-i*

Rikugun (Grün Army) ranks

lieutenant general	*chūjō*
major general	*shōshō*
general	*taishō*
colonel	*taisa*
lieutenant colonel	*chūsa*
major	*shōsa*
captain	*taii*
1st lieutenant	*chūi*
2nd lieutenant	*shōi*
sergeant	*gunsō*
corporal	*gochō*
senior private	*jōtōhei*
private/recruit	*nitōhei*
basic infantry	*landser*
slave soldiers	*dāsa*

Special Action Commando (SAC)

SAC uses same rank structure as Rikugun
Sakura-kai (Cherry Blossoms Society)
politruks political officers (non-military)

The story continues in

Volume II

The Orion War

Exodus

Sample

The mine blows exactly on schedule, producing two lethal effects. An intense thermal blast sears metal, rock and flesh while a wave of intense pressure and expanding gases spreads out-and-upward at supersonic speed. The shock wave causes devastating injuries to internal organs while the fast expanding gases lift a mass of soil and rock and men in a swelling half-orb of sudden heat and death. At ground zero, right above the insertion chamber excavated by the engineers, ultrasteel and superconcrete RIK pillboxes simply disappear. Big gun tubes and entire crews convert instantly into hot odorless gases, adding to the rising bubble. Or reduce to small lumps of singed metal or cooked bone smoking at the apex of a lifting ball of expanding water and soil. Heavy maser batteries and six fusion cannon boxes lift 300 meters into the air, riding atop the upward burping bubble. It's made of brown and ochre clay chunks, rich black top soil, mud and rocks and water, shattered vehicles, and flailing bodies and parts of dead and dying men.

Four intact heterodiamond gun tubes, too hard to crack apart, tumble slowly upward, gracefully arcing above the cresting explosion of dirt and blood and wood that flashes with plasma lightning from within, like a great black thunderstorm seen at 10,000 meters altitude. The tubes are from the 3rd Imperial Artillery, an elite unit from Manmō. So are bits of two dozen erupted gunners. Two crystal-cannon batteries from 33rd Artillery, a regular outfit also from Manmō, rise as a mutilated and mangled muddle of smashed and torn and jagged bits of men and machines, hurtled high up inside the spreading ball of hot debris.

Four heavy Mammoths parked behind the maser battery come apart at every laser-welded seam as they rise. Three sleeping crews die instantly, killed in a nanosecond because they chose to lie down for a brief rest in a convenient nearby dry trench that no longer exists. Inside the fourth armtrak are two military workers busy with minor repairs when the mine goes off. At first they're protected by a thick shroud of carbyne armor, riding the huge ejecta bubble high up. Then they spill out, bodily intact, wide awake, and utterly astonished that gravity has so little hold on them or the hugely bulky Mammoth rising right alongside.

'*No, not ME!*'

'*This can't be happening to ME!*'

'*Why am I flying?*'

'Where are my legs?'

'This isn't real! I'm young. I'm loved. I want to live!'

'Why ME? It's not fair, it's not FAIR!'

No, it's not. You were just in the wrong place at the wrong time, drew the wrong number in the war's never-ending lottery, its random draw of life and fate. Now you're dead, son. *Next!*

Seconds of rapid expansion that take forever, then the hubble-bubble slows. It thins and breaks its overstretched skin at the epicenter, and everything it carried up starts to fall: gun tubes, rocks, armor plate, concretized gun anchors, chunks of field, bodies, cracked helmets, heavy masers, three shattered Mammoths and one intact armtrak. Along with two utterly astonished mechanics from the forest world of Unterwalden. No one hears them scream over the roar of hot air and flying clay and steam and groundwater still gushing outward in all directions below them. Mortality arrives in the looming form of gravity, reclaiming them as Genève's entire and fatal inertial mass smacks each falling man hard right in the face.

Exactly 1,402 RIK are inside the blast zone when the plasma mine goes off. Some, like the armtrak and arti crews, come from the traditional military world of Manmō. Most others are young conscripts. Two full companies of infantry are from Lucerne, a quiet Grün agro-world very much like Genève. They're just 10 days into their first combat tour. None live. Most of the Lucerne boys die fast, mercifully unaware of last moments, still asleep as bones are crushed and internal organs pulped by the expansive pressure wave of the blast. A few are not so lucky but even so die fairly fast. Painlessly compared to what's coming to others from different units unfortunately posted just outside the certain kill zone of the crater.

The descending ruin overhead is full of body parts, remnants of boys and men hailing onto the now smoking and gassy ground. Night sentries about to go off duty and early-rising cooks preparing the first meal hundreds of meters from the crater edge vomit in moral horror as strings of warm extruded gut drape slickly over a neck or arm. Or snag like mockmeat sausages on jutting branches of already scorched and now shattered trees with no bark or leaves left at all. Even the trees looked tormented, with gaping white wounds of torn and pulpy vegetable flesh.

No mother will recognize or embrace the awful things hanging from trees and rocks, or raw and bleeding and unmoving on ruptured ground, oozing blood and water and green bitter-smelling bile. Larger lumps and clumps land with sick, soft *thuds!* Torsos, legs, severed feet, loosed heads with boy's faces still frozen in an instant of uncomprehending horror and shock.

A thousand meters from the forming crater rim survivors are coated a minute later by a falling, sticky red-black mist, then drenched in rolling sheets made of falling dirt, blood and groundwater. The mix smells of natural plant oils, mangled tree roots and erupted men. Exploded rocks and artificial wreckage fall to ground all around, spreading into and around a deep and smoking crater blown 100 meters down at zero point and 850 jagged and wide. Its roofless walls form an earthen coliseum of destruction and despair, of murder and madness. It's spectacle and sacrifice. It's bloodsport theater. Primal, exciting, cruel and absurd.

Printed in Great Britain
by Amazon

51527875R00149